BANKHAUS

Library of Congress Control Number: 2023923219

ISBN (paperback): 978-1-956450-98-9
ISBN (Ebook): 978-1-956450-99-6

Thousand Acres is an imprint of Armin Lear Press, Inc.
215 W Riverside Drive, #4362
Estes Park, CO 80517

A NOVEL

BANKHAUS

NEIL GIARRATANA

In memory of Peter K. Schwarzlose.
A mentor. A man for all seasons. A friend.

Prologue
A Private Bank in the center of Zurich, Switzerland

Early December   10:42 am

The client sat on a blue velvet two-seater across from the reception desk. He was wearing a gray and white checker-board, double-breasted suit with a spread-collar white shirt, gold cuff links, and a dark blue tie. His black leather shoes, polished to a high sheen, were an elegant, thin-soled version of the heavier American wingtips.

He sported a closely-cut, three-day beard, an almost *de rigueur* prerequisite for acceptance into the world of Italian men's fashion.

In his hand he held a Swiss-German magazine he'd picked up from one of the side tables. But he wasn't paying any attention to its contents. It wasn't only that it was written in a language he neither spoke nor understood. The man had the look of someone with other things on his mind.

This was private bank territory, wealth management territory, white and black money territory.

The inner sanctum of the rich.

He felt swallowed up by the mausoleum-like stillness and the long thick-carpeted halls running off in either direction from the small reception area, deeper into the inner workings of the bank. He heard a phone ringing on low volume far down the hall to his right. To the left of the reception desk, he saw elevator doors open once, then close, with a soft whirring sound.

He noticed no scent in the air, in spite of the large crystal vase filled with freshly-cut flowers located in front of him on the top of a marble coffee table. The water in the vase barely reached to the bottom tips of the diagonally-cut stems. Even in such a place, somebody not doing their job, he thought.

Turning his head slowly, he identified several miniature security cameras, capturing all and everything in their lenses. He observed the position of each camera briefly, noting how well each one of them had been tucked away into unobtrusive corners of the drapery and the room's crown moldings.

Those were the only ones he could see. He knew there were others he would never spot no matter how hard or how long he looked.

A woman approached from down the hall, coming with sure steps and a neutral look on her face. He noticed her green eyes as she looked him directly in the eyes, shaking his hand firmly. She led him toward a small conference room a short distance down the hall from where he'd been sitting.

Only a small smile played briefly at the corner of her mouth as she opened the door to let him enter before her.

There were four chairs with leather upholstered seats grouped around a dark-paneled wood table. He took the one with the windows to the left and the door to the right.

Seated facing her, he unbuttoned his double-breasted jacket and crossed his legs, careful to avoid crumpling the sharp crease of his trousers. He looked expectedly at her.

They both spoke Italian. The client employed a manner of expression typically heard in the Province of Lazio, the location of the city of Rome.

She asked about his hotel accommodations, his travels, and other standard superficialities, questions she used to relax the atmosphere at the beginning of a client meeting. He was not loquacious. His answers were best-practice examples of minimalistic conversation.

The woman's short report on how the bank viewed the current economic situation and the bank's recent financial successes within those difficult parameters elicited no long-winded or analytic response or comments from the client. He gave a one-sentence observation to the effect that all that was happening in the world had had no negative effect on his own business.

He didn't really care about the answers he gave and neither did she. Their minuet had already been pre-programmed for another entirely different purpose. He wanted to pick up 850,000 Euros in cash from his private account, a request he'd communicated to her by phone three days before.

Her two-fold role in the whole affair was a simple one: official facilitator of his request and competent representative of the bank and its multiple services.

She'd asked for his account number which he'd given her, written down on a small slip of paper. She studied the official page of his well-worn passport, then glanced up at him, complimenting him on the way he appeared in the photo contained therein.

She opened a thin folder, handing to the client several sheets of paper clipped together containing information on his account and a detailed breakdown of the asset positions it contained. With a murmured thank you, the client turned down her offer to provide him with some of the bank's thinking in making those particular investments with his money.

The total at the bottom of the summary sheet jumped out at the client: Euro 91,537,998. He blinked once, then sat back in his chair to study the pages more closely. The numbers were impressive: total assets under management higher than the year before, the result of an overall year-to-year percentage growth of 11.3 percent from the various components of the client's depot.

The report's length kept him occupied for several minutes. He commented briefly on the cash balance contained in the summary: 23.3 percent, a good bit over the classic percentage relationship of cash to total assets. He complimented her and the bank on their good work, expressing the hope that such a performance would repeat itself in the future.

Other than that, he had no other questions or comments, no suggestions for changes in the investment strategy used by the bank to grow the value of his account. Looking at the numbers, it was obvious the bank already knew very well what it was doing.

The client adjusted the knot of his tie and smiled.

The game could begin.

He gazed at the woman expectedly. She knew the score. He requested that the money be paid out in Euro 500 notes. Less weight and easier to carry, he said. She rose from her seat, informing him that she intended to go to the central cashier's office and would return shortly with the funds he'd requested.

As Director of her Division and a member of top management, there was no need for her to go upstairs for a second signature of approval before proceeding to the cashier's office. And no need to be concerned about the amount of the withdrawal. For Wealth Management clients withdrawing or transferring funds elsewhere, there was generally no cap on the amount they could ask for. After all, it was their money. Only when an eight or nine withdrawal amount was involved did a member of the bank's finance committee, usually the Chief Financial Officer, become part of the withdrawal or transfer process.

That was, definitely, not the case here.

While she was gone, the man stood up and walked around the corner of the small conference table to the street side of the room. With his right hand, he casually drew back the velvet curtain hanging in front of one of the tall windows spaced evenly along that wall of the meeting room.

Looking down onto the narrow side street where the bank's Private Client entrance was located, he observed the hurried to and fro of the pedestrians on the sidewalk. They weren't, however, the real focus of his interest.

He studied carefully the people and the scene below him. There was no one loitering at the shop windows on the other side of the narrow street nor was there anyone standing around looking at the bank's entrance or up along the façade of the bank building itself. Everything normal. Everything cool.

As he observed the street, it started to rain heavily, forcing everyone exposed to the elements to hurry even faster along the sidewalks to their destinations. No one paused or stayed standing.

Satisfied, the client dropped the curtain back into place and sat down again.

The woman returned and handed him two bulky envelopes. Their contents one thousand seven hundred individual 500 Euro notes. He declined her offer to open and confirm its contents for him. He trusted the bank, its procedures, and certainly its precise counting machines.

She slid three documents across the table for him to sign. She handed him her ink pen with the cap off, ready to use.

Dark blue ink. Nice touch, he thought.

He signed, then watched as she signed her name quickly

alongside his signatures. He informed her he did not want or need copies of the documents he'd just signed.

He placed the envelopes in a large brown suede messenger bag he'd brought with him for the purpose. She watched him carefully as he slung the bag's sling over his right shoulder, regarding him with something close to cold detachment in her eyes.

Standing at the elevator, he mentioned that he'd most likely be returning within several weeks to withdraw additional funds from his account. That would be no problem was the measured reply.

A chauffeured limousine was waiting for him as he exited the building. Jumping quickly into the back seat to avoid getting wet, he settled in and let out a breath of air as the car moved off, attempting to negotiate its way along the narrow street with its stop-and-go traffic.

His eyes began to lose some of the opaqueness they'd had during his visit at the bank.

There'd been no problems.

He lifted his eyes toward the heavens he could not see, thanking unknown gods for their kindness.

1
Via Monte Ortigara
San Remo (Italian Riviera)
Italia

July 17   A Sunday morning   3:17 am

He'd had to fully open the driver side window in his car. The heat of the night, the lack of a breeze, the bad air in the car from the sweat and desperation had made it necessary.

The darkness of the night was almost complete. Only one street light a few paces further up the road provided some small measure of illumination to the deserted road and the cars parked along it. *l'aube*, the dawn, was still more than an hour and a half away.

Maurizio Lorenzini sat hunched over the steering wheel, looking up through the bug-splattered windshield of his car at the balconies and windows of a dated, five-story apartment house facing out to the via Monte Ortigara, and then over it and beyond to the dark sea in the distance.

Large, faded red awnings, contrasting to the dirty beige exterior of the building, reached out from its façade, some partially, but most fully extended to protect the balconies and the interiors of the apartments against the strong midday summer sun and its oppressive heat.

Not one light on in any of the windows, only a few clothes and undergarments, evidently laundry from the previous day or evening, still hanging out to dry on sagging clothes lines draped across the length of several of the pre-cast, gray concrete balconies.

The previous evening, he'd made a short visit to the Salon Prive of the Casino San Remo, standing listlessly at the roulette table, betting at every several turns of the wheel a few hundred Euros, all that he'd been able to find in a desk drawer in his small, *pied-a-terre* apartment in Villefranche-sur-Mer across from Cap Ferrat.

He'd lost them all.

Leaving the casino, he'd driven aimlessly around the center of San Remo before seeking the road leading up to the six lane A-10 running parallel to the sea in the hills high above the town. A numbing tiredness, an almost debilitating heaviness in his limbs, had made him drive slower and slower until finally he'd pulled into one of the apartment building's empty street parking spaces situated perpendicular to the narrow two-lane road.

There were cars parked in the slots on each side of his, but they were dark and empty, their owners most likely still asleep in one of the apartments overhead.

It had been more than a half hour that he'd sat there, thoughts, emotions, feelings, anxiety, panic, frustration, disappointment, recriminations, all caroming around in his head, the one train of thought giving up its place to another only to be replaced by yet another, sometimes in the space of several seconds, sometimes dominating his consciousness for a minute or more.

The buzzing in his head, the memory of the past two days, the now very real consequences facing him, had combined to bring tears to his eyes, tears he couldn't wipe away quickly enough.

Maurizio Lorenzini had played his hand and lost.

No one else to blame, no outside influence that could be made responsible for that fact.

The man had an affliction, others would call it a sickness, still others would call it a disease, and those who knew him well—if they'd had an inkling of its existence—would have called it an act of pure selfishness. No matter the name or the term used to describe it, it was all the same thing: Maurizio Lorenzini was a gambler, a *hazardeur*. And he'd taken more than enough liberties with his hunger for the buzz of playing blackjack or *Chemin de Fer*.

Or his favorite, roulette.

Black or red, the *chiffres*, the numbers, the decision, the wager, the bouncing and clicking of the ball in the slowing roulette wheel, the moment when he didn't want to or couldn't breathe, the improbable win, the noiseless push of the chips across the green velvet surface to join his growing or, more often, diminishing pile, all parts of a life that had proven to have increasingly diminishing returns for him, both financially and emotionally.

He'd hidden this side of his life from everyone, experiencing alone contortions of guilt, sometimes crawling through periods of withdrawal, succeeding at it for months at a time, only then to be drawn back into the pits, into the casinos from Geneva to Nice to Lago Como where his sickness had driven him to take ever-bigger risks, losing big and winning big, and then again losing big.

And then very big.

With a second pediatric clinic in Menton on the French Riviera, and his international conferences, he'd been able to be absent from home and his primary pediatric responsibilities in Lugano for extended periods of time, long enough to allow him to dash from casino to casino, his favorite, the Monte Maurizio Casino in Monaco and its Salle Medecin where he was *un client préferé*, or a whale to use the more prevalent English term.

Those liberties, that hidden sickness, had exercised the strongest pull on a man lost without a compass, had led him ever closer to a darker side of life, to a growing negation of all that was dear and close to him, of all that made his heart sing when he was spending perhaps a Sunday with his family on their motor boat on Lago Lugano.

But not enough. Those liberties had also caused him to make a series of ill-conceived decisions, decisions made sometimes hastily at many a crossroad along the way, but decisions implicitly fateful in nature, decisions which had led him, finally, to an empty parking space on the outskirts of San Remo, with his back up against a road leading everywhere and nowhere.

He sat there now, in the dark, tears in his eyes, staring at the gray concrete exterior of a nondescript apartment building, curiously counting the number of balconies, waiting for the first light to go on in one of the windows, facing an abyss, facing a trip without a return ticket.

In Lugano, Switzerland, his home and the location of the larger of his two pediatric clinics, he was the picture of male, of fatherly perfection: 42 years of age, tall, lanky, with that certain look of authority in his eyes that good doctors always seem to have, a man always ready with a quick laugh, competent to the core, a giver, casual in his dress, but disciplined in his practice, a man of his time, a man for all seasons.

His love for his wife, Charlotte, and his only child, fifteen-year-old Anulka, the happiness of an intact and loving family so evident in its many contacts with the world outside of the home, all facets of a life seemingly undisturbed by anything sinister or dark.

The affection between father and daughter was particularly strong. There were those who called it a union made in heaven, a description sometimes used to describe the love existing between a man and woman. But in this case, it was very clear that between father and daughter there existed a special feeling, a special understanding, a special affection, a love that superseded anything or anyone else.

But hell had now interceded in all, in everything that was dear to him. And there was nothing he could do to stop it.

The previous morning, at the Hotel Neptune in Menton, France, he'd had breakfast on the terrace with someone whom he'd considered a friend, a fellow doctor, a colleague of many years, a Swiss citizen like himself, someone with whom he'd attended many an international symposium on pediatrics, someone who'd done well financially over the years and who was looking to expand his own Lausanne-based pediatric clinic activities south to the Cote d'Azur of France.

The reason for their morning discussion was simple: his second pediatrics clinic in Menton represented a location which fit exactly into the expansion plans of his Lausanne colleague. And that colleague, after several months of back-and-forth discussions, had decided to come down to the Cote d'Azur to meet, and discuss with him, the final contractual details of a change in ownership.

Under normal circumstances, no thinking person would consider selling such a successful operation, particularly one which had been nurtured from its infancy, one which had been so properly and successfully managed over the twelve years of its existence, one whose revenues and profits were still growing at a double-digit percentage rate per year.

That is, unless there was a damn good reason to do so. And Maurizio Lorenzini had a very big damn good reason to sell his clinic: he had gambled so heavily and incurred such heavy debts—over two million Euros—to the casino in Monaco that he'd had to borrow the money to run them down to zero.

Nothing unusual about that: casinos generally didn't like waiting for their money.

Right at that point, there'd been a solution at hand: to cancel those debts, he could have borrowed the money from his bank in Menton, a bank which, of course, knew him and knew of his success with his clinic. There would have been more than enough equity on the clinic's balance sheet to cover any risk the bank might have seen in funding the loan.

A logical move in such an unpleasant situation.

He hadn't chosen that alternative. Instead, he'd turned to the underworld of the casino world, those omnipresent, soft-spoken purveyors of financial comfort and easy loans with generous payback terms, those "close" friends who stand along the edges of the roulette table or *Chemin-de-fer* tables playing the same game, losing and winning and clucking their brotherly understanding of how big losses can happen, offering, then loaning dirty money needing washing to those weak enough to seek immediate surcease from casino demands to cover gambling debts, because "we know each other and understand each other and there won't be any problems because of the trust between us".

No worries, baby. No worries.

He'd chosen to put aside the stories he'd heard about others who had gone down that same road. Stories about financial ruin, family problems, extortion through kidnapping, unwitting dangerous and illegal involvement in the washing of dirty money, in one case, a fatal shooting, and in several cases, suicide of those who had succumbed to the easy, the more comfortable—and non-embarrassing—solution of borrowing money from a non-official, a criminal source.

But now he needed that sale. Not later. Now. Because there had been threats due to the long delay in the repayment caused by the drawn-out negotiations with his Lausanne colleague. There would be no more accepting his excuses and waiting for another of his positive reports on the progress of those negotiations.

Their message was brutal and simple. Get it done now, get the money and pay up. Or there will be consequences.

Hearing that, he'd been stupid—or perhaps scared—enough to ask what those consequences might be. The coldness in their eyes had given him the answer. No misunderstanding that message.

When he'd borrowed the money, he'd felt that his rationale for not using the bank as a source of funds to pay his debts had been totally correct: going to a bank to borrow money against his clinic and the equity in it would have exposed him to detailed, perhaps needling questions, from the bank, such as what he intended to do with the money. Considering the amount of money involved, a justified and justifiable question on the part of the bank, even with the security of a successful clinic and the equity in it as backup for the loan.

In the case of his bank, a required part of the loan process would have indeed involved questions about the use of the money and, potentially later, a review of where the money had gone if something happened to negatively impact the clinic which represented the security for the loan. He would have had to lie, telling them the money was meant for expansion of his current clinic or the purchase of another clinic or whatever excuse he could make up, when in fact, none of that would be anywhere near the truth.

Impossible to tell them that he had been a *hazardeur,* impossible to tell them that he had run up such terrible debts to the casino, that he had been a complete and careless fool. He would never have lived down the embarrassment with a bank that had stood by him all the years. But above all, he might have exposed himself to possible criminal prosecution for telling that lie, for taking the money under false pretenses. And causing the bank to perhaps one day be required to write down part or all of its loan to him.

So, for better or worse, the die had been cast.

The breakfast meeting had broken up with a handshake and his colleague's promise to get back to him the very same day with a final decision on the clinic purchase. A curious delay, he'd thought. After all the meetings and his colleague's obvious excitement about the clinic and its possibilities for him, why not shake hands in person right there on the spot?

Late yesterday afternoon, he'd received the following text message from him:

"Je suis plein de regrette, Monsieur, mais je ne suis pas en mesure d'honorer notre accord. Vous seriez certainement en droit de me conduire en justice. Cela ne me surprendrait pas si vous le faisiez. Mais je ne peux pas faire le paiement initial et franche-ment, je ne serai pas en mesure de payer le prix d'achat comme discuté dans les semaines prochaines. Cordialement."

The message was simple: "I regret to tell you that I am not in a position to honor our agreement. You would certainly be within your rights to legally attack me. It would not surprise me if you did. But I cannot make the initial payment and, frankly, I am not in position to pay the full amount as discussed in the coming weeks. Respectfully."

No matter which way one cut it, not matter which way one interpreted the content of that message, the deal was dead.

Every single word in that message a sledgehammer blow, every single word a mockery of his hopes, every single word a death sentence.

No explanation of why it had taken months to reach this negative conclusion, no mention of why possible delays or inability to pay hadn't been discussed and solutions found. No mention of the friendship, no real believable words of regret for the lack of forewarning, for the negative decision, and for the extensive amount of time spent on negotiations. And on travel. And on contract preparations. And the preliminary agreement.

The bastard had not negotiated in good faith.

Question after question. Was it really that, was the deal killer really the demand for immediate payment of the purchase price after the contracts had been signed, conditions that could have been perhaps renegotiated, even with the pressure of his lenders always in his ear, to allow for a payment of the purchase price over a period of sixty to ninety days? Or even perhaps longer? At least, substantial monies would have started to flow to the boys in Monaco and that would have fended off the worst.

Or perhaps it was something else, something much more mundane but no less a deal killer, his colleague's well-known philandering and his occasional, joking reference to an extremely jealous wife who knew well the man she had married and didn't want him spending so much time alone down south on France's summer playground?

Definitely a possibility knowing the man's wife as he did. But of what use were theories? Or conjecture. At the end, it was as it was.

Nevertheless, he'd had to know and to understand, he'd needed to have something that could perhaps stop the choking, cloying feeling of an end-game disaster.

A series of hurried calls to his colleague, now most likely back in Lausanne, had resulted each time in an automatic connection to his voice mail. He had left only one message for him, a desperate set of questions, wanting to understand the why and the why now, all this in spite of a justifiable urge to instead rant against him in any number of two-minute segments reserved for each voice mail message on his phone.

"Mais pourquoi, pourquoi ne m'avez-vous pas dit ceci, pourquoi ne m'avez-vous pas prévenu? Tu sais que je vous ai toujours

considéré comme un homme honorable. Il faut s'en rendre compte! On en a parlé tous les deux depuis si longtemps. On aurait pu arranger d'autres conditions. Mais maintenant çeci? Pourquoi? Dites moi pourquoi!"

Desperation pure: "But why, why didn't you tell me this, why didn't you tell me this might be a problem? You know I have always considered you an honorable person. I just can't realize what has happened! We have spoken the two of us about the clinic for months. We could have arranged other conditions. But now this? Why? Tell me why?"

Ten minutes later, he had a text message response.

"Je n'ai pas de réponse pour vous, Monsieur, que vous accept- eriez. Mais si cela vous fait du bien, je vais vous dire ceci: je ne pense plus que c'est un bon investissement pour moi. Franchement je n'en ai jamais été convaincu. Aussi simple que cela. Cordialement."

The answer a sharp blow to body and soul: "I have no answer for you that you would accept. But if it would help you, I will tell this this: I do not think anymore that buying the clinic would be a good investment for me. Frankly, I was never convinced that it was the right move for me. As simple as that. Cordially."

No need to follow up on that message. It was all a lie. A damnable lie. The use of the word *cordialement* at the end of the message? An insult. The message? The sign of a cowardly man, who, for whatever reason, and really giving none, had backed away from closing the deal, and was now seeking desperately to hide behind a self-constructed wall of excuses and fabrications. There was nothing else left to do.

A call to Monaco to those waiting for news of a completed deal and a closing date when their money would be paid back had been met with stony coldness and an agreement to meet on the outside terrace of the Salle Medecin at the Casino Monte Maurizio at eight the previous evening.

The meeting had taken place in the warmth of the setting sun, at a small round metal table next to the white railing running around the edge of the terrace. Under any other circumstances, a romantic and idyllic location with its views out over the Monaco harbor to the far reaches of the Mediterranean. But this was not a romantic tryst and its result was the exact opposite of ideal.

Twenty-four hours. Not one minute more. Whatever it takes.

An impossibility.

Maurizio Lorenzini leaned back from the steering wheel, his hands fell to his lap. The traffic on the road behind him had started to pick up a bit. Dawn would soon be here. Was it time? A cigarette? A quick search for cigarettes and then there was a Marlboro between his lips. He lit it with a match, inhaling deeply, blowing the smoke out of the still-open window into the stillness of the night.

His eyes fell on the glove department where he'd put a letter he'd written to his extended family. In addition, a separate one each for his wife, Charlotte, and his daughter, Anulka, each in an envelope with the proper address on it. The letters to his wife and daughter in French, the preferred language of a Polish wife who had immigrated with her family to Switzerland and had grown up with French as a second language.

He asked himself if all that he'd written was too emotional. Was this what suicides wrote their loved ones when they left something for them to read? But he didn't give a damn. He'd written what he felt.

He'd spoken to his wife of his faithfulness and love for her over the many years, of the joy of holding her hand when they'd walked along the shores of Lago Lugano or driven out in their motor boat onto the still smoothness of an early dawn on Lago Lugano.

He'd asked his daughter to forgive him, to think back on their happiness together, to cherish his love for her, his pride in her. He'd urged her to continue her volunteer work at the Swiss Red Cross and her part-time work at the kindergarten of her school. And, finally, he'd admonished her, as he'd so often done during her young years, to always be a giver, never a taker, whatever she did in life, wherever life and her hopes would take her.

He'd wondered if there would be more tears in his eyes when the moment came, if his pulse would race, if he would hesitate, if he would involuntarily dirty himself. He felt the utter sadness in his heart and in his soul, he recognized the insidious nature of a cowardly act, of running away from tough times, from embarrassment, from failing to tough it through. He thought of how his suicide would hurt his family, of the utter disappointment those colleagues and employees closest to him would feel, the questions it would raise for all of them as to why he had not sought help.

He recognized the self-centeredness he'd often seen and criticized in others during his life, now something he would be guilty of for all eternity.

It was time.

He took the hypodermic needle out of the right pocket of the beige-colored sport coat lying beside him on the seat. He was wearing a blue, short-sleeved shirt so there was no need to contort himself in pulling off any extraneous clothing.

The injection was Nembutal, used to drug/euthanize large animals when they needed to be put into a comatose state for treatment or to be euthanized. Use of the drug in the same dosage into the human body would cause immediate death. He had visited his medical distributer that morning in Nice and bought the drug. As a doctor, there had been no questions asked of him as to his intentions with the drug.

He'd smiled at the assistant and, in the macabre mood in which he found himself, had asked that the bill be sent to his clinic in Menton. It wouldn't save the authorities from likely doing an autopsy of his body after death, but it would give them an additional confirmation of the drug he'd used to kill himself.

He clenched and unclenched his left hand. No need for a tourniquet above the elbow. The vein he would use was very visible.

He stared at his arm, at the needle. He removed the cover.

The injection was practiced. For a moment, there was nothing, then, suddenly, a creeping coldness in his left upper arm and shoulder, a hard, cloying shock to his whole body. His heart raced.

A deep breath, and a—now already impacted—sideward glance at the glove box. And a fraction of a moment's thought on its contents.

The balconies, the faded red awnings, and the draped laundry disappeared.

2
Fifth and Sixth Floors
An Apartment Building
in the via Maurizio Cattaneo
Lugano
Switzerland

July 17   The same day   11:23 am

She'd gotten up too late. Now, there was so much to do and only five minutes to do it. She shouted down the circular stairs, her voice signaling time pressure and youthful frustration.

"Mama, have you seen the blue top I brought up from the wash? You know the one, the frilly blue one with the cut off sleeves and the open neck. I thought I'd put it here on a chair and now it's gone. And I want to wear it today."

"Anulka, I told you last night I'd hung it over the shower rod in the bathroom in our bedroom because it was still damp. Take a look. It's got to be there."

A moment of silence. Then more silence. Then the triumph, a quick call to below.

"Found it. Thanks."

New Skechers. Got 'em. No socks. Torn blue jeans. Knees showing. Tight, but that's the way they have to be worn. A thin dark blue belt. That's got to be here somewhere! The blue top, now dry. Buttons a bit stiff. A white Apple watch wrapped around the left wrist, a gift from a father who loved, who spoiled.

Hurry, hurry. I'm late, she thought.

Anulka Lorenzini was getting ready to go with her friend Josiane to the Museo Cantonale d'Arte, a short drive from her parent's apartment. Klaus Fussman, a popular German artist whose specialty was painting softly-nuanced flower arrangements using watercolors, was having a showing and this was the last day. And she and Anna, busy during the week with school and their various volunteer activities, didn't want to miss it. Not for the world, at least as far as they in their young years understood that world and its diffuse, sometimes obtuse character.

But first she had to get dressed and then drive quickly to pick up her friend.

Keys. Pocket wallet. Cell phone. Lipstick. Ahh, too much. Tissue. Fast remake. Eye shadow. Concentrate! Summer freckles untouched. Hair wrapped casually on top of her head with an elastic band holding it in place.

Finished.

Down the stairs she went, and around the corner into the living room where her mother, wearing a white, short-sleeved summer dress, sat on a deep red, two-seat velour sofa, her brown coffee mug placed carefully in front of her on a small black marble coffee table, a page from the newspaper, *Le Temps,* from Geneva, in her hand, not yet completely read.

As usual, the pages she had already finished reading were scattered, willy-nilly, around the floor in front of her, the rest, except for the one she held in her hand, still lying, neatly folded, next to her on top of one of the bright-yellow, satin cushions used to decorate the couch. No new-fangled, primitive computer for her, which would have allowed her to read her newspaper every day without the bother of having parts of it scattered all over the place and having ink smudges on her fingers and having to discard those pages afterwards in the correct garbage canister.

The perfect incarnation of a modern, yet very conservative Polish woman. Newspapers were and would stay her thing.

She looked lovingly and with pride at her daughter.

"Anulka, *comme tu es belle.* How beautiful you are. I love how you've gathered your hair at the top in a bun. But can you wear your helmet when you have it like that?"

"No problem, Mama. My hair gets a little squashed, but then I fix it the way it was after I arrive and all is well. You'd still love it, believe me!"

She laughed, a happy familiar sound in the confines of a quiet apartment. A quick grab of a chocolate croissant lying on a plate on the coffee table next to her mother's coffee cup, a bite into it, a wink and a smile to her mother, and she was at the door, turning the inside lock to open it.

Her mother looked at her as she stood there. She thought, how much I enjoy hearing her soft laugh. What a joy that is, what a blessing to have a daughter like Anulka, so giving, so different from many of the other girls in their often-troubled homes who only think of themselves and don't honor their parents as she does.

How did we do it, Maurizio? How were we so lucky to have such a young and spirited and intelligent girl as that?

She sighed. Quickly, a question, now in Italian, thrown at a door now fully open and about to be closed.

"Anulka, *hai abbastanza soldi*? Do you have enough money? You know, your father is always concerned that you have enough to pay your own way!"

"Don't worry, mama. I have enough. Papa shouldn't worry his head about that. I don't ever want that to be a problem. You know me, I can't manage it anyway so I've decided that when I'm grown up, I'm going to try to always have more than enough! Then I'll have no problems."

"Believe me, Mama, Papa will be very happy!"

She laughed again, that soft, so charming laugh coming from her throat, threw an air kiss at her mother, and then quickly pulled the door closed behind her.

Out of the elevator on the main floor, she walked across its polished marble floor to the glass door entrance. Coming in were two members of the Polizia Cantanole, serious-looking men in uniform with a purposefulness about them that made her hesitate for a second. I hope no one's in trouble in our apartment building, she thought. That would be terrible.

Then, she skirted quickly around them and was out and down the steps to her motorized green moped, a gift from her parents for her fifteenth birthday. "Mr. Yamaha", her faithful transport to all places. She unlocked the sturdy chain wrapped around the bike frame and its front wheel, stored it quickly in the pack attached to the top of the back fender, then, helmet perched securely on her head and fastened, started the small motor and off she went.

As she turned the corner at the end of the street, she looked back and up through the leafy foliage of the park at the building and at her parent's apartment on the fifth and sixth floors. The sun was beating directly down on her mother's geraniums and plants in the concrete planters located at the front edge of the balcony.

Oh, oh, big problem, she thought. I forgot to water them this morning. Not good. I'll definitely hear about that when Papa comes home tonight.

3
Outside Terrace of the Café Ponte Lago

Pedestrian Promenade
Porto Ceresio
Lago Di Lugano
Italia

June 2   Twenty-four years later   13:42

Perfect weather in the Italian lake region north of Milano. For several hours, a slight westerly breeze had been coming off the lake from the nearby Swiss side, gently moving the blue-and-white striped awnings hanging over the outside terrace of the Café Ponte Lago, and bringing some measure of cooling to an unusually warm late-spring day.

The terrace was almost full, only here and there an empty table visible, the white wooden chairs arranged neatly around them waiting to be pulled back and put to good use. The lemon-glazed cakes and iced coffees seemed to be enjoying the most demand, although an occasional chocolate-covered mouth indicated that the children in the crowd had not forgotten what tastes really fine on such a day.

The sun in her face, Anulka Lorenzini sat alone at one of the outside tables with a direct view of the busy Porto harbor. The occasional throaty roar of a motorboat, large dual chrome exhausts protruding above the waterline, revving up and then booming off after leaving the "no-wake" zone of the harbor, provided the only audible interruption of an otherwise relaxing café afternoon.

Her long legs were stretched out in front of her, her face lifted to the sun. At five foot seven inches, she was above-average in height. Normal weight. Dark green eyes. Several summer freckles grouped high on both her cheeks.

An aquiline nose centered in the middle of an oval face, its flawless complexion necessitating little or no make-up. A touch of dark gray eye shadow as contrast to her green eyes, a brush of a pale-pink lipstick on her lips, they were all she'd ever needed.

Her middle long, dark blonde hair was drawn back behind her ears, a white silk band in a blue and green Greek mosaic holding it in place. She'd perched a pair of sunglasses on the top of her head, the ends tucked firmly into the hair band.

Comfortable and familiar were not just empty words for her. She was dressed in a simple pair of long white cotton shorts and a light-green, sleeveless cotton blouse, the cleavage of her bosom just visible below a heavy gold cross hanging from a gold chain around her neck. Dark blue, suede leather flats from Ferragamo on her feet. An intricately-woven, gold chain ring on her fourth left finger, a small but expensive gift she'd bought for herself during a recent business trip to Hong Kong.

A perfect picture of elegant minimalism, both in taste and style.

A book with Italian title *Vorrei Qualcosa* lay on the table next to her half-empty coffee cup, a small slip of yellow paper protruding from the top, marking the spot where, a few minutes before, she'd stopped reading. For a moment, she let her gaze sweep across the busy promenade, marveling at the number of people out and about, taking in the beauty of the Italian flag flapping gently in the breeze above the podium reserved for the municipal band and its mid-summer evening performances.

The lake, the Alps, still snow-covered, in the distance, the freshness of the late spring air made the problems, the dangers, the questions, facing her at home in Zurich seem for a moment far away.

She was waiting for her partner of eight months, Luca Moretti, to return from viewing a four-room apartment overlooking the lake on the other side of the port. If he decided to buy it, they would use it, he'd said, for long weekends during the year and short vacations in the summer. She'd kissed him tenderly when he'd said that, signaling to him her agreement and pleasure at the thought.

He'd asked her several times to come along, but she'd declined, wanting instead to give him a chance to be alone with his thoughts, and his apparent intention to build an even closer relationship with her.

She smiled, picturing him in her mind. Tall. Wavy, dark-blond hair. Wonderful, soft brown eyes. Weekends, a casual dresser with a predilection for varying shades of blue or beige in the clothes he wore.

A man with no hidden, no dangerous agenda. No superficial *dolce vita*. No la-la. A solid and respected investment banker. With the kind of money he was earning, there was no need to grasp for more.

She shuddered at the sudden desire she felt inside for him. It was always the same. She wanted to hug him, kiss him, show him in any number of ways how much she loved him. And to tell him—in a thousand ways if he had the time—how thankful she was for the measure of balance and serenity he'd brought back into her life.

Definitely better times for Anulka Lorenzini.

But that was it.

Unfortunately, there just weren't enough of those good times to stop her from thinking about a totally different issue, her situation as Director of the Wealth Management Division at Bankhaus Finsler & Cie, one of the largest private banks in Zurich. And the dangerous position in which she found herself.

She'd been so positive about life at the beginning of her career, ready for challenges, full of ambition to make something of herself and, having hopefully achieved that, see some good money, honestly earned, a portion of which she intended to devote to helping others better their lives. Her smile, her soft laugh, so infectious, her high standard of conduct, her caring attitude for those around her, had impressed even those who'd enjoyed only a brief contact with her.

She'd joined the bank seventeen years before after obtaining a degree in economics and mediaeval history from the University of Zurich, working first as an assistant in the cashier's department, a set of windowless and colorless rooms buried in the middle of the third floor of the headquarters building. In the intervening years, she'd been promoted through a series of increasingly-responsible management positions.

Dr. Thomas Graesser, a member of the Executive Management board and part owner of the bank, had been her mentor almost from the first day of her employment. He was one of the few people at the bank whom she genuinely respected and admired.

Twice during the long years with him, she'd noticed him looking at her in a way that had said this man cares a great deal for you. However, aside from those two instances, there'd been nothing in his general behavior to indicate there was anything more to those looks than perhaps a certain fondness for her person as well as an appreciation of her continued good performance.

The sad thing about it was that she knew that their relationship could change now at any minute, that her betrayal of his trust, of his confidence, should he ever know the full extent of what she had done, would be met with disbelief, with deep disappointment, and with full-bore anger.

It hurt to even think about it.

Bankhaus Finsler had thousands of customers with normal checking and savings accounts, all of them served by retail locations spotted throughout Switzerland. However, the interesting music was played in the area of wealth management, her division, a part of the banking business Bankhaus Finsler– and practically every major public or private bank around the world—had developed into a high state of the financial art with high and profitable returns.

The bank had just less than 5000 well-situated—and well-taken-care-of—clients with total assets under management of close to 107 billion Swiss francs.

Well-situated, because each new client had been required to make an initial deposit of at least 1,500,000 Swiss francs or its equivalent in another currency. This amount was substantially higher than the minimum deposit requirements set by almost every other Swiss bank for opening the same kind of account. Together with its consistently good investment performance, that made Bankhaus Finsler something very special. And that was exactly what its wealthy clients were looking for.

It fed their egos. It made them feel unique. And elite.

Which, of course, at least, in their mind's eye, most, if not all, of them thought they were.

Well-taken-care of because they were stroked and coddled by her and the bank as only lots of money can demand and expect to receive.

A smaller number of her clients weren't really interested in having any substantive contact with the bank. Once they'd opened an account, then that was more or less the end of it. Over the many years, maybe several review meetings, more the exception than the rule, maybe a call here or there, perhaps one or two discrete messages sent to the bank over the years containing questions about their investments or the strategy underlying those investments.

Other than that, nothing. No visits initiated by the responsible bank officer on an annual basis to discuss their accounts and the performance of same. Not desired. Not welcome. Tell him, no thanks.

Simple explanation: they knew their money was in good hands. That was more than enough for them. End of discussion.

The majority did not want anything sent to them. No public bank releases. No bank annual statements. Nothing. Zero. Above all, no detailed account information in any form, either electronically or physically, by mail, for example.

And I am not coming to visit either. And, oh yeah, no telephone communications. Either to or from the bank. Nothing.

If I want something, I'll come to visit myself. Period.

There were very straight-forward reasons for these concerns. Not only large-scale tax evasion in their home countries, which many clients, for obvious reasons, wanted to keep safely hidden, no matter the cost, from all and everyone, but, also, sometimes more immediate, personal worries, such as potential problems with greedy or former business partners, fear of a blatant "inside job" embezzlement being discovered, divorce proceedings on their way south, a former mistress deciding she liked blackmail, or complicated, "play-the-game" bankruptcy proceedings which meant money still available had to be hidden, and stay hidden. Or fraud, particularly cyber fraud, large sums of money hacked by a Finsler bank client from other people's or business's accounts at other banks, requiring a quick, safe, and "sub-basement" haven at Bankhaus Finsler.

The driving reason behind all this secret hick-hack was always the same: someone might get the right or wrong idea, depending on the situation at hand, if such confidential bank account information were to fall into hands not meant to know about them.

No question. In all and every situation, the black cloak had to be buttoned tight, Swiss-tight.

And then there were those who had a very simple reason for wanting no communication with the bank: many of them, a little more than just moderately paranoid, just did not want their personal or financial information "floating around" somewhere in the postal system or on the Internet.

On the rare occasion when a member of that top tier of the client pyramid did come to visit, it was usually her job to take care of them, one-on-one. Private meeting room, credentials checked only by her, cash dispersals, or new deposits, or asset allocation discussions discretely taken care of behind closed meeting room doors. Perhaps also a quiet lunch for two along the lake in Kuesnacht, a well-healed suburb of Zurich. Or up on the terrace overlooking the city in the Hotel Grand Dolder.

No one else from the bank involved, except maybe the friendly woman at the reception who wouldn't have remembered them in any case, but whose job it was to meet and greet and provide refreshments as desired, or adjust the temperature of the meeting room, if it were found to be too cold or too warm.

One of her more outspoken clients had put the whole personal visit issue in perspective during a recent visit in Zurich.

"Ms. Lorenzini, you read the newspapers. You listen to the news. Way too much cyber hacking going on. There are some real nuts out there, guys who get off on this stuff. They want to put their footprint on every bit of data they can get their electronic hands on. Not with *my* account, thank you. So, don't worry. If I want to know something, I'll come and visit you in Zurich. Otherwise, I'll leave it to you to do what you do best: manage my money and make it grow."

How right he was.

At the beginning of her tenure as Director, she'd come for the first time into contact with a small number of wealthy Finsler clients who initially were nothing more than a collective pain in the ass. They'd walk through the door of her office or into a small meeting room, hail-fellow, well-met façade intact. She saw through it all, she knew it all. The falseness, the trickery, the hypocrisy,—and, often, the criminality.

Little people, rich people playing their own little games of importance and power. And thinking no one would see it or recognize it for what it really was.

She squirmed about on the hard wooden slats of her chair, remembering once again the long string of self-centered complaints or stories she'd often had to listen to during those years of meetings with them: wife problems, or rampant boredom, or tricky deals they'd pulled off, or problems with a hotel room not properly aired before their arrival, or ungrateful girlfriends, or ungrateful children, or, God forbid, their morning toilet difficulties, or the never-ending ("I'm just so unhappy sometimes.") burden of having so much money.

Or the Dutch yacht builders who'd caused them to endure severe budget overruns and didn't seem to care. Or their paranoia about keeping their money safe from grasping relatives ("You wouldn't believe the look in their eyes, like a snake looking at a rabbit.").

Or their superficial attempts at showing how frugal they were. Wearing a cheap, down-market watch, and making sure she saw it, was one of the favorite ways, as if that watch could possibly bear witness to their ordinary, common man status when, in fact, the eye-popping total value of their assets spoke an entirely different language. Or the one-unbuttoned button in a set of four on both cuffs of their suits or sport jackets, leaned-over, in-your-face proof of its bespoke, custom-made origin for those who "understood" that language.

And gave a damn.

She'd rejected any rationale, any excuse for that kind of behavior or attitude, except for one thing: she had, at least, a grudging global respect for the system, which, after all, had produced, at least, a good number of clients who recognized the good that could be done with their money. They were the people who actively pursued ways to benefit society.

But that grudging respect didn't in any way reflect the real story. What had slowly but surely driven a sea change in her thinking about Bankhaus Finsler and many of its clients was another part of the equation entirely.

Moral issues, attitudinal issues, a deeply-seated emotional issue.

With the exception of those clients she liked and respected, most of the money, both the clean money and dirty money, the white and the black money her clients had deposited at the bank, was just sitting there, doing absolutely nothing, except earning interest and maybe, depending on the structure of the portfolio, producing some outsized capital gains. She saw the statements, she saw the money just lying fallow, hoarded for purposes of false pride or greed, or because it needed to be hidden from someone else who was equally, or even more greedy.

It ground her down, it affected her work—and her respect for what she was and what she was doing.

In particular, she condemned the easy pickings for those among her clients who played the tax evasion card, who went about life totally and completely undisturbed by the lawlessness of their actions. Or by their self-centered approach to a life devoid of any trace of social consciousness.

She knew that it was just part of the way the system worked, also for Bankhaus Finsler, at least until Switzerland, the European Union, and other countries would finally be able to conclude their negotiations to complete the establishment of a world-wide, inter-locking system of unilateral and multi-lateral agreements, international tax law aimed at damming the tide of dirty money, tax evasion money, or, even perhaps, eliminating it almost entirely.

However, despite the best intentions, the factual realization of those goals, even with the number of agreements already in force, was going to remain, for some time to come, in many parts of the international financial world, a work-in-progress.

A never-ending one in her view.

She harbored strong doubts about the bottom-line effectiveness of such arrangements. Fact was fact: dirty—and often useless—money would always manage to find a way home.

It was these clients who became, increasingly, a thorn in her side. They possessed no recognizable or verbally-expressed desire to even do a little something good for the world with the money or the returns it earned, to try to let that money live and breathe, to give it feeling, a caring heart—and a purpose.

They simply did not care.

And the money itself? Yeah, it just didn't give a damn. About anything.

The passage of time only served to increase her resentment of those clients and their mostly useless, self-centered lives, resentment which became part of the driving force in the change in her attitude toward the bank—and the financial system in which it operated.

Because the bank, too, was complicit. It knew—and she knew it knew. The bank earned a lot of its money from assets having their origin in criminal enterprises, tax evasion, prostitution, looting of a country's resources, extortion, fraud, drugs, the numbers game, cyber hacking—all of it soulless money looking for a home and finding it.

The bank didn't really care where the money came from nor did the bank care why or why it was not being used for better purposes. For bank management, the main metrics of success were AUM, assets under management, ROA, return on assets under management, the sum of the various fees and commissions earned in the management of client money, and the bonuses paid out to management when AUM and ROA grew at budget or above-budgeted levels.

The sun rose and the sun set on those flawed, non-feeling metrics. End of story.

But that wasn't all there was to it. There was also something else in play in the increased hate she felt, even worse than the lack of caring, even worse than the greed, and the selfishness of her clients.

It was something that had burned a hole in her very being, causing a wound that had never healed, something that had saddened her soul almost beyond repair. For years and forever.

Anulka Lorenzini knew that part of herself well, that part of her so deeply affected by the suicide of her father and the circumstances around his death. Her father had been a well-known, international capacity in the world of pediatric medicine, resulting in great attention being paid by the French and Swiss police to his suicide. In his final letters to her and her mother, he hadn't included names or addresses of those persons from whom he'd borrowed the money, presumably to protect the family from any retribution. He'd only mentioned having used personal sources for the money, something the police had easily recognized for what it really meant, but the reference he'd made had been too vague and not enough to help them.

In the weeks following his death, the police had made a commendable series of intensive efforts to find those responsible for pushing him over the brink. The police knew that such deals, such arrangements often went down in what they termed the dark underbelly of the gambling world. Based on past work, the detectives knew many of the players in that *mileau*, particularly those who frequented the many casinos along both the Italian and the French Rivieras. They had all been put under pressure, all had been interviewed, several of them several times, but none of them had known anything about a doctor of medicine in financial trouble.

In the end, the police hadn't been successful in their search. Her mother had been told, right from the very beginning, that finding the exact persons involved would be very difficult and that this was a case that might never be resolved. But there was never any doubt about the intention of the authorities in the case: should the police find those responsible, they would drop the full weight of the law on their heads.

No pardon anywhere. Ever.

In the years past, however, neither she nor her mother had ever heard a word from whomever had driven husband and father to his death. No demands for money, no secret contacts with threats of bodily harm if monies weren't paid. Perhaps the intensity of the police work had pushed those responsible back into their little holes.

Whatever.

That nothing, at least, was a relief for them both.

It had been twenty-four years since, but the memory of that time, of the suffering she and her mother had endured, the intensity of the anger she still carried in her heart for those responsible, and the type of human being they stood for, never wavered nor had it ever lost any of its power.

Her father still lived with her every day in her heart, his words, his admonishments, his praise, his loving guidance, his encouragement, his kisses, the way he'd put his nose in her hair and breathed in deeply and then sighed contentedly, his hand on her head gently caressing her hair, the deep love of a father for a daughter in his eyes, everything around and about him still fresh in her heart and in her consciousness, even after so many years. So very much unlike other fathers she knew who had never said to their growing daughters, even once, that they loved them.

The crux of the matter, the central reason for her hate, for her actions, was that she knew that her father had, most likely, fallen victim to some of those very same types of people she met every day in the bank, dirty money clients whose presence, whose swagger and attitude, whose very existence ate at the very core of her being. It was all she could do to not to throw their obvious criminality and their insulting, carefree attitude to the dogs and tell them all to go to hell.

In spite of everything, she'd tried over the years to maintain deep inside of herself the softness, the caring, the giving side, things that her father had so loved about her, things that, in spite of everything, still meant so much to her because they'd meant so much to him.

If someone had asked her, do you still care, do you still want to do some good, she would have answered yes. But now, with the layers and layers of years over that time when she had been young, when her father had still been alive and her mother healthier than she was now, it was clear she was no longer wholly that same person. The years after the death of her father, the years at the bank had sadly hardened a part of her, her clients had hardened her.

The business of business had hardened her.

But there was more to it than that.

As the years passed, a subconscious wish for some sort of payback had begun to form somewhere in her. She'd found herself, at times, wanting to hurt, to screw the people who screwed others; she thought about wanting to screw the kind of people who'd also, if only symbolically, screwed her father. And her mother. And her.

In spite of everything, of her despising them as she did, there was still something she had to admit to herself: in whatever manner they had done it, the fact was they were something she wasn't. Rich. At 675,000 Swiss francs per year, plus a healthy bonus in a good year, definitely not even close.

Jealousy from a distance? Maybe. Perhaps more like an observation that some of the rich, at least those she liked to call the "good" clients, often reached a stage in their life where having money wasn't even the point any more. In a twisted sort of way, she saw their behavior, while occasionally borderline intolerable, as being somehow understandable.

A recent example of intolerable behavior, however, had certainly not fallen under that category "understandable".

Dr. Graesser stood in front of the tall window in his office, falling snow just visible past the heavy, red velvet drapes falling from the high ceiling, partially blocking the weak winter light coming in from the outside. His rebuke had stung.

"I noticed a look on your face this morning just before our meeting with Monsieur Gaillard ended. You looked like you were about to jump across the table and slap him right in the face. I know he's difficult, I know he's harassed you in the past, but you have to be careful about showing your feelings that way."

"You know this. Normally, you take such good care of

your clients. That's why I was a bit disappointed in you when I saw that angry expression on your face. You know very well that's not acceptable behavior."

She'd replied, her words measured, an even tempo to her sentences. "Herr Dr. Graesser, the man is insulting. The sexist remarks he throws at me, the way he doesn't look me in the eye, but below it, right at my chest. And, frankly, sometimes lower. That smirk on his face. You heard what he said. I have to tell you, I really had to struggle to keep myself from reacting. You know we have some clients who are like that. I'm really sorry, but they get to me sometimes."

"Yes, I understand that. And believe me, I didn't overhear the remarks he made to you. I also know we have clients like that. And I haven't forgotten your other past experiences with the one or two of them."

He studied her. "However, whatever the situation, I want to remind you that we're not in the business of judging our client's behavior or what they want to do with their money. Or, as in this case, calling them to order in meetings when they forget where they are. Or whom they are dealing with."

"And whatever we do, it's definitely not our job to teach them new manners. And, just to make everything clear here, unless their behavior is really out of line, we're certainly not going to ask them to take their money elsewhere. So do me and yourself a favor. Please try to remember those things in the future."

Her eyes had narrowed, but not in a bad way. She respected her boss. She'd done what he'd asked. And she knew he wasn't wrong. But that was it. Inside, she hadn't switched off what she thought.

Gaillard was dirty money, she knew it from his file. And he was an idiot. Just like many of the others.

However, continually living that lie had turned out to be more difficult than she thought. Yes, there were some she respected. Wonderful people, people she enjoyed seeing, eating with, telling stories with and asking about families with. While not all givers, or salt-of-the-earth types, they were at least people with a social conscience and empathy for their fellow man.

Unfortunately, they were more the minority. All the others had slowly undermined her ambition, slowly destroyed her motivation. And worst of all, their behavior, their attitude, what they did, or didn't do, with their money, had taken away a substantial part of that positive feeling she'd had at the beginning for the bank and its business.

But that was just part of the beginning of the end.

4
Outside Terrace of the Café Ponte Lago
Pedestrian Promenade
Porto Ceresio
Lago Di Lugano
Italia

June 2   14:02

Hell, I know exactly what other bankers think, she thought. I know there's some of that toxic contempt in them as well. Most of them mouth the usual line about their client base and the client-friendly services their firms offer and how thankful their clients are and how thankful they are to have such clients.

Maybe some of them mean it, most of the time. But most of them really don't. When I say those words, I'm not fooling around. I know I'm playing a lying game at least ninety-percent of the time.

She looked up, a shadow falling on her table. "*Non adesso, Signora. Ho ancora qualche café nella mia tazza. Grazie.*" Not now, Signora. I've still got some coffee in my cup. I'll call you in a bit. Thank you.

Having money was something I'd always wanted. But it was always something I wanted on my terms, the way my father would have wanted me to have it and to live with it. That was the reason I never once doubted I could one day do rich better than the rich, that I could make something good happen with the money I earned above leading a comfortable life. Not that I didn't have personal wishes, but the higher purpose was always making that money mean something, making it work for something good in the world.

What I hadn't counted on was how profoundly and deeply the contempt I felt for my clients had, over time, eaten away at me. And how much that feeling had drastically changed me and my general attitude.

I got a good, close look at how much damage that contempt had done, at how much I had changed, when I met that bastard Giovanni who managed to take that contempt and gave it a purpose. And a name. And a direction. And a goal.

And a number.

Yeah, there'd been two or three relationships way in the past, but this one? This one had been off the wall somewhere on another planet.

That first summer with him years ago? Hard to admit it now, but there was a time when my world was him and absolutely nothing else. No bank, no clients, no problems at all in sight.

I liked leaving Zurich at the end of the week, taking the late afternoon Air France flight to Nice Airport. I liked hugging him tight in the Arrival Area hall, where he was waiting after having driven over from his home in Milano. That was always something really special, that first kiss on an early Friday evening, that first moment.

I liked the sound of his convertible Porsche's double exhaust system. Sort of like our own personal calling card. Raw and loud and brassy and hot. Six stick shift, gears hot. I liked the evening sun, still intense, warming our faces as we roared along the Promenade des Anglais in Nice, dodging in and out of the traffic. Rolling the traffic lights when we had the chance, listening to the latest songs from Eros Ramazotti on the radio.

Our own private arrival celebration.

And the hotel where we stayed? An absolute gem high on the cliffs overlooking the coast, Cap Ferrat, Villefranche-sur-Mer, and Monaco all clearly visible below along the coast. I liked sitting on the terrace in that hotel with my feet up on the low stone wall, looking down at the Mediterranean, feeling the morning sun burning my skin with its rays.

And then the afternoons, the swimming off the rocks after sneaking into the fenced-in military area of Cap Ferrat out by the lighthouse. The evenings eating on the outside terrace at our favorite fish restaurant on that small beach in

Antibes, the remnants of a beach afternoon still lying around on the sand, forgotten or discarded.

The waiter at Chez Michel with that funny blue handkerchief knotted around his neck who'd smiled so nicely after he'd spilled some red wine on our tablecloth. And afterwards, those tipsy, wobbly wet kisses waiting on the narrow sidewalk out front for the valet to bring the car around . . . .

Il dolce fare niente. The sweetness of doing nothing.

There was only him, that untouchable world, and nothing else.

I should have known. It was all a game. His game. He knew my history, he knew what I liked, and didn't like. He knew I liked losing myself in the sex and in a couple of other things as well.

He knew every inch of my being. I let him do it.

Universe burning.

He knew how I despised some of my clients, the dirty money boys, the tax evasion players, who sauntered into the bank with an attitude bigger than the building they were in, he knew about my father, a likely victim of dirty money dealings, he knew into what channels that dirty money often wandered, he knew—who the hell didn't?—that Swiss banks held a lot of that kind of money.

He knew where all my buttons were and he pushed every one of them.

He rolled me. He promised me release. And I bought into it.

How the hell did I let that happen, what took that nothing-in -the—way train I was on at the bank right off its tracks; how did I become a part of his crazy plan to embezzle that money? And commit the very same crimes I was certain a number of my clients had themselves committed.

It's always the same question; it's always the same answers.

Bad enough that there are times when I think about the money I now have and what it means to have that kind of money. Those are momentary, but seductive, moments, thinking about the plans I have, the good I hope I can do with a large portion of the money, money that has now been washed the other way from dirty to clean.

Okay, alright. My version of clean.

And that other little matter? That's something way out there. How, how was I able to continue living and working as I did, totally at ease, no problems, sleeping well at night, visiting and laughing with friends, no pangs of guilt whatsoever, during the many months it all went on?

How the hell did I do that?

The first reason is easy, real easy. Giovanni. A carnal relationship perhaps gone bad? No, definitely much more than that. And, certainly, way more than enough to blind me to the danger of crossing the line, a line I maybe just didn't want to see, the line between an angry but good banker and an angry, criminal, bad banker.

He was slick, he knew how to burrow into me mentally, he knew how to take my resentment and frustration and sadness and put me in a place where I thought there might be release.

Release? Payback? Punish the system? Giovanni had it all figured out.

And on top of all that, I was absolutely convinced we'd get away with it. That's not an excuse. That's a fact.

Was maybe getting those big gobs of money that weren't mine more important to me than I thought possible?

Was that it?

Or was it something totally different? Maybe I'd just started feeling invincible and thought I could do anything, steal money, fly to the moon, be the world's moral apostle, whatever.

And get away with it.

What the hell. For years, I'd had nothing but one success after another, one promotion after the other. Looking around at clapping admirers honoring me in beautiful, closed-in *separées* in restaurants or large hotel banquet rooms was all I knew.

The honor I received three years ago in Geneva at the Hotel Richemont as Banker of The Year Switzerland? My meetings with the bank's directors twice a year, overwhelmed by their compliments and praise? The newspaper journalists from Munich, from Zurich, from Geneva, from London, from God knows where, calling, asking for repeat interviews?

Under those circumstances, who wouldn't start to believe they'd developed a Teflon skin, a Teflon personality, a Teflon professional position, untouchable in the bigger scheme of things?

It's hard to admit, thinking about those times, those accolades. Where I should have felt pride and happiness, I felt the arrogance of moral superiority. Where I could have shown thankfulness, I felt increasingly only more resentment for a bank and a system which seemed to have lost its way.

My state of mind had even gone so far as to consider the most important person in my life, Dr. Graesser, to be morally complicit. Good grief.

So why am I always thrashing about looking for an answer?

Because there is only one explanation and I'm wasting my time thinking about anything else. It is and it always was Giovanni.

Yeah, the guy was good. Very good. Convincingly good.

But his plan?

That was just too damned good.

5
The Pedestrian Promenade above the Beach
Boulevard des Anglais
Nice (Cote d'Azur)
France

A late summer evening two years prior   23:41
In August of that year, their relationship suddenly changed. Sitting at dinner in the candle-lit Moulin de Mougins restaurant just above Cannes, Giovanni had spoken briefly about his desire to become really rich, exposing her, for the first time, to a parade of his own internal demons, to a full display of his greed and his egocentric impulses, small signs of which she'd already seen in the past, but had more or less ignored.

Later that same evening, they'd driven slowly along the traffic-jammed, coast road from Cannes to Nice. And the Promenade des Anglais.

They'd sat next to one another on a worn, wooden, three-seater bench above the beach, looking down at the moon-lit waves, feeling the warm night breeze, saying nothing, trying, in spite of the tension in the air, to enjoy the moment.

He'd been nervous, he'd fidgeted with his hands, moved his watch slowly up and down on his left forearm, reached down to pull up one of his socks which had slipped down to just above his shoe.

Studying him closely from the side, she'd had a good idea how he wanted to get at those riches. She loved him, but if her assumption turned out to be correct, she would know he'd led her along all those months with only one objective in mind.

But there'd been something even worse than that. As she'd waited, a sharp jolt had gone through her, an odd feeling that she might very well be ready for what she suspected he would propose.

He'd turned then to her, and it was game on.

"Listen, Anulka, you play in the world of finance. You know there's an incredible amount of money moving around the world. In the past, I've often asked myself, is there any way I could get some of that? I didn't have an answer then. But now is different. Now, I think I do. Our being together makes certain things possible that weren't possible before when it was only me alone thinking about all that money."

He searched for her eyes. "I don't know your business, Anulka. But, in spite of that, I can tell you, I think I've got a pretty good idea of what's really going on. There's so much written information out there, in the newspapers, in books and, of course, on the Internet about the Swiss banks and their wealth management activities, how they work, their tax evasion games, the numbered accounts, the types of clients, the client services, management behavior, judicial cases, indictments of bankers who stepped over the line, changes in international law affecting black money and its ability to stay hidden. All there for anyone to read. Whatever one wants to know."

He'd leaned closer to her, studying her face. "Listen, you remember, of course, my speaking about money during our dinner tonight. What I was doing was referring to something I've thought a great deal about, something I think we can do together. It's a simple idea, but I think it's one that will really surprise you."

He'd looked at her for a long moment, then taken the plunge. Direct. Straight at the black center circle.

"Anulka, I think there's a way to tap into one of your client accounts, those you always refer to as the bank's fucking, dirty money accounts, and pull out some of the cash in one of them without the client or anyone else at the bank becoming suspicious."

He'd stopped speaking. Her eyes told him she knew exactly what he had in mind. And who would be taking the lead in making it happen.

Time to get to it.

"Looking at the expression on your face, I'd guess you know exactly what I'm talking about. That's good. But there's one thing I want to tell you right here at the start. And I mean it one hundred percent. Please don't ever think I hustled you because of your position, don't ever think that we've spent our time together with me doing only one thing, plotting and planning how to get you into this kind of a deal. And not caring about you, not loving you every day. That is just simply not true. So, please, don't look at me like that."

She had played his game then, but hadn't quite been able to eliminate a trace of sarcasm in her answer. And a bit of a bite in the question she'd posed him when he'd stopped talking.

"I'm not, and I believe you, Giovanni. I'm just a little surprised at what you've just said. Tell me, what kind of an inside job were you thinking about?"

A smile in his eyes at her use of the word inside. And she had her answer.

The words had spilled out of him. Someone would call her at the bank asking for a meeting. This someone would be a substitute for one of the real clients of the bank, someone who had made large, continuous cash deposits many years ago, someone who had at least an eight-figure asset level at the bank, preferably 70 to 90 million euros, with a good percentage of it not invested and still in cash, someone who had no real personal relationships within the bank, someone with a European passport, preferably Italian, someone dirty because it's you and you would need that.

They would need a short list of such candidates drawn from the bank's data base and files. They would need copies of those clients' signature cards. They would need copies of the passport photos currently contained in those files. They would try to choose someone who had similar features to the person coming to pick up the money and create for him an appropriate matching identification.

They would create a substitute client, a Client X.

He'd looked at her. Nothing. Not a word.

"Alright, you don't want to talk. I understand that. But there's an additional element in the whole concept, something really important for you to know. It involves you—and your security. If that dirty client were ever to come and learn what had happened to his account, you would, of course, deny any involvement."

A serious look on his face. "Your message would be simple: I applied all relevant security protocols when the client came to visit, protocols I follow and have followed without a single exception since I have been Director of the Wealth Management Division. With hundreds and thousands of clients, many of whom haven't visited the bank for years, I don't think I can be expected to recognize each and every one of them and differentiate between a possible imposter and a real client."

His voice, quiet, cautious, almost an octave lower. "If, however, Anulka, if there were a breach anywhere and you were in danger, then part of the plan would be to provide you right from the start with a new identification, a set of new documents so that you could immediately leave Switzerland and go elsewhere. Good papers, secure papers. Maybe even double down on that and give you two sets from two different countries if you wish."

A flat look in her eyes.

"Okay. Okay. I'm sorry, I know you haven't agreed to any of this, but I just want to make sure you understand everything that's involved."

It had been just a bit too much for her. No way she was going to make it easy for him.

"Just a second, Giovanni. Whatever you say, but nevertheless, you're talking like I'm just going to say amen to all of this. That's more than a bit presumptuous of you, don't you think?"

She hadn't really wanted to hear anything more of his explanations. But her growing curiosity—and astonishment—had gotten the better of her.

Before he could answer, she continued. "This whole thing sounds like a lot more than just a simple one time in-and-out. How much money are you talking about here?"

He'd recognized the question for what it was, a subtle shift in attitude. She hadn't said no, hadn't told him to stop. Instead, she was busying herself with the details.

"Well, first of all, we certainly won't to do this all at once. Client X would visit the bank a number of times over the course of nine to ten months to pick up the cash. Most likely eight to eight hundred fifty thousand, maybe 900,000 Euros or about 1 to 1,2 million US dollars per visit. Perhaps more."

He'd smiled at her.

She'd stared him down. "Listen, I asked you about the

total cash, not about percentages in any account. How much money are you talking about here? How would the money be divided up? Or is this something you deliberately don't want to tell me?"

A trace of annoyance in his voice, he'd given her the details. "Simple answer. I think you should get 60 percent of the cash. It is, after all, a bigger risk for you. I'd get 25 percent. Client X the remaining 15 percent. I think that's a fair distribution."

He'd touched her arm but she'd pushed him away, the tone in her voice showing exasperation.

"Listen, Giovanni. One last time. I just want to know one simple thing, one simple answer to a simple question. How much money total? It sounds like you want to pull out somewhere around fourteen to fifteen million Euros. Is that correct? Or is it more than that?"

Contriteness in his voice. "No. Sorry. I mean yes. It'd be somewhere in that area. And no, nothing more than that. After that, we'd be done. I promise you."

He'd looked at her, thinking he saw in her eyes what her real concern was. Would the amount of money compensate for the tremendous risk she'd be facing?

Was that it?

"Ah, I think I understand. What you're really asking about is the risk, isn't it? Alright, yes, there'd be a lot of money going out. But you know very well what you have to do when a client comes and wants cash. Secondly, remember, I told you, the real client we pick wouldn't be an active one. If we choose well, he most likely won't be coming for a visit or calling the bank for a long time in the future."

She'd looked at him. No reaction.

No, the point was important, but that wasn't it. There was still something in her eyes, still something in the way.

Suddenly, recognition.

What about us?

He'd gently turned her head to his. He'd kissed her lips, then both her eyes. For a long time after, they'd sat there on the bench, speaking quietly with one another, the several years of closeness intensifying the moment, trying to react to each other's questions and doubts, trying to calibrate—or recalibrate—their feelings as they'd worked their way through an intense and perhaps life-changing discussion.

Then a question, whispered softly, close to her ear: "Tell me, Anulka. Will you at least think about it? I know you know it's a damn good plan."

He'd studied her closely, judging the impact of his question on her. She'd avoided his gaze, looked away.

He'd stood, moving away to the railing to stare down at the sea's waves rushing back and forth across the stony beach below. She'd turned and watched him go. And drawn a deep breath.

Boiled down to the basics, he'd shown her a way to grab for herself—and grab was no doubt the right word for it—the equivalent of over nine million US dollars plus in cash. With that kind of money plus her savings and the gold depot she had, she knew that whatever came—including, potentially, the dirty money client who'd had his account plundered—she'd always be, if necessary, in a position to quickly leave the bank—and the clients she hated—she'd be able to go elsewhere, and put that dirty money to good use and still have something left over for herself.

What was it she'd always wanted to do? Screw those who'd screwed others, among them, most likely, her father.

Giovanni was showing her a way to do exactly that.

She'd felt the temptation and the greed and the bravado and the hesitation mixed in with the fear of the unknown. Thoughts of possible arrest and imprisonment tumbled helter-skelter around in her head.

She'd smiled at the one thing that had worried everyone so much when client security was being strengthened at the bank, the one danger everyone had known couldn't entirely be eliminated, the risk of a top bank executive going rogue. The irony of the situation had almost made her laugh.

At that moment, he'd turned around to face her. A few steps had brought him back again to the bench. He'd reached down and taken her right hand in both of his, twisting for several seconds the gold chain ring she was wearing on her left ring finger.

She'd avoided his questioning gaze. It's one thing to want something, she'd thought, but then, suddenly, to be confronted with the possibility of actually having it. That's tough. And then, on top of everything else, knowing, at the same time, how dangerous the getting it could be. An entirely different situation.

She'd thought about him, had sensed his determination, his impatience, his conviction. Her heart beating fast, she'd taken a moment to clear her mind, then she'd raised her face to his, looking him directly in the eye, sending him a silent message, a small smile at the corner of her mouth.

He'd heard a wave break below them on the beach, rustling across the small stones at the edge of the shore as it rushed forward. He'd recognized the look on her face, the slight glow of the moonlit night reflecting in her eyes, two deep pools of luminous darkness in her pale face.

In them, the silent force of want and temptation. And the possibility of retribution.

6
Outside Terrace of the Café Ponte Lago
Pedestrian Promenade
Porto Ceresio
Lago Lugano
Italia

June 2   Current year   14:51

In just over ten months, 13,300,000 Euros in dirty money cash gone from Sala's account, sixty percent of it mine.

Every single visit, every single withdrawal, a clean in-and-out deal. No one had suspected anything.

And there was something else, something that made me feel very strange, the pride I'd felt in how everything went down, by the book, a book I'd written years before when I'd worked on tightening the security parameters at the bank. The security video system? No problem. I'd had my finger-prints all over that installation as well. The rolls of security tape? They showed nothing but standard-set client meetings just like any other meeting with a top client of the bank.

Just crazy, crazy successful, crazy stupid—and crazy criminal.

But then suddenly, that email from Dr. Graesser last year in August on some customer matters, those several sentences at the top of the second page referring to recent large cash withdrawals by one of the bank's top clients.

My client. The false client. The bagman.

Nothing more was said, but those sentences carried weight. And something far worse: a definite hint of further management concern. I knew it right away. The negativity, my go-to source of support, suddenly turned into a weak and brittle accomplice. Why hadn't I known I'd just panic, why hadn't I known I'd immediately cave in if anything suspicious, or the least bit dangerous, ever happened?

Game over.

I didn't waste a second. Out of the office, a ten-minute powerwalk to the lakeside promenade and its bridge. Speed dials on a throwaway phone using a pre-arranged call sequence. And then he was there. And I was ready for him.

So damn ready.

"No, Giovanni, you don't understand. First of all, somebody noticing those cash withdrawals like that and then remarking on it, particularly in an official bank internal memo? That's really unusual. And Graesser isn't just anybody. He's top management, for God's sake. He has a nose for such things. And that means he'll ask more questions at some point. That would be bad, really bad."

"But that's not all. On top of that, we have your stupid gofer friend and what he pulled off during his last visit. You remember, I told him over and over again: do not do anything out of the ordinary, do not do anything that could make people notice you. And remember you."

"And what does that damned idiot do? He lets his hormones go completely nuts."

Voice tense and measured. "Normally, I go alone and get the money at the cashier's office. But this last time, I made an exception. I had the cashier bring the money to the conference room. With a normal client, a clean, thirty second in-and-out of the room procedure. No big deal. But what does that gofer of yours do? Instead of remaining neutral, professional, client-like,—with the cashier leaving as quickly as she has come—, he starts flirting with her. And keeps on doing it. Good grief! Unbelievable."

A biting tone in the words, anger up. "She spoke to me about it afterwards. Can you believe it? Somebody remembering the client. Totally dangerous. That's not what we wanted and not what we agreed upon, damn it."

A turn to face the lake. "What'd you say? You're breaking up. Move around a bit. I can't hear you."

"Ah, now it's better. What? So you don't think those things are dangerous? You don't think they're a deal stopper? Particularly that memo? Well, I happen to think they are.

And it's me who's sitting here right in the middle of it, not you. If anything happened or somebody discovers something, it's me they'll pick up."

"You know exactly what we discussed. If something came along that endangered this deal, we'd stop. That was exactly what we agreed. Nothing more, nothing less. And now something has."

"What's that you're saying? No, I don't see any sense in your coming up here to talk. It won't change my decision one iota."

"I'm telling you. Forget it."

That conversation. How could I forget it, me standing at the railing of the bridge, chipping furiously with my right forefinger nail at several encrusted rust flakes on the steel struts, loosening them, watching them float down to the slow-moving water below.

Talk about strung out.

"Stop yelling, damn it. I don't care about the rest of the money we wanted to take out . . . and stop interrupting me."

"What the hell, you're going to force me to get the money? Really? Wow, I can't believe it. You're a real asshole, Giovanni."

"Speak louder, I can't hear you again!"

"Okay, better. Talk."

"Wait a minute. What the hell did you just say! You're daring to threaten me like that? Listen, you bastard, I don't care what you say. Or what was agreed upon. I'm telling you, damn it, it's over. No more money. We already got most of it. Isn't that enough for you, for God's sake?"

"Well, that's your problem, isn't it? If I go down, you go down. And make sure your gofer friend understands that as well!"

"Wait, what, what was that you just said? Well, fuck you, too."

People had started looking. Funny, even at that anger level, I hadn't forgotten the important things, like looking along the sidewalk in both directions for a garbage can to toss the throwaway phone into. Or where the police car at the end of the bridge had disappeared to.

Almost ten months gone since that final shouting match on the bridge. No further contact. I live and I sleep and I work. I've got no damned alternative. I have to keep doing what I'm doing and try not to become guiltier than I already am.

And thank God, the real client hasn't showed up.

But the real question is what's with the quiet? It's been a long time. Not a peep from Italy.

I just can't stop thinking about it. What's he doing? Is he planning something? Or has he given up? Was it enough money for him after all? Or is he off doing some new kind of deal?

I've moved on. Has he done the same?

What?

7

The Terrace Restaurant at the Hotel Villa Visconta Di Magliaso

Magliaso
Tessin
Switzerland

June 2   Later the same day   19:08

Luca and Anulka closed and locked the door to their garden-level hotel room, remarking again how glad they'd been to be able to get a reservation for that particular room. And for the hotel in which they would be spending three nights on *demi-pension,* breakfast buffet and a four-course dinner included in the price per night.

They'd chosen the Villa Visconta for its coziness—only 21 rooms—and its quiet countryside character. The hotel had been an abandoned country manor almost twenty years ago, but the new owners, tremendously creative in their approach, had recreated the hominess of the place, keeping and restoring almost all of the furniture and decorative touches that had once made it such a splendid place to live. Its large garden with its swimming pool and putting green was currently a sea of color, flowers, purple irises everywhere against a backdrop of mature, deciduous trees and a deep-green lawn, cut and trimmed at its edges to perfection.

They were not in any particular hurry as they moved down the hall. Their lovemaking had left them in a relaxed mood, the heat of those moments now gone, but the effects still lingering on in their bodies and their minds.

Several times, she'd been moved to tears by the way he'd looked at her. His hands placed tenderly on her cheek, his direct gaze penetrating deep into her eyes, took her every time it happened to an emotional place she'd never experienced before.

She paused for a second, checking. Yes, she could still feel the wetness of him deep inside of her. She hadn't washed it out afterwards in the shower. Her cheeks flushed at the thought as she turned to take his hand.

While dressing, they'd discussed his afternoon visit to the apartment. If half of what Luca had told her were true, then it was perhaps the "second home" he'd imagined for them, but thought didn't exist. Luca had called the real estate agent from their room and arranged a second viewing for the next afternoon at three. She was already hanging framed, black-and-white photo blowups of them both on all the walls.

Thankfully, no conscious thought remained of the troublesome time she'd spent that afternoon in the cafe in Porto

Ceresio, waiting for him to come back and tell her if he liked what he'd seen.

They walked slowly down the long, terracotta-tiled hallway toward the hotel's small reception area. The yellow dress she'd chosen to wear had been a success. Luca had watched her put it on, and then fasten a dark blue suede belt with a gold buckle around her waist. The afternoon sun, the freshness of a slightly-suntanned skin on her face—and her happiness at being with him–had done the rest.

She was, in his opinion, the most beautiful woman he'd ever seen.

Smiling, she'd said to him, "Let me give you a tip, Luca. You can say that to me every day. And even more often if you want to . . ."

He replied, his eyes smiling at her, "Well, if that's all it takes, then..."

She'd let that comment go by. She knew what he meant.

She noticed one of his Davidoff cigars sticking out of the top of his shirt pocket, a medium-long, mild cigar with the number 2 embossed on its paper ring. Twice, when visiting her in her apartment in Zollikon, a suburb along the lake near Zurich, he'd smoked a cigar out on the terrace overlooking the lake, albeit with the sliding doors open. She'd watched him for a moment, then mock admonished him for such silliness—and for producing such a penetrating smell.

She reached over and touched the pocket holding the cigar. His answer to her touch was to the point: she should be happy that smoking was prohibited in the hotel. If she wished, she could sit later and watch him walk around the garden, enjoying that cigar. Far enough away so she wouldn't be able to smell anything.

She smiled. "Ah, yes, men and their little amusements!"

His answer was to pat her lightly on her bottom. "Amusements. Right you are, woman. You one of them?"

She poked him gently in the ribs, a slight smile showing at the corner of her mouth. Not just one of them, she thought. When I think about what we do together and how we are, the best one.

Ever.

In a corner of the hotel reception, an ornate, dark wooden table was set up for a chess game. Two carved wooden chairs in half-moon Renaissance style stood on each side of the table. Thick, red velvet cushions on each seat, yellow tassels dangling from the four corners of each cushion, provided a measure of soft sitting comfort. The chess figures were a study in uniqueness, an elegant combination of dark and light green marble and embossed wood, soft green felt glued to the surface under each of them to protect the polished wooden surface of the board from any scratches.

Luca and Anulka decided to start a game. If they weren't able to finish before dinner—their chess sessions were usually hard-fought exercises in tactical and strategic chess warfare—they knew they'd be able to come back and do so afterwards. The director of the hotel would simply put a little sign next to the board indicating "Game in Progress." Serious chess players would respect that. And it would keep the table and the board reserved for them for after dinner.

A special gesture for special guests.

She commented that perhaps the more suitable wording for the sign should be *Defeat in Progress.*

"Luca, I don't have a chance at winning when you play like you do. Why don't we just make a sign with those words on it and put it right in front of me now and be done with it?"

He smiled at her. "No, we're not going to do that. Frankly, I really enjoy playing with you and, believe me, you are getting better. Besides, what better way is there to admire you than sitting directly across from you at chess?"

She sighed. What can one say in answer to that kind of compliment? Nothing. Absolutely nothing.

They sat down and ordered drinks. Five minutes later, the waiter was back with their order. For Luca, a Pilsner *bier*, and for her, a Cinzano *bianco* on ice, no lemon. He'd also brought them a small dish of salted peanuts and a spoon.

Luca was incorrigible. Instead of using the spoon to put some peanuts into his hand and then pop them in, he simply picked several of them up with his fingers and did the same thing. No napkin use in sight. She handed him one. He smiled.

Several minutes later, they were deep into the game. As usual, she was having problems with his particular style of play. It was maddening. It seemed to her that Luca antici-pated her every move. He didn't study the board for long. He would just grab a piece, make a particularly aggressive move in the direction of one of her pieces, then look up at her, challenging her with an innocent smile to counter the move he'd just made.

Damn, he was good.

She took a moment to look at him. She noted with satisfaction the gold cuff links and the light blue shirt he was wearing, gifts she'd brought back for him from a recent business trip to London. She couldn't have designed a better look for him.

She breathed in and out, deeply, once, twice. Was there anything better than this, right here, right now?

The gong sounded for dinner. They made sure the director took care of the "Game in Progress" sign, then made their way through the main sitting room, admiring for a minute the several small pieces of Art Deco art hanging, softly illuminated, on the walls and the large antique piano tucked away into the corner, stray pieces of music spread out on its shiny surface.

On the terrace, Luca caught the attention of the waiter, who promptly pointed to a table for two at the front edge of the terrace next to the newly-mown lawn.

The sun had not yet set and it was still very hot. Their view of the scene before them was blocked somewhat by several grown rosebushes located directly in front of their table between the lawn and the terrace. They moved their chairs and the table a bit to the right so that they could enjoy the whole expanse of the garden and the view to the surrounding mountains.

Directly across the hotel lawn on the other side of a small road dividing the hotel property from its neighbors was the fourth green of the local golf club. Some younger members of the club were just finishing up play on that hole, apparently, however, in a relatively dissatisfying manner, because there'd been no high-fives or loud yells coming from them, signifying a birdie, or even an eagle putt.

On the terrace itself, there were nine other couples, plus two foursomes, all seated under the large awning hung from the ivy-covered façade of the hotel. Guests of the hotel, they assumed, all quietly talking with one another while enjoying the early evening atmosphere. Anulka counted three waiters who would be taking care of their collective needs during dinner. Always a good waiter-to-guest ratio here, she thought.

Dinner on the terrace at the Villa Visconta was an elegant affair. Guests made a special effort to dress accordingly. The food was first-class; the service, friendly and correct. Above all, one could sit for three hours or more if one wanted to and nobody would say a word.

The director of the hotel walked along the terrace, greeting the guests and wishing them a good evening and an enjoyable meal. In four different languages. The chef cook stuck his head out of one of the double doors leading to the kitchen, checking on the tables and confirming the guest count.

It was *bon appetit* time.

They ate in their usual leisurely fashion. By the time dessert appeared, a *panna cotta* with thick honey syrup on the top, the evening had turned to night. The murmured talk coming from the other guests, noticeable during the meal, had faded away somewhat as everyone seemed to be captivated by the calm of a warm night and the brilliance of the star-filled heavens above.

The last formalities of the evening had been adequately attended to. The director of the hotel had come along the terrace once more, expressing his hope that everyone had eaten well and that the coming night would bring a good night's sleep for all concerned.

They'd spent a major part of the evening discussing some of the current economic, political, and human affairs of the world. The day before, they'd read that another eight-year-old girl had disappeared on the way home from school in Lausanne, a city on the western shore of Lake Geneva. The authorities—as well as the local citizens of the town—were intensely involved in looking for her and for the person, or persons, who'd abducted her. Sadly, they felt, a news item one saw much too often.

"I have to tell you a short story, Anulka, something that happened to me several years ago in a small village near Augsburg in southern Germany. I was on a business trip to Munich. One morning, I read in the *Suedeutsche Zeitung* about a seven-year-old girl who'd been snatched off that village's main street by a repeat child molester. Tragically, the girl was found dead. The molester, that bastard, was caught a short time thereafter."

"At his arraignment, he pleaded guilty. That was a surprise. But now comes the worst part. He explained to the court why he'd felt it necessary to kill the little girl. She'd fought him, he said, and she had ripped off the mask he was using to hide his identity. He was worried she could recognize him later if he were to let her go, so he bashed her head against a tree and then threw her unconscious body into the reservoir behind a nearby dam. That little girl drowned, Anulka, and it blew me away thinking about it."

He swallowed heavily, tears now in his eyes. "A couple of days later, I drove over to that village, I went to the memorial church service for that girl, I stood with thousands of other people, mourning. I cried that afternoon for that little girl, for her family, complete strangers to me. I couldn't stop myself; I just felt her loss so intensely. And I guess also the loss of everything that was good in the world."

She saw his pained expression. She took his left hand and pressed its palm tightly against her right cheek. She looked at him. A fine man, she thought.

My God, how lucky I am.

She turned and waved to the waiter, asking him to bring them two snifters of Hennessey XO cognac. "Please make it as quick as possible", she told him, then turned back to Luca to say something that finally had to be said.

She reached for his hand again, the effect he'd had on her strong and deep, the shadows in her now in retreat. If only that had been the case in the past, she thought, sadly. Then I'd be in a different place and not facing what I am.

She raised her eyes to his. "You know, Luca, when I hear

you talk like that, I find myself comparing what I am to what you very clearly are. And somehow or other, I find myself coming up short. You know I'm not really into children, if you understand what I mean. I've never really thought about having them in my life. Yes, I know, bankers have families and children, but I've never seen that as my goal."

She could feel several tears coming. "Nevertheless, hearing you talk about mourning a child you never knew, hearing you talk about life in general, and about the goodness of that life, I hear humility, I hear caring, I hear the voice of a man who doesn't take in life, but gives. My father tried to give me that. How wonderful that you're actually like that."

She studied his face, her eyes filling with tears. "Maybe you see me differently, Luca, but I often sense in myself a real feeling of emptiness. It's strange. I search inside of me for those very same elements of character, the very same things you are and you describe. I had them once, I know I did. They were really me, maybe they still are somewhere, but, at least, now they seem somehow to have moved out of my reach. I don't really like to admit all this, my being supposedly the blessed child and sunny girl of the bank and all that that entails. But when I listen to you, I'm almost jealous of the quality of life you have and the way you approach life. And that makes me very sad. And even, can you believe it, angry at myself!"

"How I wish I could look at life again like you do, free to think like you, feel like you, how I wish I could be someone who doesn't exclude or, many times, have to ignore the things that are really important. I am happy, so very happy, when I think of us, don't get me wrong, but there are corners and places in me, regrets in me, that I have a hard time controlling. They often get in the way of everything else. And that makes me sometimes so terribly sad."

He held her hand tightly, touched to the core, then reached across the table with his right hand and softly stroked her cheek, wiping away a tear slowly rolling down it.

"How I love you, Anulka. But I really think you're selling yourself short. Take a step back for a moment and think about all the many different things we've discussed with one another. Remember all that? Months and months of discussions and shared experiences. You may not realize it, but every time you speak, every time you react to something, the times you refer to your father and what he meant and means to you, you choose words which tell me you do possess those qualities you just spoke about. It seems the problem is that you just don't recognize their existence in yourself. Or perhaps they're blocked by other things that seem more important to you at the moment. Or other things which weigh upon you, and don't let you see clearly what is and what isn't."

"Whatever it is, I tell you, I see those qualities in your eyes. I just saw them in your face as I talked to you about that child being killed. And I've heard and hear them in the words you've just spoken."

He smiled gently at her, then looked quickly around the terrace. The hour was late. They were almost alone.

"Listen, I have an idea. The waiters look like they might

want to go home soon. What we're talking about is really important for you, I sense it, I know it. How about this? It's a beautiful evening. Let's sit out later on the garden terrace after we've finished with our chess game and discuss this some more. How does that sound?"

She looked at him, tears pushing into her eyes from the love and feeling she felt for him at that moment.

She took a breath, shuddering inside of herself. She heard a voice somewhere inside of herself whispering repeatedly the word *help*. Squeezing his hand tight, she spoke, her voice husky with emotion, but also thankfulness.

"Yes. Thank you, Luca. Yes, I'd like that very much."

It was getting on toward ten o'clock, but there was still one more thing on the agenda before they could get back to their chess wars—and to their discussion. Luca reached into his pants pocket and took out his cigar cutter and gold lighter.

He smiled at her. She knew.

He stood up, reached down to kiss her, and then walked the several steps across the lawn to the high bushes located at the back end of the garden. She watched from afar as he lit his cigar. She could see him well, puffing on the cigar, its round tip at the end burning a steady, bright orange-red as he drew on it, pulling the smoke into his mouth and then expelling it back into the mild night air.

No doubt about it. The man loved his cigars.

8
The Villa Visconta di Magliaso
Magliaso
Tessin
Switzerland

June 2   22:01

He smiled in her direction. "Anything bothering you over there yet?"

A short, happy laugh, a bubbly laugh, an Anulka laugh. "No, nothing. You're doing a good job staying downwind from me."

"You know, this is a really nice cigar. Got a good draw. You wouldn't know this, but it's a different cigar than the one I usually smoke. Not bad. Not bad at all."

Contented, she sat there, sipping on the last of her Hennessey, enjoying him, watching him walk slowly back and forth on the lawn. She smelled the perfume of the freshly-cut grass. The warm air of the evening moved gently around her, caressing her skin. She could smell the perfume of the blooming irises coming from the garden, deep yellows and purples against a dark night.

She watched the different-colored spots of light, soft, dancing flickering luminous flashes thrown out onto the lawn and him and the bushes behind him by the candles still burning brightly inside the chiseled crystal candle holders on the tables around her.

A perfectly-framed picture.

He moved a couple of steps again, his face turned to the terrace and her, drew again on the cigar. She saw its hot, orange-red tip —and suddenly started. Above it, curiously, she saw another orange-red circle, but this one was fixed in the center of his forehead, and, strangely, not moving in the same erratic manner as the flickering light of the candles.

Suddenly, to her left, she heard a slight crack, caused, she would later learn from the Lugano police commissioner, by an ineffectively silenced rifle shot, coming from behind the far corner of the hotel. She looked at him—and saw the upper part of his forehead explode in a flare of red and solid matter.

The bullet's hitting power was enormous. He flew back into the nearby leafy bushes lining the back fence of the hotel garden. No sound had escaped his lips.

Time ceased its movement. The cadence of time suddenly altered its steady beat. The individual scenes of that horror took on for her a jerky, irregular rhythm.

Frame one: She gaped at the bushes where he'd suddenly disappeared. Frame two: she leapt up from her chair, the table, and what was still on it, crashing to one side against the nearby wall. Frame three: she ran across the lawn to where he lay. Frame four: brushing the low-hanging branches aside, she threw herself on him, now finally screaming over and over again one word—"no, no"—in a desperate but hopeless attempt to reverse what she'd just seen happen. Frame five: she tried but couldn't lift his head to hers.

She saw to her horror that part of it no longer existed. Her cheek to his, she held him tight. She moaned deeply, felt the terrible, warm wetness of his blood touch her skin, saw its dark redness smeared on the front of her dress.

Suddenly, the disjointed time frames snapped back into their correct sequential rhythm; the normal cadence of the day resumed its measured beat. Time caught up. She started to think again. He was gone. Forever.

For her, free fall into a deep black hole.

Later that same night, after the police, the doctors, the medical examiners, and the forensic people had left the hotel, after the police commissioner had asked her to please come to the police headquarters in Lugano *centro* at noon the following day, after he'd questioned her briefly—and gently—concerning Luca's business and personal life or possible threats he might have received, after he'd enquired if she'd noticed anything different or peculiar about Luca's demeanor during the day, after all that, she stood with the hotel director at the hotel reception desk.

Before leaving the hotel, one of the detectives had informed her that they hadn't found a brass casing at the

assumed shoot location. Indication, apparently, of a professional hit. A horrible thing, he'd sadly noted.

The director had managed to calm the guests and get
them all safely to bed. He saw the deep hurt, the ravages of
the murder in her face. He tried his best to help her find some
form of peace.

"I can make you a sleeping potion if you wish. You might
like to have something like that for the night."

She turned to him, under control for the moment,
speaking slowly every word. "Ah, that's very kind of you,
Signor Caprini. But it's really not necessary. One of the police
medical staff already gave me several sleeping pills for when
I finally go to bed. I'm just not ready to do that quite yet. You
understand, I'm sure . . ."

"Yes, of course. I hope they'll give you some relief from
the horror of this night. If there's anything…"

She interrupted him, telling him gently she needed to be
alone for a bit. The director briefly touched her arm, understanding fully her frame of mind. He spoke a few more words
of consolation and regret, then turned and, with head bowed,
walked slowly down the long dark hall, the sadness he felt for
her inside recognizable in every heavy step he took.

She was still wearing the yellow dress. In its right
pocket, her fingers suddenly touched something, his cuff
links. Blood-covered and still a bit sticky.

She'd somehow unfastened them from his shirt cuffs
as he'd laid there, his body twisted in the dirt and the low
branches of the bushes.

She turned away from the reception and saw the chess board with the small sign, "Game in Progress", next to it. She was hardly able to focus on it. She moved slowly over to the side of the table where Luca had been sitting. She sat down, looked at the pieces on the board, then lowered her forehead onto her folded arms near to the spot on the board where his king and queen stood close together, still untouched, still safe, side by side in their proper places.

She reached out, touching the king, her hand trembling, her vision blurred. No more Luca. Gone the apartment in Porto Ceresio, gone the chance to have a life with him, gone the chance to share its ups and downs with him, to laugh with him, to speak with him, gone the chance to drive back the worries, the darkness, and find a way to a more balanced life.

She whipped slowly back and forth in the chair, small whimpering sounds escaping her mouth, her eyes seeing nothing.

Suddenly, she stopped, grasped tightly the arms of the chair, bringing finally a needed breath of air into her lungs.

The dam broke.

For a long time, she cried the cry of pain, of desperation, of deepest sadness, of anguish, of desolation, of hopelessness.

She felt deep, white-hot, uncontrollable rage. Because she knew, she *knew* damn well who had pulled the trigger.

She'd heard nothing from Italy. All those months nothing, all those months questioning what would he do. Now she had an answer to her question. There could be no other reason for the killing than that.

But that wasn't anywhere near all of it. The worst of it, the absolute worst feeling of all, was that she knew, she absolutely knew who was really guilty of his death. The horror of that thought, the horror at what she had done, at what had happened, crushed the very spirit, crushed the very life out of her, leaving only darkness and emptiness and deep despair behind.

9
The Offices of Hofmaier & Partner Gmbh
Zimmerweg
Frankfurt am Main
Germany

June 17   11:23

The letter that changed everything was delivered on a hot summer forenoon to Felix Hofmaier's office, located on a quiet, shady side street, an eight-minute walk from Frankfurt's city center and its main thoroughfare, the Kaiserstrasse. For fresh air, Felix had opened the windows of his office to the outside, since his office building—like many of those constructed after the war in the Sixties and Seventies—had been built without air conditioning.

The letter was among the twenty or so which arrived daily at his consulting business, Hofmaier & Partner. Also, as every day, it was one of only a few whose contents contained something relevant to his business or his person. The rest of them were usually nothing but junk mail.

His secretary had placed the letter, unopened, in one of the empty sleeves of a well-used, tan-colored mail dossier. The dossier, something like a book with many pages, had individual slots where individual letters and internal memos were placed, either outgoing documents waiting to be signed or those received from other people within the firm or from outside the firm in the daily mail. Looking at the dossier from the side, Felix guessed it had been another slow mail day.

He felt a vague sense of irritation. The month of June had been simply too hot. Ten days of very unusual weather. Temperatures had since receded somewhat, but one would never know it, considering the level of humidity.

But was that it? Maybe the source of his irritation was not so much the weather, but instead a more minor issue: that morning, he'd discovered that every decent shirt he kept in his closet was at the laundry being washed. He'd had to wear an old one, one of several he'd recently put into a plastic bag lying on his closet floor, intending to toss it and its contents as soon as possible.

Strange, he thought to himself, how inconsequential things, smaller things, were increasingly aggravating him and getting in the way of the bigger things in his life.

A smile of resignation. And then a big reality check.

"What the hell, Felix. If you want to be honest with yourself, the real problem is a totally different one: where, tell me, when you talk so big and grand about them and their importance to you, well, where are those big things in your life you keep referring to?"

Tough question he thought. And no ready—or uplifting— answer. That could mean only one thing: no really big things at all.

Or, at least, not any of the things that put a nice, successful sheen on life, that put a successful buzz into one's daily activities, and could mean a hurried call to one's tailor ordering that too-expensive suit for that event-of-the-year garden party coming up the following Saturday evening.

Well, wait a minute, he thought. There had been one big thing which had come along and moved the needle, but, unfortunately, not exactly in any positive way.

His Swiss mother had recently died, a sudden and unexpected event.

At first glance, Felix had digested quite well the news of her death. He'd been in Hong Kong the first day of June when the call from his office had come. He was convinced his being that far away had helped keep the emotional impact of her death to a minimum. On the other hand, he asked himself, do I really care one way or the other where I was or what I did or didn't do?

No, not much, really.

With two exceptions, he hadn't seen his mother in more than ten years. Their relationship had been, at best, strained. They'd had their last telephone conversation a little over a year ago about some will she'd supposedly made. But that was it. A little sadly, he noted he'd heard his mother's voice a total of three times during all those long years.

He sat back in his chair. Perhaps I'm just out of sorts because I really do have a bad conscience. Fact is, I did choose not to fly back from Hong Kong for her funeral.

He'd been conferring with two business colleagues in the lounge area of the Mandarin Oriental hotel when he'd heard a series of musical chimes. Walking toward him was a young bell boy, bellboy hat and all, holding a small framed blackboard aloft. The chimes were attached to its crown. On the blackboard's black surface was his name, printed in white chalk. An urgent telephone call from Germany.

Standing in the small telephone booth, he'd heard his secretary say she'd tried his cell phone, but the call had unfortunately gone to voice mail. He'd heard her express her apologies for having to disturb him, but a call had come from the office of his mother's live-with partner in Switzerland. She had died. Unexpectedly. A peaceful death apparently. No reason given as to the cause. Condolences. And were there any travel arrangements she should make to bring him back to Europe for the funeral.

Somehow, the news had hurt. Just short of sixty and already dead. He'd twice breathed in heavily, sensed his pulse running faster.

Hearing her question, he'd known immediately what he would do, or, more accurately, not do. Told her he would be staying in Hong Kong to finish his business. Would she please inform the person who had called that he'd be in touch upon his return to Germany.

And that was it.

Hours later, in the elevator on the way up to his room, he'd thought about her again. Again, that vague feeling of sadness had permeated his thoughts. He was in Hong Kong, on the island, thirteen flight hours from Germany. And from Switzerland. He still had another three days planned for meetings, both in Hong Kong and on the mainland side in Kowloon. He hadn't arrived at his floor before he'd decided once more that the best decision was to stay where he was.

By the time he arrived back in Germany shortly before the middle of the month, his mother had already been buried, in Thalwil, a small town a short distance from the center of Zurich.

She'd spent most of her later adult life in an apartment located directly above a two-lane asphalt ribbon running along the lake from Thalwil to Canton Zug and beyond.

She'd separated from his father two years after his birth. He'd never known him, a Swiss milk farmer from Graubünden, who, after an abrupt separation, had retreated to his farm, withdrawing completely from any contact with mother or son. And not wanting any when his son had reached an age where he might possibly seek to have contact with him.

Felix Hofmaier was not a sentimental person. Nevertheless, he was still able to honor the fact that it *was* his mother who'd died and he *was* her son, this in spite of an estrangement that had existed for years between the two of them.

He knew he hadn't been an easy child. And, in later years, certainly not an easy son. But she hadn't been an easy mother either. He'd had a totally different view of the world compared to hers. Basically, it wasn't at all a matter of their having had different moral compasses. In fact, they both operated at the "looser" end of that curve. It was his mother's efforts at domination he'd rebelled against. And her attempts, when he was growing up, frustrated by not having him under that control, to double the pressure she put on him to accept her will. With no husband and only one child, perhaps understandable on her part.

His solution to the problem had been to put space between himself and her coldness and her efforts at controlling every aspect of his life. He felt he'd suffered much too much in the past to fully open his heart to her—or now to really mourn her passing.

He smiled slightly. He thought fleetingly of *The Stranger*, a book by Albert Camus he'd once read in French at university. On the first page of that book, a young Algerian is digesting the news that his mother has died the day before—or perhaps the whole thing had happened two days ago. He isn't exactly sure. The thinking effort required of him to remember the exact day bores him.

Nihilism in its purest form.

Well, he thought, at least I know when and where *my* mother died.

Sighing heavily, he opened the dossier lying in front of him. In the first slot, a heavy envelope, a letter. The type of paper and the in-cursive-written address on the front of the envelope screamed money. The return address confirmed it: an asset management firm. In fact, the firm was one he knew since its sole owner, Dr. Peter Renauer, had long been his mother's "life partner" whatever *that* meant in proper northern Switzerland society terms.

Years ago, Felix had met the man at a banker meeting in Zurich. Even though it was only a handshake and couple of words exchanged, he remembered he hadn't liked him, notwithstanding the fact that, at that time, he'd had no idea the man was involved with his mother. And Renauer hadn't mentioned it at the time either, although the family names were identical. Not even a tentative question about a possible connection.

He thought of him again. The passage of time hadn't changed his impression of the man. An ass. Cold. Distant. A real prig.

Good grief.

Well, I am already planning to spend time at the European Consultants Association convention in Basel, an event that's only several weeks away. If Renauer is writing to ask me to come to Zurich, for whatever and whichever reason, then that convention in Basel makes the logistics easier. The city is only an hour distant from Zurich by car. No problem handling both the convention and Zurich, if need be, while I am in Switzerland. With time left over to visit mother's grave and pay my respects.

He paused, looking at the word. Respects. A funny way

of saying hello or goodbye or whatever to the living or the deceased. Never really understood that part of it, he thought.

Felix had never received any separate official information concerning the existence of a will or last testament. Perfectly usual, he knew. However, he was aware that one existed. His mother had indicated that during a rare call she'd had with him over a year ago. She'd had it notarized two days before they'd spoken. She'd told him she'd given her bank a copy. And that an executor would handle all the details involved.

That's a little unusual, he'd thought at the time. Well, whatever.

He sliced open the envelope, took out four sheets of standard-sized paper, unfolded them, and quickly read the salutation and the opening paragraph of the first page. Just as he'd assumed, the letter was from Renauer personally.

Renauer had started the letter by expressing his condolences along with his regrets that he'd not as yet had the opportunity to speak personally with Felix due to the press of numerous arrangements relating to the death of his mother.

Yeah, thought so, he's the executor of the will.

Nothing but superficial "concerned" bullshit, Felix thought. The truth is he's always out there trying to earn more money and doesn't want anything—even the death of someone close to him, and the responsibilities related to it—to get in the way.

At the top of the second page, Renauer informed him he had found a carton in the office basement containing documents his mother had apparently kept from the period of her marriage to his father. It would be made available for him to pick up when he came to Zurich.

It was in the bottom paragraph on the same page where Renauer finally got down to business and made any further thoughts about old files or documents suddenly irrelevant. As executor of his mother's will, it was his duty to inform him that his mother had maintained three separate Euro-based accounts at a private bank in Zurich. The contents of those accounts were destined to fall to him as the only child/surviving member of her immediate family. The net amount of the largest account per the enclosed April 30 bank statement was 989,897.45 Euros.

Felix put the letter down for a moment.

"Holy shit. My mother had that kind of money? How did she manage that?"

Even though Felix had hardly spoken with her in the years past, it seemed from the contents of the letter that she had long forgotten that fact or that she'd considered it irrelevant. A fair assumption, it would appear, because the bank statement in his hands sent a very clear message: she'd given him some very serious money.

No mention in the letter of the value of the other two accounts, one a savings, and the other a checking account. No problem for Renauer, it seemed. He simply noted that the bank would provide Felix with separate up-to-date balances when he had the accounts transferred to his name.

Considering the size of the large account, it was a good assumption they'd probably have only minimum amounts of funds in them.

All he had to do was appear in short order at Renauer's offices in Zurich, sign some papers, then visit her bank, legitimize himself as the proper recipient of the funds, sign some papers, and the contents of the accounts would be his to do with as he pleased.

There were other matters in the letter. The contents of her apartment and their disposition needed to be discussed. Minor matters. According to Renauer, they could easily be handled when they met in Zurich.

He leaned back in his chair. Pictures of his mother from the past flashed in front of his mind's eye. She had been a young mother, bringing him into the world when she was only sixteen years old. In particular, he remembered her smile and her words of praise when he'd done something that had made her proud.

Without warning, a feeling of deep sadness coursed through him. He looked at the letter again. I wonder what she would say if she were to see me now, just north of forty, divorced, no idea where my one daughter is or what she's doing, some vestige of an athletic build in spite of a slowly-growing girth, and a consulting business which is just barely surviving.

Strong, growing competition as well as a series of self-inflicted wounds had not made it easy for the firm to win lucrative consulting assignments. There'd been so many consulting shop startups around Frankfurt and the people running them knew more than a thing or two about how to sanitize or restructure companies.

In contrast, Hofmaier & Partner was living from month to month, incurring losses that had depleted its once strong financial position.

There'd been a scandal four years ago when the firm had been caught grossly inflating its billings to a large client in north Hessen. Both Frankfurt newspapers, the *Frankfurter Allgemeine Zeitung* and the *Frankfurter Rundschau*, had reported extensively on the progress and resolution of that case.

His refusal to respect the law, to be completely honest in his business dealings, was born of a casual approach to life and its rules. Felix had handled the whole thing with a certain amount of equanimity. Simple reason: he moved in a business society for whom power and money were the ultimate aphrodisiacs. And a straight line was definitely not always the best way to achieve that kind of "success".

A criminal suit against the firm had been resolved through a *nolo contendere* plea. That plea, including, among other things, restitution to the company involved, had not helped to improve the reputation of his firm, and certainly not his own. At least, he hadn't been arrested, tried, found guilty, and sent to jail.

Unfortunately, that experience hadn't altered his basic

approach to business and the conduct of his life. He'd escaped punishment. He was convinced he would escape again if he ever got himself into a similar position.

Hofmaier and Partner, however, had suffered long-term damage. Before the case broke, Felix had employed twenty-eight consultants plus five office staff in his firm. Germany's *Manager Report* had even cited his company as being one of the top financial workout consulting firms in the country. Now, there were just five consultants and an administrative assistant remaining on the employee list, a list which did include, thankfully, Ben Ritter, an excellent colleague and loyal friend left over from university days. Ben was the kind of guy who really didn't care what he did as long as he could spend adequate—and, at times, excessively long—periods of time in one of the many wine *lokale* in and around Frankfurt.

While at university, both he and Ben had been members of a local wrestling club. Felix had lost most of his matches. Ben, however, quick and fast on his feet, and tricky in his moves, had won most of his. What had it netted them both after all was said and done? Some good stories to tell at the local beer establishments when they met others who also, at some time in their lives, had "gone to the mat". And that was it.

They'd become even closer friends after Ben had lost his sister almost sixteen years ago in a multi-car auto collision on the A9 *Autobahn* just north of Ingolstadt in Bavaria. Felix had handled many of the burial arrangements. His helping hand at a time of great sorrow for his friend had created a bond between the two of them that, over the years, had not lost one iota of its intensity or strength.

While Felix was the more serious element in their friendship, Ben, in contrast, tended to operate from the more edgy side of things. Before joining the firm as a minority partner, he'd spent almost ten years working for a French-Arab bank consortium in Sharjah in the Gulf.

Who the hell knew what he'd been doing or not doing down there? Legal. Or not legal.

In the earlier years of his work with the firm, that experience and the contacts he'd made there had certainly helped him gain some lucrative consulting assignments for the firm. However, after the scandal with the billings, things had even gotten difficult for Ben in acquiring new clients or working again for existing clients within the network of relationships he'd built during those Dubai-Sharjah years.

Nevertheless, Ben was just one hell of a consultant and businessman. He had a certain aura about him that seemed to fascinate his contemporaries. Smart, erudite, well-read, well-traveled, that he was. But there was also something about him people couldn't put their finger on. A kind of vibe seemed to surround him, definitely not something so apparent that everything else he projected as a person faded into insignificance, but rather a subtle, almost calculating, at times, diffident manner he used to interact with his surroundings, all of it carried off with finesse and smoothness.

And without it raising any questions about who he really might be.

Get him out of the office, and Ben went instantaneously into player mode. He loved money. Everything he did revolved around getting and spending more of what he called the grease on the skids of life. And, strangely enough, he always seemed to have more than enough of it. Of course, it helps when one is earning a large salary, isn't married, isn't going through a divorce, has no kids, and thinks life is just one great big, long, twenty-four-hour party.

He'd once seen him by chance on a weekend in Munich at Hirmer, the six story, upscale men's store in the Kaufingerstrasse, the main shopping street of the city. Ben had been in the middle of one of his purchasing frenzies. When he saw Felix, his very first comment to him had been: "Hey Felix, welcome to my little bit of six floor heaven." Crazy bastard, Felix had thought at the time.

Felix suspected that Ben still had any number of hot irons in some fire somewhere, but he'd never asked him about it. Actually, he didn't care whether he did or didn't. They were close friends. They worked very well together. The clients thought highly of Ben and his work. That was enough for Felix.

They were due to meet that evening in one of their favorite wine *lokale*, most likely puffing themselves up again, as the night wore on, with dreams of possible growth in the company and the fast life. Dreams that, at least, for him, he suspected, would never become reality, even if he continued cutting corners and pushing the legally-permitted envelope.

In fact, life was really in the process of passing him by,

fast turning him into a jealous observer of other people's successes and their enjoyment of life's rewards. His eyes showed
it, his demeanor bore witness to it, and physically, his growing
stomach didn't make him, at least visually, part of that fast,
fashionable crowd he'd have liked to have been part of.

The news in the letter, however, was something entirely
different: definitely, a life-changing event. A "big thing" for
damn sure.

Felix decided not to call his old friend and partner right
away. It'll be more fun to watch him when I drop this bit of
news on him this evening. Should be good for a laugh or two.

He paused for a second. Dammit, he thought, cold hard
reality suddenly pushing its way back into his consciousness.

Unfortunately for him, there were just too many times
when he couldn't hold that reality back, couldn't stop it from
shoving him hard right into the middle of one of his failures.
And tricky games.

From the feel of it, it looked like this was going to be one
of those times again. He put his thoughts about Ben aside.

In the past year and a half, Hofmaier & Partner had
been heavily involved in consulting to the Loretz Maschinenfabrik Gmbh, a financially-troubled company located in
the hilly Spessart area about twenty-five kilometers east of
Frankfurt. Part of the firm's work had involved it helping the
client to obtain additional outside financing in order to continue operating its business. The NHF Handelsbank AG, the
client company's house bank for many years, had supplied the

money, secured primarily through inventories and receivables. And a good dose of hope.

The infusion of new money hadn't helped. Six months later, Loretz had found itself in liquidation, a shell of a company with nowhere to go.

The bank's Credit Committee chairman, Mueller, had criticized a number of statements Felix had made months before when presenting, with glowing words and convincing data, the survival chances and future prospects of his client company. The bank had worked with him then in supporting the client. A loan of two and a half million Euros had been made to Loretz, money which, unfortunately it appeared, was now no longer recoverable.

The bank had believed and trusted him. But that was then. Now was now. Mueller had asked to see him. He was to get his chance at four that afternoon at bank headquarters.

A shake of his head. Anger in the eyes. And a sudden need for a coffee and some fresh air.

Café Krone, the best in the area and near the office, would do the honors. That was part of the advantage of having offices in downtown Frankfurt where everything one wanted was always within walking distance. Felix made no excuses to anyone. A boring life required quick, readily-available, non-problematic fixes.

The elevator was empty and the lobby as well. Out on the street, the humidity of the day hit him full blast in the face. A hotter-than-normal but typical summer day in middle Germany, that was, until the usual late-afternoon thunderstorms arrived and drove the temperatures down twenty degrees. Then one had to wait sometimes weeks for the weather to calm down and get back up to some meaningful, summer-like temperatures. Very frustrating in a country with such short summers.

A lot like my life at the moment, he thought: an occasional hot flash and then lots of dark down time. Absolutely depressing, he concluded, as he entered the café and took a seat at a window looking out to the street.

He conjured up a picture of his mother seated across from him when he'd seen her for the last time. A politically correct meeting, mother and son talking around all the issues that would never be seriously addressed.

And then her parting words to him: "Be brave".

She'd repeated that very same phrase on the phone the year before shortly before she'd rung off. What an odd statement, he thought. People who say something like that are usually speaking to themselves.

He finished eating his small sandwich and the piece of cake he'd ordered. He noticed an ant making its erratic way across the polished tabletop, heading straight for the cake crumbs left on his plate. His right thumb reached out and crushed it.

An empty gesture, he thought, as he made his way back out into the hot sun. On the other hand, maybe I'm that ant, a sign I could possibly be squashed by some random event I don't see coming.

Whatever.

10
Wagner's Weinlokal
Schweizer Strasse
Sachenhausen (Frankfurt am Main)
Germany

June 17   19:22

Sitting in traffic crossing the Main river bridge, Felix was finally able to relax for a moment. It's not every day one inherits money like that, he thought.

On the other hand, there's something funny about the whole thing. I'll bet there are many more questions than answers on the table in Zurich.

Felix was the kind of guy who tended to get pissed when he suspected that somebody was attempting to take him down the road. His mood would get worse if he discovered that he'd already been taken down that road or, even worse, when he found himself already at the end of that road with no way back.

Nevertheless, money was money. And there was apparently a lot of it.

A quick call from his secretary to Renauers's office in Zurich had netted him an appointment with the man in his offices in Zurich the last day of June.

In a moment of misplaced enthusiasm, he'd thought about calling Barbara, his sometime bed partner, to let her in on the good news. Five seconds after the thought had entered his head, he'd shot it down, questioning, among other things, his judgment and whether or not it had been perhaps seriously impaired by the recent news. In the kind of relationship they enjoyed, where the only central point was exclusively a therapeutic one—you scratch my itch and I scratch yours—, he asked himself what he'd been thinking about when a call to her could very well have created an additional itch on her part, this one totally unwanted.

What was profoundly unsettling, however, was the tough meeting he'd just had with the NHF Handelsbank. And with Mueller.

Long years of experience with lawyers and such meetings had taught Felix to be very careful with his statements in whatever context he made them wherever and to whomever he made them. He'd gone alone to the meeting, having decided to listen first to what the "gentlemen" had to say before taking any further steps, including the possibility of having to lawyer up. Appearing with a lawyer could be interpreted in a negative way, a sign that, in fact, he was involved in something bad and had therefore asked legal counsel to accompany him.

A recent letter he'd received from the bank had spoken of a need for the parties to meet and "discuss certain issues relating to the consulting work carried out by your firm and you personally for the Loretz Maschinenfabrik Gmbh". Interestingly, it had also contained the phrase, "possible exploration of alternative solutions to resolve the current problem". That phraseology had seemed to signal that the bank was perhaps not going to take a totally hard line in the matter.

At least, that had been the hope prior to the meeting.

From a private source within Loretz, Felix had learned that the bank already had third-party forensic audit staff inside the company going over the books as well as all written communications between Loretz and Hofmaier & Partner. While he'd thought there might be some problems with several of the payments made to third parties (potential preferential third-party treatment prior to bankruptcy), Felix felt that he'd otherwise acquitted himself vis-à-vis the bank and the client in an appropriate and legal fashion.

Thought is here the key operative word. In fact, Felix was seriously kidding himself.

In previous telephone conversations with bank management, he'd made the same statement over and over again.

"We all know that continuity in revenues and profits are subject both to market vagaries as well as to effective company execution of its tactical and strategic plans. We gave you our best opinion. And the best forecasts we had. And our best efforts in working with the company to secure its survival. And you received a confirmation of the company's credit worthiness in writing from us."

Felix had smiled as he'd spoken those words, convinced he had an iron-clad wall built around himself and his work. Unfortunately, the people listening on other end of the line hadn't been smiling at his line of bullshit.

The whole thing is a joke, he'd thought. The bank knew exactly what kind of things can happen when it makes its own forecasts and then the market or markets or the economy turn against it. Those people should get off of their high horses and get real about what happened at Loretz.

What should have caused Felix to pause, however, was something that went well beyond possible liability problems associated with any third-party payments made in the weeks before the official bankruptcy filing. Or any potential arrogance on his part.

The rub was this: Felix Hofmaier knew, one hundred percent *knew*, that a number of the key forecasted numbers in the loan application had been, in fact, massaged so that Loretz would appear to be in a more favorable market and financial situation than it really was.

How he knew? First of all, Loretz management, and its financial people in particular, had not been shy in discussing how they were "putting together" some of the more critical benchmark forecasts for the loan application at the bank.

To his credit, Felix had spoken out against some of the

more egregious examples of that duplicitous approach. That had stopped, at least, a part of the game.

Nevertheless, he had allowed other numbers, numbers he knew to be, at best, spurious or inflated, to be used in supporting the company's sales and cash planning forecasts. He had personally discussed with Loretz management their possible impact on the bank's thinking and the chances of the company getting a loan from the bank.

Smoke and mirror numbers scattered about and hidden between good numbers. But, nothing, he'd thought, that would really endanger the company's continued existence if they weren't achieved. Still a good chance to make those numbers happen.

Unfortunately, reality in the form of incompetent management and some negative developments in several of the company's main markets had served to magnify the risks already embedded in the perfumed assumptions and unrealistic benchmark targets.

The damage was done. The smoke and mirrors approach had crashed and burned. And, with it, the hope that all would turn out well.

He knew the bank most likely suspected that the forecasts in the loan documents had been partially manipulated. Although it didn't yet have a final report, its opinion was clear: Felix and his firm *must* have had knowledge of their existence and their dubious nature. And had willfully accepted them. And if that weren't the case, then Felix and the firm should have had knowledge of the possibility of their existence. After all, they were the consultants. What the hell were they getting paid for?

Felix knew insurance law. The firm had good corporate liability insurance protection. However, it was only valid for mistakes/bad recommendations, i.e., simple negligence, made in the course of the firm's normal consulting work. Not, however, for gross negligence.

Or for intentional fraud.

Gross negligence would mean no insurance coverage of any eventual settlement between his firm and the bank. Legal bills would very likely eat up whatever was remaining in the firm's accounts. And Hofmaier & Partner would be driven into bankruptcy. He personally would have nothing left because he'd kept most of what he'd earned over the years in the firm, money that was already now almost depleted due to the firm's recent losses.

He would have to declare personal bankruptcy.

In addition, any battle of this sort would require him to spend a great deal of time on the specifics of the case. As a consequence, he wouldn't be able to work as much. Less work would mean less invoicing. And lower revenues meant exacerbating the already serious cash flow problems in the firm.

And finally, there was the matter of reputational loss. Felix knew he'd never survive it. His time in Germany would be over. Immediately, or, worst case, after several years in jail. He'd already had a problem several years ago with the German judiciary. This new screw-up might be just the straw that would break the camel's back. And also get him thrown out of the country.

For those reasons, Felix had arrived at the bank's headquarters ready to talk about some form of compromise solution to the problem. Less than two hours later, he found himself walking across the street to the underground garage at the *Opernhaus*. The meeting with the bank had been everything he'd not expected. No sign of compromise. The bank was going to pursue its interests with all the means it had at its disposal. There would be no room for maneuvering or negotiations.

The head of the Credit Committee, Mueller, had made his position—and his expectations—very clear. With the final report from the forensic auditors expected within the week, the bank would be able to definitively prove that Hofmaier & Partner "had not conducted itself in a professional manner" during the loan application phase. Then he'd dropped the bomb on Felix. Gross negligence, possible fraud, were the words he'd used.

The bank had a letter from him on Hofmaier & Partner letterhead citing in detail the creditworthiness of the Loretz Gmbh and recommending that the loan be approved. The letter had created a direct legal relationship, and thus formal connection, between the firm and the bank. Its existence gave the bank the legal right to attack the firm directly and put a claim on its assets. And potentially put its owners in jail.

Worst case scenario.

Arriving in Sachsenhausen, he found a parking spot near the bridge over the Main River. It was still warm. He threw his jacket and his tie onto the back seat of his car, then rolled up his sleeves. He walked slowly the several blocks toward Wagners. He wasn't sure if a couple of glasses of apple wine were going to be enough for him. Something harder, maybe a couple of those high alcohol-content apple schnapps, might help mellow somewhat the hyper activity of his brain cells and their constantly nagging, apocalyptic concerns.

He turned into its cobblestoned entrance and there was Ben, already apparently well into the evening. Smiling, his somewhat round and already flushed face lit up from the wine and perhaps some undefined expectations for the coming evening hours. As usual, he was dressed to the nines, even when it was only a pair of blue jeans and a blue polo shirt.

And bright yellow, suede leather loafers. No socks.

"Yellow suede loafers? What the hell is that?" Felix asked himself. But he knew, of course, the answer: just Ben being Ben. Even with his somewhat rotund figure and ears that popped out a little too far from his head, he always managed to look like somebody who constantly cut it.

Damn it, thought Felix. What is it with the guys who aren't the best-looking one around, but always seem to end up with the A-list super women? When Felix had asked him once about that particular talent of his, Ben had simply characterized himself as one big, plugged-in electromagnet. Well, what the hell did that make the women around him? Blonde or brunette hunks of iron? What a crock of bullshit, Felix had thought. But he always forgave his friend.

Life would only be half the fun if Ben weren't around to throw one-line zingers like that at him.

His old friend stood, gave him a big hug. Because of the number of people already celebrating the beginning of the evening, Ben had only been able to find places at a table just inside the narrow, covered entrance of the *lokal*. At least there, the noise level was somewhat lower than in the main interior courtyard.

The waitresses didn't waste any time at Wagners. There was money to be earned with such a crowd. Their waitress brought Felix a glass of cold, unsweetened apple wine, putting it on a circular piece of printed cardboard on which she also put a small mark with a pencil to show that the customer, in this case Felix, had been delivered one glass of apple wine. Felix knew there would be many marks on it before he and Ben finally stood up again.

Ben sensed immediately that his friend was in a bad place.

"Alright, Felix, we can't talk here too much, but right out of the gate, the first and, I promise you, last business question of the evening. As soon as we've discussed that—and I know, just looking at you, that something has not gone well this afternoon—we can get down to the more important things in life like checking out which one of the waitresses running around here is baggable. Agreed?"

Felix smiled, in spite of the heat, the noise, and his old friend's usual line of crap and macho remarks. Nodding to him in assent, he touched his glass to Ben's, then took a long pull from its contents.

He looked at him closer. Even when they'd seen each other only infrequently during the time he was in the Gulf, Ben had always impressed him as someone who always knew exactly what he wanted. One thing for damn sure: when Ben wanted, he went and got. He often acted like he was tuned out, but Felix knew he was anything but. His modus operandi never got lost in the shuffle. Straight at it. No detours.

They needed a private moment together. They swung their bodies around on the bench in order to face away from the table. Bent over with their elbows resting on their knees, they leaned closer to one another.

Ben didn't waste any time. "Ok, Felix, give it to me. Tell me what happened."

"Well, first of all, I can tell you the whole meeting took place in a very nice conference room. The view from the 57th floor over to the Taunus Mountains was just great. The NHF Handelsbank tower has very clean windows—and I got my ass kicked from one end of that conference room to the other. They talked; I listened. Result? We're fucked."

Ben had one word for that. "Shit."

"They have some preliminary information from the forensic work being done at Loretz. They don't know yet for sure, but they're assuming some of the back-up calculations the Loretz people used to support their forecast numbers,

numbers that were put into the profit and loss, cash plans, and balance sheet projections for the loan documents, were not even best guesses. You won't believe it, Ben. At the meeting, Mueller repeatedly referred to them as fantasized, 'dream-on' numbers."

"He made a big deal of trust, of the bank having believed in our integrity, of the bank having had confidence that the numbers were, as he put it, good. And a serious and economically-sound reflection of the possible."

A pull on a glass now almost empty. "So, there you have it. They're expecting a final report from the forensic auditors within the week that, according to them, will substantiate everything they suspect."

"Not good, Felix, not good."

"Yeah, well, ready? There's even more if you can believe it. They also went for the letter we sent to the bank confirming those numbers and the continuing creditworthiness of the company. I had it with me at the meeting. I read it again while they were blah-blahing my ass half silly. They may have a point there. We were positive in that letter. Maybe too positive."

Ben nodded. "Hmmm, possible. You might be right there."

"Okay. Be that as it may. But what really pisses me off is the anger, the total, non-professional over-reaction. Think about it. We put some detailed statements, some "best-estimate" boilerplate crap into that letter. Okay. Disclaimers we do standard in any letter we write to anyone. Okay. We emphasized the precarious market conditions, the future attitude of Loretz's customers, the projected possible success of a new machine line they'd just launched, and the need for the quick and complete recovery of some larger, older accounts receivables. Okay there, too. Hell, we left lots of doors open where things might not work out for Loretz. Perfectly okay, and perfectly defensible."

Looking very serious, Felix took a deep breath, then continued.

"Nevertheless, old friend, I have to tell you, this is turning into a *very* sticky situation. What came across was their feeling that we were either blind, or incompetent, or looking the other way, or, worse, complicit in cooking some of the numbers to make the overall Loretz situation, and its future prospects, look better than they were."

"At one point, it got really fast and furious. Can you believe it? They explicitly mentioned gross negligence. And fraud. They talked about compensation for damages and about nailing my sorry ass to the wall and then sending it to jail."

He cleared his throat. "And no offer put on the table to resolve the issue; no we-can-make-this-all-go-away-if-you-would . . . blah, blah, blah. Nothing. My opinion? They're not interested in any compromise offer. They want blood. And guess whose blood that is."

Ben looked at him and swore. "Damn it to hell, we're getting screwed by those guys at Loretz. They're blaming the whole thing on us. They're the ones who said do something, for God's sake. We tried to stop it."

"Yeah, you're probably right, but with one big difference. We both know we let those guys at Loretz wink at us occasionally when they showed us their best-estimate calculations. Hell, we even fucked over some of those calculations ourselves. And why'd we do that? Because we wanted to keep billing Loretz for as long as the company was financially good for it. It was good money for us. You know it and I know it."

Felix leaned forward closer to Ben so that he could speak directly into his ear.

"Look, my friend, let's not forget where we are. This is not the time or the place to discuss this any further. We're both in the office tomorrow. Let's meet at nine in the morning and go through this whole thing."

Ben looked at him hard. "Ok, but one last question. Did they mention what the next step would be?"

"Yes, they have some things they still need to check. Whatever that is. Then they intend to write us. They want to outline their position in writing and the steps they intend to take. They said we'd be given time to respond before they'd initiate any further action. We'll play that game. No problem."

Felix studied his friend closely. "You know, I've been asking myself, could there be a possible softening of their position in those words, maybe a wink that a compromise might be possible? Maybe there is. I just don't know."

Ben gently grasped his friend's left forearm with his

right hand. "I know, Felix, but all that does give us some time. At least that."

They both turned around to the center of the table again, a signal it was time to turn to the more fun things of the evening. Felix took a deep breath and exhaled. He leaned forward across the table and looked at Ben. Now was the time to tell him about his mother.

He smiled broadly. "I have something else to tell you, Ben. But, this time, it's something good."

Ben stared at him. "Hold on a second. Let's order something for the old stomach."

A quick signal to the more attractive of the two waitresses to come visit them at their table. Felix looked at him. Damn. No matter what's going on, small or large shit, he thought, the guy never missed a beat.

They ordered another round of apple wine, a couple of schnitzels, two mixed salads, some pretzels, and then, just for laughs, checked out the conversation going on right next to them. Yup, there it was, right and left: the usual one-centimeter-thick layer of sexist superficiality.

They both guessed that the young woman at the end of the table would be the first to succumb to her immediate neighbor's vacuous, hustle bullshit. Always the same game, they concluded, not feeling at all conflicted by the fact that they themselves were often guilty of doing the very same thing.

Ben leaned forward to him. "Okay, let's hear it. What have you got that's so good?"

Felix grinned broadly in anticipation.

"You know, my mother passed away several weeks ago. I just received today the letter from her paramour lawyer friend—damned idiot in my opinion—who informed me as her trustee . . . ready? That I'm to inherit what looks like over a million Euros. Before taxes. The money's sitting in several accounts in a bank in Zurich. I can pick it up anytime I want to."

He cocked his head at his friend and waited for the usual over-the-top comments. No reaction. He waved his hand back and forth in front of Ben's eyes. Nothing. Eyes didn't move. He just sat there and regarded him with a blank stare.

"What the hell's going on, Ben? Didn't you hear what I just said?"

Ben focused on him suddenly and smiled. "Oh, no worries, Felix. I heard you alright. Sorry about not answering right away. In fact, if you want to know, I just spent a pleasurable minute or two making a list of all the things I'm going to have to pack for the tropics. A hot pair of Bermudas, yeah, that's what I'll need. Maybe something in red and purple. Yeah, and I'm reading the Maldive Islands off the southwest coast of Sri Lanka are just the place this season. My sources tell me they're awesome. Hundreds of little tropical islands right out there all alone in the middle of the Indian Ocean. Sun every day. White sand. Warm water. Bars humming. So tell me, are you going to be getting business or first-class tickets for us? And how long are we planning on being away?"

Ben sat there, grinning broadly and enjoying himself.

"Damn it to hell, I'm serious, Ben. And no, we're not

going to the Maldives. And no, you don't have to run out and start buying some crazy-ass sandals or some horrible new shorts. I'm going to put that money to work because, when I think about all the shit that's going on right now, I have a very strong feeling that I'm going to need it."

Ben smiled. "Sorry, Felix. I was just giving you a hard time. Honestly, I think that's just great what's happened. I know you didn't have the best relationship with your mother. But she's done something wonderful for you. I guess I should just say congratulations," he said, smiling warmly at his friend.

"Thanks, really made my day, that I can tell you."

Ben looked at him intensely, bothered by a sudden thought. "Hey, Felix, something just occurred to me. You once told me your mother lived in a rented three-room apartment in Thalwil. Nothing against the apartment and its modest size, but something doesn't fit here. Did you have any idea she'd squirreled away that kind of money?"

"No, no idea", waving as he spoke to the waitress to bring them two apple schnapps with which to toast their friendship—and his good fortune.

"At least, she never spoke of it. But what the hell. It's a lot of money and I'm not going to say no to it!"

Ben looked at him closely. "Of course not."

A thoughtful look at his friend. "Question for you. How are you going to handle the tax side of it? You know, you might have to pay inheritance taxes here in Germany and you'll certainly be subject to taxes on any interest or capital gains you make. Remember, Germany and Switzerland have made new arrangements on the double taxation treaty between the two countries. At some point, most, if not all, of the remaining black money held by German citizens in Swiss banks is going to see the light of day. A lot of it already has. But you, my friend, you are a Swiss citizen. You could just park the money elsewhere, of course, and then pick up what you need when you go to Switzerland. Nobody in Germany would be the wiser."

"On the other hand, I honestly don't think you want to get involved in any way, shape, or form in that kind of game. My personal opinion. Look at what is going on at the border between Germany and Switzerland. German border authorities stopping German cars to check for cash from Swiss bank accounts passing over the border into Germany or some German tax guys writing down license numbers of German-registered cars parked in the streets of Zurich and then passing those numbers on to the border control so that the car in question can be stopped when it passes from Switzerland into Germany."

"It's really unbelievable, you know. The news is full of stories about things like that. Really stupid things. But, as usual, there's always some damned fool who decides to risk it and sets up an account in Switzerland. And then what? He gets caught. And you know what happens after that."

He gazed sternly at his friend. "You, Felix, you definitely don't want to be that fool."

Felix looked Ben directly in the eye. "You're right, Ben. I don't want to be that fool. So, no worries, my friend. I'm going to toe the tax line in Germany right down to the last comma and period."

"You want to know why? I'll tell you why. Several reasons. We're in a serious fix here, Ben. You know it. I know it. I have enough serious problems in my life, what the hell, we both do. Really serious ones. So, the answer is quite simple. I am just not interested in piling any potential additional shit on top of the pile of shit I've already created for myself."

Felix leaned back a bit, a bit bemused at a thought. "Besides. we live in a rich country. We profit from that. So, personally, I've never really had a problem with supporting what the government wants."

He looked Ben right in the eye, reflecting, serious and fearful at the same time.

"You know, Ben, it might seem strange to you as a German citizen. But, bottom line, my biggest worry isn't really taxes, yes or no. It's an entirely different worry I have. Even if we get some kind of a financial deal with the bank, I am just damn afraid that I might be forced to leave Germany because my work permit and visa would not be renewed. If that were to happen, then, I tell you, my friend, that would hurt really bad."

Felix annunciating his words. "Why hurt? Simple, Ben. I love this country, I love living here, I love the women,—you know that very well!—, I have great friends here. I do not want to endanger my situation any more than it already is. For me, a disaster to even think about having to leave Germany."

"So, for a myriad of reasons, enough is enough. And if

you think you hear in that statement some form of regret for the number we pulled with Loretz and the bank, then I can tell you you're damn close to being right."

Ben smiled a broad smile. "Felix, you're a first-class guy. No matter what the outcome, we're always going to remain good friends. Of that I'm sure."

They stood up, asking their neighbors to keep their seats free for their return. They both had to take a quick trip around the corner before their order came. Halfway across the inner courtyard, Ben turned to Felix, stopping him.

"Look, I've been thinking about this, too. Personally, I think we're going to come out of this alright. Don't worry about the bank being so hell bent on taking us all down the road. This is not big money for them even if they want you to believe otherwise. I know these banker guys and their little arrogant games."

"I think they're more pissed that their egos and their supposedly good judgment have been blindsided. Particularly Mueller. It happens every time. They get a drop or two of catsup on their ties. Or a greasy spot on their one hundred forty-gram light wool pants and they get all huffy. And then they go nuts. And they threaten like the world is going to come to an end for the person who has crossed them. Personally, I think they even enjoy that kind of a situation sometimes. Gives them a chance to do their macho number and scare the hell out of everybody."

"So yeah, first of all, they'll go after us with a hammer. Standard bullshit. Then, when they think they've cooked our asses long enough, they'll want to reach a compromise solution, which will involve us paying them some form of financial compensation for their damages. And, most importantly, a salve for their little damaged egos. And also their reputations. And we'll be off the hook. No jail time. And they'll look good to their superiors. Everybody gets theirs. Win-win all around."

Felix's facial expression was still filled with doubt. Seeing that, Ben grabbed his friend's shoulders with both hands, looking him directly in the eyes.

Time for some straight talk.

"Listen up, my friend. Relax a bit. Remember, they've got their own worries. They probably suspect their Credit Committee might have been too dependent on one source of information for the loan call they had to make. And those numbers they called "dream-ons"? They were numbers they themselves accepted when they approved the loan. Yes, we were the consultants when that call went down, and we're for damn sure not free of mistakes either. But that's why we have liability insurance. And the bank knows that, too."

Ben looked around before continuing. "When I think about the legal shit that bank has gotten itself into in the United States, and then compare that to the two and a half million Euros they're telling us they're worried about, then believe me, this is not going to have them declaring all-out war. They're human. And they run a business. They have to prioritize their time and people resources and pick their battles. I tell you, they have much bigger problems than the one they have with us."

Ben looked at him calmly. "Yeah, we might have to admit to some kind of malfeasance. Yeah, the damn lawyers will cost us money and there'll be a stink in the papers about it. It's even possible we might lose the company. And it's possible we will have to put some of our own money down on the table to make everything go away."

He paused for a moment, looking for a moment at the scene around him. "But bottom line, we'll do what's necessary and what will let us go on with our lives. And we'll still be alive and still able to enjoy an apple wine or two. So, cheer up, my friend. I stand with you. We'll handle this just fine."

Felix knew that Ben was probably right. They might be able to make a deal. On the other hand, he hadn't spent the afternoon being eaten alive by the Handelsbank.

A deep breath. "I hear you, Ben. It's okay. I understand you. Believe me, I'm going to try and relax and take it as it comes."

"By the way, speaking of things to come, don't forget I'll be going to Basel in less than two weeks for the consultant convention. Afterwards, I'm planning on going to Zurich to meet my mother's old boss. It turns out he's the executor of her estate. Not happy about that, but it is as it is. He wants me to sign some papers so I can take immediate ownership of her accounts. So, in just about three weeks, I should be somewhat wealthier. At least, temporarily so. At least, that's the plan."

"Right", said Ben. "I know you're gone during that time. We'll celebrate when you get back."

He smiled, the impishness in his eyes back. "Yeah, and too bad about the Maldives. Staying on one of those small little islands and drinking a couple of Mojitos every day would have been fun."

He laughed and punched his friend lightly in the arm. Felix raised his right fist in mock displeasure and shook it.

"Oh, one thing, Felix, before I forget. I don't think you mentioned it when we were talking at the table. What was the name of that bank where your mother had her account?"

Felix thought for a second. "Uh, I don't know. I think it was Bankhaus Fixler or Fieber or something like that. But I'm not sure."

11
Bar della Pace
Piazza Alfieri
Asti
Provinzia di Piemonte
Italia

June 24   8:52 am

Giovanni Vincoli sat at one of the small tables outside the Bar della Pace, waiting for Saverio to arrive. There wasn't a damn thing he could find in his head that might entice him to sit back, relax, and think pleasant thoughts for a change.

"A pox on every fucking thing in my life", he said to himself.

He hated it when he had hard grounds of coffee left in the last sip of his espresso; he hated it when he found himself still burping up the effects of yesterday's long and heavy late lunch with some friends at Al Sorriso; he hated it when it was so hot that the leaves on the trees were already either drooping or starting to turn, in June, a suspicious shade of brown;

he hated it that he was spending much too fast the money both he and Saverio had stolen; he hated it when women he slept with decided he was spot-on marriage material after the first night spent together; he hated the thought of Anulka Lorenzini and her stubborn ways; he hated it when his damn Porsche Carrera S—he was still waiting for delivery of a Fiat 500 Abarth—couldn't even get up enough legs, even with a six speed box, to beat some damn Audi R8 at the stop light just off the Autostrada; he hated it when he put on a clean pair of jeans and found that a disgusting grease spot on the upper right leg of those jeans that should have disappeared in the wash hadn't disappeared one bit.

And he hated it when his buddy, Saverio Marino, was late for important meetings.

Shit, what a mess.

He knew a bad mood was definitely not the best precondition for finding a solution for the whole Finsler-Lorenzini situation. And it certainly wouldn't have either of them joking about how the bitch had found a damn good way to run them both down the road and out of town.

There was, at least, one small consolation for it all: after Luca's brutal murder, Giovanni was pretty sure she wouldn't be trying to run anybody down any road anywhere for a long time.

He had a good view of the tree-lined street that circled the piazza. When he'd chosen the day for the meet, he'd been careful to pick one when there'd be no farmer's market clogging up the piazza. That would have meant no parking spots available anywhere in the center of town until after 13:30.

That would've really pissed him off. Massively.

Driving into the piazza, he'd glanced at his watch and determined he was still a bit early for his meeting with Saverio. He'd parked, then remained seated for about ten minutes on his cell phone, checking in on two of his building projects in Milano and speaking with the foreman of a renovation job he was supervising on a private villa near Bellagio on Lago di Como. Afterwards, he'd gotten out and walked to the front of his car, scanning the piazza for the parking attendant in order to buy a parking ticket to put on his car's dashboard.

He hadn't paid attention to where he was putting his feet. That was a mistake. The result was a thoroughly-flattened pile of fresh dog shit located right next to his left front tire.

Hell knows no fury like someone who has just stepped into it. His mouth ran away from him. Seconds later, he'd looked up and checked around to see if there'd been anyone within hearing distance.

Good God, I hope no one heard that, he thought.

Washing and wiping clean his shoe afterwards in the toilet of the bar had been everything but a pleasant experience. Even the bar girl, smelling the situation when he'd walked in, had hit him with a look which had done nothing at all for his general state of mind. And the damned shoe still smelled to high heaven, even after he'd purposely chosen a table outside the bar on the breezy colonnade.

Suddenly, the chair next to him scraped backwards and

there was Saverio. Guy always looked good: white Adidas shoes without socks, blue jeans, no belt, one of his beloved Zegna shirts, this time in straight purple, gold chain around his neck, a suspicious-looking, irregular bruise on his left neck, and a smile on his face a mile wide. If past history were any guide, Saverio had used the previous night for something a little bit more interesting than just sitting around drinking and talking about nothing the way he had with his friends at the LaVilla Hotel where he'd stayed the night.

Giovanni asked himself, "How the hell does he do it? We've got big problems here and he just slumps down in his seat, the bar girl comes running over like a lap dog to take his order, and then he just sits there, rubbing his hands together, as cool as anything, ready for the day's action."

No question up to now about the stink still coming from his shoe. Well, that shouldn't take too long, he thought.

It didn't.

"Hey, Giovanni, you looking where you're walking these days?" he asked, and waited for the push back.

"Always, damn it. Shit. If it bothers you that much, then move your ass over to the other side of the table. Or get downwind."

He took a quick, inspecting look at his shoe, then looked up at Saverio. "Can you fucking believe it? Fresh dog shit. That damned dog survived only because it was no longer around when I stepped on its dinner. And, just to keep things straight here, your comments aren't helping things either. So, get yourself some coffee and something to eat. And let it go, damn it. We've got more important things to discuss here than dog shit."

"Okay. Okay. Relax, Giovanni, coffee's already taken care of. So, okay, let's talk."

Saverio looked at him for a second. They were both friends, but Saverio knew the bad moods Giovanni could get himself into upon occasion. This one appeared to be one of the more virulent ones.

Giovanni studied his friend's face. "Look, we've got to do something about this whole Finsler-Lorenzini thing. Believe me, I'm not complaining about the money we already got, that's all good, even though I think the bitch got way too much from the whole deal. We really screwed those percentages up. But okay, it's done. Can't change it."

"I have a different problem. And it's something we should do something about. We wanted a total of 14,500,000 Euros out of the whole deal, that was the cash amount in the account, and we didn't get it. And that pisses me off. That bitch still owes us 480,000 Euros, damn it."

A pause, a smile at the thought. "On the other hand, I have to admit we did get our asses clean out of Switzerland after the hit. And what's really good is that nobody seems to know anything. So okay. Everything great from that point of view. But, frankly, that's not the point here."

Saverio knew exactly what subject Giovanni had on his mind: Anulka and her not reacting to his threats and what had happened. Not one word from her. Not even after they'd whacked Luca, the poor bastard.

Giovanni looked out over the piazza, then turned to his friend, leaning closer to him so he could speak more discretely.

"Look, what she's essentially doing here is blowing us off. I hate that. That story she told me about the email her director sent her about the withdrawals still sounds to me like she made it up. And since my talk with her that day on the phone where she blew the whole deal up, nothing. Even with Luca gone, nothing. Can you believe it? We just murdered her squeeze and she doesn't react! Unbelievable."

"The only way I can explain it is that she's so scared about getting caught that she can't think straight. But then, what the hell do I know? Maybe she did suspect discovery. I mean, you told me yourself you didn't have your best day the last time you were there. And putting some moves on that girl from the cashier's department you told me about wasn't very smart either. Shit, maybe somebody even took another look at the video of your visit. And saw something suspicious. And then asked Anulka about you. You know, any number of things are possible. And none of them good. None of them."

He took a sip of his coffee. "Luca. That will be hurting her bad. Wouldn't be hard to assume we pulled that one, would it now? And so, she says to herself. Fuck 'em. I'm not going to do anything more, even if they start to threaten me again with something else. Let 'em stew, the bastards. No more money. No nothing."

He adjusted his chair to get even closer to Saverio and his ear.

"I mean, she's also got another alternative. And it's not a good one, particularly for us. If she's really pissed, which we don't know for sure, she could completely lose it and go to the Lugano police and tell them what she knows. That would really fuck things up. On the other hand, I don't think she'd do that. Because she knows if she did, we'd take her down with us."

"So, what the hell. Fact of the matter is, she's not contacting us and not reacting to us. So, I ask myself. Is she planning something against us? Or is she protecting us for some reason? Or is she looking for a way to get us out of the way without implicating herself? Or maybe, that would be a real miracle, she's even working to get the rest of the money she still owes us. Who the hell knows?"

He grasped his friend's arm, frustration in every whispered word. "So, what, Saverio? What do we do now?"

Saverio knew his friend well. Very definitely not having a good day.

But he was right. They had to come up with something.

He sighed. "You're right, Giovanni. I've been thinking about this whole thing, too. And, I gotta tell you. It pisses me off just as much as it pisses you off. And you're right. We gotta do something. So, listen up. Here's what I've been thinking."

He took a sip of his coffee, looked around. No one at the next table. Only a couple of people walking along under the arcades, but not in their direction.

For starters, an important warning.

"The first point I want to make is yeah, you're right, we did get a lot of money. But that's part of the problem, my friend. We both are so screwed up, we're spending it way too fast. There's only one solution for that. We have to slow down a bit with the la-la. And what's really important, we don't want anybody asking questions about our suddenly throwing big money around like we've been doing in the last few months. That would be bad news, my friend, and you know it."

Saverio looked at him closely. "You agree with that? It's gotta stop, Giovanni."

"Yeah, yeah. Okay. Got it. Go on."

"No, damn it, don't grin like that. I'm right and you know it. We need to be much more careful. And I mean in everything we do. Are we okay with that?"

"Yeah, okay. I got it. So, let it go now."

Definitely a real bad day, thought Saverio.

"Okay, just so you understand the dangers involved. So, alright, let's move on. The second point I want to make is that you may be right about the girl. And the video. It's very possible someone could have become suspicious if they looked at it closely. I gotta tell you, that day at the bank? The whole thing just didn't smell right. And I probably got a little bit too horny when that girl walked in. Great ass. But, yeah, I guess I really fucked that up."

"So, when I think about this whole mess, I have to think she just might be right about somebody smelling something wrong. For God's sake, just look at the facts. Video. The girl.

Bad feeling. And then a lot of money going out. No wonder her boss questioned that. Hell, I'd probably have done the same thing in his place."

"Yeah, okay. So, what! You had a bad day. And her boss got itchy. But that doesn't help us further."

Saverio looked at him, his face serious.

"Yeah, you're right, but what that means, of course, is that we're burned. And, if *that's* the case, which I think it is, then all the cards are in Anulka's hands. If she doesn't make a move, then she's effectively put us out of business. There's no one else we could send into the bank to do what I did. And even if we could, I don't see any other major pressure we could put on her that would force her to set up the deal again. Her boss is onto her. I fucked up. We threatened her. And we've murdered her lover. So, bottom line, we're at point zero. We have nothing."

"Of course, we could make a couple more threatening moves. Some really hot ones. Like confront her in Zurich. Threaten her life. All possible. Hope that something like that would change her mind. But in my opinion, it'd be a waste of time. For the time being, at least in the short run, she's made the call that sticks and we have to accept it. I don't like it. You don't like it. But it is as it is."

Giovanni started to speak, but Saverio waved him off.

"Hold on, Giovanni. Just wait a second. You know me. Would I leave it at that? Just calm down a bit and listen to me. There is another alternative. And, beyond that, I have a suggestion, something I think we should seriously consider, independent of what she does or doesn't do. So, just sit back and relax, would you."

Giovanni smiled. Good old Saverio. Always the same. Smart, tricky Saverio would know what to do.

A half-smile on his face, Saverio starting setting up the game.

"Personally, I think Anulka has really been deeply affected by all that's happened and all that we've done. But she's a smart woman. Yeah, okay, she's shut down the deal. But she's also chosen to remain quiet. She's playing the Lugano police the way I would play them if I wanted to protect something or someone from being identified. And, secondly, doing that gives her an option."

Saverio looked up at Giovanni. "Don't give me that smile stuff, damn it. Believe me, that kind of behavior could very well be a sign she's got something in mind she wants to be free to do."

Giovanni looked at him.

"Hey, easy. It's okay. I'm listening to you. And, just so you know, I don't think you're wrong."

"Good. So, listen. One thing I don't think she's doing is thinking revenge. Frankly, I don't think she's the type. However, and this may surprise you, what I do think she might be thinking about, in spite of us murdering Luca, is finding a way to get us the money because she believes, or she assumes, that we'll always be out there threatening her if she doesn't. She may hate the thought, she may be really pissed, but that may be enough to move her to get us off her back by giving us the money we're still missing."

"I tell you, I think it's very possible she may be considering exactly the benefits of that kind of solution. And that means, I hate to say it, we have to be patient and continue to wait a while for some sign from her. And I think it may come sooner than we think."

He glanced over at Giovanni. "So, what do you think? Am I right?"

Giovanni looked out over the piazza. Cars. People climbing in and out, walking about. Lots going on. But nobody yelling about stepping in dog shit.

I'm not a patient person, he thought to himself. But, yes, Saverio could very well be right. He'd also mentioned something else in addition. What was that?

He looked his friend in the eye. "Look, I'm not going to say right now if I think it's a bad or good strategy. So, let's move on for a minute. You said you also had a suggestion. I want to hear everything you have to say first. So, what is it?"

"Well, you probably won't like it. Very simply, we just put a stop to everything. We go away and live to fight another day."

Giovanni almost jumped out of his chair. "Fuck that. No way I'd do something like that," he said.

His voice loud, spittle at the corner of his mouth. "You don't have to go any further with that screwed-up suggestion. Shit, what a stupid idea."

Saverio still quietly in the game, still setting the scene.

"Damn it, Giovanni. Calm down. Just listen for a minute. I'm not nuts, believe me. Look, you know, we both did the hit and I'm in no way sorry that we did. I hate the bitch just like you do. And she still owes us some serious money. So, give it a break. I don't need to prove to you what I'm willing to do to get it. That should be damn clear to you."

He shot a look at Giovanni's face. Eyes flashing. But not much else to see there. And at least he was quiet, listening again.

"Look, there are advantages to what I'm proposing. Say we do decide we want to cut and walk. We keep a low profile on the whole Magliaso thing and don't piss her off anymore or possibly drive her to do something that might screw *us* over big time. That's always been a big risk for us and you damn well know it."

He continued, now looking him directly in the eye. "We go on with our own lives. We both have professions. We still have some extra money. It's still high summer. Lots of action on the Côte d'Azur. Hell, we grab your new Fiat 500 Abarth when it arrives next week, drive over to Nice, gamble a little, hustle a little, drink a couple of glasses of wine and eat a salade noiçoise at the Neptune Plage on the beach, tan up a little bit, and enjoy life. *Basta cosi.* That's it. End of story."

"Just a minute," Giovanni said.

He got up, touched Saverio's shoulder, and went inside to tell the bar girl he needed to order something and to please come and check if his friend also wanted anything.

She came and took their orders, still regarding him with

a look of distaste, then flounced off again in the direction of the bar.

Always the same. Nothing but snotty bitches running around.

He stretched his legs out in front of him. Time to give Saverio's idea its due.

He felt a calmness, a feeling of conviction inside himself. "Okay, here's what I think. I'm sorry, Saverio, but I just can't agree with your suggestion that we drop everything and let it go. We've come too far for that, and, besides, I personally don't think the game has played itself out yet to a point where we'd be forced to say it's over and then just walk away."

"You yourself mentioned a couple of minutes ago the possibility she just might be working on getting us the money somehow. If so, I want that money. Architecture just doesn't do it for me anymore."

He hesitated for a minute, thinking, looking for the right words. "Yeah, you know, when I think about it, she could be doing exactly what you say. And, if that's the case—and I'm not saying it's not possible—, then you're right, the best would be for us to just relax. And yeah, what the hell, go to Nice and push it a bit. Wait until the end of August or the beginning of September. If nothing happens, then we sit down again and discuss the whole thing once more. Yeah, better."

He paused, looking off for a moment into the distance, then turned back to face Saverio, a positive note in his words.

"You know, listening to you, I'm even thinking it's very possible she might even try to contact me. Why not? The

Lugano police are due to make some closing statement soon about the case. That would take some of the pressure off. Hell, we may even get a call from her telling us she has some money for us. Really, who knows what that bitch has in her mind?"

Saverio looked at him and smiled that little smile of his. Giovanni was there where he needed to be.

"Alright, I know, dream on. But ok, Saverio, I give you the point. Yeah, I may have been pushing it too hard. That's true. We're only a little more than three weeks past Magliaso. And yeah, I agree, your alternative to wait a bit is good. I'm okay with that."

His face darkened somewhat, the eyes clouded over, his look faraway. "But, you know, Saverio, there is something I have to tell you, something that really haunts me, something I thought would never bother me. It's Luca. I don't sleep well some nights. Damn it, I was looking right at his face through those sights. Wasn't exactly easy to pull that trigger. The poor bastard, he might have been a good guy, but then again, I'm thinking, business is business. It was necessary. Unfortunate, but necessary."

His eyes, narrow slits, now focused. "I'll tell you something else. I bet she feels directly responsible for his death. In her situation, I know I damn well would."

Saverio touched Giovanni's arm. He didn't have a comment. He'd said everything he'd wanted to say on that subject.

"Listen, Saverio. I know you've got to leave soon and so do I. And we still got those drinks we ordered. Give me a couple more minutes. I have one more thing I want to say to you and also one quick question."

"No worry, Giovanni. I can call the people from my car and change the time of my arrival in Turin. But make it ten minutes. Then I really have to go."

"Okay, good. First of all, whatever I may feel about the hit itself, I want to tell you, your planning and arrangements were spot on. Good job."

Saverio smiled.

"Hell, you know me. I would have gone into Switzerland, done the number the same day, then run like hell that night for the border. Instead, you arrange for us to go to separate hotels and spend a couple of days relaxing until things are, yeah, back to normal. That definitely was the better, safer move. Probably saved my ass."

Saverio smiled at him. "Not probably, Giovanni. Definitely. But whatever. We both got in and we both got out. And we're sitting here. In the end, that's what counts, my friend."

The bar girl came back with their orders, coffee for him and a Martini for Saverio. Another quick, turned-up-nose glance at his shoe and she was gone.

"So, and now my question. I know how I got back to Italy. Just normal, put-it-in-gear and drive stuff. But you stayed a bit longer. How did you get back? And what did you do with that rifle? Be a shame if you had to leave it behind. Did you get it back into Italy. And if you did—I think I'd bet on that—then what'd you do with it?"

Saverio leaned back and smiled. No way he wasn't going to enjoy telling this story.

"Don't worry. It's all taken care of."

He smiled. "Listen. You ever seen those day tour buses and those bicycle nuts with all their racing bikes and gear and what not stored in those big enclosed trailers behind the buses? That gave me the idea. Guess who became an amateur *Giro d'Italia* racer. You'd have laughed your ass off seeing me dressed like that. Even had a little Italia cap. And all the advertising bullshit. The rifle I broke down, put it in a sports bag, and attached that bag to my bike. Then off I went in the bus, bike with the bag in the trailer, right back over the border to Italy. I should have taken a picture of it all just for fun."

Giovanni shifted his body, laughing, almost knocking his cup over. "You are such a wild ass, Saverio. Yeah, I can just picture you like that. A real ringer rider standing there looking like he belonged. And yeah, a photo. That's definitely what we would need for our little trip scrapbook."

Saverio looked at him in mock surprise—and hurt.

"Ok, ok. No worries. Great style. Great move. So, you got back over the border in good shape. But what'd you do once you got back? That's one fine rifle. After all the trouble you went to, it'd be a shame if you decided then to just dump it somewhere."

Saverio snorted and reached over to touch his arm. "You underestimate me, my friend. No way I'd ever do that. That rifle is in Italy. But nobody will ever find it, except you and me. It's hidden really well, I can assure you."

He leaned back and laughed at the expression on Giovanni's face.

"Hold on tight. This is really going to blow you away. You know those old cemeteries we have in this country. I'm talking about the ones with all the mausoleums, those low tomb-like buildings that look like small houses grouped together, one right next to the other, in a large square or rectangular form."

"Looking from the outside at any one of the four sides of the cemetery, you have the feeling you're looking at the back sides of a single, solid line of small, one room stone houses, all of them packed in one long row. There are at least one, and sometimes, several coffins in each one of those mausoleums. Logical. People, families, put their dead in there. And you can move around in those things standing up."

"The whole cemetery has a single, iron gate entrance that is usually open. Inside, one can walk freely around in the middle court section. Nothing there except some stones, a couple of walkways, and lots of weeds with some flowers interspersed between them. The mausoleums are located along the four outside perimeters of the open middle section. You ought to go visit one yourself sometime. A very edifying experience, I can tell you."

Giovanni looked at him, knowing—and shivering—at the same time.

"What I did was very simple. I went to the cemetery near my girlfriend's apartment—you know the one, right on the edge of Alessandria—and broke into one of the old mausoleums that had gone half to hell because it was built in the 19th Century. Didn't look like anybody had been in there since the last burial took place. That was Anno 1851."

"Visualize a ledge running directly under the ceiling all the way around three of the four inside walls of a typical small mausoleum. Ledge must be at least ten feet above the ground. Coffins on the floor in the middle. That ledge is about two feet wide at any given point. So, what I did was simple. I put the case up on that ledge. I shoved it way back to where the outside wall and the sloping roof meet so that it's not visible no matter where you stand below. Don't ask me what I stood on to do that."

He looked up at the sky and took a deep breath. "You have no idea what a hellhole that was. First, the creepy feeling one gets in such a place, then all the bugs crawling all over the inside of the walls."

"Then the air—dusty, dead air. Probably from the middle of the 19th Century as well. I gagged a lot. Once I was done, I shut the front door behind me and put the old lock back on. Threw some dirt on the two steps in front to hide my foot-prints and then went and had a tall cool one at a local bar."

He hesitated. "Well, to be honest, several tall cool ones."

"And oh, yeah, I almost forgot. I crossed myself several times after I closed the door to that damned place. Didn't want to be accused of having forgotten to show respect for the formalities, you know."

Giovanni just stared at him. Then he laughed and shook his head. "Absolutely incredible. I can't believe it. You are one sneaky son of a bitch, Saverio. It's a damn good thing we're on the same side. Otherwise, I'd be really worried."

Saverio smiled his Cheshire cat smile.

"Yeah, well, I thought that was pretty good move myself. If we ever need it again, it's there for us to pick up. I'll let you have the pleasure of doing that. Just a small tip for you: take a can of bug spray with you when you go."

Giovanni couldn't get over his friend's good spirits. It seemed to him Saverio thrived on the risk of what they were doing. He himself wanted only the money. Big balls were not exactly his strong suit. He compensated for his lack of aggressiveness with other "qualities"—cold-hearted greed, anger fits, and laziness were the names of his games.

It was late morning. High time to drive back to Milano. He had an afternoon meeting at a construction site near Milano's Malpensa Airport. A late arrival was not an acceptable alternative for the hard-assed client who'd be waiting for him there.

They walked together down the steps in front of the bar, crossed the road to the piazza, and shook hands. He remembered the minefield near the left front fender of his car. Instead of approaching from the front, he came at the driver-side door from the back, got in, and then drove past Saverio, waving to him a last time before heading out of the piazza and out of Asti.

I'm late, he thought, as he reached the Autostrada A33 and headed east toward its junction with the A26 running up to Milano. He undid the wrapper from an orange-flavored lollipop—one of his favorite flavors—and shoved its business end into his mouth.

It was time to roll up the windows and push some metal down the highway.

12
The Trustee and Asset Management
Offices of Dr. Peter Renauer
Renauer Treuhand AG
Florastrasse
Zurich
Switzerland

June 27   The same year 16:52

Peter Renauer slumped down in the chair in his office.

It hadn't been a good day for him. Nothing but long meetings with two dissatisfied clients. Endurance contests involving judgments and guesses during which nobody had really won. Both clients had complained that he'd not been living up to his promises to provide them with over-average returns and vacuum-tight safety for their capital.

What the hell is a man to do, Renauer asked himself. He'd repeatedly explained everything to them, regretting as he did so that he'd brought them and their money into his firm those many years ago.

In his opinion, ungrateful bastards, considering all he'd done for them and their wealth over the years.

Fact was the whole damn world economy had been standing for too long on shaky legs. Volatility, inflation, supply chain issues, a major pandemic, terrorism, negative growth, austerity programs in some of the rim countries pushing those countries into depression, the European Union on a tear to rip itself apart, a war going on in Ukraine.

Only in the last twelve months or so had the markets changed for the better. The firm had used that time to produce its usual, well-over-the-average, results for its clients.

Prior to that turnaround, Renauer had reacted in the appropriate fashion. He'd moved a substantial percentage of the money under management out of equities into short-term cash instruments. However, interest rates of 1 to 2 percent were just ridiculous for a firm promising growth-oriented asset management. But following a conservative strategy, he'd had no choice. That necessity had impinged negatively upon asset growth/returns in his clients' accounts in the past several years, although the growth in the market starting in the early Fall of the previous year and lasting, with several ups and downs, up to the present, had significantly reduced the damage incurred prior to that time.

Bottom line, the two-step strategy had protected the asset value of his client's accounts over a very tough time in the markets. And they looked positively-enough set up so that the recent, albeit, high single digit growth in the equity indexes looked like it would continue for a considerable amount of time.

But for those two he had just seen in his office, nothing he had said had changed their minds. And they'd let him know it.

It didn't matter where one had looked in that bad economy. He knew exactly who the major perpetrators had been.

Yeah, okay, the pandemic. Not possible to change that. And a blind Federal Reserve believing inflation was transitory.

But the bankers. Yeah, the bankers. They were the real "heroes" of this story.

Massive mistakes in judgment, bad forecasts, unchecked greed, ignorance, the launch of poor-quality IPOs, inflated egos, narrow-mindedness, rejection of economic reality, trickery, treachery, prevarication, inability to compromise, selfishness, and a big dose of superficiality were just some of the failings he'd seen during the recent upheaval. When he took a minute to think about it, he saw there was actually nothing new in his current conclusion: they'd been doing the very same thing for a long time.

Damned idiots.

There was no doubt in his mind: he was the only sane one left standing.

Renauer could look back on almost thirty years of asset management—both for his clients and for himself. In spite of the bankers, government incompetence, and haphazard macro-economic policies with their often-negative impact on asset values, he'd managed to build a successful business, client by client, investment deal by investment deal. He'd only had one down year, something that still ate at him when he looked at the yearly performance metrics of his firm through the years.

A significant number of his clients had invested white money. These were clients who paid, in their home countries, the appropriate taxes due on whatever income or return their assets generated. No problem there. Honest clients like that were always welcome—and always respected.

He also had a fairly decent number of clients from Asia and Europe as well as South America who had no wish whatsoever to have the source, as well as the uses of their money, known to any regulatory instance, above all, to any tax authorities in their home countries. This was black money, untaxed money, money moved around in secret. Such clients relied on him not only to guard the secret of the existence of those assets, but also to do with them what he really did best: produce exceptional and consistent growth in their value.

No problem there either. He'd had over the years a single-minded approach to their needs. They knew it. And they certainly appreciated it.

His secretary knocked, bringing him two documents to sign. Two swirls of his pen and it was done. Not a word was exchanged. She shut the door gently behind her.

He paused with his thoughts, suddenly distracted, and looked around. Renauer, he thought, you've got a nice business office here. It fits you.

Any normal businessman, knowing what was really in it, would have had to be a little bit off the rail to agree with him on that one. Renauer was a minimalist *in extremis*, meaning that if he'd been able to get away with it, he'd have had no problem sitting on the floor and asking his occasional visitors to do exactly the same thing.

In actual fact, he did have a desk and a semi-comfortable high-backed leather chair on which he was sitting as well as two metal chairs facing him on the other side of his desk. No upholstery or cushioning on the seats.

The desk structure in black metal. Not a single finger-print to be seen on the inch-and-a-half thick glass plate serving as its surface. Not a single piece of paper on its top to detract from its polished perfection.

Not a single personal photo or framed letter from some obsequious client on the wall. Not a diploma or honorary certificate in sight. No flowers. No magazines, no newspapers on the coffee table. In his opinion, all extraneous bullshit items which had nothing to do with taking care of business.

He himself the definition of the word ascetic. Fifty-nine years of age, over-average stature, short, gray hair, clean-shaven, white skin on his lean face, with dark eyes that bored into one when he spoke. He kept a Mont Blanc ballpoint pen, the one he'd used to sign the documents, in the left pocket of his shirt. He never left it on his desk after using it for fear its shiny black surface might suffer a scratch from the glass desk top or be smudged by someone with unwashed hands picking it up and using it before he could stop them from doing so.

To his right, on a small black velvet pad, there was an engraved silver tray upon which his secretary had placed a glass and a large bottle of mineral water. The polished tray didn't have a single fingerprint on it. The bottle was always full, its seal always intact. When Renauer did open the bottle and pour himself a glass of water, his secretary had a standing order to immediately replace the now only partially-full bottle with a fresh, full one.

To his left, on a small side table next to his desk, a black telephone console. To its left, one personal item, a small silver framed picture of his daughter, Ophelia, the result of a long-ago relationship with a Parisian woman he'd not seen in decades. His daughter was the one single human being in his life whom he really cared about.

He didn't give a shit or a damn about anybody else.

His desktop computer was located behind him on a narrow table shoved up against the wall. It also in black. Table top also in thick glass. A set of simple metal drawers in black neatly tucked under the glass.

Although he no longer did any active trading, he had a small flat screen television set up on that table. It was tuned to CNBC International, the business channel. His English being perfect, he would occasionally turn up the volume to listen to interviews or discussions or reports on the market progress or lack thereof. Most of what he heard was either vacuous nonsense or self-serving blah-blah. On the other hand, he did hear occasionally something that was quite useful for him and his business. So, it stayed there.

On the other side of his office, near the door leading to his secretary's office, stood two stiff, uncomfortable-looking black leather chairs. His employees in the office smiled behind his back when they heard him say how effective those chairs were in keeping discussions or meetings moving along smartly.

Amused though they might be by him and his habits, when compensation was the subject, they spoke in hushed tones, revering the man who'd created such a money machine and who paid them as well as he did.

What really differentiated his office from a normal one were a number of items he'd added a number of years ago. His office had seven 17th and 18th Century oil masterpieces hanging on its walls. The biggest one, a country pastoral scene in the Normandy area of France, its canvas and frame almost covering one of the whole walls, was his favorite. To avoid possible theft, each was attached by a wireless connection to a central security system. And that system to a local security firm on call, 24-7.

He liked to show visitors his knowledge of the world of art, expounding at length on the merits of the one or the other artist's steady brushwork or feeling for the nuances of color. For anyone wanting more information, he would show his visitors the contents of a large art book about the period. He kept it in one of the drawers behind him and not laid out open in his office because he did not want uninterested parties pawing or dirtying it or bending its pages.

Anal does what anal does.

Art is art, but it can also be used for other purposes. In one of the ornate gold-leafed frames, Renauer had had a local security firm install two items: a small, wide-angle fiber optics lens and, just above it, a super-sensitive pickup microphone. Both of them (supposedly) invisible to the casual eye, hidden as they were among all the ornate carvings and gold leaf of the frame.

He'd had a separate wireless transmitter attached to the side of his phone which, when pressed down, would turn on the recording system. To turn it off, he had only to press the same switch again. Except for his secretary, none of the people in his firm knew of its existence. The recordings were transmitted real-time to a sender-receiver hidden in his outer office. From there, they were passed on to an outside firm. A small battery pack was available at the back of the picture frame to power the system when it was turned on.

A really interesting touch was employing the wire on which the painting hung as the system's antenna. Clumsy, not exactly state-of-the-art, and certainly not necessary in a digital and wireless world, but he was proud of that little number. No one else had thought of it.

He used the system for recording his conversations with clients or those bringing him deals or investment opportunities. This, of course, always took place without their knowledge. If necessary, he had no compunctions about using what was on the DVDs for purposes of blackmail. Or for putting the one or the other miscreant investment firm in its place. He had a perfect record. He'd never lost one deal, never missed any objective he'd set for himself when he'd used his art for such purposes.

Just part of taking care of business.

To the other professionals in the finance world, he was the personification of a pure bastard. He didn't give a damn about the industry, the competition, and the people who worked for the competition. And he made sure they knew it.

Conversely, his colleagues, looking at him and his personality, looking at his single-mindedness for business and money, asked themselves how such a cold and anal person could have managed to build such a profitable business. They could have saved themselves the trouble. He wasn't even going to give them the time of day.

There was, of course, a method to his madness. By giving everyone the impression he didn't give a damn about his reputation or image, he was, in fact, doing the exact reverse: building that reputation and image. Renauer was convinced the more he played hard ass with his environment, the more he dropped an occasional dime on one of his "professional colleague", someone whom he alone thought deserved it, the more he thought his reputation and standing would profit from it.

Fact was, it did. He liked that. In his opinion, that was real image.

Really fucked everybody up.

His internal management style was entirely different. His employees seldom, if ever, left his employ. Hardly anyone could remember any one of them being out in the market in recent years looking for new employment. They were paid extremely well, and, interestingly enough, considering the kind of person he was, had a fairly broad canvas to paint on. They liked the kind of freedom he gave them. They were good at what they did and they rewarded him with solid results for the firm and its clients.

His external partners, the banks, knew it was the rare exception when one of them was approached by a Renauer client who was thinking of switching his account elsewhere. How the hell he'd managed to create that kind of loyalty was the stuff of many a lunch conversation. No one had any real answers to the continuing riddle.

For Renauer, it was no riddle at all. Exactly the opposite. He knew exactly what he was doing and how he continued to create and maintain enormous client loyalty.

It was all really quite simple.

Peter Renauer was a very wealthy man. He'd achieved that status, not only by paying himself well, owning his company one hundred percent, and making smart money investments, but also by being very patient. And very tricky. Being patient in business matters is normally a sound strategy. Renauer followed that principle without exception in all of his firm's operations. Those which were legal—and those which weren't.

Normally, when someone sought anonymity for his capital, that usually meant, assuming proper legitimization and adequate funds, that that someone would open a numbered account at a Swiss bank or at an asset management firm such as his. He'd opened a lot of such accounts for his clients in his time. They were his Category B clients. Anonymity-seeking, wealthy clients.

Their affairs were taken care of at his main offices in the Florastrasse in Zurich

However, for the special type of client *in extremis*, Renauer's Category A clients, the world they wanted and needed was structured in a very different way. A simple numbered account or standard management contract wasn't enough for them. In their world, anonymity meant capital-letter secrecy in everything related to their assets.

It also meant that under no circumstances should anyone else, particularly family members, relatives, family lawyer in the home country, former wife or old girlfriends, God forbid, the tax authorities, or even people within the firm's offices in the Florastrasse ever have access to the fact that the client had at some point in the past squirreled big money away with Renauer in Switzerland.

No one. Ever. Never.

That was one of the reasons why the physical, organizational, and financial management structure of the Category A operation was located in Winterthur, so to speak, off-campus, and thus far away from the Florastrasse. Such confidentiality, such extreme concern about secrecy, was also in his interest because he "managed" the assets of this special group of Category A clients in a very special—but also very self-centered way.

Normally, the process of defining Category A or Category B clients started with the first official contact between himself and an interested potential client. It was like the branding of cattle. Some got one brand. Others got a different one. Everyone sorted and slotted and put out to pasture, according to preset criteria.

The Category B clients always wanted a vacuum-tight contract as the formal basis for their association with his firm. No problem. The arrangement included not only the specific way their money was to be managed, but also addressed something very important to them: the disposition of their assets should they die. The B clients never forgot the reality of their existence—and reality post that existence. Consequently, they always made sure that the steps to be taken upon their passing were all formally anchored in the documents they signed.

He had no problem with bringing such new clients into the firm. Money was money. Fees were fees. Percentages were percentages. Profits were profits.

Happy Category B clients. Happy Renauer.

But not as happy as he was with his Category A clients. He turned these people's secrecy paranoia to his singular advantage. In the account documents they were given to sign, there was no reference whatsoever to what Renauer must do, or, if he were incapacitated, what the firm should do with the client assets if the client were to die. Because of his reputation and because of the firm's strong performance, potential Category A clients already trusted him explicitly, taking little or no time before signing to look carefully at the required documents or read the fine print.

Bad move.

More often than not, no thought crossed their mind that they might also be just a little bit mortal and, at some point, perhaps sooner than expected, pass away. For them, his assurances that secrecy was the highest law of the firm were more than enough. Everything else would take care of itself, now and in the hereafter.

They trusted and looked at him as perhaps only a dog can look trustingly at his master. Pat. Pat. Good, old, trustworthy Renauer would know what to do when the time finally came.

He loved the initial "recruiting" moments with those Category A candidates, relished observing close-up their foibles and weaknesses. When he noticed a potential client's paranoia, he'd just wait for a couple of minutes. Then he'd lean across his desk, fix that person with a well-meaning smile, and propose that because of "the important nature of the investment", the client's money might be better managed and administered by him personally in Winterthur, instead of by one of his people in the Florastrasse.

One could put it into a trust, for example, or create a corporate entity with the funds to be managed contained in its accounts. Of course, the company in question would be administered and managed by him personally. Which, of course, was nothing but a fairy tale, because he managed all client accounts and all spun-off trusts himself, whether they were held in the Florastrasse or in Winterthur. Or elsewhere.

The potential Category A client, confronted with such a special invitation, thought he knew very well what that meant. He was to become a member of the select inner circle, the special fraternity, the Council of Brothers, an owner of the key to the elephant burial ground. Or, as one client put it bluntly but, nonetheless, accurately, investment Valhalla.

There would be the usual exchange of pleasantries after such an offer: Client says, "You honor me". "No", says Renauer," you honor me." That, and similar bullshit, usually flew back and forth for about five or ten minutes or so until everybody concerned was covered with honor and respect and loyalty and humility and thankfulness for the grand opportunity and God knows what else.

What fools they were, he thought to himself.

If the potential Category A client did unexpectedly notice there was no section in the contract explicitly referencing the disposition of his assets after his death, Renauer would excuse that with a few mumbled words about recent changes in Swiss law. An administrative error. The contract—"please excuse this unfortunate omission"—was not the appropriate one for foreign clients.

A minute later, a new contract, a Category B contract, would be produced. The new client would sign it—and then join the ranks of Renauer's regular client base in the Florastrasse.

The client never knew the difference. He thought he was in Winterthur when, in actual fact, he was a client in the Florastrasse. No elephant burial ground or Valhalla in sight.

In all this back and forth, there had to be some good reason for his making such a fuss about contracts and category choices and disposition of funds. Constantly using a different-strokes-for-different-folks approach.

In fact, there were two very good reasons. Fraud and embezzlement were their names. Having successfully taken care of all the initial formalities involved in the recruitment of his particularly beloved Category A clients, Renauer then proceeded to take care of business. Sometimes for years, sometimes—unfortunately or fortunately, depending upon the health of the person involved and one's point of view—for a much shorter period of time.

Since many of the Category A clients didn't call or visit the firm, Renauer would not have been Renauer if he hadn't made sure there was continuous follow-up on every private client's life in his home country. He never missed a beat. Through unofficial contacts in Germany and France and the Netherlands and other client countries, he always had a reliable read on the lives of his clients. Or, more importantly, for him and his special brand of fraud, any possible public or official announcement of their demise.

When a client died, he didn't stop managing the client's assets. Instead, he would patiently wait at least twelve months, sometimes longer, to see if anyone showed up to claim the money. If someone did come, and that did occur from time to time, then no problem whatsoever. They got the money, assuming proper documentation and legitimization.

If, however, no one came to him during that year, he, as the trustee of record, simply transferred the monies into another account outside of the Winterthur operation, but still within the group of companies he owned. A few days later, there would be a "slight accounting bump in the dark" and the money would flow in different-sized tranches into one of his private accounts around the world.

Patience and patronization and asset growth and the well-meaning smile had won another victory.

During the many years of his legal as well as fraudulent management of the firm and its client accounts, he'd been able to accumulate so much money he'd stopped counting after he'd passed the 200 million Swiss franc mark.

Several years ago, he'd started putting some of that money to work in smoothing out some of the rough spots which occasionally popped up in some of his client's portfolios.

This was not an altruistic move on his part. Nope, it was just damn smart business. Rough spots he defined as lousy returns. Talk about developing and maintaining absolute client loyalty. Reinauer was a client relations expert *par excellence.*

His method was very simple. He would, upon occasion, signal directly or indirectly to a private client, who had not seen his portfolio grow in the accustomed manner, that the firm,—"without any legal obligation to do so, of course"— had stepped in to help "get the overall asset level moving back in the right direction."

These were not dumb people. Every client got the message. No wonder no one was looking for alternative financial advice.

His pride in his firm knew no bounds. He knew he'd

created a brand-new variety of the infamous Ponzi scheme. He just couldn't blowhard it all over the market. In crass terms, the game was just so simple: take from the dead and give to the living.

To be fair, he did have a right to be proud of his firm—or, at least, of its legal business model. He was successful. His life was orderly.

Everything in the green, literally, in the world of Dr. Renauer, asset and arts patron par excellence.

Except for one thing, a little sticky—and potentially dangerous—problem involving the soon-to-be-completed transfer of the assets of his former private secretary, Chantal Hofmaier, to her son Felix. Aside from that bothersome little issue, however, the sun shone every day for Renauer. And that in a climate where sometimes weeks passed when the sun never came out from behind the fog and the rain and the clouds stacked up on the north side of the Alps.

He thought about his reputation—and that of his firm. And of the games he'd played. He sipped some more water. Those damned innocents, he thought. They don't even know the half of it.

They most certainly didn't.

More than two decades ago, Chantal Hofmaier had come into his employ. She'd started in the general accounting office of his then small firm and moved steadily upwards within the organization until, seven years ago, she'd become his private secretary.

She'd been an attractive woman in the prime of her life.

She'd had what in the 19th Century would have been characterized as an "hour-glass" figure. Years later, "voluptuous" or, even later, "hot" would have been the more appropriate, but also more distasteful word of choice to describe her.

In the formal environment of the firm, she'd acquired a reputation for being both competent and loyal. She had sparkling brown eyes, a ready smile, and a musical laugh that charmed everyone who heard it. Many of her fellow workers had commented on the absolute polarity of the two personalities involved: she, positive and happy, he, dour and controlling.

As it turned out, it didn't matter either way. Opposites are supposed to attract one another and, in this case, they'd apparently done so. In spades.

She'd already separated from her husband before she'd started working for him. No matter which position she had within the firm, she'd always focused on only one thing: the firm. When she thought about her son, something she did only very rarely, she surmised that her one-sided approach to life was probably the reason they both had become almost strangers over the years. She could handle multiples tasks, but apparently not multiple emotions.

Early on, he'd noticed her total concentration on his firm. As the years passed, he was more than happy to promote her based upon that loyalty and her contribution to the growth of the firm.

During those same years, he'd also experienced a need for some therapeutic exercise with someone of the opposite

sex. She was the best talent around. Easy answer to the problem: seduce her. Which he promptly did.

Or thought he did.

Part of Chantal's being true to her focus on the firm
and moving up in the organization had involved her seduc-
ing him. Which she promptly did. The net result was, so to
speak, a meeting at the midfield stripe. They enjoyed a carnal
relationship of mutual convenience with a small side order of
affection.

Over time, Chantal became privy to just about all and
everything the firm did. Simple reason. She was available
both day and night, something Renauer also appreciated,
both day and night.

Since his daughter had long ago decided to live in Paris,
he could move around in Zurich as he wanted. He would
spend months living with Chantal in her apartment, then
she would move into his home on the Sonnenberg in the
hills above Zurich. Their three am discussions in bed did not
involve dissecting in detail the lousy Zurich weather forecast
for the next day.

Back and forth went the clothes and the toothbrushes,
and back and forth went the emotions. Sometimes, she was
the more affectionate, he then the less affectionate of the two.
Then, for no reason other than the fact that they perhaps
thought subconsciously it might be fun the other way around,
they would switch roles. She would then become the less
interested one, he the more interested party.

A friend of theirs, observing the whole kerfuffle,

had reduced it all down to a single observation: whatever will do you.

At the beginning, other employees in the firm, observing the hick-hack relationship they both seemed to have, had occasionally sat together trying to find an answer to that most interesting of questions: who's on top this month? They'd formulated that question, however, in both the figurative and the literal sense.

Good for a laugh or two at noon in the firm's lunchroom.

Several years into their relationship, the whole thing had become a non-issue. Both of them were still together, still doing their thing. It was as it was. The employees reacted to this increasingly boring state of events by moving on to making fun of or laughing about other scandals, both in and outside of the firm.

In the course of her work, Chantal had become quasi-friends with one of the clients of the firm, a German citizen by the name of Reichert, who, in definite contrast to the other clients, came relatively often to visit.

She knew his file. He was Category A, a Winterthur client.

However, Winterthur itself was very definitely not his favorite flavor of the month. Ergo, he made it a point of arranging his visits at the Zurich office, it being almost right next to Lake Zurich with a great view, and also much more convenient for visiting friends in nearby Kuesnacht.

Chantal maintained hard copy files of the Winterthur clients in her office. This allowed Renauer to have some basic account and investment information physically in his hands when, rare as it was, a client like Reichert came to visit him in the Florastrasse. The files were located in a state-of-the-art Gardall safe, built into the wall directly behind her desk. *Bankenmaessiger Schutz.* Bank-style protection. One of Renauer's less valuable paintings hung over its small black steel door.

The original and complete Category A client files were held in Winterthur in a computerized central *Datei*, accessible only through code and password. Continually updated flash drive copies of the data base were held at a safe location elsewhere in Zurich.

When Renauer ran over with one of his meetings, and Reichert had to wait for fifteen or twenty minutes or so, she would chat with him about his life and his family while he waited. He had three kids whom he loved very much. He was also a very private man, someone who, surprisingly, had a strong inferiority complex. "No one should know how I really am and what money I really have," he'd once told her in a moment of frank discussion about himself and his life.

A nice man, she'd thought the first time she'd met him. That positive opinion of him had not only remained the same over all the years he was a client, but had grown as she'd gotten to know him better. She always hoped the best for him—and told him so every time they met.

Seventeen months ago, Reichert had, suddenly and unexpectedly, died. Because he knew of her nice relationship with him, Renauer had informed Chantal of his passing the day after it occurred. He wouldn't be coming any more.

She was shocked and dismayed at his death. She would miss him.

Normally, Chantal received only official written information relating to the deaths of the Category B clients. This news she always passed on dutifully to Renauer who usually wrote a personal letter to the immediate family regretting the fact that the client had passed on. With certain exceptions, she'd never seen him write anything to deceased Category A families or relatives.

The only information Chantal received concerning the deaths of Category A customers was a short email note from Winterthur telling her that Mr. or Mrs. So-and-So had passed on and would she please shred the file contained in her wall safe relative to this person.

She'd never been directly involved in any of the clearing and settlement details involving the disposition of a deceased Category B client's assets. It was just not part of her duties or responsibilities. All that, she knew, was handled by several people in a separate department on the floor beneath hers.

As far as Category A clients were concerned, she'd always assumed that all death-related matters were taken care of in Winterthur in the same conscientious way as they very obviously were in the Florastrasse.

In this particular case, however, she'd known and liked Reichert and appreciated it when he'd had the chance to chat with her in her office. Thus, she decided to ask Renauer if there were anything she could do to help reach the family so that the account could be properly closed or, if the family wished, continued on active status.

She'd broached the subject at his home one night three weeks after Reichert's death. It was as though she'd set off a bomb in his living room. He threatened to hit her with an empty bottle of wine. She feared for her life.

His message to her had been simple: stay out of things that do not concern you. Do not try to contact or talk to any of the client family or any representatives of Mr. Reichert. No exceptions. None.

She was pissed at his reaction. And suddenly suspicious. She'd felt strongly that this case did concern her, so she'd done a little checking. And then a little more checking. And then she'd added some major hacking to the mix. She secretly made a flash drive as well as selected hard copies of the documents and money transfer records she'd found.

Afterwards, viewing those hacked documents in her apartment, she'd discovered the cause of his explosion and his anger at her: Renauer had made Winterthur a criminal enterprise. The detailed information indicated very clearly what he'd been doing with the assets of his paranoia-driven clients, clients who had died without having made any prior arrangements for the disposition of those assets.

The cost of trust—and Valhalla.

It was almost genial, she had to admit. The bastard had taken it all for himself.

Not only was her client friend's family being cheated,

but many other clients' families as well, going back many years, had never seen a single franc or Euro of the money their family member had deposited so securely, and so very secretly, in Switzerland.

Her loyalty to him had always been strong and blind. For a long time, that had been all she'd needed in order to accept any aberrations she saw or discovered in his character or behavior. Including the secret recordings being made in his office.

But this was an entirely different kettle of fish. This, she knew, was egregious criminal conduct of the highest order.

What really angered her, however, was not only the fact that he'd been defrauding client families for years—that was bad enough—, but that he was cheating the family of some-one who'd become important to her, knowing full well, as he did, that there'd been a special relationship between her and the client before he'd died.

During the years, many people had maintained to her that Renauer really didn't give a shit about anybody except himself. She hadn't wanted to believe it. Now she did.

She despised him for it.

Three weeks after that discussion at his home, she'd met with him at the Kronenhalle Restaurant in downtown Zurich for dinner. The atmosphere between them had been icy. They'd sat at a corner table next to the small bar in the larger of the public rooms reserved for dinner guests. They'd eaten venison with spaetzle, a dish they both often ordered in the fall when the hunting season was fully underway. As always, the room was crowded and she'd had difficulty making herself heard above the general noise level.

In spite of his previous warning, but now armed with new information, she'd inquired again about the Reichert money and when it was going to be transferred to the family. She demanded from him that he confirm to her that he'd passed on Reichert's money to his immediate surviving family. Why would he otherwise threaten her if he weren't doing something else with the money, she asked him?

She knew, of course, exactly what he was doing. She just didn't let him know what she knew and how she knew it.

His reaction was anger. He'd stood up, paid the bill, and beckoned for her to follow. That night at his home, Chantal got a good look at the depths of hell, courtesy of Renauer. And she learned the limits of her own abilities. And character.

He'd admitted his crime to her. Fraud he'd called it. For the crime he was guilty of, the law prescribed, depending on length and intent and the amount of damages, at least twelve to eighteen years in in prison.

A terrible punishment.

He told her he would cause her serious harm if she were ever to do anything with the knowledge she now possessed. If she informed the authorities, he'd make sure she was arrested, just as he would be, once they'd gathered enough information to prove the existence of his crime. He'd describe her as a direct and active participant in the crime. And who would believe her when she maintained she'd known nothing of his doings and hadn't aided or abetted him in any way in perpetrating his crime?

Who had the better cards in the hand? She knew exactly who that was. It wasn't her.

"Chantal, let's get a couple of things straight here. First of all, you're not well. Your work has suffered because of that, creating a difficult situation for me. As for your future, if I were to fire you, you'd have a hell of a time finding another job. Either in our industry or out of it. I know exactly what I would do to stop you getting anything besides a cleaning job somewhere. You'd be finished."

"On top of that, your financial resources are limited. I know what I've paid you in bonuses in the past years. Even if you've saved everything you got, it still wouldn't be enough for you to live on. Pension or no pension."

Then he'd hit her with the lowest of blows. "If you land in jail, you wouldn't last a year. That hell would finish you off. And even before you got there, you'd go down psychologically. Why? Think about it, Chantal. You'd have to endure a trial and you'd have to endure being sentenced to prison for crimes you didn't commit. Are you prepared to go through something like that? Do you really think you would survive that kind of punishment?"

He'd put on his sorry face. He regretted having to talk to her like this, he told her. She deserved something for staying with him and for being loyal in such a situation. He told her he would start putting a certain sum into an account for her every month. Within a year, the total amount would probably add up to at least three quarters of a million Euros, if not more.

And that wouldn't be the end of it. He'd continue to pay her as long as she lived. The money, he knew, he'd take from his Kunst Treuhand AG account, an account he used to bunker the official profits he made in the Florastrasse and which he drew upon to satisfy his appetite for buying unique and rare masterpieces. Clean, legal deal.

A reward to her for her loyalty over the years if anyone asked.

She was shocked. But he'd won. She'd let herself be bought off, albeit with the proviso that she be able to make a will that would guarantee her son would inherit any and all monies and assets in her accounts on the day she passed on.

Her demand was non-negotiable. No games. No tricks.

He'd agreed to it. She would have her will notarized by a notary public in Zurich so that he, as executor of the will and as an appointee of the probate court, would have to write Felix and hand the money over to him when she was no longer there.

He'd have no other choice in the matter.

If she regained her health, she might be able to escape from him one day, and, using the money, move elsewhere. The thought for her was a pleasant one, but unfortunately one of very short duration. She knew she no longer had the energy or the drive to make that kind of a decision and then see it through.

She'd sat back on the sofa she knew so well from so many previous evenings in his house. She'd bid adieu once more to her client friend, she'd said goodbye to the good intentions she'd had, and finally, she'd said goodbye to the person she thought she'd been throughout her whole life.

Later that evening, he'd taken her upstairs to his bedroom and raped her. She knew then what hour the clock had struck.

After the horror of that night, her life went on. Her work in the firm went on. But every day of the following months, she endured a torture that had become her life, a torture that was breaking her, psychologically, and now also seriously affecting her physical health.

On the next to the last evening in May, more than a year after that night in his home, both of them had another long and heated discussion, this time at her apartment in Thalwil. She had little strength left, but she'd wanted one last time to attempt to right what she considered to be a big wrong.

The buzzing in her head which had started many months ago had reached a stage where she'd begun to have trouble hearing what people were saying to her. The arrhythmic cardiac disturbances she'd occasionally experienced had caused her moments of panic, sending her off to her doctor who could only barely calm her fear of experiencing a more serious, perhaps mortal, event.

That evening, she'd threatened, in spite of the money, in spite of his threats, to go to the authorities and tell them what she knew. She felt it was her last chance to redeem herself, to take a stand for herself, to fight for something and for someone who had not been able to help himself, her old client friend.

He'd gotten up without a word and gone to bed.

Early the next morning, she was dead, killed at his hand. He'd spiked her morning tea with poison with no reservations or regrets whatsoever for doing what he considered to be a necessary evil. She could have ruined everything, he thought, as he called the police, asking them to come immediately.

She'd died quickly and quietly. Without great pain. There were no marks on her body. No reason to suspect anything other than what the police found in the apartment. And what Renauer related to them about the events of the early morning, his waking up and finding her lying dead next to him.

The authorities had gone through the usual required motions in such a case. They'd checked the records and the treatment her doctor had provided her in the months preceding her death. They'd interviewed the psychiatrist who had been seeing her on a weekly basis. They'd interviewed Renauer several times at his offices.

But they didn't order an autopsy. First of all, there was no prior order or approval from Chantal giving the authorities permission to conduct an autopsy upon her eventual demise.

In addition, and perhaps in this case more important, the person involved made a difference. Renauer was well-known in Zuricher circles. Although many considered him to be a real bastard, his word—and his firm—represented weight and authority. He owned one of the leading financial management firms in Switzerland. In addition, both he and Chantal had been for years a well-known couple around Zurich. There'd never been any rumors of any dissonance whatsoever between the two of them.

He'd told the authorities, she'd been in ill health for some time, and her heart must have failed. He informed them that the son, the surviving member of the family, was currently in the Far East, and apparently not interested in coming back to take care of his mother and the final arrangements for her burial.

Everything real easy, everything low key.

After several days, there were no further questions from the police. The authorities didn't have an autopsy done. In their opinion, it wasn't necessary. No medical advantage would be gained by conducting one. They'd closed the file within a week. Cause of death on the official death certificate: heart failure. She was buried in a private ceremony the following week in her beloved Thalwil.

A week or so after her death, Renauer had written a personal letter to Felix Hofmaier expressing his regrets and his hope that they both would be able to meet soon in Zurich in order to take care of a number of matters relating to his mother's passing.

Felix had called the previous day from his hotel in Basel, again confirming the meeting. He would see Felix in three days in his offices.

He wasn't looking forward to it.

13
Anulka's Apartment
Goldhaldenstrasse
Zollikon
Canton Zurich
Switzerland

June 29   19:47

Anulka sat in her favorite lounge chair located directly in front of her apartment's large picture window. She had a direct view of the lake and the still partially-snow covered Alps behind it. The evening was still warm. She'd opened the sliding door to her terrace to allow some fresh air into the apartment—and into her thoughts.

The television was tuned to SAT 1, a German TV station she was able to enjoy through her cable TV connection. She was only half looking at the flat screen, something about acrimonious debates in the German parliament. The television was on mute. Politics had never really interested her. Now, it seemed that not much else did either.

For the first time in weeks, she'd declined a dinner invitation to eat with some friends at the Kronenhalle in Zurich. She wanted be alone and to think. Hard as it would be, she needed to develop a plan of action, something to neutralize the horror of that day, something to free her from the dangers all around her, something to give her a chance to move on in some fashion with her life.

She'd thrown herself back into her work after returning from Lugano two days after Luca's murder. She'd tried to give herself as little free time as possible during any given day so as not to be forced to think about what had happened. She'd spent extra hours working in the bank, developing detailed plans to acquire new client accounts. She'd met more often with her own people, discussing with them how the bank might take its already first-class service and performance to another level.

All that work, all those efforts ran counter to her feelings and attitude vis-à-vis the bank. But she didn't care. Anything, anything to keep her mind off the horror of Luca's death and the insidious path it had cut through her being and her soul.

She'd spent one extended weekend visiting her mother, now living in Neuchatel in the western part of Switzerland. Although a visit there could sometimes be a problem for her psychological balance, her mother's obvious concern for her and her well-being had touched her deeply and helped her keep her sanity and her drive.

In Zurich, she'd accepted invitations to the theater and to dinners, ostensibly arranged for everyone in the group involved, but, in reality, only for her. She appreciated every-thing that had been done to help her, but she still slept alone in her apartment, accompanied every waking minute by the memories of the nightmare that had been Magliaso.

Together with Luca's parents, she'd made all of the arrangements for his burial. Suffering every minute of the way, she'd helped them take care of his affairs. Going through his things and his files, she'd found old receipts of times and pleasures past, she'd found her name doodled on the side of notes he'd made about his business or on his things-to-do lists, she'd read her name scrawled on ripped-open envelopes lying on his desk still not thrown away. Sharp, sudden, unex-pected emotional blows she'd found almost impossible to counter or to neutralize.

They struck deep, they struck hard, they broke not only skin but heart. They didn't heal.

His mother had comforted her as best she could. But the words, the gestures, the caring, the concerned looks, the long affectionate hugs, were no match in assuaging the hell going on inside of her.

For several weeks after his murder, she'd run on auto-matic. Sometimes, she would appear to black out in the middle of a conversation, as if a movie projector had clicked on behind her eyelids, pulling her with its black-and-white film to another place and another time.

She'd visited her personal doctor. For the first time in her life, she'd begun to swallow prescription pills designed to calm her and reduce her anxiety attacks. Their bitter taste matched the bitter taste in her mouth. They rounded off the sharp edges of the symptoms of her problem, but never its cause.

Not only had she to carry around with her the loss of the man she'd loved, but she also had to bear the constant, devastating thoughts of guilt, of having been personally responsible for his death. There was no rest, no surcease, no respite from the beat of those drums.

Guilty. Guilty. Guilty.

In the morning, she'd spoken with Luca's mother by phone. Another difficult conversation with a mother who could not fathom at all what had happened to her son, who could not imagine that he'd done anything in his life to warrant someone taking that life, who wanted, if possible, answers from Anulka, answers Anulka could not give, a slippery slope she dared not ever step onto.

Her heart had broken as she'd heard his mother crying. She'd been helpless to stop herself from doing the same. Afterwards, the awful recognition had come: she'd reached absolute bottom.

Twice in the weeks following her return from Magliaso, she'd driven back down to Tessin and gone to the Lugano police headquarters to answer questions concerning Luca, his life, and their time together. She was under no suspicion that she'd been in some way involved in the shooting. The police would probably continue their investigations until they were satisfied they'd considered all and everything involved with the crime. Fine, that was their job. She wasn't going to stand in their way if they wanted to continue doing that job. And think what they wanted to think.

But now, after all the pain, she knew, it was time, time somehow to get real, time to pay attention to somehow getting her life back on track. One way or the other, she had to find a way to shut down the desperation she felt, to still the hate she had in her, to staunch the accelerating hemorrhaging of her soul, bleeding her out emotionally, taking away—with no mercy—everything worthwhile living for in life.

She took a deep breath, the air smelled so good, so summer-like.

She knew it had to start somewhere. She knew very well if she didn't get a grip on herself very soon, she might very well lose control of her sanity. And with it, possibly her life.

In that moment of absolute despair, she sensed a slight surge of energy, of resolution, of intent. She took a breath, then another, and then another. Then several more, slow deep breaths like a swimmer putting large amounts of oxygen into his blood before starting a fifty-meter competitive race.

The calm before a race with no certainty it could be won. Keep going, she thought. Keep going. Keep breathing. You have to do this. You have to.

She glanced up at the slowly-darkening evening sky. Now? Was now the time? Am I ready? Can I do this, can I find the way? Doubts starting to make room for intent and the burning necessity to fight for and get an upper hand in her life.

The minutes passed as she sat there. At the beginning,

the words, the thoughts came slowly. So slowly, so very slowly. But one by one, they began to form a logical sequence, to provide her with an outline of how to proceed.

A sentence here. A thought there. Another sentence. Then another. And another. And then another.

Her breath quickened. She sensed inside of herself a breakthrough. She felt it intensely, felt it getting stronger, the emotions in her at that recognition almost overwhelming her, the chance to finally, and effectively, confront and neutralize the doubt and hesitation grasping tightly every one of the senses of her being.

She let that emotion, that intent come, pushing her, shoving her, forcing her to confront herself, her reality, to find, at last, some tangible course of action, a way to escape from clear dangers she knew could massively hurt her if she did nothing to defend herself. Or set her life right.

She knew damn well what was on the table. There had to be hardness. And controlled anger. And focus. And sustained intent.

She stood suddenly, and walked back into her living room, closing the sliding door behind her, then sank down onto the couch.

Strong intent in every breath she took, in every thought, in every fiber of her being.

It was time to make a list.

The number one concern for her was an extremely critical one. She needed to make a final judgment call on the risk of the bank discovering what she'd done. In all the time that had passed, the real client had neither called nor contacted the bank. Based on his past behavior, something she'd carefully researched, it seemed, light years ago, she doubted he would call in the foreseeable future.

A video issue involving the gofer's last visit seemed to have been a one-day matter. Someone in the bank's Security Office had spoken to her several days later, after having viewed the security video tapes from that particular day. Some vague feeling that not all was right with the client and what he had seen on the tape. Thankfully, she'd never received another call or question on that subject, particularly after she had, in very clear words, questioned the caller's motives in making such a statement when she personally had cleared and vetted the client in question.

She'd noticed not one iota of change in anyone else's behavior vis-à-vis her person and her management of the division. It'd been almost eleven months since the last cash tranche had been picked up by Giovanni's gofer. More than enough time for something to happen, for some alarm bell to go off somewhere in the bank, for Dr. Graesser to follow up on the email he'd sent her.

Nothing. Zero. Niente.

Scratch concern number one from the list.

The second concern involved Giovanni. For Anulka, there was no doubt he'd been involved in Luca's murder. It just wasn't possible that Luca himself had done something that had warranted some other person other than Giovanni taking his life. The police may think that, she thought, but

I don't believe that for a minute. At her core, she was certain he'd been involved, that he was the one who'd pulled the trigger.

Giovanni had killed him. No one else. No doubt about it.

Scratch concern number two from the list.

Then there was the third concern, one that directly impinged upon her continued well-being—and upon her life. Why hadn't Giovanni contacted her immediately after the shooting? She certainly hadn't been in a strong position right after his murder. Why hadn't he come to Zurich and tried to pull one of those little scare-everybody-to-hell games he'd tried when she had, early on, expressed a slight doubt or two about the mechanics of the deal?

Did he think that perhaps she should be the one to initiate contact *with* him? Or had he finally decided he'd gotten a lot of money and was that then not enough? Or did he think that shooting Luca was a just and terrible punishment for her quitting the deal and that that in and of itself was enough payback?

She knew she had to find a way to quiet her fears about what he might still be capable of doing. Including threatening her. Or even eventually killing her. If he could kill Luca in such a cold-blooded fashion, then she had no doubt he could do exactly the same thing to her if he still felt enough wasn't enough.

She couldn't take the third concern off the list.

Sitting there, she knew she needed a short-term plan to counter that threat or, even better, neutralize it before it became reality. But what? Revenge? Find the rest of the money and give it to him? Ignore him? Get help? Tell the police everything? Kill him?

What?

Unfortunately, up to now, every solution she'd thought of had included one or more serious downside risks for her.

There'd been one alternative which had been her initial—and spontaneous—choice to take care of the problem.

Pay him off.

It would have meant her giving them both a total of forty percent (Giovanni's twenty-five percent and the bagman's fifteen percent) of the difference between the 13.3 million Euros which they'd pulled out of the bank and the 14.5 million Euros, the final target objective. In net terms, 480,000 Euros of the 7,980,000 Euros—in US dollars just north of $9,000,000—she had in a safe deposit box at another bank well outside Zurich.

She hadn't been able to touch or spend any of the money. It was still all there, in 500 Euro notes, waiting for her to come and do something with it. However, giving them a part of that money would have wiped out a part of the financial cushion she'd need if the bank were ever to discover what she'd done and she would have to flee.

Borrowing a half million Euros from her bank or another bank *am Platz* in Zurich would have the same effect: even in her position, too many potential questions like what do you need the money for? And, of course, she would have to pay it back. And that would have the same effect on her future financial security.

And, besides, she thought, and most probable, who knew if that idiot Giovanni wouldn't try to come after her for more, if the both of them wouldn't try to blackmail her for even more money? And little by little drain down to empty the safe deposit box where she kept the money she'd grabbed?

Maybe not realistic because they might go too far and thus push the whole cart over. But nonetheless possible.

No, it was just too dangerous to give them anything. She had to keep all the money intact. It gave her the ability, if necessary, to escape Switzerland and then disappear. It gave her a chance to live on in secure fashion and to find a vehicle for doing something good with the money she'd taken. Otherwise, everything would have been for naught, both rationally, but, above all, in her eyes, morally.

Finally, there was a real and hard and personal emotional reason behind her thinking: she'd be damned to hell if she would give those murderers anything that now belonged to her.

They'd taken Luca. An enormously high price. No. Nothing more. Not one damn Euro cent more for them.

There did exist a second possibility, a very logical one: find someone else whom she might be able to persuade to do the very same thing both she and Giovanni had done. Under the right circumstances, and with adequate preparation, another round with a client from the original list—there'd been more than several appropriate, i.e., dirty money, alternatives to choose from the first time around—wouldn't make things that much worse for her, she thought.

Fraud was fraud. Embezzlement was embezzlement. Going back to the trough one more time would just raise the amount the bank would have to pay to the real client to reimburse him for his losses. No real problem there. And potential jail time if she were caught? The first time would put her away potentially for life, what the hell could or would a second one do?

The major issue with that solution was a simple one: she didn't know anyone whom she could involve in such a plan.

A third possibility, telling the police all she knew and hoping for a fair trial, would represent nothing but a self-inflicted wound. She'd be able to take down Giovanni and Saverio,—all to the good when her punishment was being considered—but, at the same time, she'd be putting herself directly in jeopardy, and, most likely, for a long while in the slammer. She knew she'd never survive that.

Then, there was a fourth possibility, a real crazy, emotional one she'd had in the days immediately after Luca's murder. She'd wanted to take part of the money and find someone who would go down to Italy and do to him and his accomplice what they'd done to Luca. Conceived in the heat of the moment, she'd later discarded that solution as well.

I may be someone who can lie and embezzle, she'd decided at the time, but murder is another story entirely.

Whatever the final answer, she knew she couldn't continue to live with the uncertainty, with a pulse she could hear in her quiet moments, raging, banging around in her head, and deep inside her very core. Her whole being cried out for resolution and an end to the nightmare.

She stood suddenly. It was almost too much. She needed a quick distraction.

Looking around her living room, she felt again that good feeling she'd always had when surrounded by the things she loved. A painting from the German artist, Carl Wilhelm Seiler, hung on the wall to the left of the sliding door to her terrace.

She'd always had a predilection for the classical modern, a form of art produced in the early 20th Century in Germany and Austria. It had, aside from its beauty, a quiet classiness, a fineness in its execution. Most importantly, it had an ability to calm her. And, God knows, she needed that now.

Seiler had outdone himself with a painting of a young man standing at a high writing desk in his library, browsing through a book he'd taken from a shelf behind him. His clothes were period 18th Century. When she'd seen the painting at an art gallery in Munich eight years ago, she hadn't hesitated. It had become one of her favorites.

After she'd rented her apartment, she'd decided to decorate the rooms in a more elegant style than she'd had in her previous apartment. She particularly loved the matte white, green, and blue colors she'd chosen for the living room walls and ceiling. The polished tan brown of the oak floors complemented those colors in the room perfectly.

Her white silk couches with blue and green pillows

spread about on them were her special pride. People visiting her would stand with their backs to one of the couches, then fall back onto it, almost disappearing into its soft luxury.

The depth of the couches had been a particular concern of hers. When she'd visited friends in New York City two years ago, she'd been impressed by how much room there was to lean or fall back deep into the many pillows and cushions placed at the back of their couch.

When she'd returned from New York, she had searched for and found a custom furniture maker in Zurich, someone who could replicate, in sitting comfort and style, what she had seen and experienced in New York. The result of her efforts—and his—stood in the living room, all nineteen feet long and almost five feet wide of it, two separate pieces, in rectangular form, directly in front of her black marble fireplace.

A large Louis XV mirror with a silver-leafed frame she'd purchased on a rainy day at one of the small shops in the *Marché aux Puces* in Paris years ago hung over the mantle. On the mantle itself, she'd placed some mementos from her travels, a carriage clock that ticked a little bit too loudly for her taste, and a framed picture of Luca and her taken during the last winter when they'd spent three days together in Paris.

It showed them sitting together at a small outside table having breakfast at the Les Deux Magots, a favorite bistro among Parisians on the Boulevard St. Germain. She was leaning into him while smiling directly into the camera. He had his left arm wrapped tightly around her, kissing the top of her head, her hair blowing wildly from the windy effects of the swift-moving weather front that had reached Paris early that same morning.

Damned hair, she thought, even as a more important reality overwhelmed her senses: this is the best picture of my life.

The previous evening, they'd been up on the Boulevard Montparnasse eating a late dinner at the Bar à Huitres, a seafood restaurant preferred by many Parisians when out late after an early evening movie. Several glasses of a chilled Sancerre together with two dozen Imperial oysters, slices of lemon lightly-squeezed on top of each one, had been simply culinary heaven on earth.

Afterwards, walking slowly down the broad, tree-lined Boulevard St. Germain on the way back to their hotel, Luca and Anulka had passed the still dimly-lit interior of the Deux Magots. They'd resolved to have breakfast there the following morning.

She remembered their slow, short walk after that breakfast down the narrow Rue Bonaparte to the banks of the Seine. Along the way, they'd stopped at an antique map store owned by Gerard Rossignol where Luca had bought her a map of France dating from the 17th Century. An original from Willem Blaeu, the Dutch cartographer.

She'd had it framed upon returning to Zurich. It hung on the hall wall directly across from the entry door to her apartment. The map reminded her of her loss, but also how wonderful such trips—and the time with him had been. She liked that. She wanted those reminders. Forever.

For a long time, she'd reflected on whether she should keep any pictures of Luca in her apartment. At the end, she'd decided it was better to confront, and perhaps, in that way, beat back the horror of his death by reminding herself of the happy times she'd spent with him. Thus, she not only had his picture on the mantle alongside one of herself as a young girl and her father, but also two others, one on the night stand in her bedroom, and one propped up on her desk just under the table lamp to the left of her desktop computer.

The picture in her bedroom had been taken the evening of their arrival in Magliaso, one day before his death. There'd just been enough light left in the evening sky to capture him and what he was doing without using a flash. Luca had been standing next to their parked car, helping the porter to get their baggage together to bring to the room. She'd called to him as he stood there and asked him to turn around to her and smile. There he was in the picture, loaded down, among other things, with her brown leather computer case, his hair falling over his forehead, smiling directly at her in his special way.

The phone rang. Anulka sighed. "Damn it, not tonight."

It rang again.

Ah, whatever, she thought. Driven by a sense of discipline as well as curiosity, she stood up, walked to her desk, looked at the phone id number, then picked up the receiver.

It was Michaela, her old university friend, calling from her home in Wolfratshausen, a small Bavarian town about twenty-five miles south of Munich in the foothills of the German Alps. She punched the talk button and greeted her.

"Hello, Michaela, I saw your number on the telephone id. How nice of you to call. How are you?"

Back across the distance came that husky voice, that caring voice of Michaela's, a voice she'd heard several times on the phone in the last several weeks.

"Ah, Anulka, I'm always fine. You know it's you I'm worried about. I don't think there's a day that doesn't go by where I don't think of you. So, I just thought I'd call again to see how you're getting along. I hope I'm not disturbing you."

Anulka smiled, happy to hear her voice. "Not at all. I was just sitting here, thinking."

"Not good, Anulka, too much thinking. You told me the last time we spoke that you were very busy at the bank. I hope that that's still the case because, God knows, you need it for reasons you and I don't need to discuss any further."

"Yes," she sighed, "I'm very busy, thank God. I've been traveling a bit around Europe on business and I'm expecting some new clients this week. It's just incredible. Money never stops weaving and dancing. And you're right. I need a lot of distraction at the moment."

She sat down again. She smiled slightly at the thought of what she wanted to say.

"Now, Michaela, I know you're going to ask again about my weight so I'll just tell you up front. And be done with it. I've lost about eight pounds since we last saw each other."

"I know. I know. You're right to worry that I don't eat

enough. But I tell you, I do eat. But I just seem to keep on losing weight. But honestly, I don't think it's a concern yet."

She smiled at the thought. "On the other hand, I can tell you there is at least one good thing about it all. I can wear some of the smaller size things I've been hoarding in my closets for so long. But that's," she paused, suddenly speaking very softly her next words, "very small compensation for the hell I'm going through."

She started crying softly.

Michaela was distraught. Her friend was suffering and there was nothing she could do. "*Verdammt*. Damn. What the hell was I thinking even asking her personal questions at such a time", she asked herself.

She waited several moments for her to gather herself. She heard a slight rustling. Tissues, she thought.

"Anulka, can you hear me? Maybe I should hang up and we talk later."

"Yes, Michaela, I hear you. It's okay. Believe me, I'm okay."

"Listen to me. All of us are just heartsick about what has happened to you. We have so few possibilities to really express our feelings and support to you. I just want you to know that I'm always there with you on that phone when you want. All you have to do is call. Or if you want me to visit or you want to visit, just say the word. Listen to me, Anulka, I mean it."

"Ach, Michaela, you're a true friend. I'll be okay. I'm a big girl. I just have to get my thoughts a little better organized. I've got a lot to think about now and in the next few days."

"Then, by all means, do that. If you want to talk about anything, then call. I give you a big hug through the phone. Ciao, dear Anulka, take care of yourself."

"I know that. Thanks so much for your call. I hug you, too, Michaela. Ciao." She pushed the disconnect button.

She stood, her eyes darting from one corner of the room to the other. I can't breathe. Air. Fresh air. I have to have fresh air, she thought.

She went out on her terrace. Leaning on the railing, she looked out over the lake to the far shore and the house lights now coming on. She breathed in deeply, then turned and sat down on the edge of a chaise lounge she'd pushed into the corner of the terrace.

Sadness. All the time sadness. And feelings of rage, And guilt. But now, this evening, she thought, finally, also, some rational thinking and rational planning.

And some focus and hardness.

She sensed that, at some point, the kind of thinking she'd been doing would also enable her to consider what she needed to do, long-term, to punish Giovanni and his gofer. However, at the moment, that definitely wasn't what needed a fix. Or immediate rational thought.

It's the damn short-term, that third concern I need to solve, she thought. I need those guys gone, off my back, at least for a while out of my mind, if not permanently.

For that, I guess I have no real choice. I need to get my hands quickly on some serious money. With someone else as the gofer at the bank, using another client's identity. Or, perhaps there's another totally new way I haven't thought of yet. Whichever way I do it, I need to pay off that bastard in Italy and his gofer as soon as possible.

A moment later, a soft sigh. Enough thinking.

I need a new gofer. It's as simple as that. I don't know how, and I don't know where I'll find one, but that's got to be it. The most impossible, the most difficult, the most dangerous solution, yet the only solution.

A thought suddenly struck her, a possible further real and present danger for her in that decision. She worried she might be compelled to do something really beyond the pale, something so cold-blooded, something so beyond what she'd ever done before that she'd be, both mentally and emotionally, permanently damaged by it. That would be major collateral damage. For her, and, very likely, for anyone else involved.

Not actually a pretty picture, she thought, but then, we're past all of that, aren't we. It is as it is. God, it's all so far away from that August summer night in Nice when Giovanni worked my resentment, when he pried open deep cracks in the moral integrity, I thought I had as a person. And as a banker.

Or, perhaps, I should call it more correctly by its real name, moral virginity. Morals and integrity never really tested, the holier-than-thou banker putting on a smoke-and-mirrors show to the world about the right way, the fair way, the supposedly moral way of a conscientious banker, when, in fact, no real temptation had ever really crossed my way to sorely test me and my integrity. Until that day finally did arrive, when the stronger drive of human revenge and venality finally did succeed in taking its pound of flesh, want and ego and opportunism and weakness toppling any loudly-proclaimed or assumed moral integrity from its false pedestal.

And the hypocrisy of it all? Hatred of the moral desert which characterized many of her clients balanced against the ease with which she had slipped over the line into straight-out criminality?

Not going to go there, she thought.

At the end of the day, it doesn't make any difference. I know very well what I did. But also, what now needs to be done.

Can I really do it, really find someone like that? I don't know. Damn hard. Difficult. Perhaps, or maybe, just simply impossible. But I have to give it a shot. I have to. I have no other alternative.

Night had come. She got up and went back into her living room, turning on two of her table lamps, the soft light illuminating gently the polished dark wood of the small side tables on which they stood.

She still had some bank files to read before going to bed. Perhaps there would be some time left over afterwards to check her own emails, something she hadn't done for several days.

Sitting at her desk, she caught a glimpse of her reflection in the glass of one of the silver- framed pictures she'd placed alongside her computer. Luca looked right back at her. She looked closer. In the glass, her face somehow superimposed over his.

She smiled.

14
Restaurant La Tour de la Pelote
Quai de Strasbourg
Besançon
France

June 29   19:51

The convention in Basel had ended at eleven that morning. A lot of hot air and hot conference halls. Every year, he asked himself why he went, and every year when the invitation arrived for the following year, he dutifully signed the registration form, sent the required fees along by bank transfer, and put the dates into his desk calendar and computer diary. Actually, a little crazy, he thought.

It had become a tradition for him to treat himself every year to a special dinner on the evening of the last day of the convention. He preferred somewhere far away from his so-called colleagues, some of them successful, some of them not so successful (like himself), every one of them adept at bullshitting the other with stories, the contents of which most likely born of a collaborative effort between the tooth fairy and several half-drunk ghost writers.

This year, he'd chosen Besançon, about an hour and a half southwest of Basel by car. Years ago, in another life, he'd studied French there and had had a wonderful but short relationship with his French conversation tutor. She'd been older than he was by six years.

The time was the late Eighties, years after George Marchais, the head of the Communist Party in France, had tried and failed to win more legislative power in the National Assembly. In the Seventies, almost twenty percent of the popular vote in French national elections, a lot of it from the younger age groups, had gone to the Communists. While that percentage had since dropped considerably, some of the country's young people were still talking socialistic and communist firebrand politics.

Among them, his tutor.

Her enthusiasm for Communist principles had led to some heated conversations, Felix speaking in his broken but steadily improving French, and she, exasperated, that he couldn't comprehend how important the Communist movement was for *la futur de la France*.

On the other hand, he'd been able to learn many "useful" French phrases relating to such unimportant things as cleaning up a room or carrying out the garbage or, definitely more important and, thankfully more frequent, demands to *viens enfin au lit et baise moi*, come to bed, damn it, and fuck me.

He'd never forgotten those words. Nor her seriousness. And certainly not her passion.

The meeting in Basel had been exhausting. It was just so damn difficult to cut through all the noise and glad-handing and rushing to this or that seminar or the toothy smiles from people who called you their friend within thirty seconds of shaking your hand. A disheartening experience all around— albeit with three interesting exceptions.

There'd been several speeches that had kept him listening carefully. He'd also had several substantive discussions with two colleagues about the ins-and-outs of restructuring mid-sized companies. And he'd made several good contacts at director level with two French consulting firms. Each one of the firms consulted to large French subsidiaries of German companies.

The director of one of the consulting companies had claimed that a prospective client with which they were currently negotiating needed the kind of senior consulting weight Felix could supply. The potential client was anxious to conclude the negotiations on job scope and timing in the next three to five weeks. It would be good, he said, if Felix could come in short order to Paris to meet with the firm's management as well as with the potential client. His presence, his language capability, and business experience, would help the firm lock up the assignment. And, of course, give Felix months of revenue-producing consulting work within the scope of that assignment.

Why isn't it always like this, he thought.

He hadn't hesitated. He'd arranged to go there on the 17th of July, three days after France's annual Bastille Day celebration on the 14th. Thinking about that coming visit, Felix decided that maybe the convention—and all its usual bullshit—hadn't been so bad after all.

Felix took another sip of an excellent Meursault. The wine had everything: the right temperature, the right year, the right taste, the right aftertaste. He had the bottle sitting in an ice bucket next to his table. He'd be damned if he were going to wait for the waiter to come by and pour more wine into his glass when the one he was holding was empty. He would do it himself. Good wine like that shouldn't be kept waiting.

He was sitting next to the fireplace in one of those restaurants one finds quite frequently in France. The French love their grand history and they love their historic architecture. There were stone walls, lances, tapestries, candlelight, and subdued lighting, rough-hewn wooden tables, lots of velvet and flags, stone floors, big red wine glasses, the personnel dressed formally in white dinner jackets and black bow ties, and above all, first-class food and a wine menu that just shouted quality and careful thought.

An important recipe for a successful restaurant in France.

And that was the reason why Felix had made the long trip from Basel down to Besançon, just to the east of Champvans-les-Moulins. After the din and noise of the last few days, he also needed a moment's peace to prepare himself for his meeting with Renauer, scheduled the next day for three in the afternoon.

Felix had called him one day after receiving the letter. Thankfully, Renauer had not been available. Felix was glad he hadn't had to listen on the phone to any bullshit platitudes about his mother. One fawning performance from him at their forthcoming meeting was going to be more than enough.

He'd spoken to his new secretary, a nice woman who'd told him of her sorrow at his mother's passing. She'd informed him there was a carton in her office waiting for him to pick up. Personal files and pictures and stuff from her office. A second, somewhat beat up carton, a Personal-Private note pasted to its side, had been put on top of the first one. That carton, Felix knew, would most likely contain the files from his parents to which Renauer had referred in his letter of early June.

He was still puzzled by the size of his inheritance. Where had it all come from? It was big money. His mother had only been an employee, albeit a well-paid employee, of a relatively small company.

Something somewhere didn't fit right.

Renauer had not mentioned the cause of her death in his letter. His mother had been in her late Fifties, too young to die. What had caused her death? Had she been sick? Had she had some serious medical problem? Had she suffered in any way? Had that bastard perhaps worked her to death? Or maybe literally caused her to worry herself to death about something having to do with their relationship?

Felix had decided to take several days of vacation after his appointment in Zurich. Neuchatel for the wine and some hiking, or, perhaps better, Lucerne for a little swimming. The lake water would still be cold from the melting snow, but it would certainly help to clear his mind before heading back to Frankfurt.

For a brief moment, he'd considered setting up camp in his mother's apartment in Thalwil, but he'd discarded that idea as quickly as it had come. He'd have had to sleep in the same bed in which both Renauer and his mother had slept. And where she had died.

Definitely a guarantee for a sleepless night.

A hotel in Zurich was the better solution. The driving distances between the two places where he had to be were minimal. He'd booked a room at one of his favorites, the Hotel Schweizerhof, in the center of Zurich.

He looked at his watch, then over to the bar and saw the waiter hurrying toward him with the steamed trout and spring potatoes he'd ordered.

A culinary moment of quiet before the storm.

15
On the Lake Side Across From the Corner
Bellerivestrasse and Florastrasse
Zurich
Switzerland

June 30   14:32

The drive up to Basel and then on to Zurich had been easy. No traffic to speak of, even when coming into downtown Zurich.

Finding a parking spot had been another story entirely. Parking garages in the whole area full, trams flitting loudly back and forth on their metal rails, their bells ringing, warning the pedestrians trying to illegally cross the street in front of them, no left turn here, no right turn there, no U-turn, no stopping allowed, unused driveways, unused garage doors facing the street, no unloading, small cars only, parking only for street residents with valid permits, cars parked double in the streets, no one moving, no one in sight looking like they were going to get into their parked car and then drive away.

Finally, he found a spot, six blocks away from Renauer's office. Unfortunately, that small success hadn't been enough to get him off and walking quickly to his appointment. He'd discovered, to his exasperation, that he needed at least five Swiss francs to feed the parking ticket machine in order to buy a time tag to put on the dashboard of his car. Even though he'd stopped for coffee at one of the Autostop complexes on the way, he hadn't thought to get some small change for when he got to Zurich.

"I need a quick solution here," he said aloud to no one in particular, as he looked along the sidewalk for someone coming toward him.

Nobody.

Five minutes later, a quick espresso at a corner bar, a couple of steps down the street from his parked car, a smile at the young girl tending the bar *and* the cash register, and he'd solved his problem. He had enough small change in his pocket to buy two hours' worth of parking time.

His cell phone rang just as he was about to cross over the Bellerivestrasse to the Florastrasse, the small street where Dr. Renauer's office building was located. A quick glance at the number told him Ben was calling. The sun was hot so he moved quickly under several large shady trees that lined the sidewalk, punching the talk button as he went.

Ben spoke immediately. "Hey, Felix, everything okay?"

"Hi, Ben, everything's okay. I am standing right across from the entrance to the street where Renauer's office is located. I'm sorry, but about to go in. I'm afraid I have only a little time to talk. What's up?"

"Sorry, I thought you'd already been there. Well, look, give me a call when you're through. You and I have to discuss some client stuff. And it'll take a little while to explain it all to you. Besides which, it's too loud to talk right now. I can hear the traffic on the street."

In spite of what appeared to be a serious reason for the call, Ben couldn't resist the temptation to tease his friend. "You know, it sounds like you're standing right in the middle of the street. Don't forget what your teacher used to say about what to do before crossing the road, Felix."

"Damn it, she wasn't very good looking and besides, I didn't listen for one second to what she said. And okay, we need to talk. I'll call you back as soon as I can."

He slammed the phone shut. With all respect for his friend, he wasn't in the mood for fun and games at the moment. And whatever the client had wanted, that could wait until after he'd finished with Renauer and his games.

He crossed the street quickly and entered the Florastrasse. Not far from the corner Renauer's building. He saw a bronze metal plaque on the side just to the left of the entrance. On it, the name he was looking for: Renauer Treuhand AG. A smaller plaque right below it: Ninth floor-Reception.

He looked up at the facade of the building. Clean lines, attractive. The antithesis of the man Renauer had once met. A thought occurred to him. If it turned out Renauer had his personal office located on the west side of the building, he might be up high enough to look out over his neighbors as well as the leafy trees lining the lake further away. That could then give the bastard an unobstructed view across and along the lake.

Too good for him, he thought. Way too good.

16
The Offices of Dr. Peter Renauer
Renauer Treuhand AG
Florastrasse
Zurich
Switzerland

June 30   15:03

He pushed the buzzer at the side of the entry door. Someone upstairs buzzed it open. Inside not really a hall, rather a small enclosed reception area with an almost sitting-room quality. White marble floor with an intricately-woven Oriental carpet centrally positioned just behind the entrance door. Several pieces of art on the walls. Dimmed-down halogen lighting in the high flat ceiling. Brown leather couch and two tan leather easy chairs. Side tables. Bronze, dimmed table lamps placed on their polished dark wood surfaces.

Big money speaking its own visual language.

He took the elevator at the far end of the room. Arriving on the correct floor, Felix announced himself to the receptionist. Nice, friendly person. She offered him a cup of coffee.

Renauer had asked to be excused for several minutes. He was on the phone with someone in New York. His secretary would come for him when he was through with the call. Please be seated. The daily papers were lying on the coffee table should he wish to read something.

Felix sat down. He noticed his pulse rate had increased somewhat. Renauer is probably sitting in his office, enjoying his little game of making me wait before he personally comes down the hall, full of excuses, rushing in order to impress me with his regret at being late.

He would be addressing him using his formal family name and title. While they knew each other, they were not friends. In such a situation, the German language required the formal use of the mister and the surname. It gave both parties the ability to maintain a certain formal distance from one another while still using the name of the person sitting or standing across from them.

It would be Herr Dr. Renauer and Herr Hofmaier during the whole duration of the meeting.

Felix could look down the hall. Someone was coming rapidly toward him. Suspicions confirmed. Here we go.

Damn, he's aged, thought Felix, as he looked at him more closely. He'd always had a good height on him, but now, as he got nearer, Felix noticed a slight stoop to his frame. I hope it's the weight of all of the stuff he's pulled in his life that's weighing him down.

Felix stood up.

Ice Age handshake. But formalities were formalities,

Renauer expressing the hope that the trip over from Basel had been a pleasant one, and Felix confirming that it had been. Compliments on both sides about healthy appearances. A nice-to-see-you-again expressed, but almost gagged on when spoken.

Pure bullshit.

They walked back down the hall. Corner office to the west. He had a clear view of the lake and beyond. Damn.

Felix drew a deep breath. This is where my mother worked, he thought, as he passed through a smaller office, shaking hands with Renauer's new secretary. He thanked her again for her kind words on the phone and for passing along the news of his mother's death. She pointed to two cartons on the floor right next to her desk, indicating they were his and could take them with him when the meeting was over.

He took a seat directly across from Renauer at his desk. His secretary brought Felix a coffee, the cream and sugar sitting on top of little doilies on a polished silver tablet. Doilies? One rather odd-looking cream-colored cookie lay on a small white saucer directly next to the coffee cup. Another small doily peeked out from underneath the saucer underneath.

He looked at her. Why didn't you just bring a plate of them, dear lady?

What the hell is she doing now, he thought, as she took the almost full bottle of water from his desk and replaced it with a full one. If that is what I think it is, thought Felix, our guy here is anal as hell.

Doilies? Full water bottles? Polished silver tablets?

Good grief.

Felix considered what would happen if he were to drop a crumb from the cookie onto the carpet. Would it be the inner courtyard at dawn and my back pushing up against a crumbling brick wall? Would Renauer be the shooter?

Renauer shuffled a small pile of papers in front of him, apparently checking for something. A green dossier lay on his desk next to his right arm.

Felix stole a quick look around the office. Antiseptic feeling. Office and furnishings boring and impractical. Only the art on the walls spoke to him about a side of Renauer which, under other circumstances, might possibly have made for an interesting discussion.

He looked back again at him, saw him cleaning his eyeglasses with a tissue, a separate one for each lens, for God's sake. *Complètement dingue.* Completely crazy.

Enough of this. He decided to take the initiative.

"Herr Dr. Renauer, I want to thank you for taking the time to meet with me. I know you have a tight schedule so I'd like to propose that we dispense with the opening ten or so minutes of normal chit-chat if that's alright with you."

Renauer nodded his agreement. Felix met his gaze. No way to know how he was taking his attempt to get down to business. His eyes, like those of a viper snake in attack mode, flat, cold, two dimensional, betraying nothing.

"Good. Thank you. Let me start by saying that your letter to me was a very kind gesture on your part and your words were definitely helpful. Thank you for that."

Renauer nodded slightly again.

Still no verbal reaction. Okay. If he wants to play it that way, so be it.

"You know, of course, that I had a very tenuous relationship with my mother, so I'm sure you can imagine my surprise when I read the parts of your letter pertaining to the money she'd left me. I had no idea she'd managed to accumulate such assets during her life."

"Yes," replied Renauer, suddenly speaking. "During the whole time I knew your mother, she was a very thrifty person. She was also well paid as I'm sure you can imagine. She spoke to me about leaving you the money in her will. Personally, I thought she was doing the honorable thing, no matter what had happened between the both of you in the past."

He smiled slightly and glanced for a second out the window, then turned back to Felix. His look spoke volumes, as if he'd just discovered Felix were some kind of undefinable insect crawling across the floor, headed directly for his pants leg.

"I always took very good care of your mother, Herr Hofmaier. You know we spent a good deal of time together. She meant more to me than I can say. I miss her every day. And seeing you here as her son makes it not a bit easier on me, I can assure you."

Truer words had never been spoken. Felix studied the man closely. Not a muscle moved in his face. No teary eye, no tilt of the head. His white hands, folded together in front of him on his desk, were like sculptured stone. His voice monotone and flat, his words an attempt to show some degree of emotion.

The man is wound up like a top.

"I'm aware of that and I know you've also incurred a deep loss. But I am sure you can imagine that I am curious about her death. We both know my mother was relatively young. Even though we didn't speak very often, I wasn't aware that she had any major health problems. Tell me, what happened? What was the cause of her death and how did she die?"

Renauer leaned back in his chair. The air seemed to hang heavy in the room.

"Yes, your mother. So sad. I assumed you didn't know this. Your mother's health had unfortunately declined in the last years. In the past twelve months alone, she'd had a number of fainting spells and continuing weakness in her limbs, particularly the legs. She also complained to me occasionally about pain in the area of her heart."

"She'd also lost some weight, something really unusual for her because she was, as you might remember, a good cook, and also liked to eat well."

Serious face. Serious demeanor. The flat tone of a statement being made to a court of law.

"About seven or eight weeks before her death, I noticed she'd begun to totally skip meals, something she'd *never* done in the past. That worried me greatly. I urged her to go to the doctor. I think she went twice. Not enough in my opinion. The doctor diagnosed a somewhat elevated blood pressure and gave her something for that as well as for the anxiety attacks she'd apparently been having. I knew nothing of the latter. Otherwise, she refused to go more often to have herself looked at, always saying to me, 'I'm fine. It's only a spell. It will pass.' I can tell you I was not happy about that."

"As we both know, it didn't pass. It would seem her heart finally failed. We went to bed relatively early the night before she died. The next morning when I woke up, I turned to her to say something about a subject we'd been discussing the previous evening and saw suddenly that she was gone. Her eyes half closed. At peace somehow."

He looked down for a moment, his words coming now very slowly. "You must understand. It was a terrible shock for me. She lay, please excuse the word, dead next to me. She was . . ."

Felix raised his hand, taken aback by the drama of the moment. "My God, how terrible that she died that way. And right next to you. Terrible. I understand you completely. That must have been a real shock."

Felix shook his head slowly. "You know, it's just all so sad. For both of us. Just so damn sad."

A short silence in the room.

Felix studied Renauer.

The question that had to be asked. "Herr Dr. Renauer, you stated my mother most likely died of heart failure. Why don't we know this for certain? Wasn't there an autopsy to determine the cause of her death? What were the authorities doing and thinking? Good grief, a woman dying in her sleep, no real recognizable cause of death, in ill health perhaps, but nothing really serious. That really begs the question, don't you think?"

Renauer looked at his hands, both of them sliding slowly back and forth across the surface of his desk. Felix didn't take his eyes off them. And the long moist streaks they were leaving on the polished glass surface.

You bastard, I'm watching you. Tell me the truth, damn it.

"Yes, Herr Hofmaier, it's a good question. I also wondered about it. Here's what I can tell you. That morning, the medical emergency people and the police came very quickly. They saw no external evidence that she'd been injured in any fashion. She lay very peacefully in the bed, turned slightly to her side away from me. She'd obviously died in the night. The medical examiner and I spoke at some length about her and her medical issues. He also told me he'd be checking with her doctor. I gave him his name and address so that he could do that."

"Two days later, he called to tell me her body was being released. And would I, please, give him the name of the funeral home so that when their people arrived at the morgue, the body could be handed over with the proper papers and authorization. They told me that they had put heart failure in the death certificate as the reason for her death. Apparently, they saw no reason to do an autopsy. I did as he requested."

He continued, giving Felix no chance to interrupt him. "You know, I'd hoped that you'd be able to attend the burial. However, we heard nothing from you except your secretary calling to say that you'd chosen to continue your business trip in Hong Kong and not return for the funeral. I knew of the difficulties you and your mother had with one another. Your behavior and your reaction—or lack thereof were, therefore, not unexpected. In fact, it may surprise you, but somehow. I understood you reacting the way you did."

He paused for a second, thinking about something, putting his hand on the green dossier lying before him on his desk. "Ah, yes. Before I forget it, I've gathered together a number of newspaper articles and clippings and such concerning your mother and those days around her funeral. I thought you might like to read and perhaps keep them. They're all in this dossier together with copies of the original documents we will be discussing this afternoon."

It was worth a try, Renauer thought. Anything, anything to get Felix away from asking further about the particulars of that morning, of the picture he had in his mind of Chantal silently gagging on the poison, of the surprise, the panic, the anger, the deep disappointment in her eyes as she looked at him, dying right before his eyes.

"You will see in one of the photos contained in the dossier that I had the honor to speak at the celebration of her life. Such sadness, such an honor for her. I can assure you, it was all a very moving moment for me."

Nice speech, Felix thought. And a nice clean out for you relative to her death—and its probable cause. And a nice clean shot at me and the fact that I did not attend her funeral.

What do you know about what was really going on between my mother and me, you presumptuous prick? Hell, you look worse than my mother probably looked when she lay dead next to you in that bed you shared with her.

It wasn't all that easy. Felix felt a deep sadness. He wished he'd been there for her funeral.

He looked at Renauer. Something definitely wasn't right. He saw little flashes of light, pearls of perspiration on his forehead. He saw his eyes wandering about the room, his face drained of color. Emotion at the thought of his own personal loss? Or was he lying? Or a combination of the two?

Or was it something else? Something worse?

"Well, thanks for your explanation, Herr Dr. Renauer. But, you know, frankly, I would have thought that the authorities would have ordered an autopsy in such a situation. But they obviously didn't. Don't really understand that. But, okay, it's past. At any rate, I thank you for arranging the burial and taking care of all the details surrounding her death. You did a great deal for her. And I'll definitely be reading those articles you mentioned. It's a nice gesture on your part."

Enough of this bullshit, he thought. I've heard all I need to know. There's some real gaming going on here, but I'm not going to take the time to figure it out now. That can come later. Time now to get down to some brass tacks.

Felix took a legal pad out of his case, removed a ballpoint pen from his shirt pocket, and leaned forward.

"Herr Dr. Renauer, we have some important formalities to go through. Perhaps it would be good now if we turned to them. Would that be acceptable to you or is there something more you'd like to relate to me concerning the death of my mother?"

Renauer nodded in agreement. His one thought: we're moving on. Thank God. No more questions. I did it. He accepts what I've said.

"No. Nothing more. I think we can get started."

Felix studied his face, checking for any sign of relief that the discussion about his mother was at an end. Nothing, except that now his eyes had again gone flat.

No life in them whatsoever.

"Good. Then, first of all, I'd appreciate you giving me the keys to her apartment. I assume I have immediate and free access to it. Correct?"

Renauer nodded and reached into his vest pocket, removing two keys bound together with a leather thong. He handed them to Felix who took them and deposited them in his right jacket pocket. Felix didn't need the address. He knew where the apartment was.

Renauer cleared his throat and looked directly at Felix.

"I want you to know I've taken the liberty of paying forward six months of rent for your mother's apartment. I thought you might like to take your time in going through the apartment and arranging for what needs to be done in order to vacate it. I hope this arrangement meets with your approval?"

That was a surprise. "Yes, it does. Thank you very much. If you'd be so kind to provide me with the name of the rental firm and the contract, I'll handle any remaining issues directly."

"It's already taken care of. I've had the complete file with the rental agreement and relevant correspondence put in the same carton containing your mother's personal files. You probably saw it already. The carton is in my secretary's office. One of the files in it is tagged 'Apartment'. You'll find everything I've arranged for you in that file."

Felix took a deep breath. He'd had a funny feeling as he'd held those keys in his hand. Actually, more an electric feeling, as if he'd suddenly come into physical contact with his mother. Talking about her has perhaps made her alive—and important for me again, he thought.

How strange is that? I still have deep feelings of anger for her because of the way she treated me in the past, but now those feelings are mixed in with a growing sense of regret and sorrow at her passing.

Renauer was waiting. He cleared his throat.

"Yes, I saw the carton when I came in. I'll be taking it with me when I leave. Thank you again."

Now for a couple of questions to shake things up a bit.

"I also saw a second carton when I passed through your secretary's office. Is that the carton containing the files from my parents? Did she keep all that stuff here at the office? What about other personal files, or are those in the other carton you mentioned the only ones that exist? Are there no other files anywhere? Nothing more here in the office? And what about her apartment?"

Felix looked closely at Renauer. The man seemed to be in some sort of physical trouble. Perhaps the whole discussion about his mother too much for him? After all, she had worked closely with him for seventeen years and they had been a couple for a number of years during that time.

I really should give him that, he thought.

"Are you feeling alright, Herr Dr. Renauer?´

No answer.

Renauer opened the bottle on his desk, poured himself a full glass of water, then slowly swallowed half its contents.

He raised his hand to his mouth, coughed once, then replied.

"I'm fine. Just a little pollen in the air from the early summer flowers, he said. Nothing serious."

What was troubling him so much, of course, was his fear that he'd in some way give himself, and what he'd done, away. If he weren't careful with his choice of words, he might provide Felix, even unconsciously, with some kind of signal that his mother had not died a natural death, but instead death at his hand.

That would be fatal.

There was also the danger that Chantal had somehow managed to get her hands on some incriminating documents which would make his life very uncomfortable if they were to land in Felix's, or anybody else's hands for that matter. The problem was he'd searched everywhere. And found nothing.

He paused, drank the rest of the water in his glass,

steeling himself to enter the minefield of questions Felix had posed to him.

"First of all, the carton with the files from your father and mother was found in our archive room. I'd asked one of my people to go down there and do a thorough search for anything your mother might have put down there for safe-keeping. It would seem I was right in my assumption because we did, in fact, find the carton. It's not the type we usually use in storing our paper files and client documents. Your mother must have brought it into the office at some point in time—we're not sure when or even why–and put it in the basement archives where we keep our other old files."

"As you will see, on the side of the carton it says "FILES-GRAUBUNDEN" in big capital letters. We checked the contents and found files and whatnot from your father and mother's life together."

He hurried on. "None of us knew of its existence because the writing on the side of the carton was turned to the wall. Whatever the reason, it is yours now. I'm sorry to say it was also somewhat dirty from all the dust that seems to collect in that room so I had my secretary clean up the outside for you."

Felix was listening carefully, suddenly fascinated by the opportunity he'd have to find out about the life of his parents when he was still very young.

Renauer spoke in a somewhat stronger voice.

"Perhaps a word or two to the other carton I mentioned earlier. Some of its contents include her personal correspondence, insurance documents, bills, and the like. You will appreciate that your mother worked long hours. Therefore, I had no problem with her taking some time here or there during the day to devote to her private affairs."

He paused for a second, then spoke again, looking intently at Felix.

"There is a framed picture of you and your mother in that carton. A very nice picture, I might add. She had it on the shelf behind her desk. Otherwise, there are some knick-knacks that your mother liked to have around her on her desk. I personally was not a fan of her doing that. But I suspect you know your mother was sometimes a very determined woman. And I must say she knew her value to the firm."

"Otherwise, I have no knowledge of any other things or files belonging to your mother. When I spent time at her apartment, I saw some folders with some mail and what-not lying around. There was also a small pile of dossiers in the living room in the book shelves next to the fireplace. But formal files? Nothing that I can remember seeing or running across when I was there. You'll be going to her apartment. Perhaps there's something in one of the rooms or inside one of the French armoires which I didn't notice. That could be possible."

Renauer's mind was racing. Damn it. I checked every-where. Everywhere.

Nothing.

A thought suddenly occurred to him. "Oh, yes. Some-thing else. There's a closed storage compartment in the cellar that belongs to her apartment. The number on the wooden door is the same number as the number of the apartment. I was once down there, but it contained only suitcases, some Christmas decorations, I think, an old floor lamp, some clothes hanging on a horizontal pipe, and, oh yes, a bicycle. From what I can remember, I don't think there was anything else down there such as files or the like."

"Aside from that, I really don't know what else I can say, Herr Hofmaier. I'm sorry I can't be of more help to you."

Damn, Felix thought. Maybe a caring bone or two in his body?

"Well, thanks. That's good information, Herr Dr. Renauer. Frankly, I don't remember my mother being much of a pack rat. However, I'm sure you understand that I want to take care of everything properly."

Renauer nodded. Face impassive, hiding a constant feeling of near panic inside.

"While we're on the subject of her apartment, I'd like to open an account at a bank somewhere near her apartment. I want to have a safe deposit box close by, so that I don't have to cart what I want to keep all the way to Zurich. Do you know a bank I could use in Thalwil?"

Renauer smiled. Easy question.

Pressure coming down again. Better.

"Yes, I do. The man you want to speak with is Dr. Heinz Althaus. He's in charge of Customer Relations at the Thawiler Regional Bank. I'll be happy to call him to introduce you to him. The bank is located on the main street right next to the City drugstore. You can't miss it when you're there."

Felix wrote down the information.

Okay. Now for the big points.

"Well, I think that takes care of everything except for the matter of the money and perhaps any other things my mother might have left me in her will. You're the executor of that will. I don't know whether or not you knew this, but I knew of its existence through a call my mother made to me last year. She informed me she'd written a will, had it notarized, and had asked you to execute it upon her death."

He stopped speaking, looking directly at Renauer. For several minutes, he'd seemed quite normal. Now, something was definitely wrong again.

Renauer swallowed hard, asking himself what the hell else Chantal might have told her son on the phone. His eyes, opaque, went out the window again, seeking God knows what.

A minute passed.

Felix waited, then pushed the point, leaning toward him as he did so.

"As I mentioned earlier, I'm quite dumbfounded at the amount of money my mother left me. How was this possible? You knew her well; both of you worked closely together. At the end of the day, she was your life partner. Tell me, how do you think she managed to put that kind of money aside? Do you know where the money came from?"

Renauer turned to Felix, nodding at him. He had some measure of control back again.

"Yes, I can tell you what I know. But, first of all, please excuse my lack of courtesy for not responding immediately to your previous comments. I was just thinking again about your mother. ..."

A deep breath. A short, penetrating look.

"I want to answer your questions, but before I do that, I think it'd be appropriate, and also make things clearer for you, if I were first to explain to you the legal situation relating to the probate of wills in Switzerland. Can we proceed that way?"

Felix nodded.

He was right. But don't give me the whole book, for God's sake.

Renauer took a deep breath. "As you correctly say, your mother took her will to a notary public here in town to have it notarized. That notary sent me a copy. At her direction. I read it and discovered that your mother had named me to function as the executor of her estate. I saw also that she had instructed the notary to send a copy to her bank. Somewhat unusual, but nevertheless. At any rate, it would seem that that was done, because when I spoke to your mother's bank, they knew about the will."

"As you perhaps know, it's necessary to apply to the Swiss probate court in order that an official certificate of inheritance can be issued. That has been taken care of. The probate court has appointed me, corresponding to the wishes of your mother, as executor of her estate. Once that certificate is on the table, and assuming all debts are paid, the persons or persons inheriting the estate can then dispose of the net-remaining estate as they wish."

Felix looked at him. Standard probate procedure.

Get to the point.

"You will certainly remember that long before she made her will, your mother gave you, and you signed, a power of attorney empowering me to execute on your behalf the provisions of any will she might make where you were the beneficiary of her estate. That specific power of attorney was, of course, referred to in the will your mother made. As a result, I can now tell you officially that I have completed all of the necessary legal arrangements required of me, both by you and by your mother."

"At the same time, I also want to emphasize that I have done so, not only because it is my duty as executor, but also because of the close relationship your mother and I had over the years. It was important to me that this matter be handled promptly and correctly."

"Thank you, I appreciate that very much.", Felix said, the tone of his voice not revealing some of the irritation he felt at hearing things he already knew in such detail.

How the hell did I forget that, he thought? He's right. I did sign something like that way back when.

"As stated in the will, you now have the right to the contents of all three accounts maintained by your mother at whatever their net balances should be on the day you sign the papers at the bank. In addition, all the contents of the apartment in which your mother lived now also belong to you. There's a car, a Mercedes 330, which she bought one year ago. I've had it washed and cleaned and polished. It's parked in the underground garage of her apartment house. Stall 23. I left the keys to the car as well as the insurance slip on the table in the entry hall of her apartment. The two transmitters for the garage door opener are also there right next to where I left the keys."

Have to admit that's nice of him, Felix thought.

Renauer tried to accelerate the pace of the meeting. He laid his hand on the green dossier again.

"Finally, as I said before, I've provided you in this dossier copies of all the relevant documents resulting from the probate procedure, a copy of her will, as well as correspondence from Bankhaus Finsler relating to your mother's accounts."

Renauer looked suddenly pained.

"I'm sorry, Herr Hofmaier. I should have mentioned it first. I'm so sorry. I've also included in the dossier information regarding the address and the location of your mother's grave. I know you'll want to visit it. I understand the gravestone is already in the ground. I had her favorite flowers planted along the perimeter of the plot as well. Tulips. She so loved those flowers."

"Thanks. Yes, I know she did. I remember that well."

Nice of him. I need that information, but for God's sake, let's move on.

Renauer drew a breath, looking directly at Felix. He had to be very careful now with what he said and how he said it.

"So, allow me to turn now to turn to your questions about the money. Your mother was a good woman and a tremendously important part of my firm for many years. I was very thankful to her. During all those years, but particularly in her last year, I rewarded her with some extra payments for her services. Sizeable sums, I can tell you. I'm sure you'll understand that I also helped her to put those extra payments to work. That is what I do. Now you are the beneficiary of her good work and service."

Felix nodded, looking at Renauer carefully. The good doctor seemed to have calmed down somewhat. He even had a slight smile on his face. Hell, no wonder. He's thinking he's wound his way through the worst of it. Whatever that was. There'd been no disaster. No confrontation.

"Thank you, Herr Dr. Renauer. I thought it might be something like that, but your explanation is very satisfactory. Please accept my thanks for your work and for also thanking my mother in the manner you did. How sad that she didn't have a chance to spend it. I know, however, that she worked hard and that she was very devoted and very committed to your firm—and to her work with you."

Felix wanted it done as well. "I have just one more question. Whom do I need to speak with at the bank? I would like to go there, if possible, tomorrow, or at the latest, the day after tomorrow. Can you give me the name and telephone number of the person I should call in order to arrange an appointment?"

Renauer answered quickly. "Of course. In the dossier, you will see the name of the person you should speak with at the bank. Her name is Ms. Anulka Lorenzini. She is the head of the Wealth Management Division. Her telephone number is in there as well."

He smiled, in spite of himself. "But you don't need to concern yourself. I took the liberty of calling her yesterday on your behalf. I've known her over ten years. I checked her availability for this week. She's in town and, of course, as always busy. Nevertheless, I asked her as a special favor to me to meet with you during your visit here in Zurich. She's awaiting your call to set up a meeting. She's assured me she'd be happy to personally handle the transfer of your mother's accounts to your name."

"Unfortunately, I haven't received the latest account statements from the bank for the two smaller accounts. However, I'm sure Ms. Lorenzini will be able to sort through all of that for you. I've already sent her all the necessary official documentation empowering her bank to carry out the appropriate transfers to your name. I hope that's all satisfactory for you."

Felix nodded again. Keep going. Keep going.

"Yes, just fine, thank you."

Renauer handed over the dossier. "On top of the documents, you'll find several sheets I would like to have you sign. Two important pieces of paper. The first lists individually all the contents of the dossier. You need to sign and date that list on the bottom of the second page. Please also sign the second document confirming that you accept the term and conditions of the will and the transfer of the goods and monies contained therein."

Felix took the dossier and opened it. Without reading or checking anything in detail, he signed and dated everything. And asked Renauer for copies of both the documents he'd just signed. Of course, no problem was the answer.

Renauer buzzed for his secretary who came, picked up the two signed documents as requested, telling Felix she would prepare copies for him and put them in an envelope he could take with him when he left.

All well and good.

Felix looked across the desk at Renauer.

I don't trust the bastard. However, I think he's probably handled this matter in an orderly—and proper fashion. At least that, he thought.

Renauer leaned back in his chair and crossed his arms. Body language message to Felix: looks like we're done here, and am I glad.

Felix smiled slightly. I'm reading you loud and clear, my friend. He leaned back, sending him the same message.

A short silence. Both men mentally checking their respective mental lists to see if there was anything else that needed to be discussed.

Felix spoke first, making sure diplomacy got its proper due. "Well, frankly, I think we've covered everything, Herr Dr. Renauer. I appreciate very much the complexity of what you've had to accomplish. I think you've done a very thorough job. I want to thank you for that."

"You're perfectly welcome, Herr Hofmaier. It was my sad duty to do so."

Felix nodded and stood up. "Before I go, would you permit me to spend a moment looking at the art in your office? Perhaps you could give me a short tour?"

With that, Felix moved to a medium-sized Renaissance portrait of a young woman hanging to his right on the wall. He leaned in close to take a look at the brush work. As he did so, a small flash of light from something on or in the right side of the frame struck his eyes.

The sun was now shining across the room from the west and, because of the angle, reflecting off something metallic or glass in the frame. Felix leaned closer to look at the picture— and at the ornate frame.

And almost lost his balance—and his composure.

He was looking at a small fiber optic lens, about half the size of the end of a pencil eraser. He'd never have seen it if the sun and its rays hadn't at that moment been at that precise angle to the lens. He'd pulled back, praising the picture and its beauty.

The son of a bitch, he's been videotaping this whole conversation, he thought. Can you believe that?

Renauer drained the rest of the water in his glass. He stood up and spent the next ten minutes providing Felix with an overview of five artists whose paintings hung in his office. Normal words, normal word tone, normal conversation.

Felix pretended to hang on his every word, full of compliments for the artists, and Renauer's fine feeling for good art.

Inside, he was in turmoil—and severely pissed.

There's no doubt in my mind. The man's as dirty as they come. The real question was where was he dirty? What had he done? Or maybe the better question might be: what hadn't he done?

The art tour was over. Felix kept his emotions under control. He thanked Renauer for his time, shook hands with him, and exited his office. His secretary was waiting for him in the hall. She informed him that she'd asked one of the younger office staff to take the two cartons, including the envelope with the copies in it, to the elevator. The young man would be waiting there for him and would go with him to his car so that he'd not have to carry those heavy things himself.

He sits enough at his desk, she said, smiling mischievously. He can use the exercise. Felix smiled at that, and thanked her again for all she'd done for him.

He walked back down the hall to the reception area, then pushed the main entry door open. He looked across the corridor. He saw the young man with the cartons standing in front of the elevators. Felix waved to him. He looked at the cartons the man was carrying. A sudden sadness. They should be playing a dirge somewhere, he thought.

He gathered himself and strode the last several steps to the open elevator door. He took a deep breath. He was ready to take the few remaining vestiges of his mother's life at the Renauer Treuhand AG down to the lobby and out into the outside world.

17
Chantal Hofmaier's Apartment
Seestrasse
Thalwil bei Zurich
Switzerland

July 1   11:41 am

It stopped raining as Felix slowly drove past the sign indicating he'd arrived in Thalwil. Fifty-nine degrees Fahrenheit on the car thermometer. Middle of summer and the weather forecast is indicating four inches of new snow in the Alps above the two-thousand-meter elevation by late afternoon.

Typical capricious summer weather in Switzerland, particularly on the north side of the Alps. One day summer, the next day, January.

Felix parked along the right side of the Seestrasse, just below the steps leading up to his mother's apartment building. He rolled down the driver side window to get a better view of Lake Zurich and the Alps beyond. Beautiful, he thought.

God, my mother saw that beauty every day.

He still had the two cartons in the trunk of his car. The previous evening, he'd just been too disturbed to open them and check their contents. Better to carry them up to the apartment and do it there, he'd decided.

Felix's evening had been spent enjoying a stroll in downtown Zurich. He'd walked along the lake front, then down the Bahnhofstrasse to the main railroad station. He'd been struck again by the number of high-end watch and jewelry stores on both sides of the street.

"Who buys all this stuff?" he'd asked himself. "And look at the prices. Time is time. I don't need to blind myself with hundreds of small diamonds mounted around the face of my watch, glittering and sparkling no matter what time of day or night it is. And having the bloody thing repeatedly tell me what a special person I am."

Perhaps being rich is the biggest curse of all, he thought. Terrible when one has so much money, can afford everything, but, at the same time, is never able to satisfy, no matter what the price or purchase, one's internal demons crying out for more, and then even more.

Materialism was definitely not Felix's bag.

As he'd walked, he'd reviewed in his mind the meeting with Renauer. The man was hiding something. And Felix had a very good idea what that was and why he was doing it: the story he'd dished up about the death of his mother was very possibly not the true story. And, if that's the case, he's worried I might discover the truth one day.

Now, sitting in his car, Felix wondered if he'd ever be

able to determine what really happened to his mother. The man is as slippery as an eel. He suddenly thought of the recording Renauer had made of their conversation. He was glad he hadn't called him on it on the spot.

I have the advantage. I know what he did, but he doesn't know I know.

"Besides, where the hell's the problem?" Felix asked himself. It had been a standard conversation about life and death and money. Everything legal. Everything above board. The man had a meaningless tape.

Screw him.

He looked up suddenly, searching for the source of a loud voice outside his car. Someone was standing on the side-walk next to his car, pointing out to him that he was parked without a time slip having been put on the dashboard.

Hell, fire, and damnation. Just what I need at the moment, he thought, a busybody Thalwiler citizen defending law and order in the village.

Okay, okay, he mouthed, signaling his intention to take care of the problem. He got out of the car, walked to the ticket machine, got a ticket for one hour, and, after putting it on the dashboard, took the two cartons out of the trunk.

He looked around. The guy was still standing there, just down the sidewalk, grinning at him, happy now that order had won the day. Felix resisted firing off a verbal broadside in his direction that probably would have netted him a summons for besmirching the honor of a law-abiding Swiss burgher.

But he couldn't resist taking a small shot at him. Idiot, he mouthed in his direction.

The door to his mother's apartment was double locked. Felix turned the key twice and pushed down on the door handle. And suddenly stopped. This is my mother's apartment. She died in this apartment. She was carried out of it on a steel gurney by the orderlies from the morgue. He turned around and looked at his surroundings. Saw the stairs he'd just used. She went down those same stairs every day, he thought.

Shit.

What a strange feeling. Now that she's dead, I suddenly feel closer to her and more responsible for her. And I care about her, in spite of always having turned myself away from her in the past. Her three accounts, now mine, speak volumes about her having apparently felt the same way.

He'd received a voice mail message early that morning. Ms. Lorenzini had called to suggest a meeting at the bank that afternoon at 14:30. Could he please call her or her secretary as quickly as possible to confirm that time or to arrange a new meeting time. That had surprised him. Renauer was moving fast. Almost like a get-him-in-there to the meeting, give-him-his-money, and get-him-out-of-there feeling. Nonetheless, Felix had confirmed the time with an assistant secretary. If he wished, she'd told him, he could use the private garage with its underground parking. All he needed to was to tell the attendant in the garage whom he was scheduled to see.

He looked again at the door in front him. Okay, let's do this. He pushed it open. The air inside was stale, an antiseptic aroma mixed in with the old and the stagnant. He picked up the cartons and carried them into the living room, placing them on the coffee table.

Place needs a good airing, he thought. He went to the balcony door and opened it wide, then walked through the apartment.

This is going to be tough, very tough. How am I going to get through these days, how am I going to clean up this place, and go through all her clothes and belongings?

I'm just not prepared for this.

He looked closely at the large bed in the master bedroom. Here's where she died. What was it like that morning when Renauer discovered her dead next to him? He remembered there'd been no autopsy. Funny that, he thought, in spite of Renauer's explanations.

Slowly, scarcely breathing, Felix did a second tour through the apartment, moving this time much more slowly from room to room. Opening the one drawer here, checking what lay behind a mysterious door there until he'd checked all corners of the apartment and its contents.

His mother had lived well. The furnishings, particularly the armoires—they looked to be French 17th and 18th century originals—were first-class pieces of furniture. He looked over at the full bookshelves around the fireplace in the living room.

"What's that there," he asked himself suddenly. A framed picture of Renauer and his mother stood in one of the still-open spaces next to a pile of paperbacks. Felix strode quickly over the bookcase and turned it face down.

He sat down on the couch. He could just hear the traffic noise coming up from the Seestrasse below. From where he was sitting, he could look over the plants hanging on the balcony railing to the small towns and villages scattered along the shore on the other side of Lake Zurich.

He looked around. Here she'd lived, here she'd laughed, here she'd slept—and here she'd died. He lifted his hands to his face and, for a long while, rubbed his eyes with his fingers. Again, doubts came to him that he might not be up to doing all that was necessary to properly take care of his mother's affairs.

An inner voice yanked him back from the easy way out. This needs to be done.

Go do it.

He stood up. Okay, he thought, I'm going to need lots of folding cartons and large plastic bags. When I'm finished organizing everything, I think I'll call one of the non-profit organizations in the area and have their people come and pick up everything I decide not to save or keep for myself.

Suddenly, another thought. Dammit, I forgot to call Ben back yesterday.

He grabbed his cell phone and turned it on. Three missed calls came up on the screen. Two of them Ben's number. From early this morning. The third from his soon-to-be former girlfriend in Frankfurt.

He speed-dialed the number. Ben came on the line after two rings. Felix apologized for not returning the call earlier.

Ben brushed off his apologies. He was on his way by car to Munich to meet with two possible client prospects.

Not a word or question about what Felix was doing or how he was feeling. Ben cut to the main point immediately. "We need to talk urgently," he said, "but not on the phone. Just so you know what it's about, it concerns a client of ours and a bank relationship."

Felix knew exactly what that was all about. The bank has written us after my recent talk with them. Ben has seen the letter and opened it as I asked him to. This sounds like the shit has hit the fan.

"I know it's on short notice, Felix, but can you come to Munich while I'm here?" Ben asked. Felix said he could, but not today. Tomorrow morning with Swiss or Air Berlin would be possible. Ben said fine. Do it.

Felix replied, "I'll check the flights and text you the details of my arrival. But I can only stay for the day. Is that okay? Is there anything else we need to take care of while I'm there?"

Ben said that the day trip would be fine. Nothing else major going on. Two acquisition appointments early in the morning. And one in the late afternoon. He'd handle those meetings himself.

"I've nothing planned for lunch, so get here before noon. We'll eat at Franziskaner in the Residenzstrasse in the city center at twelve or as close to it as possible. Depends on the reservation situation."

Ben paused for a second on the phone. "By the way, forget the damn taxis from the airport. Way too expensive. Take the S-Bahn in from the airport to the Marienplatz station in the center of the city. That'll be the easiest for you. Then you only have to walk ten minutes to get to the restaurant."

He closed with a warning: "And Felix, for God's sake, come to Munich with a clear head. Got it?"

He wanted to reply that he would but Ben had already shut down the call.

Boom. Clear head with all that's going on? Is he joking? Those bankers are going to screw us bad, he thought.

He speed-dialed the number of his lawyer, Heinz, in Frankfurt. Felix knew he'd be back in Frankfurt the next Monday, now that he'd canceled his little two-day vacation in Neuchatel.

The phone started ringing. I don't give a damn what he's doing that day, he thought. I don't care if he's pleading a case before God in heaven. I'm already on his calendar.

He just doesn't know it yet.

18
The Banking Offices of Bankhaus Finsler & Co

Adlerstrasse

Zurich

Switzerland

July 1   14:20

Felix turned into the bank's underground garage entrance, waiting for the rolling door to open completely so he could drive in. A tinny-sounding voice coming from a small box next to the driver's side of his car had asked what business he had with the bank. He'd given a two-word answer in response: Anulka Lorenzini.

The garage door had started moving immediately. Arriving at the underground entrance to the bank, Felix gave the car to a valet driver who, with a small squeal of the tires, hit the gas and drove the car away.

Always the same deal wherever there were valets, he

thought. Punch it to get the hot shot effect, a small strip of rubber, even in the garage of a private bank in Switzerland.

A young woman approached him from the enclosed waiting area. She asked for his name. Felix smiled and gave it to her. The young woman nodded, then asked him to please accompany her to the elevators.

Twenty minutes later, Felix was still sitting alone in a small conference room next to the Wealth Management reception area. He'd accepted the receptionist's offer to bring him a cup of coffee.

"Double espresso would be better," he'd said. The *Neue Zuercher Zeitung* and the *Basler Zeitung* lay next to the tablet. She'd brought them with her with the expresso, perhaps knowing there'd be a delay in the start of his meeting.

He hadn't looked at them. He thought briefly about his trip to Munich planned for the next morning. He'd booked an early morning flight with Swiss that would get him to Munich shortly after ten. No problem with making the meeting at twelve noon in Franziskaner.

Felix looked again at his watch. She's late. A sigh.

He picked up a newspaper and started reading the lead article about the Swiss parliament and the country's budgetary problems. Misguided politicians everywhere, he thought. Even in Switzerland.

Two minutes later, a short knock on the door and Anulka Lorenzini entered the room. She was dressed in a long-sleeved, low-cut, green silk jacket with two gold buttons buttoned at the front. Underneath a light-gray, checked blouse with a high, wrap-around patrician collar, a heavy gold cross hung around the outside of its folds. Her skirt a slightly darker shade of gray.

She shook hands with him, greeting him with a *Guten Tag*. Good day. The high German version, not the Swiss-German one.

She'd brought with her a sheaf of papers and several small file folders. Felix studied her as she sat down across from him. Fine looking woman, he thought.

He looked her in the eyes. Saw the green in them, saw also the traces of sadness, the opaqueness in them. Oh, oh, something bad has happened to this woman, he thought.

Anulka shuffled her papers, then looked up, mustering him carefully from across the table. Felix nervously straightened his tie.

I must look like a piece of shit, he thought to himself.

She addressed him, her voice soft, but with a heavy intensity that surprised him.

"Herr Hofmaier, I do hope you'll accept my apologies for being late to our meeting. Business today is so unpredictable and, sometimes, one has to balance two equally important priorities at the same time. That was my problem during the last half hour. I hope I haven't inconvenienced you in any way."

He smiled. "Not at all. It's I who must apologize for having had to ask for such a quick appointment with you."

She smiled back at him. Felix flushed.

Anulka in all-business mode. "I've known and worked

with Herr Dr. Renauer for many years. I can tell you that when he calls, I'm either immediately available or I try to make myself available as quickly as possible for whatever he has on his mind. He's one of the best financial management people we have here in Zurich. I know you're visiting from Frankfurt and that you're only in Zurich for a couple of days so no problem whatsoever. I assure you I'm happy to take care of this matter personally."

He murmured a quick thank you.

She looked at him closely. "A sad occasion has brought us together, Herr Hofmaier. Your mother, I've been told, recently suffered an untimely death, considering her relatively young years and, also, her importance to Herr Dr. Renauer and his firm. I didn't know her personally, but my people tell me she was a client in good standing for many years here at the bank. Please accept my heartfelt condolences for her passing. I hope you're doing well in spite of your loss."

He was startled—and also touched. She already knew something about him. That surprised him. Renauer had probably blabbed more than what she was just telling him. No matter. She was simply doing the required honors.

"Yes, Ms. Lorenzini, my mother is sadly gone. Thank you for expressing your condolences. I was at her apartment this morning, looking at everything she left behind. Very difficult, I can tell you. We didn't always have the best of relationships, but I must confess, I find myself very much affected by her passing."

His voice softened, then dropped an octave.

"I think everyone reacts differently to such a loss. And then having to confront what's left is also not very easy. Above all, one never knows exactly how one will react until something terrible actually happens. A loss of someone one cares for is a loss. It hurts, sometimes very much, sometimes less so, but one thing is surely true, I can tell you from my own experience. Deaths like that never fail to leave gaping holes in our lives no matter what kind of a relationship one had with that person or persons."

Not a sound. He saw her swallowing rapidly several times. He saw her eyes glaze over. She blinked.

Good grief, he thought, focusing on her face. Those are tears in her eyes. What have I done? What have I said? Was I too maudlin?

He moved his writing pad closer, then smiled at her, hoping she would understand the signal and what he intended by the smile he was directing at her.

He quickly moved on. "But enough of my sadness, Ms. Lorenzini. Life goes on and I also have to move on. I see you have brought several files and dossiers with you. Would it be alright with you if we started with the accounts and what's in them?"

She breathed in deeply, looking for a moment at him, a slight smile now at the corner of her mouth. She understood what he was trying to do. She put her sadness on hold. She pushed back the wetness in her eyes. She forced herself back into the present.

Yes, he's right. It's time to take care of business.

She started off with the large account, containing now a total of 1,265,375 Euros per the June 30 closing. She noted that the account had experienced a recent, double-digit percentage increase in value due to several market trends she would explain later in more detail.

The checking account (Giro account) had only eight hundred and some Euros in it.

"What is the balance in the savings account, please?" he asked, looking at her profile from the side.

She opened the file and checked the number she had for the savings account. It showed a balance of 391,573 Euros. At less than 2 percent interest per annum.

Whoa, how this, he thought to himself. Why didn't my mother have the two larger accounts lumped together into one account? She could have earned more.

With a start, he suddenly realized he was missing the whole point. Much more important, but perhaps also more ominous, the sum in the savings account was itself probably more than large enough to cover what Renauer had told him he'd given his mother in recent years to reward her for her work.

If that's the case, then what was the story behind the other account that had over a million Euros in it? Where had that huge sum come from? Was that what Renauer had referred to when he'd spoken of extra payments which had taken place in the last year? Why hadn't that money been simply paid into the savings account? Was it because the bank—or Renauer—had convinced her she could earn more by having the new incoming monies managed within the Wealth Management division? Or something else. Her own decision perhaps?

What?

He hesitated. Thinking. Just ask standard simple questions, Felix. Remember, she knows Renauer well. And those two go way back.

"I'm somewhat surprised that my mother kept two separate larger accounts. One with a very low rate of return, the savings account, and one a managed account, apparently producing annually well over a 10 to 15, maybe 20 to 25 percent annual return when I extrapolate the results of the last two to three months. Why do you think she arranged things this way?"

The question didn't faze her.

"A good question, Herr Hofmaier. First of all, I can tell you, many of our clients follow that kind of a strategy. They divide up their investments. And their accounts. It's not what I would call unusual. Some of our older clients like to have two legs to stand on, if you understand what I mean."

"Remember, your mother had the savings account for years and years. The amount you're seeing in the larger account represents only the sum of the payments made into it in the course of the last fourteen months. And, of course, our investment efforts afterwards with that money."

"Let me be precise here, Herr Hofmaier. When you look at the account documents for the larger account, you will note that the transfers to that account were made by the Kunst

Treuhand AG. Your mother opened this account just last year and the payments into it started shortly thereafter. As you will also see, no further payments were made into that account after April 30 of this year. For us actually, nothing unusual."

"However, if I may say so, what you should be concentrating on is the fact that the strong growth you're seeing here is not automatic. In our business, there are good years and then there are years where things are somewhat tougher."

She took a breath, expelled it softly again.

She droned on with her explanation. "During the relatively short time your mother had this account, and, in particular, during the last several months, we've had a rather unique confluence of several positive developments in some important sectors of the international financial markets. You can imagine encountering such a situation is just what every investment manager—and, of course, every investor—dreams of and hopes for."

"First of all, we've had a turn up in bond prices due to lower interest rates. As you've seen, your mother was very heavily invested in Euro-based bonds. That alone produced a substantial boost in the value of her account."

"More importantly, the bank made several very profitable judgment calls relating to the recent currency market volatility and its effects on the relative value of the world's major currencies. As you have seen, your mother's account also contains a significant number of bonds denominated in other currencies. What we here loosely call currency plays, although, strictly speaking, holding bonds is not necessarily the classic version of that kind of a play, such as buying or selling forward currency contracts or options."

She smiled at the thought. "Having that kind of portfolio structure with the market development we have had recently meant very good things for the value of your mother's account. However, going forward, no one can guarantee there'll be that kind of positive growth every month or every year. I do hope you understand that fact."

Felix didn't care about any of what she had just said. Not a damn. All interesting stuff, to be sure. But, while she'd been speaking, he hadn't even been half listening.

He had another totally different, and much more immediate problem.

"What was that she just said?" he'd asked himself. "Kunst Treuhand AG? Who or what the hell is that? What did my mother have to do with art and artists? And what's that date? The account is only fourteen months old? Why did she open a brand-new account for that extra money? Was it perhaps because she wanted to highlight the source of the money? Damn it. Is there some kind of message here I'm missing?"

His face was a mask.

I knew it, he thought. I just knew there was something not kosher about what that bastard told me yesterday.

He'd almost missed the whole timing thing. The overwhelming detail in all the documents would have had him lost in the sums and divisions of the bank's detailed rendering of the account's growth. At a later point, he might have seen the date the account had been opened. He doubted that. If he hadn't asked and she hadn't referred to the time period in giving him an explanation for the size and growth of the account, he'd never have gone looking for it.

He'd never have understood that, because of that date, there was possibly a sinister uniqueness to that account. And the amount of money contained in it.

His mother had become a rich woman in an extremely short period of time. He recalled she'd made her will making him the beneficiary at almost the same time the account had been opened. She'd even called him on the phone about it, one of the three times he'd spoken with her in the last ten years.

That will and its existence must have been extremely important to her. Was there a connection there somewhere? Was this the "dirtiness" he'd sensed yesterday during his discussion with Renauer?

Question after question. Could there be another reason his mother had received such large sums of money? Was it just simply a more generous second thank you to her? Had that been his way of showing his devotion to her during the time she was in declining health?

Difficult to believe that, he concluded. Renauer would have known that her constant ill health would not allow her to spend or enjoy much, if any, of that money. He might even have thought she could possibly die within a short period of time. So, what were the large payments for?

Felix felt a spasm in his stomach. Oh, oh, maybe we're dealing with something totally different here. Could it have been some kind of a payoff to keep her quiet? Was Renauer involved in something illegal his mother had discovered? Could he have been the cause of her continued bad health? Or, damn him, even her death?

She saw that he was deep in thought. More than a minute had already gone by. She leaned forward toward him with a concerned look on her face.

"Is something not in order, Herr Hofmaier? Is there perhaps a problem with one of the accounts? Are you feeling alright? Can I get you a glass of water? Or perhaps something else?"

He looked at her and waved his hand.

"No, thank you very much. I'm fine. I'm sorry for being so quiet. You must understand, it's been a very stressful time for me these last few weeks. I was thinking about my mother, and the fact that she won't be able to enjoy what she's now passed on to me. The thought of that made me for a short while very sad."

She was moved by his words. Here was a man who'd recently lost his mother, a man who obviously was very much affected by it. Here also was a man who was surely also a little bit out of his element. And very clearly depending upon her to guide him and make sure he did the right thing. From her point of view, she understood perfectly his thought processes. After all, weren't they all similar to hers when she thought about her own loss?

She decided she liked Felix Hofmaier.

She spoke with an undertone of feeling in her voice. "Perhaps it would be best if we took care of the formalities now. I know you have requested that all three accounts be combined into one. The documents you will sign now will reflect that."

He nodded his agreement and took out a ballpoint pen from his shirt pocket.

"If you don't mind, I think it'd be best if I were to come around to your side of the table and show you, one by one, the confirmation and transfer forms and exactly where you must sign each one of them. We're going to transfer the three different accounts to your name, then combine them into one investment account, and I want to be sure we don't confuse the one with the other. Afterwards, I'll give you copies of each of the documents you've signed for you to take with you for your records."

And with that, she simply stood up and walked around the table and sat down next to him. She had three dossiers in three different colors laid out in front of her on the table. Looking at them, Felix thought, what I'm seeing here is a whole life reduced to three colored files with several loose scraps of documents contained between their respective covers.

How sad, he thought. How *very* sad.

For the next twenty minutes, they both were absorbed in working through the asset positions of each one of the accounts, as well as the paperwork required to officially transfer account ownership to him and then combine those same three accounts into one. Felix did as he was told, signing where appropriate, nodding when he understood, asking questions when he didn't.

It's always the same, he thought. Lots and lots of text, nine-tenths of which I don't want to read and, even if I did, wouldn't understand anyway. And the rest, important, but couldn't the whole thing be handled with just a couple of signatures instead of multiple ones?

He signed the last document. Everything was taken care of. The money was his. He would keep it at the bank as his mother had done.

Suddenly, she was standing. She asked him please to excuse her so that she could go and have copies made of everything.

"Would you like another cup of coffee," she asked. Felix was Bened out on coffee.

"A Fanta orange would be good. Does the bank have that kind of thing in its refrigerator?" he asked.

Amused at his manner, she cocked her head and smiled. She would check, she replied, then she was gone.

Beautiful woman, he thought, powerful woman, but then there's that sadness about her. When I look her in the eyes, I see a wall, a curtain, I see opaqueness. Her eyes are only alive on the surface. Underneath, there is injury and hurt. I see that. I don't know why I see that, but I see it.

Ten minutes later, the door opened and she was back. Behind her came a young woman holding a small tray, a can of Fanta, and a glass with some chipped ice in it, balanced on its polished surface.

She smiled at him, waiting for his reaction. Felix laughed and told her if, excuse the expression, a conservative private

Swiss bank can produce a can of orange soda in that short period of time, then there should be no doubts about its ability to manage client money successfully. Definitely a class act.

She handed him the copies of everything in three separate folders, then sat down across from him. Damn, he thought, why didn't you come back around again and sit next to me?

He caught her looking at him, her eyes suddenly with a sparkle in them. With a start, he wondered if she hadn't guessed exactly what he was thinking. Or was it just his comment about the Fanta?

She moved a note pad over in front of her. She had a pen in her hand.

Back to business.

She looked sternly at him as she leaned forward to speak.

"Herr Hofmaier, I have several things I need to say to you. The first one involves the way you handle your tax obligations. Times have changed in the world of Swiss banking. For several years now, Switzerland's finance laws have made it increasingly more difficult to park black money, particularly cash money brought to the bank, in Swiss bank accounts. In addition, and in particular, the German tax authorities have been more than, shall I say, industrious in finding ways to control its citizens' international financial dealings and, specifically, any relationship those citizens may have with Swiss banks."

"As I am sure you've seen in the news, there have been several formalized, reciprocal changes in our respective laws to strengthen Swiss control over German citizen accounts in Switzerland. In addition, the German authorities have become even more active in pushing to penetrate the Swiss banking system, and thereby determine which German citizens, or foreign citizens living in Germany, have Swiss bank accounts, in which assets or income are hidden from the German tax authorities."

"Quite astoundingly, the German tax offices have even bought lists of client names and accounts from people who worked within the Swiss bank industry and had stolen client data. All these developments have implications for your investments and your approach to your future returns."

She was serious. "As a Swiss citizen living in Germany, I would advise you to consider the fact that, in the short, but also in the long term, you will have no benefit in keeping your money hidden from the German tax authorities. Since you live on a visa in Germany, you should consult a tax advisor there in order to acquaint yourself with the current and potentially future tax law situation between Switzerland and Germany. And, above all, exactly what the reporting requirements are in Germany for someone in your specific situation."

She leaned forward. "My personal opinion? Play it safe and declare everything."

She flipped a page. All business. "Shall we continue? A second matter involves inheritance taxes. I would assume you'll have to pay some form of inheritance tax in Germany. Again here, it would be best to toe the line and pay those taxes as well. Please think about how you want to handle your affairs with us. In any case, I would appreciate you letting us know as quickly as possible how you wish to proceed after you've done your homework in Germany."

Felix didn't miss a beat. "Thanks for the detailed information, Ms. Lorenzini. First of all, I want to assure you I will certainly keep the bank aware of my tax situation, and my thoughts on that matter. However, I can already tell you this. I'll be declaring all of what I've inherited to the German tax authorities. I have no problem with that. In addition, I have no problem in paying income taxes there on what I earn with the money you'll be managing for me. Even though I am a Swiss citizen, I love working in Germany. To put it plain and simple, I do not plan on getting into any sort of problems with the German authorities."

Exception being the danger of my being arrested and found guilty of fraud, he thought.

She smiled at him.

"Fine. Then that's cleared up. One more question for you and then we're done. It concerns your approach to risk. Do you wish to maintain the same investment strategy your mother used or have you got something else in mind?"

Time to pass out the chocolates.

"Ms. Lorenzini, Bankhaus Finsler has a sterling reputation among Swiss banks. I'm very appreciative that you and the bank are willing to continue the relationship you had with my mother. I never spoke with her about her financial affairs, but I can see she was very astute in her choice of a bank partnership. My answer to your question is a clear yes."

She smiled at the answer. "Well, thank you very much for that. I hope you'll continue to be impressed by our services. And our work on your behalf."

The meeting was over. She stood up. He felt a vague disappointment he wouldn't be seeing her again very soon. He thanked her for her time. She indicated it had been a pleasure for her as well.

They shook hands at the elevator. She remained in front of it, looking quietly at him until the doors had closed and the elevator had started its descent.

Down in the garage, the valet brought his car around. He got in and sat for a minute before driving off. He'd become a wealthy man. He searched within himself for a feeling of joy or happiness. Nothing. It was as it was and he accepted it as fact. There was nothing more there than that.

Suddenly, out of the corner of his eye, he saw someone pushing through the double glass doors from the lower-level entrance hall where the elevators were located. It was her. She was looking around for something. Then she saw the car with him in it. She waved with her right hand held high. She was holding some papers in it.

He turned off the motor and got out. She hurried over to him, somewhat out of breath.

"I'm so sorry. Thank God, I found you before you were gone. These copies were found at the copy machine. When I printed copies of the documents you'd signed, the machine apparently held back several pages and ejected them only after I'd turned around to come back to our meeting. Please excuse this terrible *malheur*."

She smiled at him and handed him what she had in her hand. Felix smiled and thanked her.

Suddenly, an entirely separate thought came into his mind.

Hell, why not?

"You've been so very kind to me, Ms. Lorenzini. I hope you will not take offense, but may I ask you something? Would you do me the honor of having dinner with me while I'm in Zurich? I'm over for the day in Munich tomorrow, but back in town late tomorrow afternoon."

"I'll be spending the day after tomorrow working in my mother's apartment and then going to Lucerne for several days of vacation. But, if you have time tomorrow evening, or after my return from Lucerne three days hence, that would be wonderful."

She was quiet, looking at him with a thoughtful expression.

He added quickly. "I hope I'm not offending you. Somehow or other, I feel it's the proper thing for me to do. I know I'd enjoy it. I hope you would, too."

He looked into her eyes. Holy shit, he thought, they're greener than green can be. She looked at him. No surprise in her eyes. No how-could-you-dare-to-think-that look. Had she somehow expected the invitation? He couldn't tell from her facial expression.

Then, suddenly, a nod. "Thank you for the invitation, Herr Hofmaier. How kind of you to ask. Yes, I think it would be very nice to have dinner with you. And tomorrow evening would also be fine."

She gave him a small smile. "You know, you are, in fact, an important new client for the bank. I'm sure we'll have many things to talk about. You have my number here at the office. Please call me before you leave Munich to return to Zurich. We can meet where you wish for dinner."

And now a brilliant smile. "And, oh yes, please don't ask me what I like to eat. You choose. Whatever it is, it'll be fine."

He couldn't get over what he'd just done. He stammered a reply to her yes.

"Yes, I'll certainly do that."

He shook her hand hurriedly, then almost banged his head on the car roof as he slid into the driver's seat of his car. The car didn't stall when he put it in gear.

He got out of the garage without hitting any of the other cars or scraping any of the walls along the exit ramp leading to the street.

But it was close.

19
Restaurant Zum Franziskaner
Residenzstrasse
Munich
Germany

July 2   11:42 am

Felix had arrived at Terminal 2 of Munich's Franz Josef Strauss Airport at 10:10 in the morning. Having no baggage—just a brown leather messenger bag slung over his shoulder—, he'd passed through customs and passport control into the Arrivals Hall without any delay.

He was hungry. To the right of the exit from the Security Area was a delicatessen with tall round tables set in front of it. High bar-like stools surrounded each table. The varieties of sandwiches in the vitrine, some open, some closed, overwhelming. A little early for that kind of stuff, however.

Further to the right a small Bavarian bakery. Better. Felix ordered a croissant and a double espresso. He hadn't had breakfast in Zurich because he'd overslept and almost missed the plane.

The airplane coffee had been a non-starter. The espresso was gone in three swallows.

Lots of noise, lots of movement, travel chaos pure.

He looked at the crowd of people waiting for arriving passengers. Kids in prams, dogs in abundance, excited words of greeting, businessmen shaking hands with one another, a "true blue" Bavarian dressed in short, suede leather pants, high gray wool socks, and a leather vest with white shirt underneath, the sleeves rolled up over the elbows, older people standing off to the side, probably waiting for some friends, maybe also pensioners, coming from northern Germany to visit the "real" Germany.

It was time to go. He quickly bought the *Sueddeutsche Zeitung* at the *Pressekiosk* near the exit of Terminal 2, then started the long walk to the underground railway station located under the Central Service Area of the airport.

His cell phone rang. Ben on the line. Felix confirmed he'd be arriving on time at the restaurant. Ben sounded stressed on the phone.

Not going to be a good day, he thought.

Munich was one of Felix's favorite cities. Just north of the Alps, its skies a special kind of blue when the warm *Foehn* wind from the south was blowing, an elegant and energetic style. And great beer.

Forget thirst-quenching qualities. Think pure nectar.

Felix wasn't visiting Munich for the pleasure of it. Sitting in the train, his thoughts went back again to his yesterday meeting at Bankhaus Finsler. And, even more specifically, to Anulka Lorenzini.

The previous evening, he'd been almost desperate to come up with an idea for where to take her to dinner. He'd finally decided upon the Seehotel Sonne in Kuesnacht, located directly on the lake close to Zurich. He'd made a reservation there that morning while driving to the airport. He knew the hotel from having spent several nights there two years ago. He'd also eaten in the restaurant.

A safe choice.

He also remembered something unique about it. He'd sat at one of the tables right next to heavy, yellow-toned silk drapes, drawn back and held in place on each side of tall windows by a heavy, twisted cord. What had fascinated him were the subtle colors of orange and red and yellow woven into the cord, as well as the oversized tassels, each one attached to and hanging from the cords holding the drapes in place. He vaguely remembered having taken a picture of the one hanging closest to his shoulder. Anyway, he thought, it'll be fun to check if they're all still there.

Before going to bed, Felix had checked his clothes. Nothing to wear. The one suit he'd worn in Basel was wrinkled and spotted. A sport coat and slacks combination were marginal at best. Every dress shirt except one already worn. Not to forget whatever he wore needed to do, namely cover a belly that had hung somewhat over his belt, when he'd checked his profile in the full-length mirror of his hotel room.

Why is it I always look like a mess? Shit.

I've got one alternative. After our meeting, I'm going to go over to the men's department at Loden Frey. It's really only around the corner, a two-minute walk from the restaurant. That'll take care of the problem, assuming I find a good saleswoman to help me make the right choices. Several suits would be good. If I do it by myself, I'll just spend a lot of money, and still look like hell.

The train began to slow. Maybe I'm just getting excited about nothing. It's probably just a business meeting for her. After all, I am a new client for the bank, so to speak. And she has a special relationship with Renauer. And your mother has just died. She feels sorry for you. So that's it. Accept it.

Bong. Marinplatz. *Aussteigen, bitte*. Please get off. He left the station, using the main exit. He located the Residenzstrasse, running off to the right past the City Hall. The restaurant—and the meeting with Ben—ten minutes away.

The hell of it was they had to do this kind of thing in person. One had to be careful in Germany. Who knew who could be along for the ride and listening to what was being spoken on the phone? Even if that conversation were only being listened to "inadvertently," meaning the authorities were actually looking for something else, but had "stumbled" by chance onto his and Ben's conversation.

The NHF Handelsbank was no small bank, and surely better plugged into any number of different possibilities to act or react to the specifics of the case. If the German state had "free" and unhindered access to its citizen's bank accounts,

270

making them, as the press liked to say, "transparent as glass", then the possibility for it or some other organization to plug into telephone conversations or to check up on someone's actions or movements on a broader scale couldn't be too far behind.

Felix knew his dispute with the bank was a small one, at least in terms of money involved. Nevertheless, being super careful was the more prudent choice. Hell of a situation when one can't even trust the phone to speak about private or legal matters.

As he approached Franziskaner, dodging all the while errant bicycle riders determined to force him off the bicycle path reserved for them in the middle of the pedestrian zone—he usually walked in their path on purpose just to piss them off—, he thought about his coming chat with Ben.

He had many concerns, but one very immediate one: the letter and what could possibly be in it. The bank seemed determined to take him and, possibly, his firm down. The recent meeting he'd had with the bank had certainly pointed to that possibility. However, hearing something said at a meeting is one thing. Seeing the same thing contained in a formal letter and signed by several upper-level bank muftis is another thing entirely.

He reached for the door handle and pulled on it.

Lunchtime. Franziskaner was full. Ben was already sitting at their table, a red-and-white checked tablecloth covering it. Noise level: moderate. Acceptable for talking and not having others listen at the same time. They greeted each other standing, shook hands, then sat down, looking with strained faces at each other.

"Ben, first things first. Please order me a beer, half a liter will do. And if that's the menu at your elbow, then let me have it so that I can order something. And while you're at it, give me the letter, please. I can read it while we're waiting for the food to come."

He checked Ben's expression. He looked somehow beaten down.

That bad? Damn it, he thought. Maybe I should just run for it. Just north of forty, no real prospects, little money left except for what was in Zurich, the bank in Frankfurt threatening to take me and the firm down, reputation ruined, nothing left to keep me in Germany.

Hell, Ben's recent comment about going to the Maldives was, definitely, beginning to look better and better.

The waiter came. They ordered. Marinated smoked salmon with potato pancakes for Felix. Suckling pig with dumplings on the side for Ben. Cucumber salad with minced onions on the side for them both.

Ben reached into his jacket pocket, took out the letter, and handed it to Felix. He reached over and touched his arm briefly.

He spoke slowly, measuring his words.

"Before you start reading, Felix, I have to confess something to you. You remember our discussion at Wagners a couple of weeks ago. When you and I spoke that evening, I didn't believe the bank would go so far as to put us right up

272

against the wall. However, I have to admit I may have been mistaken. It's a hard letter, Felix."

"On the other hand, my friend, saying that doesn't mean I'm ready to give up. I'm still convinced, we'll find a way out of this mess."

Felix leaned back in his chair. "It's okay, Ben. Hell, who really knows what people are thinking sometimes? But I did appreciate your thoughts that evening, that I can tell you."

Felix looked down at the letter, then back again at Ben. A couple of questions were bouncing around inside his head.

"Have you sent a copy of the letter to our insurance company? We need to do that immediately. Also, did you bring a copy of the insurance policy with you? Have you checked if we're covered or not?"

Felix in light panic mode.

Ben recognized it, leaning across the table, speaking softly.

"No worries. I sent a copy of the letter to the insurance company the minute it came in. Called our guy there, but he wasn't in. Left him a message. No response from him or the company yet. On the insurance thing, I didn't bring a copy of the policy with me, but I can certainly send you one at your hotel in Zurich. Count on getting it tomorrow."

Felix nodded.

"As for the coverage, I've read the relevant clauses of our policy pertaining to that issue," Ben said. "We're insured to a maximum of 500,000 Euros. We're also paid up on our premiums, thank God. However, here's the dicey part. The policy stipulates that the insurance company is obligated to defend us only if the issue involves consulting errors, or mistakes, we made when conducting our normal business."

"That means, for example, if we were to recommend a course of action to a client and it turned out to be the wrong one and that course of action cost the client money, then we would be protected if the client decided they wanted to take us to court because of it. If we lost the case, the insurance company would cover any damages award up to a maximum of 500,000 Euros."

"Hell, you know the drill, Felix. To defend ourselves, we'd argue we made those recommendations. based upon our best knowledge of the facts and that we'd adhered to the highest principles of integrity and professionalism while doing so. The usual bullshit buzz words."

Felix was feeling somewhat constricted. He loosened his tie and unbuttoned his collar.

"However, here comes Part 1 of the hard stuff. We had a consulting contract with the Loretz Maschinenfabrik Gmbh. Our liability insurance covers only direct contractual arrangements and simple negligence. There is no insurance out there in the market that comes into play when a firm, such as ours, is accused of being an accessory before the fact or directly guilty of gross negligence or fraud. That type of insurance just doesn't exist. In addition, our registration as a limited liability company may not hold back the Huns either, even though it would, under normal circumstances, not expose our personal assets to any claims. Clear so far?"

"Yeah, I know that. Unfortunately, very clear."

Felix looked at the letter in his hand. Ben leaned closer, touched him arm.

"If you don't mind, Felix, let me give you a couple more thoughts here before you start reading."

Felix nodded. "Yeah, okay. Go ahead. I'm listening."

"Ok, Part 2. Now the whole situation gets stickier. A third party, with whom we have no contractual relationship, could perhaps come to the conclusion that they'd also suffered some specified or unspecified damages because of what we recommended to or did for our client company. In that case, we would also be covered, but only because we have the direct contractual relationship with Loretz. What that means in plain German is that the third party would have to sue Loretz and Loretz would then have to sue us. But that's not possible because Loretz is all shot to hell. Got that?"

He nodded. Felix admired the way Ben was approaching the problem.

"Now comes the real bad part. You know the letter we sent to the bank—they're a third party, Felix—confirming our opinion that Loretz was a creditworthy company. We've talked about it a number of times. You know that letter was a formal representation from us to the bank on behalf of our client."

"That's the shitty part. Our old friend Mueller knows that. He mentioned that in his meeting with you and now he has apparently made his decision. It appears he's chosen to use exactly that letter and its contents to attack us. And, unfortunately, I think any lawyer will tell us he has every right to do so."

Ben looked like hell.

"In the letter you have in your hand, even though they don't say it *expressis verbis*, the bank implies that we qualify as an accessory before the fact, meaning they think we directly and consciously let the people from Loretz deceive and defraud the bank. They also think we might be in some way complicit with Loretz—they use that word in the letter— because we 'approved' the unrealistic forecasts or estimates their people made."

"And not only that, Felix. If this thing were ever to go to court, you can just imagine what the Loretz people would say under oath. The judge would warn them about perjuring themselves and that would, no doubt about it, open the flood-gates. Or should I say turn on the flood lights. And they, my friend, would be aimed directly at us. Because Loretz is no longer there, we would be directly in the bank's line of fire."

"For me, the whole situation is clear. The bank thinks it got whacked because we fucked them. Directly or indirectly. And, most likely, deliberately. And they think they can prove it. That's why you heard them use the words gross negligence at your meeting with them. They didn't use those words in the letter, but I think that's very clearly what's in their heads."

"Of course, in legal terms, if they were to discover the whole story—some damn idiot from Loretz blabs out of turn and they believe what he says about our behavior, they could easily make a case for gross negligence, if not out and out fraud. If that were to happen, the bank would opt for a solution that gets them the most money possible from us. There'd be no deal possible."

"They would sue us in court. The law, the district attorney, might get involved. There would be a court case. We would most likely lose and money, company money, maybe potentially even our own money if fraud were involved, would flow, certainly not enough to satisfy the bank's losses, considering the way the insurance is structured and the company situation, but enough of it to satisfy a major part of the bank's losses and make Mueller a hero again. And whether or not we went to jail afterwards wouldn't bother him and the bank in the least."

"So, the long and the short of it is, there could very well be a court case if they see gross negligence or, worse, fraud. So, what's to do in that case? Simple. We work with our insurance and we try to cut a deal in advance to save our asses. But I can tell you, in my opinion, any deal we make isn't going to very pretty either. Whichever which way we look at it, we're deep in the shit."

Felix slumped further back into his seat. This is bad. Really really bad, he thought.

Ben clenched his right hand into a fist.

"However, I can tell you, Felix, there are, thank God, several redeeming factors in all of this we shouldn't forget. Number one is the liquidation of Loretz and whatever the bank can get out of that kerfuffle. And, number two, there is our insurance, assuming we can prove our conduct was only simple negligence—meaning stupidity on our part. In effect, we'd have to prove that we were simply dumb, and didn't have a clue about what the hell we were doing and what was going on. And the insurance company would then defend us dumb shits because our 'crime' was simple negligence and not gross negligence—or fraud."

"Of course, if it's gross negligence the bank wants to make stick, then we'd obviously have a much more difficult— and much more expensive—problem."

"I imagine they might also like to sue our friends at Loretz for fraud. But there's a small problem with their doing that, at least as far as Loretz concerned. It's bankrupt. And who knows what their executives have in their bank accounts? Or if they'd lie their heads off. Or what their insurance would do, assuming, of course, that the premiums on their insurance had been paid in full. And we don't know any of that at the moment."

"On the other hand, in the eyes of the bank, we, my dear friend, at least in the case of simple negligence, do have insurance and we're not bankrupt. Not exactly deep pockets, but then again, not exactly empty ones either."

Ben's facial expression was hard.

"Felix, the word complicit is the key here. It's a dangerous word for us. So, bottom line, if we're not able to prove the opposite, that it wasn't gross negligence, or, heaven forbid, fraud, then we have no insurance."

"And, as I said earlier, the possible end game picture is

definitely not a pretty one. Potential time in the slammer. Real shit, I can tell you."

Felix didn't want to read the letter anymore. The thought of it and its contents made him sick to his stomach.

"Goddammit, Ben. What the hell do you think we should do?" he asked, his voice raw and low.

"Well, the text of the letter from the bank increases the chances of our insurance company getting involved. That's good. And as I told you, there's no mention or intimation of gross negligence anywhere in it. At least, Mueller hasn't gone for the jugular yet. That's also good."

"So, here's what I've done. I contacted our insurance guy several days ago. Told him about possible mistakes in our work. He seemed to accept that. I sent him a detailed memo summarizing what I'd told him on the phone. A copy of the letter went to him by fax. He said, they'd be writing us quickly with a decision."

Ben smiled slightly. "By the way, even complicity or negligence can also be viewed as something not willfully done. It could mean, as I said before, that we just didn't do our job. That would mean, we're just damn lousy consultants. But, and that's the important point here, definitely not criminal consultants."

Felix looked around the room. He knew how he wanted to play it.

"Ben, if that's what it'll take, you're looking at the dumbest shit consultant who ever walked the face of this earth."

Ben had a good laugh. Relaxed somewhat. Took a long swig of his beer. Encouraged Felix to do the same.

"Question for you, Ben. The insurance only covers 500,000 Euros. What do you think the bank would accept to let the whole thing go away?"

"Well, there's always a little negotiating to be done between the demand and the get. Let's assume it comes down to simple negligence. Stupidity in our terms. My bottom line read is this: the whole thing could go away for us for somewhere between 500,000 and 600,000 Euros, assuming they get a little something from the Loretz liquidation. Most of that money would then come from the insurance company. The rest from the firm."

"If it turns out it's gross negligence they're after, then the gates are wide open. I can't give you a figure there because, if there were ever a deal to make, we would, of course, be hit, in addition to the higher cost of the deal, with additional costs for lawyers, not only ours but potentially theirs as well."

He looked at Felix, the man a mixture of conflict and worry.

"We need to move quickly to get ourselves an outside lawyer to work with us. And perhaps, at the beginning, before the insurance company decides how it will proceed, have him informally talk with the bank's lawyers to see if there is any common ground to be found for a possible settlement. That will cost something in lawyer fees, but I think it'd be money well-spent."

"Hell, he might even get us a *nolo contendere* which would

solve the whole problem. We pay some form of restitution, don't admit guilt or innocence, and we're done."

Ben smiled. "Be nice if it worked out that way. Am I confident we have a chance for that to happen? Frankly, not really."

"But no matter what we hope or want, we definitely need that lawyer, particularly if the insurance company tries to find a way not to honor their policy obligations to us. That could turn out to be a fight, too. You know, at the end of the day, insurance companies don't really care. They're on the outside looking in. And they don't like to pay. Anytime. Anywhere. But you and I? We're completely exposed."

Felix felt sick. "Look, Ben, I'm not feeling very good. I'm not going to read this letter. Maybe next Monday. Besides I think I already know everything in there so to speak. Wish I didn't, but I do."

He took a breath, then continued. "Your idea to engage an outside lawyer is spot on. Just so you know, I called our old buddy Heinz in Frankfurt yesterday. He'll meet with us on Monday at 11am in our offices. I assumed that time would work for you as well. Maybe we'll also have some word back from the insurance company by then. That'd certainly help when we talk with him."

Ben nodded, understanding very well his friend. "Yeah, well, I'm glad that's taken care of. And the letter? Yeah, well, I can understand you not wanting to read it now."

Ben looked over at Felix after the waiter had brought their food.

"I'm really hungry. The way you look, you could use something, too. Life goes on, damn it. So, eat something, Felix. Food's always good here."

Felix sat there, thinking, wishing he were anywhere, anywhere else but where he was.

20
Restaurant Sonnengalarie

Seehotel Sonne
Seestrasse
Kuesnacht bei Zurich
Switzerland

July 2   19:52

Damn. The same beautiful drapery tassels and cords were still there, holding the drapes back from the very same window next to which he had sat alone, having dinner. two years ago. He'd smiled when he saw them.

However, in contrast to that long-ago evening, this time he was sitting across from what had to be the most attractive woman in the room.

No, make that all of Zurich.

He looked around while she studied the menu. The Sonnengalarie Restaurant, as always, compelling and inviting, the quiet ambiance of a restaurant managed by people who knew what the word class and service meant.

Her silk dress, off-white, with no sleeves, a purple silk sash wrapped around her waist and knotted at the side, intertwined with a gold chain, the end of which hung down her side. Her dark blond hair pulled back and held with an almost matching sea-blue hair band, her gold cross just visible above the low neckline of her dress.

He sighed. Well, at least I don't look like a mess this evening, he thought. In fact, Felix was very pleased with himself and what he was wearing. Dark gray suit, blue-and-white, narrow-striped shirt with gold cuff links, and a dark blue, plain silk tie. Black oxfords on his feet.

When Anulka had arrived, her eyes had fixed on his face, then dropped down to his shoes, then reversed course and x-rayed their way slowly back up to his face. Then she'd smiled, a smile of approval worth every one of the thousands of euros he'd spent on new clothes that afternoon in Munich.

As agreed, he'd met her in the bar. They'd chatted for about fifteen minutes about the weather and the warm summer and the traffic problems in Zurich and the unacceptable high cost of flying short distances in Europe.

Then the waiter had arrived to take them to their table.

Sitting across from her, Felix sensed he was in for an unusual evening. This was not him getting ready to hustle a woman into bed. This was not a woman who was looking for adventure and ready to flirt her way there in any way possible.

This was also not going to be an evening of superficiality or boredom or empty commentary on what had been ordered for dinner. These hours with her were going to be a serious affair. At least for him, and, hopefully, also for her.

They placed their orders. For her, the poached lake trout with wild rice and, for him, instead of the trout he'd had the last time he ate there, the New Zealand lamb chops with potato croquettes. Before the main course, salmon *carpaccio* for them both. No bread, please. A large bottle of Pellegrino *frizzante* would be fine.

The choice of entrees, one suitable for white, the other suitable for red wine, meant splitting the wine choice. Felix solved the problem by ordering two half-bottles of wine—for her, a dry white from the Loire Valley with its own bucket of ice, and, for him, a robust red from the Medoc region of southwestern France.

Her smile told him, he'd handled the problem well.

In spite of the rough day he'd spent in Munich with Ben, Felix was feeling good enough about himself to tell her the story about the drapery tassel and how he'd taken a picture of it when he'd last sat at the same table. That seemed to really amuse her and she looked at him with a gentle smile on her face, her head cocked to one side.

A winning smile. But, again, a smile missing the last measure of heartiness. Then there were her eyes, eyes which both fascinated and disturbed Felix. They had a certain opaque look to them, a trace of other-worldliness that suggested this was a woman whose inner emotions were not in harmony with the world around her. To him, they appeared to be just a little off-focus, even when she was looking directly at him.

Anulka knew he was studying her. She'd caught his look as she'd studied the menu. She'd seen his eyes wander around her face, seen them search for and catch, for an instant, her own, seen them watch her as she'd spoken with the waiter.

She knew he'd been surprised when she'd said yes to his invitation. In fact, she'd been surprised at herself for accepting his invitation. It had been his spontaneity, and his hopeful look, that had drawn from her a positive response.

Both he and I have suffered a loss, she thought. I know about his loss, but he doesn't know anything about mine. I have lots of serious baggage. Does he have any?

She stole a look at him as he ate his *carpaccio.* He certainly has that smell about him, she thought. While she had no concrete proof for reaching that conclusion, she did have a well-developed sixth sense. And that sixth sense was telling her that Felix, too, was driven by demons he couldn't control, by circumstances he couldn't neutralize. That was enough to awaken her interest. And her curiosity.

There was one thing, however, that she hadn't discovered. Felix represented one of those rare examples of manhood who possessed an almost similar ability to sense what the other person was feeling and what emotions or concerns were making that person feel that way. She was curiously blind to that side of him. She felt secure in her cocoon of proper decorum, in her powers of observation, in her businesslike behavior, and correct dinner chit-chat. And in her conclusions about him.

As a result, she had no clue whatsoever that he'd already

been walking around inside of her, drawing some of his own hard—and sad—conclusions about her and where she seemed to be with her life.

The waiter had brought their main course, the wine had been poured, the usual questions concerning the quality of the food each was eating taken care of.

She looked at Felix. "Tell me, Herr Hofmaier, how did your trip to Munich go this morning? You mentioned you had some sort of a meeting there. I know, of course, you're in the consulting business. Were your discussions related to your business, if I may ask?"

She wasn't really looking for any concrete answers. It was simply a nice, innocent puffball question and its answer would tell her a little bit more about him. That was all she expected. And wanted. A light, pitter-patter chit-chat along with the meal.

Talk to me, Felix. Entertain me a little.

What she got, however, after twenty minutes of his talking, was the dark side of Felix Hofmaier. He didn't admit to any wrongdoing. He didn't admit to any weaknesses that had possibly got him into his current difficult situation. He used other words to describe what he and his firm had done, but she'd read between the lines. And inferred the rest.

She'd been right in her initial feeling about him.

Absolutely astounding. They both carried some major baggage.

She made a tentative list: in varying degrees, weakness of character, over-the-borderline behavior, lack of integrity, prevarication, Teflon attitude toward laws and regulations, greed, and malleability. And, finally, bitterness and perhaps a form of capitulation in the face of possible fateful and negative events affecting their lives.

The words she had in her mind, the recognition of a reality she already knew, made her sad. She sighed deeply.

It seems we're both God-awful messes, each in our own way.

To make sure she heard every word he spoke, she'd leaned forward over the table, grasping her gold cross between two fingers of her right hand. She'd remained in that position, caught up in and fascinated by the drama of the Loretz-Handelsbank-Hofmaier triangle. And by Felix Hofmaier's concluding words to her.

"We reject any accusations directed toward the quality of our work and we're going to fight them, of course. We do have insurance, but that may not protect us under certain circumstances. We have some hard thinking to do. Particularly because we're not sure yet what the bank will finally decide to do—sue us, negotiate a hard deal, or compromise with us. One thing is for sure. We have a problem, both personal and corporate, and that's why I was in Munich for a meeting with my colleague."

Anulka Lorenzini was no dummy. She knew the words he'd used to describe his situation were designed exclusively to transmit innocence and victimization. However, what he'd really exhibited to her were his guilt and his culpability.

She knew exactly what had really happened.

And so exactly did he. But he just wasn't admitting it.

First of all, Felix and his firm had been earning a great deal of money through charging high consulting fees to a company that was now bankrupt. Probably driven by bad financial problems inside his own firm. He hadn't wanted to give up that revenue. He'd lied and cheated to keep it going longer.

Second, she knew there would have been detailed profit and loss estimates and forecasts in the loan application submitted to the bank. Standard stuff. And, of course, a balance sheet per the latest quarter. Perhaps the consultants Felix had installed at Loretz had been dummies. More likely, they'd been bought off by the company or encouraged by Felix to beautify the numbers.

Bad forecasts don't just happen, she thought to herself. Mistakes in judgment can happen. After all, forecasts are best-estimate guesses of what might or is likely to happen. However, they can also be ill-conceived or manipulated. Or, worse, criminally perfumed to death.

No doubt about it: those documents had most likely contained some real bullshit assumptions. A financial fairy tale hour. Possible manipulation in the profit and loss forecasts. Possible cash plan manipulation. Possible balance sheet manipulation. Possible fraud.

No. Very likely fraud.

Bad. Very bad.

She was certain Felix had been the driving force behind the whole game. He was guilty as hell of leading the bank astray and causing it to lose money. It wasn't the company that had failed. Or the bank that had failed. He himself had failed to do his job.

However, what had really blown her away was his representation of his supposed innocence. Good God, anybody with half a brain could see through that story, she thought. One thing's for sure: if that's the way he's selling his point of view in the whole affair, if that's going to be his defense, then he'd better be damn careful. He might have a problem convincing his insurance company to step up and support him. Not to mention the bank not accepting his arguments and going instead for the jugular. And possibly a judicial process.

Good God. The man is in really deep.

She suddenly thought of her own situation. Just a minute here, girlfriend. Who are you kidding here? Who here is the pot and who is the kettle? He's stolen and you've stolen. Different venues, different degrees. But the same damn thing.

She sighed and looked at him. "Well, I can certainly sympathize with you and your troubles. A bank isn't always the easiest of partners. As a banker, I can tell you management sometimes overshoots in trying to correct any bad situation it finds itself in, particularly when inflated egos are involved or potential mistakes in analysis or judgment can be laid at its doorstep. That's just the way it is. But that same management will never admit it. Never."

He leaned forward to her, his face serious.

"Thank you for saying that. I see it exactly as you do. You know, I'm sure you can imagine how this whole thing concerns me. You know and understand the complexities of a bank-client relationship. There are never just black and white situations. Absolutely right. I just hope the people we're going to be fighting against have a similar attitude and the same understanding for such relationships."

You've certainly got that right, she thought. Did he really think he was going to escape, more or less, unscathed from what he'd done? The moves he'd put on that bank were not just simple bagatelle crimes. This was serious stuff.

He's naïve, she thought. He'll need money, potentially big money, particularly if the insurance company refuses to cover him. And that means his own money. He'll have to pump more money into the firm if he wants it to survive. I bet there's a problem there, too. Doesn't have enough to cover it.

And he knows it.

She stayed neutral. "You have my best wishes for success. Herr Hofmaier. I am sure you'll be making every effort to neutralize all the things that you might be accused of. There might even be some common ground somewhere which would allow both parties, you and the bank, to resolve the whole thing in a more or less amicable fashion. I do hope that for you going forward."

"Very kind of you. I'm glad you see the things the same way I do. I know I have a tough road ahead of me so thanks for your good wishes."

He suddenly paused. "I'm so sorry. I must ask you to excuse me. I've been so terribly impolite. Here we are sitting and talking and you've long finished with your meal. Very selfish of me. I see the waiter over there by the small bar," he said, raising his hand to attract his attention.

"Would you like a desert and some coffee? Or an espresso? Perhaps a liqueur?"

Yes, she thought, after all that excitement, I'm still hungry. Desert and a double espresso would be fine, please. And a cognac.

The desert—Toblerone Parfait—and espressos they had at their table. They drank not one but two cognacs afterwards out on the terrace overlooking the lake. As always, for her, Hennessey XO. For him, the same.

There was more chit-chat, a discussion of Swiss and German politics, Zurich's constant budget problems, and the effects of the increase in value of the Swiss franc on Swiss tourism. The rest of the conversation, just end-of-the evening banalities.

Felix walked her to her car to see her safely on her way. She thanked him for an interesting dinner and for the pleasant company. He did the same. She expressed the wish that they might renew their discussions when he was again in Switzerland.

It would be fun, she said.

He agreed immediately, promising to call when he knew he'd be coming back to Zurich. In about eight to ten days or so, he said. Still some loose ends to take care of. She smiled and said she would look forward to it. She didn't know exactly her plans. She assumed she would be in Zurich when he came back. He said he'd call when he had exact plans and hope for the best.

As she drove away, she reflected on the thank yous and the polite statements of intention that had passed back and forth between them. Her words had expressed an honest appreciation for an enjoyable dinner. However, what she'd said beyond that had had nothing to do with the usual superficial effort made by people saying goodbye after dinner, and stating how lovely it would be to have a repeat meeting soon.

Very often a lot of that was just bullshit, spoken and forgotten.

She'd meant every word of it. She'd wanted him to believe she meant every word of it. She'd give him a week to call. If he didn't, she'd pick up the phone herself and call and talk about his progress with the bank matter.

Or whatever.

She drove carefully, negotiating the steep road up the side of the hill to her apartment. She thought about the evening and the match she'd identified between herself and Felix. She'd had no choice: her analysis of him had had to be cold-blooded and without emotion.

For the moment, Luca was far away, the pictures of him in her apartment far away. Her father even further away.

In her opinion, Felix Hofmaier had suddenly advanced to the status of a possible knight in shining armor. He could be the one to help her make a second run at the bank. There'd have to be another person involved, of course, and that might be very difficult to arrange. But she had to start somewhere. And he was, definitely, a good place to start.

There was no happiness in her heart as she began mentally outlining for herself the buttons she'd need to push in order to put Felix squarely into that knight's armor, then prepare him, metal parts and all, to fight the final fight. It wasn't in her character, wasn't the way she wanted to be, not the way she felt she was, but she had to be hard.

She assigned a top ranking to the word need. Alongside it, she put another word: greed. Then she added a last word to the list, something that made her sigh with sadness, but something she knew had to be part of it.

Bed.

21
The Apartment of Chantal Hofmaier
Seestrasse
Thalwil bei Zurich
Switzerland

July 3   8:47 am

Sitting in his car on the way to Thalwil, Felix yawned several times in quick succession. He hadn't slept well during the night. Too much to eat, too much to drink the previous evening. And too fresh and exciting the memory of Anulka Lorenzini and the time he'd spent sitting across from her at the restaurant. What had really gotten his attention was her suggestion that they meet again when he returned to Zurich. Driving back to his hotel, he'd painted all kinds of pictures in his mind about what might possibly happen between the two of them a second time around.

There'd also been positive news to start the day off. He'd had a call earlier that morning from Paris. Monsieur Aron had informed him that the firm's German prospect had confirmed the meeting for the 17th of July. The company's management was becoming increasingly anxious to get started.

The assignment would take several months to complete.

The people in Paris—and Monsieur Aron—knew, of course, that Felix had had only a short briefing on the situation when he'd met with the firm's consultants in Basel. But *la vie, c'est ainsi* . Life, it's like that. Assuming all went well on the 17th, Felix would soon be part of the team charged with carrying out the assignment.

Before he'd rung off, Monsieur Aron had inquired if he'd have time to spend an extra day at the firm's offices in order to discuss the details of the assignment. *Un jour de plus? Aucun problème, Monsieur Aron. Et merci de m'avoir inclu dans votre équipe.* One more day? No problem. And thank you for including me in your team.

At breakfast that morning, he'd thought about the short vacation he'd planned in Neuchatel and Lucerne after all of his meetings in Zurich. Nice reality check. This was not the time to run off to enjoy some innocent little la-la in the mountains south of Zurich. There was just too much to think about, and too much going on, to drop out of the action even for one day.

A quick call to the hotel had taken care of the problem. The concierge had been very helpful, promising a refund of the prepaid monies to his credit card account within the week.

He stopped his car right below his mother's apartment. Excellent parking spot. This time, no irate citizen in sight.

Five minutes later, he was sitting on his mother's living

room couch, looking out the window, the cartons he'd brought with him the first time, still unopened, perched in front of him on the coffee table.

Felix stood and moved them to the dining room table. He spread the contents of the first carton, the one containing the material from his mother and father, out onto the polished surface. In addition to the normal records of everyday life, he found about forty letters they both had exchanged during their courtship and then after their marriage when he'd traveled to the livestock auctions in his home canton.

He read all of them, learning how much his mother and father had loved each other and how happy they'd been when Felix, their only child, had arrived in the world. He read how his father had terribly missed the farming life in Graubuenden. Urban life had not been the answer for him. Contrarily, his mother had wanted none of the country.

Sad paragraphs, a deep love, abject unhappiness and frustration, in letters written so long ago.

The second carton contained documents dealing with his mother's insurance, her car, her credit card accounts, her bank accounts at Bankhaus Finsler, her apartment, and her medical records. Standard records of a modern life.

He paused. Medical records. He went looking for anything dealing with the last twelve months of her life or with the problems Renauer had mentioned. He found nothing in the correspondence with her doctor relating to a weak heart or anything similar that might possibly have killed her. Tiredness, yes, lack of energy, yes, some depression and anxiety, yes, prescriptions for some tablets and pills, yes, but nothing serious.

What had really happened to her?

He took out the framed picture of himself and his mother Renauer had mentioned, he at the age of eight, his mother, of course, looking younger than he had her in his memory. He brushed over the surface of the picture with his fingertips as if to touch that time, that memory, that connection to a mother who no longer existed.

His thoughts skated back across the years, pausing here and there to remember his mother holding his head in her two hands, kissing his forehead, his mother smiling at him as he graduated from the University in Zurich, his mother criticizing him, hurting him with her coldness and indifference to his subsequent life.

Renauer did that to her, the bastard.

He stood up and went through the apartment again, checking even more closely for the existence of any further personal files in the normal nooks and crannies of each room. Except for a small pile of innocuous files in the bookcase, he found nothing.

Strange state of affairs, he thought. This apartment has been carefully "dry cleaned". Everything too orderly, everything too impersonal, everything too damn quiet.

Well, whatever. He sighed. He took out a post-it sticker package and unwrapped it. He went through the apartment, putting a sticker on those pieces of furniture he would keep. No question about the antique French armoires. Beautiful pieces of furniture, a reminder of his mother's good taste. They would definitely stay.

The other furniture and smaller items, he'd give to a church or some similar organization along with her clothes, her cosmetics, and the contents of the drawers in the bedroom tall boy and the bathroom. And what was in the medicine cabinet.

Wait a minute. He remembered, suddenly, his last, long-ago visit to his mother in Thalwil. He'd stood in the bathroom with her, right in front of that cabinet, looking with her into its mirror, remarking to her about all the things she kept behind its mirrored doors and in its little drawers. Ah, she'd replied, medicine cabinets are good for many things. They can contain the obvious, but also the hidden. They can represent a life. They can speak volumes about that life when one knows how to read and interpret those purposes.

At the time, he'd laughed at what he'd judged to be nothing more than a throw-away remark on her part. Now, he thought again about what she'd said. From where he was sitting, he could see through the glass double doors of the living room, diagonally across the hall, and into the bathroom.

The medicine cabinet hung there as always on the wall above a single sink.

A medicine cabinet representing a life? What the hell was that? She was probably referring to the cosmetics and medicine and other knick-knacks contained inside. What else could that remark mean? Nevertheless, he got up and went through to the bathroom, opened the small doors.

He peered at the cabinet from both sides, squinted as best he could behind it along the wall on which it hung. Just a medicine cabinet. Standard contents. Nothing more. Nothing less.

I'm not going to get silly about this, he thought, but I'm going to have a look behind this cabinet. He took out everything inside, putting the various bottles and tubes into the sink underneath the cabinet. Then he checked how the cabinet was attached to the wall. Four hooks held it securely in place.

No problem. He lifted the cabinet off the hooks and set it down. Two dead spiders hanging there on the wall in their small, but, now, no longer functional, webs. And one small, indefinable insect, also dead, with a funny yellow stripe running along its back right in the middle of the web.

Otherwise, nothing.

This is ridiculous, he decided. Just to convince himself, he'd rubbed the palm of his hand over the wall, dead spiders and a bug be damned. Flat. Just a wall. Its surface, maybe a little sandy. Yeah, perhaps even gritty. The color of the wall where the cabinet had hung more vibrant due to that portion of the wall's minimal exposure to light and dirt. No other discoloration.

Perhaps something hidden or stuck away in the cabinet itself? He checked the back wall of the cabinet. Minimum a half-inch size board between the inside and the outside of the cabinet. What the hell am I thinking here, he thought to himself. This is not a thriller where people jam incriminating or important documents into something like a medicine cabinet. Or behind it.

Time to get real.

He was done. Everything back in its proper place. Medicine cabinet hung back on the wall.

He sat down again in the living room, then suddenly stood up and went out onto the balcony. The air was fresh and it rejuvenated him. I need to get out of here, he thought. He took the picture of his mother and Renauer and put it into his messenger bag. The picture of himself and his mother he put alongside it in the bag, separately wrapped with some paper from the paper roll in the kitchen. He looked over again at the medicine cabinet in the bathroom and shook his head.

Well, that was much ado about nothing, he thought.

He wandered once more slowly through the apartment before shutting the windows and drawing the drapes closed.

When I come back here in about ten days or so, I'll bring some black plastic bags with me. There might very well still be the one or the other thing that I might want to keep.

And I'm going to sleep in the apartment.

To hell with Renauer and his games. My mother lived here. I'm going to stay here, even if it's only for several days. Besides, right after I leave here, I'm going to walk to the bank here in town, open an account, and rent a safe deposit box.

What was the name of the person I should contact? Ah, yes, Dr. Heinz Althaus.

In this life, he thought, one never knows.

22
The Offices of Hofmaier & Partner
Zimmerweg
Frankfurt Am Main
Germany

July 7   11:55 am

Things were starting to heat up. The morning had been full of calls and reading reports and a short meeting about possible recommendations for one of their few remaining old clients.

And a long phone conversation with his lawyer.

Now, just short of noon, Felix needed a minute to regroup and gather his thoughts. It would have been better if he'd had the opportunity to meet with Heinz personally. A short drive out to the Taunus mountain area, and he'd have been walking directly into his office. Well, Heinz had had a good excuse—and he *had* called to warn about a time problem and the necessity to do the chat on the phone instead of face-to-face.

At the end, it had all worked out satisfactorily. Everything had been covered on the phone, including signing and faxing back to Heinz the form authorizing him to represent—and defend—Hofmaier & Partner in the Loretz-NHF Treuhand AG matter.

After reading the letter from the Handelsbank earlier that same morning, Heinz had warned both Felix and Ben not to have any further direct contact with the bank. Nor with anyone from the Loretz Maschinenfabrik Gmbh. He, Heinz, would take over all contacts and all negotiations, both with the bank as well as with the insurance company.

He told them that based upon what he'd read in the letter, a compromise solution was entirely possible. He related to them that he'd had cases like this in the past. First came the heavy barrage from the other side, threats of a possible suit, then hard negotiations, and finally agreement by both parties to some form of compromise solution.

"Don't panic" was his message. Everybody always wanted to move along, get past unpleasant things. The only thing needed was to find a way, a catalyst, for both parties to be able to do exactly that.

They knew the insurance company was going to cover the initial legal expenses involved in attempting to negotiate a settlement with the bank. A letter from the company had arrived that morning confirming that fact. Two lawyers would be starting work immediately on the case. The letter had also contained a list of certain exclusions relating to the company's responsibilities in the case, the usual boilerplate and multiple outs some insurance companies cite when they try to keep themselves from having to partially or fully honor the policies they sell. They were exclusions with which both Felix and Ben could live, at least for the moment.

Heinz had confirmed that the letter from the insurance company was okay. "Standard insurance stuff," he'd said.

Felix couldn't stop worrying. He worried that when the whole thing had finally played out, he as majority owner could be out hundreds and hundreds of thousands of Euros, if not more. Ben would, as minority partner, also be involved in any restitution agreement, but nowhere near to the extent that he would be.

Unless, of course, Heinz and the insurance company lawyers managed to convince the bank to walk away with a compromise solution somewhere north of 500,000 Euros, but not enough to cover the whole loss of the bank. That would mean the parties had to agree, no, the bank had to agree, to simple negligence. With, potentially, a little help from the liquidation mass at Loretz, that would mean the insurance company would pony up the first 500,000 Euros, but, in doing so, would, of course, also require Hofmaier & Partner to contribute. There was no scenario Felix could envision where he could see the bank accepting anything under 500,000 Euros to settle all damages and claims.

No compromise, he knew, meant the bank could institute legal proceedings against his firm—and him. And then go for an amount much higher than that.

Thankfully, Hofmaier & Partner had registered itself as a limited liability company. Any liability to be part of any settlement would most likely be in the middle five figure range. That would help, as well as the fact that the capital required to form the Hofmaier & Partner Gmbh had, at the time, been fully paid in. However, even though the assets and the debts of the business were required to remain by law separate from the personal assets and liabilities of the company's owners, would that hold in a potentially serious case like this one?

Who knew?

The worst of it was the fact that he wasn't even sure the bank would accept a compromise. That was something Heinz was going to have to sort out.

His phone buzzed. Monsieur Aron on the phone. Oh, oh. Something wrong?

"Bonjour, Monsieur Aron. A pleasure to hear your voice again. How are you," Felix said, with some hesitation.

"Bonjour, Monsieur Hofmaier. Thank you for asking. I'm fine, thank you. I hope you are as well?"

"Very much so. I've just finished a meeting on a rather complex situation involving a client's problems with bankruptcy. You and I are both in the same business. We both know there's always something going on every day. Clients are not always easy, I can tell you."

"Exactly, Monsieur Hofmaier. And that's the reason for my call. Our client meeting here is going to have to be postponed by several days. Instead of the 17th of July as we recently discussed, they would like to visit us on the morning of the 19th of July."

"The meeting is now scheduled to start at nine-thirty.

As you know, the clients have already received our complete written proposal. I think they have found it to be very relevant for their needs. With the meeting taking place in the morning, we would then have time to meet privately the same afternoon so that it won't be necessary for you to stay an extra day as we'd originally planned."

"I hope that this change in dates will not cause us to have to proceed without you. We do need you and your experience in this meeting. Would you be able to change your plans so that you could be here on the morning of the19th?"

Felix smiled. If that's all it is. No problem. No way he was going to let the deal slip through his fingers. Or those of the firm.

"Just a second, please. I'm going to put you on speaker. Let me check my schedule here."

He flipped the switch on the phone console. He mumbled something under his breath, let out a couple of hmms here and there, then flipped several pages back and forth in his calendar, loud enough so that Monsieur Aron could hear what he was doing.

With a soft but audible-enough sigh, "Yeah, okay, that would work," he closed his calendar.

He spoke into the phone.

"I see two conflicting dates here, but I'm sure I can have the one which directly conflicts on that morning—the other is for the previous evening—moved to another date. I know the client well so that shouldn't be a problem."

Monsieur Aron grunted. "Excellent. I'll inform my

colleagues and, of course, the client that you'll be able to participate in the meeting. We'll have lunch together with some of my colleagues. I know a restaurant in our vicinity which I'm sure you will find acceptable."

"It is for me to say excellent, Monsieur Aron. Is there anything I should bring with me to the meeting?"

"*Rien de spécial.* Nothing special. Just you. You are what we need at the meeting."

Felix was fighting to keep from laughing.

"Then I'll sign off. *Je vous remercie de m'avoir appelé. Au revoir. Et* à *bientôt.* Thank you for calling me. Goodbye and see you soon."

Down the line came the standard courtesy response. Felix broke the connection. He opened his calendar again to the 18th and 19th of July. He crossed out the details for the meeting on the 17th of July. He turned one page, noting the appointment time, address, and telephone number of the firm in Paris under the agreed-upon date.

He had no difficulty in finding space to do that. The page for the 19th of July had been totally blank. He buzzed his secretary to inform her of the appointment. He promised to give her the travel details after he'd made another call.

Time to call Anulka.

A bit too soon? Not really. He hadn't yet called to thank her for the evening.

I'll put that down as the reason for my call and then take it from there. The word there in his mind meant, I'm going to go back to Zurich before I go to Paris. Period.

He took out the card with her cell number on it and punched in the numbers. His face was flushed somewhat. Damn it, he thought, get yourself under control.

It's just a woman, for God's sake.

He couldn't believe it. For the second time in a row, she picked up the phone almost immediately, answering it with a proper "*Guten Tag*. Lorenzini here."

He'd assumed he would just leave a message for her on her voice mail. Now here she was on the phone.

You idiot, say hello, and then tell her what you want.

"Hello, Ms. Lorenzini, this is Felix Hofmaier speaking. How are you?"

Anulka smiled. A knowing smile. She'd been right.

"Hello, Herr Hofmaier. I'm fine, thank you. I must say this is a very pleasant surprise. And totally unexpected. How are you? And what brings me the honor of hearing from you?"

"Well, first of all I wanted to thank you again for having dinner with me this past week in Zurich. A very enjoyable evening, I can tell you."

He drew a deep breath. Here we go.

"I told you in the parking lot at the restaurant that I was planning on coming back to Zurich in eight or ten days. In fact, I'm still planning on doing that, but my timing has changed somewhat. I intend to be in Zurich the 16th, the 17th and the morning of the 18th of July. I have to be in Paris early on the morning of the 19th which means I'll leave Zurich for Paris the previous afternoon and stay overnight there. I'd like very much to invite you again to dinner. Would the evening of the 18th of July be doable for you?"

"Ah, Herr Hofmaier. First of all, thank you for inviting me to dinner. It was a pleasure. As far as the dates you mentioned, I'm so sorry, but I have to tell you I'll be traveling on those days in Spain and, therefore, I won't be in Zurich. Dinner won't be possible, I'm sorry to say".

She paused. She heard him say how sorry he was that it wouldn't work out. She could almost hear his hopes crashing to the floor. Time to change the direction of the conversation.

"Just a second, please. Did I hear you correctly? Did you say you intend to arrive in Paris late in the afternoon of the 18th? Do you have some business there?"

"Yes, I do. As I mentioned, I have a client meeting in the middle of the morning on the 19th, then a lunch, some internal meetings with a consulting firm in the afternoon, and I plan to return that same evening to Frankfurt."

"Well," she said, "Sorry. My mistake. Maybe there *is* something we can do. I've planned to travel from Malaga to Paris, arriving on the 19th in the middle of the morning. I have some clients to visit in Paris and then a couple in the Loire Valley near Tours. My first appointment is at four that same afternoon. However, I'm thinking I could very well come up a day early from Malaga, arriving in Paris sometime during the afternoon of the 18th, book a hotel for the night, and then go the next afternoon to my meetings. If as you say you intend to arrive in Paris late that same day, then it'd be possible for us to have dinner together that same evening, just not in Zurich, but in Paris. Am I right about the timing? Would that be a realistic plan for you?"

She knew exactly what she was doing. She swallowed hard. The fact that it had to be Paris was particularly difficult for her. The thought of her long weekends there with Luca was like a heavy fist banging on the door of her soul, warning her off from going through that door, from doing what she planned.

The hardness had to come back. She went to where it was inside of her and powered it up, shoving her softer thoughts and feelings off into that intimate corner of her mind reserved only for herself and her deep sadness.

She smiled briefly. If that man doesn't understand what I'm really saying here, then he's beyond hope.

Felix couldn't believe what he was hearing. This was seductive play at a high level. In the next fifteen seconds, two things happened simultaneously: he swallowed hard, and turned abruptly to his side as his secretary entered the room, not wanting her to see how stiff his cock had become.

"What was that?" he thought to himself after his secretary had left his office. "An invitation? An innocent offer to have another business dinner with me? A bald- faced declaration of interest to get into my pants. Or rather her wanting me to get into her pants? Can this be? Am I hearing this correctly?"

His mouth was dry. He thought of the half-full bottles of water Renauer always had removed from his office. He needed some of that water right now.

"Ms. Lorenzini, sorry for not answering right away. My secretary came in and distracted me for a minute. Yes, the 18th in the evening, that timing would be perfect. Where do you normally stay when you travel to Paris? Personally, I like to stay at the Hotel Intercontinental. I find its service and central location to be excellent for my purposes. For your information, I'll be making my hotel reservation there."

"Well, if you don't mind, I'll do the same. The hotel is perfect for my purposes as well. More convenient for both of us with time savings and taxis and picking up and finding each other, don't you think?"

Definitely a games-people-play moment, he thought. Here we are, both of us polite and nice and businesslike, but also fully aware of what's going to happen at the end of the evening. Nobody's saying it, nobody's intimating it, but the ink of the signatures on this contract is already dry.

"Yes, certainly. A good idea."

"Good, then it seems that everything is set. I'm going to be looking forward to it."

"Looking forward to it? Did she say that?" he asked himself.

He almost slipped off his chair as he considered the implications of that statement.

She added quickly, "Please do ring me or send me an email to confirm your booking and I will do the same. Please also include the details of your arrival. And I'll do the same. By the way, whatever restaurant you choose will be fine with me. I like everything as you know."

Then she said goodbye. And he to her. Barely. The sound of his voice sounded more like the guttural croak from the throat of a frog in heat.

She smiled. There'd been no appointments in Malaga for the set of dates he'd mentioned to her on the phone. But one goes with what one has—or is given.

A deep breath. She buzzed her secretary, telling her she should start setting up some client meetings for the 19th and 20th in the Paris area. We can't keep these people waiting so long for a bank/client chit-chat as we sometimes tend to do, she told her. Her secretary said she'd get right on it.

The secretary knew what she was talking about. There was a list of clients Anulka had her keep, clients who required—and welcomed—frequent hand-holding by the bank. She would use that list, searching out those who fit geographically, to make the appointments.

In Frankfurt, Felix put down the phone. He looked at her name in his calendar, thought about what they'd arranged, and what might happen when they met, then slouched back deep in his chair.

He was finished, absolutely finished, for the day.

23
Golf Club Varese
Via Vittorio Veneto
Luminate
Italian Lake Region
Italia

July 11   17:52

Nothing like a hot summer afternoon spent on a challenging golf course. Giovanni and Saverio sat on the terrace overlooking the first tee, commenting, after their round, on the difficulty of the course, and the horrible humidity they'd endured during the round.

Right from the start, a difficult par four. From the tee box, absolutely no view of the flag, hidden, because the fairway, out at the one hundred ninety-meter mark, dropped off at that point, then ran straight down a steep, uneven hill to the small green. Bunkered on every side. The golfer, playing this hole for the first time, had no exact idea where the proper landing zone for his first tee shot should be. Somewhere on the hill running down to the green, but where?

Just hit it straight, Giovanni had said, after quick-hooking his first shot into some tall trees to the left of the fairway. Every golfer knows it. Hitting the ball straight ahead is generally the best policy on any course. Unfortunately, Saverio had then topped his ball, rolling it only about one hundred meters out onto the fairway.

That was just the start. The course had dog leg fairways and water. Its hilly location above Varese required good physical condition, particularly in the heat. There were only two ways to play the course: one either walks it with a golf bag mounted on a two-wheeled trolley. Or one carries.

Upon arriving at the club, they both had decided they would carry. Macho decision. After four hours and thirty minutes of play in the hot sun, definitely a bad decision. They were exhausted and glad to be able to sit down and enjoy a couple of cold beers.

Giovanni looked over to Saverio, weighing carefully his next words. "You know, Saverio, I've been thinking about the situation in Zurich. I know we discussed this in Asti and I know we agreed to wait until the end of August to see what Anulka would or wouldn't do. However, we've heard nothing in either direction. Just nothing. And that in spite of Luca's death."

"You know, I still have that sneaking suspicion she may think we're going to let her go and not do anything more about the money. Well, she's definitely wrong there, damn it. Since when do we let anybody set the pace for us? I tell you, all things considered, I think that's exactly what she's still doing and I don't like it one bit. And bottom line, that means we have nothing."

He became even more serious in tone. "Frankly, I don't think the silent treatment is going to work either. What I think we ought to consider doing is something entirely different. Nothing physical, but something that will put a knife into her heart, figuratively speaking. She needs that. She needs to piss in her pants. What I'm thinking about is a serious warning, a shot across her bow delivered to her right inside the bank, right inside that secure cocoon of hers. Or what she thinks is a secure cocoon. Why do I want to do this? Well, that's simple. I want my money."

He drank the rest of the beer in his glass, now already warm. "So that's where I am, Saverio. What do you think?"

Saverio wasn't surprised by what Giovanni had just said. He himself had had the same thoughts.

"Look," he countered," we discussed all of this already about three weeks ago. Remember, she's not just some dumb bitch. She knows what the deal is. We know she's still working at the bank. That says to me that nothing of what we've done has been discovered. And it also says to me that it's still possible for her to do something to get the money we want. Why that? Simple. Because she's still there where the money is."

"I'm sure she knows other ways to skirt the security systems they have. Hell, she knows everything about that damn bank. I'll bet she was even involved in putting some of their current firewall policies and security procedures into place."

He looked out over the golf course.

"For example, would making a decision to somehow find a way to go back to the trough mean higher risk for her? Sure it would, but she knows in her heart of hearts she's already burned. It's no longer a question of her staying and growing old in that bank. She knows that possibility doesn't exist anymore. At some point, a small fire could start in the bank about some missing funds or the real client could show up at the bank for a visit."

"At that point, she has to run. Immediately. She has no other choice. She has all of the false papers and passports from us, and she has enough money. She can go anytime she wants, but where? No, I think she stays put, at least for the time being and waits."

Saverio studied his beer glass. Still a swallow or two in it.

"The whole fear of discovery issue? The embarrassment? Us? I think she has to be asking herself what's really worse. The bank finding out what she did or what we potentially would or could do to her if she doesn't come across with the rest of the money. That's why I think she has only one thing in her mind: find a way to escape the pressure we've been putting on her and hope for the best at the bank."

Giovanni started to interrupt him but Saverio cut him off. "Let me flesh out my thoughts a bit here. Okay?"

He nodded and leaned back again in his chair.

Saverio swallowed the last of his beer, then continued.

"First of all, fact: her Luca is dead. Second fact: she's guilty of fraud and embezzlement. And she's probably feeling doubly guilty because she knows that her actions, indirectly, or directly if you will, caused his death. And she's scared. In her place, I'd definitely be thrashing about trying to find a way to solve the problem of paying us off."

"Look, what I'm trying to say here is, fraud is fraud. People say, the second time around is easier than the first. The threshold is lower. So, for her, in spite of the shitty situation she finds herself in, another run at the money is certainly doable. And, of course, in our case, murder is murder. I'm sure the second one would also be easier for us than the first."

Saverio looked his friend directly in the eye.

"You want my bottom line opinion? I think we should continue to wait. Don't think for a minute I'm letting her off the hook. In my view, I think that hook is already very deep in her. She has to do something. So, there you have it, my thoughts."

He saw the waiter out of the corner of his eye, stuck two fingers up in the air, ordering two more beers for them both. He turned swiftly back to Giovanni, touching his arm to get his attention. And an answer.

"However, having said all of that, I am interested in hearing how you would go about giving her that warning. What do you have in mind?"

Giovanni considered his words. He had to admit Saverio wasn't wrong. Nevertheless, something more needed to be done to get the ball rolling in the right direction.

"Okay, I hear you, and I agree with much of what you say. But I'm still convinced we must move on this. Here's my idea.

What I'm thinking about is a hard nudge, a direct push to get her reacting more quickly to the situation, meaning letting us know not if, but when money is going to start rolling again."

"I'd get one of those burner cell phones, a throwaway. I'd call her direct office line at the bank—I have the number, as you know—until I hear her pick up and say hello. Then I'd simply say: 'You know Latin, Anulka. Remember. *Tempus fugit*.'"

"Time flies. That's it. Nothing more."

"After that, I'd get rid of the throwaway and it's done. Nothing on paper. No traceable call or contact."

"Even if she's in a meeting when she picks up the phone, that one sentence will send her straight to hell, knowing as she does that such conversations are sometimes recorded at the bank. Those weeks with no contact from our side speaks a language she may have misinterpreted. She needs to know we're still serious."

The two beers had arrived. Saverio looked out over to the garden directly in front of them, then down into the maze of trees and fairways that comprised the Golf Club Varese. Nature is so beautiful, he thought, and here we are, sitting here, plotting unnatural things, rough things. But he's right. It has to be done.

"Yeah, I agree, it would have an effect. When would you want to make the call?"

"I'd call it in about ten days' time. Give her a little more time, which I think you'll appreciate. If I don't get her the first time, I'll just keep trying until I do. You'll hear from me the minute I've been able to put that warning into her ear."

Saverio paused for a second, looked at him without speaking, then emptied his glass in big gulps.

He stood and looked down at Giovanni. "Ok, do it."

24
The Apartment of Chantal Hofmaier
Seestrasse
Thalwil bei Zurich
Switzerland

July 17   8:46 am

Felix had spent the night at his mother's apartment. He'd slept well. He hadn't had the strange feelings he'd expected to experience by staying there.

In fact, he'd actually enjoyed it.

The breakfast dishes were still on the coffee table in the living room. Felix sat reading the *Neue Zuercher Zeitung*. Earlier that morning, he'd walked up into the center of Thalwil to get a half dozen *broetchen* , rolls, from the bakery, and to buy the newspaper at the local *Zeitungskiosk*.

He looked through the hall into the bathroom again. That damn medicine cabinet was still hanging there, still staring at him, still bothering him. He got up and went into the bathroom and looked at it again.

I need to check something here again, he thought. He emptied the contents of the cabinet into the wash basin, then lifted the empty cabinet off its hooks. He looked at the back wall carefully, ran his hand lightly over the plaster surface once again. As before, little pieces of sand fell from the surface directly where the cabinet had been hung.

Suddenly, a thought. He checked the wall to the left and the right of that spot, rubbed his hand over the surface. No sand. Smooth surface.

He looked closer at the sandy part. Something has been done to this wall. But what? With his knuckles, he rapped gently on a part of the wall where he'd felt the sand particles. He did the same with the wall directly to the right and left of the cabinet. Somewhat different sound. Not hollow but somehow different.

There's something behind that wall, damn it. And I want to know what it is.

He went to the basement where his mother had kept a small set of tools. He found a chisel and a hammer, then returned to the bathroom. Fifteen minutes later, he'd opened up a ten-inch wide hole in the wall. He reached into the open space behind the now-broken bricks and touched something. A plastic bag. It came out easily. Inside a large, sealed envelope, the word FILES written on it in large letters.

In the same plastic bag, a second envelope with his name scrawled on it. He recognized his mother's handwriting. He could feel folded sheets and something hard inside.

His heart was beating. There was perspiration on his forehead, not so much from the exertion of opening the wall, but from what he'd just discovered. And what he assumed it might be.

He quickly cleared the coffee table of the morning's dishes. He opened the large envelope. In it, hard copies of financial transfer documents and account information, fastened together with a large paper clip. A yellow stick-it note fastened to the top sheet with words on it written in her hand: SAMPLE HARD COPIES (SEE FLASH DRIVE IN SMALLER ENVELOPE FOR COMPLETE DOCS).

Damnation. His mother had really meant what she'd said. There'd been a life tied to that cabinet. He reached for the second envelope, his pulse racing. He opened it, saw his mother's handwriting. A letter from her.

He held his breath and started to read:

My dear Felix, if you are reading this letter, then it is because I am no longer able to speak with you personally about the documents you now have in your hands. I am so very glad you remembered my comment about life and the medicine cabinet.

You will certainly have heard that I was sick and under a doctor's care. You will also have heard that I'd changed in the last months of my life. The reason for that state of affairs you now have on the flash drive I included for you.

To understand what it all means, you need to know the following: Dr. Renauer has for years kept a separate wealth management operation in Winterthur. The Florastrasse operation is his legal business. The Winterthur business is also a legitimate side of his operation, but it has a criminal component to it that is reprehensible in the extreme.

Normally, he put all those clients who desired secrecy for their investments into an account in the Florastrasse.

These were clients who were smart enough to provide for the formal disposition of their investments—and the contents of their accounts after their death.

About ten years ago, he created a second category of wealth management clients. These clients were taken care of separately through his offices in Winterthur. He used that operation for only one thing: it was reserved for those clients who were so extremely paranoid about secrecy that they, as strange as it may seem, didn't even think to worry about how and in what form their assets would be distributed after their death.

They were blinded by one overriding objective: no one should ever know what monies they had under management. Nobody. Anywhere.

With one exception: Dr. Renauer.

The contracts those Winterthur clients signed did not include anything about asset distribution. Theirs was an erroneous assumption, a blind trust that Dr. Renauer would do the right and fair thing, meaning, making sure after their death that the money was passed on to the appropriate person or persons.

However, he did nothing. He didn't make any attempt to find those to whom the money now possibly belonged. He didn't inform anybody about the change in the "status" of the deceased client's money. He didn't want to nor did he need to.

Nobody beside him and the individual Winterthur clients knew of the existence of the money in the accounts. There was no contractual obligation to do anything differently. So, when a client passed away, he would simply wait a while to be sure no one would come to claim the money. Then he transferred the client's assets in tranches into his own accounts.

Through these criminal acts, he has become wealthier than you can possibly imagine. He steals from the dead and gives to the living.

In the last year, he admitted this quite freely to me.

I imagine you are probably wondering about why I would be talking with him about such things. Good reasons exist for that circumstance.

During the years I worked for him, I knew, of course, about the existence of the Winterthur operation, but I never knew what he'd arranged or not arranged for in case of a Winterthur client's death. I saw the Winterthur clients who came to visit with him from time to time in the Florastrasse. I noticed nothing extraordinary about their visits or their attitude about the firm or that they were worried in any way about their money.

I was confronted with the criminal side of the Winterthur business after a Winterthur client I liked, Herr Reichert, died. This client had told me upon occasion about his family and about his devotion to them. After his death, I didn't see Dr. Renauer making an effort to find any members of that family who should have been, under normal circumstances, at least informed about the existence of the money in his account. No letter, no personal call from him.

That surprised me so I asked him if I should do the informing or if I could help him do it. He became very angry. He refused, telling me it was none of my business.

I became frustrated about his attitude and his coldness so I checked everything I could find concerning his operation in Winterthur, the results of which you now have in your hands. Please note that the client files and transfer documents contained in the flash drive were "removed" without his knowledge or permission from his computer system in Winterthur.

I have also included a selection of hard copies for you in the large envelope. The documents contained therein are clear evidence of his crimes. Now they are yours to do with as you feel appropriate.

The larger amount of money you have inherited from me comes from Dr. Renauer. After having analyzed the data I'd pulled out of his system, I confronted him again. I did not, however, tell him about what I knew. I wanted him only to take care of "my" client friend's family. That was the driving force behind my repeatedly speaking to him.

He continually refused to do anything. I pushed back hard. He in turn put me under massive pressure. He raped me. The horror of it!

And told me he would see me in prison because I was "involved" in the fraud. His point was clear: if he went down for the crime, he would take me with him. He had the stronger hand. So, I accepted the money he wanted to give me to keep me quiet, hoping that I could use it one day to escape from him.

Felix, you must understand that I was scared and thus accepted the situation as it was. The will with you in it was my one demand and my one precondition to carry on, as before, with *him. I want to assume he has fulfilled that demand because I reg-istered the will with the authorities and gave a copy of it to my bank. He knows that.*

I have suffered terribly these last months, both physically and psychologically. During this time, I have also regretted terribly not having been a better mother to you, not having seen that we were, in fact, different, and that that is actually alright in a relationship between a son and his mother. And that a mother must sometimes accept the fact that her son may think differently than she may about certain things.

I was often too rough with you. I am so sorry for that. Instead of pushing you away and criticizing you and your life, I should have embraced you and the differences that existed between us. You refusing to have anything to do with me was sadly the result of my not doing exactly that.

You know how much of myself I invested in the firm. I was blind to the really important things in life, like you, blind to the effect my negative attitude had on you. As I write these lines, it hurts me so much to think about what I have missed in my life and what I did to you.

In spite of everything, I loved you and never stopped loving you. You were my only child and, during all that time, I missed you more than you can know.

Visit my grave when you have a moment. Sit on the grass and say some words to me when you're there. Touch the letters of my name engraved in the gravestone. Perhaps you will feel my fingers touching you back.

My doctor has told me that, aside from a generally weakened

*condition and occasional bouts of depression, my health is good. No
organ problems, no sign of heart problems. Nothing.*

*Do not mistake it, Felix. Peter Renauer is capable of any-
thing. You having found this letter should indicate to you that he
was, at the end, apparently capable of the very worst of crimes, the
murder of your mother.*

*I kiss you and hold you tight, my dear son. Take care of
yourself.*

Adieu.

Your mother

Felix dropped the letter on the floor and lay back on the
couch. A devastating letter.

His head buzzed, he broke down. How does one handle
tears and sobs and, at the same time, try to breathe?

Felix attempted to do both without choking himself.
For long minutes, he sat in one position, bent down over his
knees, everything else gone except his constant horror at the
words he had just read. He cried for what had happened to
her, he cried for what could have been with his mother, he
cried for the times he'd wished her to hell for her attitude
and coolness to him, he cried because he wished he could still
speak with her but couldn't, he cried for his childhood, and he
cried for his future existence, an existence without a mother
who had, in fact, loved him in a way he'd never known existed.

And he raged at Renauer. There was now no room for
doubt. Or lies. The man had killed his mother to protect him-

self and his criminal behavior. Selfishly, without a care in the world for her or her life.

She'd stood in his way. She would have ruined him, his reputation, and his life.

He lifted his head, stared at the documents on the coffee table in front of him, shuffled them back and forth, picked up the one or the other page to study its contents more carefully. No doubt about it. Renauer had committed multiple financial crimes. Fraud was written all over practically every piece of paper he now held in his hand.

He looked out the window, tears still welling in his eyes. The sun had gone behind the clouds hanging over the lake. That bastard sits over there in Zurich, he reflected, still thinking he has sold me a bill of goods. I knew he was dirty. But murder?

He stood up. His immediate urge was to drive over to his office and confront him with what he now knew. In spite of his emotional state, cold reason held him back from doing that.

If I attack him now, he thought, if I go to the police, he might kill me as well. And, if not, then there's the possibility that the authorities in the case might possibly demand I return the money I've inherited. The money could be important for me, considering my situation in Frankfurt.

Shit, what a situation.

He unclenched and clenched both of his fists, then hit the side of the living room wall with the right one. Hard.

He went out onto the balcony, trying to calm himself. He heard the cries of the birds flying high above him. He felt the wind from the lake on his face. He stared at the sky, at the lake, at the distant mountains.

Finally, long minutes later, he began to think clearly again. A phrase he'd heard once jumped into his head: revenge is a dish best served cold.

Exactly. That's what I'll work toward, he thought. I'm going to take the time to find something that will really settle Peter Renauer's hash, once and for all.

He packed his things, cleaned up a bit in the kitchen and in the bathroom, throwing away in the garbage the sheet he'd put over the sink below the wall to catch the falling bits and pieces of plaster. He glanced around the apartment once more, a deep sense of sadness clutching hard at his heart.

Descending the stairs, he checked once more that he had the flash drive and letter secure in the inside pocket of his suit jacket. Before heading to Zurich and Kloten Airport, he planned to stop at his bank and put everything into his newly-acquired safe deposit box. And something else needed to be done as well, he thought.

I'm going to go to the cemetery just above Thalwil, sit on the grass, and talk for a while with my mother.

And touch the letters of her name on her gravestone with my fingertips.

25
Main Lounge
Hotel Intercontinental
Rue Scribe
Paris
France

July 18   22:51

Felix sat in one of the lounge chairs in the main reception area, waiting for Anulka, who'd excused herself to go the ladies' room. They'd just arrived back at the hotel after their dinner at Jules Verne, a top-of-the-line restaurant located one hundred and twenty-five meters up on the first platform of the Eiffel Tower.

Magnificent, panoramique view of Paris. *Absolument quelque chose de spéciale*, absolutely something really special, they'd both agreed.

The Vichyssoise, a cold potato soup, as appetizer, had been first class. Actually, so spectacular that they'd almost ordered a second round. The two bottles of red Bordeaux wine they'd drunk together with a main course of *steak au poivre* and *pommes Dauphines* had started a nice warm fire inside each of them.

In the taxi coming back to the hotel, she'd moved across the seat right up against him, the whole length of her body pressed against his. She was so close he could feel the heat of her, smell her skin, look down at the soft whiteness and curves of her breasts rising and falling in the bodice of her black dress.

He could smell the subtle sweetness of her perfume. And the faint scent of the wine on her breath from dinner.

Waiting for her to come back, Felix didn't waste any time. He had a couple of serious matters on his mind. First, there was the horror of what he'd learned in Thalwil. His subsequent visit to the grave of his mother had been more than emotional, the sadness he'd felt as he'd touched the letters on her gravestone, deep and profound.

A plan to give Renauer his just due was already beginning to form in Felix's mind. The timing part of it already clear. He'd be returning to Zurich several times in the months ahead to finalize all of his mother's affairs. Sometime after those visits, he would initiate what he was determined to do: avenge her murder in a brutal—and hopefully effective—fashion.

The morning and afternoon meetings with the French consulting firm and its German client were planned for the next day. He had a good feeling about the whole thing. According to an email he'd received two days ago from Monsieur Aron, the prospective client would make final his decision at the meeting. Its management had found the contents of the proposal more than acceptable.

The discussions, perhaps here or there, a small change in the one or other detail, would be nothing more than a formality. Standard client behavior. The client just wanted to have a little breathing room before making the final decision and signing the contract.

Under any circumstances, a done deal. Just the signature was missing. And the start date.

He hadn't called Ben yet to tell him how close the French client was to closing the deal. Wait until he hears the project will need more than one consultant. Nice scheduling problem for him. He'll have to come to Paris as well. That'll get his attention, he thought.

Besides, if something does break in Munich, we can send one of the other Frankfurt consultants down there to handle the assignment. With Ben spending Benimum a week per month in Munich, we shouldn't have a problem handling both jobs if it comes to that.

He'd heard nothing from Heinz. However, he did know that two exploratory—thank God, also constructive— meetings with the bank had already taken place. The insurance company was also keeping its word. Ben had told him one of the insurance company's best liability lawyers had accompanied Heinz last week to a meeting at the bank.

No word, however, on whether or not the insurance company would want to or even be able to talk with some of the people at Loretz. In any case, the whole Loretz management will probably not want to say anything. Their lawyers will have taken care of that risk.

Also, no request from Heinz to change the way he was currently arguing the firm's position vis-à-vis the bank. That spoke for the fact he was good with the arguments he was currently using. Felix knew that Heinz would soon make a recommendation on the best way to reach some form of acceptable agreement with the bank. That was the reason why Felix had always sought his advice. Heinz was smart, effective, and, above all, quick at finding a way out of difficult situations.

He saw Anulka coming back into the hall, looking around for him. He stood up and waved, then pointed with his right hand in the direction of Le Bar, located on the far side of the lounge next to the La Verriere restaurant.

As he approached the bar, he looked in at the restaurant next to it, the ambiance of the garden, the tables set around it, the elegant decoration, the soft lighting. Damn, he thought. There's Paris. And then there is just whatever is left over after that.

They met just in front of the entrance to the bar and entered together, selecting a small table a distance away from a group of well-lubricated guests sitting in the far corner.

She'd taken his arm as they'd walked in, pressing it against the upper part of her body. Full soft breasts. He'd swallowed hard.

Their dinner together had been a small surprise. A quiet affair. They'd spent the time talking about politics, banking, about his coming meetings, what she liked and didn't like about her job, his friend Ben about whom she'd specifically asked, and his approach to life.

He didn't wonder why the dinner had had a kind of low-key character to it. For him, the reason was clear: They both knew full well what was going to happen afterwards. No longer a question of if or where, but rather one of when— and then, perhaps even more important, how it would be. Each one of them would have had a different answer to the question why.

He could hardly wait.

Anulka looked at him, a feeling of sadness, even of capitulation, in her heart. This whole thing is nothing but a necessary evil, she thought, something that needs doing. And nothing will change that fact.

She caught him smiling at her. She returned the smile. Maybe, just maybe, I will enjoy sleeping with him. She let her eyes wander over his body. I haven't had a man in a long while, she thought. Just thinking about that first touch, that first shiver. God, I like that. It's always the same: the body and the mind sometimes at odds with one another.

I wonder what kind of a lover he'll be.

He looked at her, drinking in her smile and the way she was looking at him. Aside from the sex angle, this was a woman he liked. And respected. And if he wasn't mistaken, he felt sure she liked him as well.

He lifted his glass, touched it gently to hers, then took a deep swallow of his Hennessey XO. Nectar. Pure nectar.

She looked him right in the eye. In spite of everything going on in his life, he sensed that the evening—and the night—would bring about a change in that life. He hoped for it as he signaled to the waiter to please bring him the check.

It was going to be his room.

"Anulka, I've just looked at my watch. I love chatting with you. I know it's rather late, but I'm not tired at all. Would it be too forward of me to ask you if you'd like to have another short drink in my room? I had room service put some of my usual things up there when I arrived this morning. There's a bottle of cognac. You know the brand", smiling as he spoke to her. "And I have some other things to choose from if you want something *plus légère*. If you'd like some ice, I can order that as well."

She looked at him and cocked her head. Catching his eye, she smiled, then quickly closed and opened her own in assent.

Bong. The elevator arrived. In they went, the doors closing behind them. Due to the lateness of the hour, there were no other people in the elevator. A slight tenseness gripped the both of them. Neither one of them spoke. Everything had already been said. And they both knew it.

The wine and the cognac they'd consumed, the anticipation of a touch, of a kiss, of the first touch of the tip of the tongue, fueled the heat in their minds and their bodies. He turned to her and she towards him. He had a good seven inches on her. He lowered his head to her left cheek and brushed it gently with his lips, breathing in as he did. In his lifetime, he'd never smelled anything so perfect, so enchanting and subtle, so overwhelming.

If just a slight touch of her cheek and her perfume get me going like that, he thought, then what's going to happen when we get upstairs?

For God's sake, Felix, get yourself under control.

She turned slightly more to her left and their lips finally met. They stood there, the tips of their lips just barely touching each other, gently, softly, caressing, sensing one another, their breathing, short, shallow, quick intakes of air, comingling with one another when expelled, as they waited for their floor, frozen in the moment—and in the expectation.

Bong. 8th floor.

They walked down the hall to his room. She entered before him. He stepped in behind her. The door behind them fell into its lock. It was dark in the room. A dim glow from the street lanterns below came in through the half-closed, heavy curtains and sheers framing the two high windows of the room.

They could hear the muted sound of traffic through one of the windows he'd left partially open, a soft busy humming on a warm Parisian, late summer night.

He turned to her, putting his arms around her, sensing her heat and the fullness of her body. She squared herself to him, pressed herself against him, feeling, rubbing her lower belly gently against his erect cock. She reached up with her left hand to the back of his neck and pulled his lips down to hers. Their kiss, now full, was tender, haunting, and complete.

The moment overran them. She ran her tongue along his upper lip, touched with her right forefinger his cheek, wet both his lips from left to right with the tip of her tongue, the necessary evil now far away.

This was good. Very good.

She began to breathe heavily, matching his breathing in the cadence, feeling the same excitement and desire, the body heat rising in her, her face flushing. He took her hand and kissed its palm with the tip of his tongue.

Suddenly, for a brief second, her thoughts flew away to another place, to another time, to another life. She remembered who'd done that with her once upon a time so long ago. But she came back as quickly as she'd gone away, the pulse in her forehead now beating a rhythm of want, and a need for animal satisfaction.

Now. This moment. Not later. Now.

She reached down to him and gently stroked his groin. She felt him tense, then relax, then his body shudder as she moved her hand up and down along the length of his stiff cock. He raised both his hands to the back of her neck, grasped the zipper of her dress and pulled it down to just above her bottom. He slipped her left, then her right arm, out of the sleeves. The dress fell to the floor.

He looked down at the whiteness of her skin, at the outline of her breasts, he saw their fullness, their softness, the up and down of her breathing.

He reached behind her, undid the pearl buttons of her silk top—not a bra but a small short, loose, sleeveless undershirt with two straps over the shoulder—loosely covering her breasts and let it drop to the floor. His mouth was bone dry. He placed the palms of his left and right hand gently on each of her nipples, moving them in a circular motion, at times faster, at times slower. She felt faint. She pressed herself closer to him. She could feel his cock pressing against her, the wetness of his tongue, of his saliva mixed with hers.

There was no holding back. She shuddered, let out a cry, arched into him, grabbing him tightly, soft, moaning, whimpering sounds escaping from her lips.

For more than a few seconds, she went far away. And then she came back. From a sweet darkness that had enveloped her whole being.

"Good God", she asked herself, "where did that come from?"

Three steps and they were lying on the large bed in the middle of the room. She was still shuddering. He held her gently for a moment. They kissed again, this time penetrating each other's mouths with their tongues as far as they could reach. The taste of the wetness of her mouth, her perfume, the softness of the skin on the nape of her neck, the touch of her warm skin on his, captured his senses completely.

She swung her right leg over his body, pressed herself to him, stroked him again, then sat up and took off the rest of her clothes. He smiled when he saw that she wasn't wearing a thong—something he considered so completely *déclassé*, so tasteless—but rather a pair of loose, white silk underpants. Something like the loose boxer shorts men wear.

Class wears class stuff, he thought.

She undressed him, telling him to hold still. All the while looking at bulge of, then exposing the hardness of his erect cock, waiting there for her touch. When she was finished, she leaned down over him, her heavy breasts resting on his stomach, and put him deep into her mouth.

She stroked his cock with her lips, her tongue, moving it gently back and forth, taking him as deeply as she could into her mouth. She cupped his balls in her left hand, and with the tip of the forefinger of her right hand, slowly and gently traced a line up and down his scrotum. She caressed both his balls with the tip of her tongue, starting, stopping, fast, then slow.

Felix was lost somewhere between the darkness and the light, his body humming a tune he'd never heard before.

His brain almost completely shut down.

He lifted her body higher up on the bed, kissing her deeply as he did, the wetness in their mouths combining into an elixir he felt he could swallow forever. She was biting his lip; she was moaning; she was gasping. She whispered in his ear, now fully lost in the moment, "Come to me, come deep to me, Felix", and pulled him to her.

He touched the wonderful soft skin of her upper inner thighs; he felt the welcoming openness of her pussy. He entered her slowly, her wetness drawing him easily and ever deeper into her. Slowly, centimeter by centimeter, he slid into her until he was fully inside. She pulled her legs up so that he could penetrate her further, wrapping them around him, moving her hips in a slightly circular motion against him as they lay there, now fully joined together.

He moved slowly back and forth inside of her, over and over again, sometimes stopping for a second or longer, sometimes tensing and then releasing his cock for several seconds when he was fully inside her to signal how deep he could be in her.

The jolts of passion she felt as he did that almost made her faint. She bit his ear, she breathed words he had trouble hearing because of the buzzing in his own head.

He heard her whisper, her voice raw, "When you come, Felix, come deep inside of me, come as deep as you can."

The buzzing sound redlined in his head. He did exactly as she wanted. She felt the first surge, then the second, then the third surge of his sperm deep inside of her. And she climaxed again, sliding along its waves, up and down, her body jerking at the sensations smashing into her, astonished and completely at a loss to explain her excitement and desire for him. She kissed every part of his face, his eyes, his forehead, his nose, his mouth. She rubbed her cheeks on his.

And she moaned and told him, "Don't. Don't move. I don't want to lose a drop of you."

They slept through the night, holding each other close, only a light sheet covering them as they lay there. When the dawn came, he entered her again. She was still full of his wetness. And again later, just before the telephone rang with his wake-up call.

She looked at him as he turned back from the phone.

No embarrassment. No downcast eyes. She smiled at him and kissed him gently. He murmured to her that he had to be at his meeting at ten that morning. She said she would sleep a little longer, then get up and return to her room to get ready for the day.

His heart stayed with her in that bed, even after he arrived for his meeting at the Porte de la Chapelle. Before leaving the room, he'd told her he would be coming back to Zurich soon because of something he needed to quickly take care of. She hadn't asked why or what, simply told him she'd be waiting for him. And would he please call when he got back to Frankfurt so that she would know he'd arrived safely.

When his Air France flight landed late that same evening, he did as she'd asked. She told him she'd been thinking about him the whole day. She told him she could still smell his scent on her, even after showering that morning and spending the afternoon in meetings. She loved the smell of him, she said.

What she didn't tell him was that, after he'd left, she'd put two of her fingers deep inside of herself, then taken them out and raised them wet to her mouth.

She loved the taste of him, too.

Felix managed to stammer something to the effect that Paris was a good place to lose one's heart.

Over and out.

26
Gare Cff de Genève Cornavin
Rue de Lausanne
Geneva
Switzerland

August 1   17:12

Anulka was going to be late to pick up Felix at the main railroad station. He was coming from Zurich where he'd spent the last two days taking care of the last of his mother's affairs. He was looking forward to seeing her again, no matter where that took place. The possibility of being with her in Geneva for one day was something really special for him, he'd told her.

He loved the city. The Jura mountains vaulting high just behind the airport and the border to France. The vineyard-lined road stretching along Lake Geneva to Lausanne, and then further on to Montreux.

And he'd be able to speak French, his favorite language, now, of course, a necessity because of the work he'd be doing in Paris. She'd been charmed by what he'd said. Anybody who can look forward to speaking a language one likes and be happy about it can't be all bad, she thought.

She herself had arrived in Geneva three days before for meetings at the bank's branch in the Rue de Rhon. Originally, both she and Felix had planned to spend those same several days together in Zurich, but there'd been a major mistake made by the Geneva branch in scheduling the four days of meetings. She'd had to leave Zurich and come south before Felix had even arrived in Zurich.

Actually, she wasn't unhappy at all about their having to meet in Geneva. In Zurich, there'd have been some issues with the overnight situation. Using her apartment would have been the first problem. Definitely, a no-no, with pictures of Luca and her still-vivid memories of his having slept there.

Sleeping in his mother's apartment in the same bed where she'd died? Also, a no-no.

No doubt about it: difficult circumstances.

In contrast, Geneva offered a simple and neutral solution. He would stay with her at her hotel. Everything was arranged, including making sure his favorite beer and a bottle of his favorite whiskey would be there waiting for him when he arrived.

The meetings at the bank had gone well. However, meetings often have a tendency to last beyond pre-arranged timeframes. She'd been involved in one of those in the afternoon. Nevertheless, a taxi she'd wisely ordered in advance had rushed her quickly to the train station, less than ten minutes away by car.

Only thirteen minutes late. She hurried into the station and checked the arrival times. Felix's train was running forty-eight minutes late. All that hurry? For nothing? What had caused that? A quick check with a ticket agent provided the answer: light signal problems on a stretch of the main line just north of Bern.

Well, okay. Time enough for a coffee at one of the small, standing-only cafes in the lower level of the station. Definitely a better way to pass the time than waiting in the middle of the Main Hall, in danger of being run over, right and left, by early evening commuters.

She sipped her coffee and studied the shoppers and passengers heading for their trains. Or the exits. Everyone with their own lives, everyone with their own priorities and problems.

Her eyes narrowed as she recalled the shock she'd received the past week. Sitting in her office, a call had come through on her private phone line. No number ID. Only eight or nine people had that number, including Giovanni.

She'd been too lazy. She hadn't felt it necessary to ask the bank for a change in the number because he'd used it only twice in all the time they'd been together.

It was a mistake.

She'd been in the midst of examining some quarterly portfolio results for a client. There was a serious problem with several of the key benchmark numbers. A bit behind in her time plan, she'd turned, distracted, toward the buzzing phone on her sideboard, quickly lifting the receiver. Totally unexpected, she'd heard his voice speaking to her. Her heart had raced; her throat had closed. No breath possible.

His last two words, *Tempus fugit*, still rang in her ears as she heard the beep-beep-beep coming through the phone receiver. He'd already hung up.

A fear such as she'd never known had held her for a moment in its grip. She'd stood up, turning, involuntarily sweeping, with that sudden movement, one of the dossiers in front of her onto the floor. She'd walked to the window, then to the door, then back to the window, and finally back to the chair behind her desk. She'd fallen into it, breathing hard.

Then, as quickly as it had come, the fear had fallen away, to be replaced by hard spurts of anger and rage. The bastard. The absolute bastard.

There'd been the anger at herself for reacting in the way she had. But, more so, there'd been the rage at him for what he was still demanding.

She'd sat there, slowly breathing in and out, slowing her body down, slowing her impulses down, slowing her emotions down. A couple of minutes later, she'd returned to normal. More or less.

She'd taken a sip of the apple juice her secretary had brought her. The coldness she needed had returned. If this were other times and other places and other possibilities, she'd thought, she could imagine finding him, wherever he was, and whacking him personally, close up. But these weren't other times and those other places didn't exist.

She'd felt once more that bitter determination to get

her life back, to steal more money, enough to secure her freedom, to finally put the past to rest, no matter what collateral damage that determination might cause.

She knew very well Felix might become a part of that damage, part of that necessary evil. It was so very sad, a cost she had to accept, in spite of her growing affection for him.

That night in his room in Paris had been a surprise. It wasn't the fact that it had happened, because that had been, well, to be honest, pre-planned and anticipated. No, it was the intensity of the act itself which had caught her completely unaware. In fact, the whole time with him had been quite extraordinary: the dinner, the night in his room, and, then, finally, his amusing and confused comments to her on the phone from Frankfurt Airport.

But no matter. She had her opening. She was going to use his dark side and his current financial problems to entice him to take part in a second round of embezzlement at Bankhaus Finsler. She remembered their first evening together at the restaurant in Kuesnacht. She remembered the conclusions she'd drawn about him, her sense of his desperation in searching for an escape from his precarious current situation, an escape from the forces that held him captive, an escape from all those explanations and discussions and modeling of possible solutions, all of which had been heretofore for naught.

She remembered the similarities she'd recognized in their situations. She'd seen nothing in the meantime to cause her to change her mind.

It wasn't going to be easy to convince him to take such a giant step. His transgressions, at least those she knew something about, had been relatively minor ones up to now compared to what she had in mind for him. On the other hand, he certainly wasn't an innocent babe in the woods either, that was a fact. And that made it somewhat easier to imagine he might very well go along with what she wanted him to do.

Fraud and embezzlement were major felonies. Bad enough, but, of course, she knew that only too well. But he was the only alternative she had—and she intended to make the best possible use of the chance he represented. And also, of course, of his colleague in Frankfurt.

That one must really be a number, she thought.

She drank the rest of her coffee. Don't think about it anymore, she admonished herself. Just go do it.

Loudspeaker blaring. The delayed train from Zurich was arriving on Track 5. She hurried to the escalator that would take her back up to the Main Hall. The narrow platform was full of passengers streaming toward her from the open doors of the train. And there was Felix, smiling as he hurried along the platform toward her.

She smiled and reached up to take his kiss.

They arrived at the taxi stand, got into an empty taxi. She gave the driver the address of her hotel. Rue du Puits-Saint-Pierre 1.

He knew the hotel. "Very nice choice," he said.

She looked at him. "You had signal problems? That's

a new one for me, considering the train system we have in Switzerland."

"Couldn't believe it myself, but the train had a car with a bar in the middle so that's just about where everyone went after the announcement was made. Good crowd, and, surprisingly, the beer was cold—and plentiful. I actually enjoyed the time."

The Hotel Les Armures is one of the finest and most attractive old-building hotels in all of Europe. Built in the 17th Century, it is located in the oldest part of Geneva, once a strictly conservative Calvinist city, something difficult to imagine when walking the hilly pedestrian zone of the Old City. Hedonistic attractions on every side: women's boutiques, cafes, restaurants, bookstores, art galleries, furniture boutiques, shoe stores, bars. And steps going up and down away from the cobble-stoned pedestrian zone, leading to little hidden nooks and crannies, filled with history—and sometimes more tourists than one could stand.

They arrived at the hotel just before seven in the evening, perfect timing for what was to come. Her room was on the third floor at the front of the hotel. Junior suite. King-sized bed, separate sitting room area in front of the windows, old wooden beams cutting parallel lines along the whole length and width of the room's ceiling. Between each of them, multi-colored geometric and floral drawings of a by-gone era.

Nice room, he thought. I don't know what it's costing her per night, but it sure isn't going to have her leaving just a few hundred Swiss francs with the cashier when she checks out two days hence.

He noticed the set-up on the coffee table in front of the window. She'd had ice, a bottle of single malt whiskey from his favorite Scottish distillery, *Old Pulteney*, and several different brands of German beer in an ice bucket brought to the room.

Nice.

Anulka sat across from Felix on one of the two large easy chairs positioned around the coffee table in front of the window. They both had opened cold beers and toasted their *Wiedersehen* with one another. Felix jabbered on about his pleasure at being again in Geneva, and, in particular, being able to share that with her.

One beer led to another as they talked, Felix turning somewhat mellower in the process. Also enjoying the moment, Anulka was nevertheless distracted by the thought of what she was facing. She remembered, unfortunately much too vividly, how Giovanni had propositioned her with the same plan many evenings ago in Nice.

It had been that long conversation with him that had helped drive her finally to the edge. And then right over it.

I'd been waiting for that kind of an opportunity, she thought, but I didn't consciously realize it until he'd started to speak.

Is Felix also waiting for something similar but doesn't know it? She knew there were major differences in experience and history between them. She sighed. I'm not sure he's going to give me the same kind of opening I gave Giovanni. Hell, she thought, I'm not even sure I'll be able to find any opening in him.

He's hurting badly, but is that enough to push him over the edge? Particularly now when, at least, part of his immediate cash flow problems appear to have been solved by the full-time consulting work he'd be doing in Paris. And hadn't he said that his lawyer had gotten a good initial grip on the bank case in Frankfurt?

He finally noticed the look of worry on her face. He thought of the sadness and the, at times, vacant opaqueness he'd seen in her eyes in the past. There was something in her letting her be there with him, and, yet, at the same time, not be there. He decided there was no better time than now to broach the subject.

"Anulka, there's something I have to ask you. I think you know very well how much I care about you. And, so, I know you know that when I ask you for an answer to a question, I'm not asking that question just for the fun of it. Or to embarrass you. Or because it's a way to make small talk with you."

He looked at her intensely. "Do you understand me?"

Her breath caught. Concerned, she nodded and waited for the question.

"When I look at you, Anulka, I see, I feel sadness; I see and feel terrible unhappiness. You can't imagine how unhappy that makes me," he continued, "because I think there's something destroying you inside. I need to talk with you about this. Do you understand that? May I speak with you openly? And will you speak with me in the same way? "

She looked at him, not saying yes, not saying no. Her face pale, her eyes opaque, distant.

Felix now very concerned. "Please tell me what's troubling you so much. Tell me what it is that seems to be tearing you apart. Is there any way I can help you, is there anything I can do to help you solve or resolve whatever seems to be bothering you so terribly?"

A small voice from her, a trembling voice. "Yes, Felix, I'll try".

She straightened herself in her chair. Hers was no make-believe or sympathy game play. It was naked despair and deep-seated anguish that Felix saw in her face and recognized now in the tears filling her eyes.

During the many tortured months she'd lived with her crime and its consequences, she'd had no one with whom she'd been able to talk, she'd never been able to release the pressure of the terror she felt inside of herself, never been in a position to voice the regrets she'd constantly experienced for doing what she'd done, never been able to rid herself of the doubts, the feeling of helplessness, the guilt that haunted her in the night, or to stem the tears that welled up in her eyes every time she relived that night in Magliaso.

She'd been totally alone with her nightmare—and with her wrongs. There could be no worst torture than that, she thought, not being able, not even once, to share or reduce the kind of continuous horrible pressure she constantly felt inside herself.

For the first time in her adult life, she was in a position of extreme vulnerability.

She ignored the utter selfishness of the request she would make of him. She had to, she had no choice.

She wiped away the tears on her cheeks. She would make a last effort to call upon a harder part of herself, the cold and calculating part she would need to get through what she had to say. She needed its energy, its strength to make her unfeeling for when she would look Felix in the eye and beg for his help.

But not enough to just have the power to do it. She needed, desperately needed, to be finally able to talk about what she'd experienced and what she was experiencing, to save herself from total ruin. And perhaps even death.

She knew she would be taking Felix into her soul. She hoped she was right in her judgment of him. She knew there was a risk in talking to him about herself and attempting to involve him in her crime. He would bear witness to her most innermost thoughts and emotions. He would know that she'd crossed any number of lines in the past. She'd already seen that questioning look on Felix's face as they'd sat drinking beer.

She'd known he was going to ask the question he had.

It was just too much. She thought of her father, of times long past, of his face smiling at her, still so clear in her memory, and a terrible sadness came over her.

And the flood came.

She sat there, bent over, sobbing and crying in the true meaning of those words. She cried for everything that had been but was no more. She cried because she was scared. She cried for her frustration, for her helplessness. She cried for what she had once been and was no more. She raged at those who had put her in such a desperate position. And at herself that she had been so weak, so stupid—in spite of her contempt for the bank and its clients—to let herself be taken down such a dark and horrible path.

She cried for a love lost, for the terrible guilt she felt. And finally, she cried for her act of selfishness and for her regret that she had no choice, no other choice but to steal again from her bank. And to use other innocent people for that purpose.

For what seemed like an eternity, she sat, bent over, in that floral-covered easy chair by the window, in the deepening shadows of that warm summer evening, and cried her heart out.

Nothing affects a man more than a woman crying tears of anguish, tears that come from way down deep in the soul.

"Good God," he said to himself. "What have I done here? Why is she crying so?"

Desperate, he jumped to his feet and almost ran to the bathroom, looking for the paper tissue dispenser on its wall.

He watched her carefully as she slowly regained her composure. His heart went out to her. He put his hand on the back of her head, holding it gently, using a tissue to dab the remaining tears away. Then, he went back into the bathroom, took a wash cloth from the rack, wet it with cold water, and brought it to her to put on her flushed face.

She looked up at him, smiling gently. Her body still shuddering intermittently.

But the tears had stopped.

She spoke slowly, haltingly. "Felix, thank you. I'm so sorry for being in such a state. There's nothing to worry about. I'll be fine."

He looked down at her, gently helping her to run the wet cloth over her flushed face. Then he sat down again.

"I'm sorry. My God, I'm so sorry, Anulka. What is it? Talk to me. Tell me what's wrong. Whatever it is, tell me."

She spoke softly to him. "Felix, I understand your worry. And you not understanding my behavior. Believe me, I understand everything."

She reached over and touched his arm.

"You see, you're right in what you say. I'm sad, very sad. I want to tell you, more than you can ever know, why I'm so sad. And I'm going to do exactly that. Here and now. I've given up. I can no longer not talk."

She looked at him intensely. "But there is one thing I must ask of you. Please do me a favor when I'm finished talking. It's really important to me. Otherwise, I can't go on."

"Of course."

She paused, gathering herself. "I ask you, I beg you. Please don't ask me any questions afterwards. You may notice a hole or two in some of what I say. Or something may puzzle you. Or something may seem to be missing. This is already hard enough for me. So, please, let it go. Let it go. Don't ask me about anything. Accept that it is as it is. *Je t'en prie.*"

She grasped his hand, holding it tight. She looked pleadingly at him. The expression on his face told her he didn't fully understand what she was saying. She had to make him understand.

She moved closer to him, meeting his gaze, willing herself to finally find the right words.

"Believe me, what I have to tell you isn't going to be easy for me to tell or for you to hear. Or bear. Or understand. You might even become angry. But discussing these things with you in too great detail would be too much for me. It's already hard enough for me to give you answers to your questions without having to go through a long and drawn-out discussion afterwards. Are you okay with that? Will you respect my wish?"

He smiled and nodded his assent. He touched gently her left cheek with his right hand. He wanted to hear whatever she was willing to tell him and in whatever detail she chose to do it. And if she needed help or assistance with something, well, one could talk afterwards about that as well.

She stood and walked around the easy chair to the open window behind her, looking down for a long moment at the back and forth of the pedestrians on the street below her in front of the hotel. A warm, early summer evening in the Old City of Geneva slowly drawing to a close.

She gathered her thoughts, steeled herself, then turned back to him.

She smiled tentatively at him as she sat down again. She took a deep breath, leaned forward, and started to speak. For almost forty-five minutes, she spoke to him. He did not once interrupt her.

She spoke of her life and what she'd experienced, how she'd grown up. Of her aspirations and her later disappointments. Of moments of happiness along the way. Of moments of sadness, of the tragic death of her father, and how much she'd missed him all the years. Of her increased rejection of the superficial, moral virginity she'd seen among many of those who practice the profession of banker, of her rejection of the immorality she'd seen and saw in much of what her bank accepted as normal business practice, of her inner fight against and her deeply-felt, increasing resentment of the bank and many of its dirty clients. She spoke of the fact that she'd finally lost that fight, that the resentment and hate had become too much for her, that she'd chosen to strike hard at the bank and its client system, steal from it, but, in doing so, had put herself simultaneously so severely in harm's way.

No more than that, but the message was already clear: I'm in serious trouble.

She spoke of the hard and dirty blackmail being used against her, the demands for money she could not meet. She spoke of its insidious nature, of the pressure from it having become an integral part of her life, woven into its many folds like a poisonous viper wrapped around her body, biting her continuously, the only problem being that she didn't die from its poison, but lived on with the torture of its presence, with

the toxicity and the horrible pain of its continual, poisonous bites.

Every single day—and every single night.

Several times, it seemed, she would lose again her
composure. Several times, her facial features tightened up
and tears glistened in her eyes. Her hands were in almost
constant motion. She bobbed back and forth on the chair.
She took repeated deep breaths, pushing as best she could her
emotions back down inside of herself, steeling herself, urging
herself to carry on.

It didn't always work. In spite of everything, there were
also moments when the hold she had over herself completely
failed, when her feelings fell out of sync with the story she
was trying to tell, when the words tumbled out of her in a
hurried, almost jumbled cadence, their sharp edges cutting
him to the very quick of his being.

She had to tell him. "I think you know I'm telling you
all of this because I need your help. I am so desperately afraid,
but I have no other alternative but to speak to you of these
things. Can you imagine living such a hell, Felix? I tell you I
can because I am right in the middle of it. I can't sleep; I can't
eat; I can't function properly; I can't be a human being with
this torture, this nightmare inside of me. I must have some
resolution. Otherwise, I am lost."

She paused, looked up at the ceiling, then back at him,
for a moment, in spite of her anguish, a hint of tenderness in
her eyes.

"Am I happy having to tell you all of this, am I proud

of what has happened? Not in the least, damn it, that I can tell you. But I have no alternative. Do you understand that?"

She looked him deep in the eyes. She spoke the words that had to be said.

"For God's sake, Felix, please help me," the heaviness of the pain in her in every word.

Not a sound. Her cry for help hung in the room. She saw the milky look in his eyes. She saw his face, the shock on it from the words she'd spoken, from words communicating an anguish that almost suffocated the room.

She knew she had to go on. There could be no waiting for his answer. Or his reaction. She had to finish. She had to get the whole story out.

She saw him start to draw a breath to speak to her, to respond to the terrible emotion of that moment in which they both found themselves. She reached over quickly and touched his lips with her right forefinger, asking him with the gesture not to speak and to please let her continue.

He reached up and squeezed her hand. And nodded. Go on.

She shuddered several times deep within herself. She had herself under control again.

She was ready to put the core problem on the table.

Her voice low, she spoke of her need to finally satisfy a blackmailer, to get rid of him once and for all. To protect Felix and his feelings, she did not identify him nor did she reveal the reason for the blackmail itself. She spoke of the amount of money she needed, she spoke of the one remaining alternative that existed for her, an alternative that would involve her—but also him if he agreed to it—in defrauding her bank, but, in the doing, would secure enough money for her to rid herself of the blackmailer.

She described how everything would work. She explained the need for the client lists, the need to check the sources of the money on deposit, to identify all or any dirty money involved, to create passport copies. She listed the steps necessary to create Client X.

She told him she was confident the plan she'd developed would work. After all, it was her backyard, so to speak. She knew every in and out of the bank and its systems and procedures. She just couldn't tell him in detail how she knew the plan would work so well.

She cited also the danger and the downstream risks, risks that had convinced her there was a real need to take out a significantly higher amount than she needed. They would all need it to survive if the authorities were to get on their trail.

Five million Euros was the amount she had in mind.

She told him what would be hers. To make it fair, she would keep only 50 % of the total amount taken. As for the remaining amount, Felix could decide how he wanted to divide it up. Divide it up meant that, since he was already a client of the bank and, therefore, burned, so to speak, there would be a need for a second person to slip into the role of Client X, the one who would visit the bank and pick up the money.

She looked up at him, saw his eyes go opaque, realizing what her words meant, what that could mean going forward.

She injected some hard, real-world facts into her words. She cited indirectly, diplomatically, but clearly enough for him to understand, his current and potentially significant, future financial difficulties. If the insurance played games, he'd have to come up with some very serious money. His firm would be insolvent. And he'd be left with almost nothing. A sum such as she had mentioned would go a long way, if not all the way, in solving any potential problems with the bank in Frankfurt. And in neutralizing the danger of criminal fraud proceedings against him—and the possibility of prison.

She spoke of the wonderful night they had spent together in Paris, her surprise at the feelings she'd experienced that night, of her knowing and understanding the kind of hellish life he was leading, and of his need to reshape that which would be his life in the future.

There was a deep coldness wrapped around her heart now as she spoke. She used words designed to appeal to his weaknesses, to his malleability, and to his naiveté, words that would manipulate his thinking, and hopefully cause him to seriously consider her proposal. She stressed the need for a new beginning for each one of them—and perhaps both of them—and the need to have the freedom to make that new beginning happen.

She told him everything he needed to know. She mixed truth, half-truths, and lies together. She didn't feel any shame. She was simply beyond that.

He hadn't interrupted her once. As she'd spoken to him, now meeting his eyes, now touching his arm, now cocking her head at him, she knew that what she was saying was not missing its mark. Just as Giovanni had gotten to her that summer night so long ago sitting on a bench on the Promenade des Anglais in Nice.

He hadn't been mistaken in his judgment of her. And she hadn't been mistaken in her judgment of him. What irony that is, she thought.

She had what she wanted, a confirmation. No doubt about it. If that weren't the case, she thought, if the pressures on each of them, each in their own separate way, hadn't been equally intense, he'd have already told me minutes ago to go to hell.

He hadn't. And he didn't. And he wouldn't.

She knew it already.

Felix knew his own weaknesses and now he'd seen hers as well. Even with the consulting fees he would get in Paris and the inheritance from his mother, he knew he was in grave financial and, very likely, also legal danger.

He knew also that he didn't have many alternatives available to him. In fact, up to now, he'd not seen anything even approaching a hint of a viable solution for his problem. In the cold light of day, what she was proposing was a possibility. And a way to possibly survive.

He wanted to know more about the blackmail and the reason for it. He felt a need to strike out at the person who was blackmailing her and to eliminate that horror for her. But he remembered his promise. And he kept it.

He looked at her. She's asking for help. She needs that help. Think about that instead, he said to himself. Everything else is secondary.

As he'd sat there listening, he'd experienced a feeling of sadness. While it all sounded feasible, it would mean for him another crime on the wrong side of right. But this time, a really serious crime. He felt for a moment the need for moral integrity, but only for a moment. And then it was gone.

The practical in him, the overwhelming superficiality in him, was attracted to its possibilities. And he was surprised. It had never occurred to him that someone—least of all Anulka—would be the one to provide him with the possibility of using such an alternative to finally and perhaps permanently change his life and the track it was on. And in doing so be able to free her as well.

She'd stopped talking. She was exhausted. She felt exposed and naked. But, somehow, it all felt right.

She didn't go for the close. She sat back in the easy chair, a soft, warm breeze blowing in at her back from the open window onto the small beads of perspiration that had formed just under the hairline at the back of her neck.

She waited.

Felix got up from his chair. The beer she'd ordered brought to the room was gone. He went to the small icebox provided by the hotel, and took out a Heineken beer. He held the bottle in her direction, asking if she wanted one as well. She declined. What she needed was a reaction, any reaction, perhaps an answer, something verbalized, but she wasn't going to beg for it.

He looked at her, no anger, no disappointment in his face. Expressionless.

The question he finally posed exhilarated her. For reasons that had nothing to do with its specific content.

"Who would actually come to the bank as the Client X to pick up the money? I can't do that. You know that, you mentioned that. So, then, who could do that?"

Good God, he's really in, she thought.

She had an answer ready. "Good question, Felix. I have a feeling my answer will surprise you. What do you think about this possibility? We've spoken several times about your colleague and friend, Ben. You've told me a little bit about him, his history, and, above all, his love of money. And the fact that, in your opinion, he might have been involved or might even still be involved in some interesting, off-the-grid activities."

"Didn't you also tell me in Paris that night that he'd spent almost a decade working for an Arabian-French bank consortium in the Gulf? That'd be optimal, of course. He knows the banking business. And I would guess also the wealth management business."

"Don't worry. I know you don't know anything specific about what he actually does outside of the office and I know you've never been involved in anything he's done. It probably doesn't even interest you. That's not what I'm implying here."

"I know that, Anulka."

She smiled, relieved that they were discussing details, and not the overall moral issue of the plan.

"But, seriously, Felix, wouldn't Ben actually be the perfect candidate? Think about it for a moment. Look at him and think about how he really is and what he values."

He looked at her and nodded slowly. Yes, possibly true. He thought about all the issues standing in the way of even getting his attention to discuss what she'd proposed. The on-going problems with the NHF Handelsbank. Probable, perhaps immediate financial damage to the firm, and to him as partner, and maybe even to him personally.

He thought about Ben's skitter-scatter life style. Perhaps some other things he might also be involved in. Who the hell knows what the guy really does or is thinking sometimes?

He stopped. If I were to put all those issues aside for a moment and just let Ben be Ben for a moment, would that work? The answer came quickly. A no-brainer.

A boffo choice.

But would he do it? Would he be interested in taking his possibly semi-illegal bent up several notches and doing something like this?

He got up from his chair, the details of the proposal, but also its potential rewards, bouncing around inside his head. He was tired. He felt confined. He needed some fresh air.

He needed to be alone.

"Anulka, it's getting a little late. I'm really not in the mood to go out this evening. Would it be okay if we ate dinner here in the room? I'm going to go for a short walk, maybe a half hour or so, to think about what you've just told me. I'm sorry, but I just can't talk with you about all this at the moment."

His eyes bored into hers. "Please don't misunderstand me. I'm not angry at you or disappointed in you or what you've said. I just need to be alone for a while. If you're okay with dinner here in the room, then please order us anything you see that looks good and tell the waiter to bring several bottles of beer in an ice bucket with him when he comes up. Okay?"

She rose and went to him. She put her arms around him, raised her head and kissed him.

"I understand. I'll order something. Go take your walk."

The dinner took over forty-five minutes to arrive. Felix arrived back just as the waiter was leaving the room. *Steak au poivre* for the both of them. *Fois gras* topped with drops from a light orange sauce as appetizer.

He stood, still at the door, looking at her. Their eyes locked. No words were spoken. He walked over to her, pushing the dinner cart and the table set for dinner gently to one side. The enormous emotional stress of their conversation had not left them untouched. The enormity of the act they were contemplating hung over them both like a dark thunder cloud, bolts of lightning shooting out from underneath it in every which direction.

She stood up as he approached her. He kissed her, first softly, then harder. An enormous passion gripped them both. She clung to him, wanting his skin on hers, wanting him to put his cock deep into her as quickly as he could.

They fell onto the bed. A tangle of limbs and clothes, an intensity of desire, a raging fire in their heads, and in their bellies, that one round would never be able to extinguish.

The next morning, as they lay in bed, he gave her an answer. He wanted to help. He understood perfectly her intentions. He asked her a couple of questions about the details of the plan.

He told her that, for the moment, his answer could be neither yes nor no. He needed time to think. He would need to speak privately with Ben in several days' time. Probably invite him in the evening to his apartment in Bad Homburg for something to eat and a couple of beers. Or maybe breakfast on the weekend so they'd have the space and time for a serious talk.

He would call her immediately afterwards, indicating that they would or, unfortunately, would not be accepting her invitation to the "party" she was giving in Zurich.

The bigger risk lay with Ben, he observed, since he would be the one going into the bank to pick up the cash. He told her, frankly, he didn't know what he would say. However, one thing was clear: it would have to be a joint decision between himself and Ben. That, he felt, was the most important thing he had to say to her. Everything else they could discuss later when a decision had been made.

She smiled at him. It was a fair answer and a fair proposal.

She was hungry. She needed a coffee—and some breakfast. She looked for the phone to order something. And to have room service come up and pick up the room service cart. How embarrassing, she thought. What will they be thinking about us downstairs when they see those uneaten dinners?

His hand gently grasped hers as she picked up the receiver. She turned and looked at him. He was right.

The fire wasn't out yet.

27
The Penthouse Apartment of Felix Hofmaier

Landgrafenstrasse
Bad Homburg vor der Hoehe bei Frankfurt
Germany

August 4   10:32 am

Felix sat in his favorite easy chair, looking out at the large park bordering the Landgrafenstrasse. Beautiful, warm August morning. The sliding doors were open to the terrace, the flowers in full bloom in the pots hanging along its outside retaining wall.

They need water, he thought.

Damned weather in this country. When it shouldn't rain, it does. Copiously. And when it should rain, it doesn't, often for weeks on end.

The pages of the Saturday edition of the *Frankfurter Allgemeine Zeitung* lay scattered around his chair, most of them already read. The rest of his breakfast, on a small tray, was shoved onto the side table next to him. The coffee was still warm, with more in the kitchen ready to go.

Ben was due to arrive at eleven and Felix didn't feel like making another pot. What the hell, the guy wouldn't even notice it. Probably hung over again from some exhausting trolling exercise the previous evening in one of the hot new clubs out by the Frankfurt Airport. Well, let him have his parties and what comes afterwards. He's a big boy. He can handle it.

His face darkened. Renauer. The day before yesterday, that lying bastard had actually called him on his cell phone while he was still in his mother's apartment in Thalwil. As if nothing had happened. As if he hadn't killed her at all. He'd asked, perfectly cool and collected, how he was coming along with sorting out his mother's apartment. If there was anything he could do to help, he'd wanted to know.

Nothing, thank you.

Hard questions had haunted him after he'd hung up. How does one begin to hold back the temptation to fire a verbal broadside at another person when one knows how much they deserve it? How does one control oneself when one knows the murderer of one's mother is on the line? How does one calmly listen to that someone talking on about the hard client work he's involved in or spouting sweet nothings about how terribly much he misses his mother and her quiet, effective counsel?

He'd known the answer to every question. One does it with self-control and discipline. And patience because one knows another day is coming, bringing with it, justice—and payback. He knew that any, out-of-control, emotional confrontation between them both might possibly lead to Renauer murdering him, knowing that Felix knew about the murder, just as he'd brutally taken the life of his mother.

For his part, there was no way he would—or could—murder Renauer. If that were to happen, the bastard would be gone forever and would only suffer several quick moments of fear and pain before everything went permanently black: the first moment knowing he was facing death, and the second, suffering the deadly effects of the instrument that would cause it.

Definitely not enough. There was a much better punishment for him, one that would cause him constant mental anguish, that would have him, every second of his waking hours—and, hopefully, his sleepless nights—, regretting the fact that he'd committed fraud, that he'd murdered, that he'd brutally taken a life for his own selfish reasons.

From the very start, he'd known he would wait several months before initiating his plan. Too much going on at the moment. Delaying any action would also have Renauer believing he'd gotten away with what he'd done, that he was also in the clear with Felix. And, when the blow finally fell, when it was time for revenge, Felix would have the opportunity to enjoy his pain without any distractions. And without fear of any repercussions. Whatever Renauer thought, he would never suspect from what direction the blow had come.

He smiled slightly as he stood up to go to the kitchen

to refill his coffee cup. He took a sip. He looked at the pot. Damn it to hell. I'm going to buy another brand of coffee the next time I shop. This stuff turns strong and bitter way too fast.

He went back into the living room and sat down. Cynicism was not his game and, certainly, not a weapon he liked to use. However, the events of the last week, particularly that one night with Anulka in Geneva, had thrown his life into even more turmoil.

What a mess.

Up came the screen. Even without Anulka and her proposal, a whole, long shit list scrolled slowly down in his mind like the credits for a lousy film: still no definitive word from the Handelsbank in Frankfurt, possible financial ruin, an uncertain professional future, his mother's murder and its effects on his emotions, meetings with his tax advisors to make sure he was on the legal side of the income tax laws, his teenage daughter with a birthday next week—or maybe the week after, he wasn't sure, and no way to communicate directly with her, the possible Paris assignment and the extreme stress it would put on him, and Ben's increasingly excessive, after-hour antics that could possibly impinge upon his ability to do substantive and effective work, no matter who the client was.

And, if all that wasn't enough, there were crumbs and pieces from the breakfast rolls all over the floor, some of them with little globs of honey still sticking to them. No wonder his shoes had stuck a bit to the kitchen tiles when he'd gone to get more coffee. Must have stepped on them as I got up, he'd thought. Damn it. Now I have honey sticking all over the soles of my shoes.

Shit. Everything is going south.

He shifted his weight on the couch. And, then suddenly, there was Anulka in his head again, the main event, the giant of all giant issues.

This was serious stuff. What she'd proposed in Geneva had interested him—how could it not?—, but also made him seriously worry. On the one hand, he knew he was falling in love with her. She needed his help. Her plan, carried out successfully, would help solve, if worst came to worst, any short-term, major financial problems he might face with his firm.

And she could restart her life.

On the other hand, the worry he felt was not only logical in such a situation, but also intensive because of the extreme risks involved and their possible, long-term consequences for his life. One minor hiccup and he would, no question about it, spend the rest of his life in the slammer.

He knew she hadn't told him everything, holding him to his promise not to ask questions about the blackmail or the blackmailer. Or anything else. Even after a short discussion in her hotel room the following morning, reviewing the whole mechanics of the operation, Felix was still uncertain as to his correct course of action.

There was also a little nagging voice at the back of his mind, asking him if he were not somehow being led down the garden path, if not all the lovey-dovey and the sex and her intense focus on him were just a form of subterfuge to soften him up, to make him take that kind of a serious step from which there would be no return.

But in his heart of hearts, he wanted to believe her, he did believe her. It was a credible story. And she was in danger. Those were convincing arguments speaking against any trickery on her part.

Malleable and superficial Felix, Felix in his own dark world, larcenous Felix would not have been Felix if he hadn't been attracted by the idea of being able to play the knight in shining armor, to help her solve her problems and, while doing so, simultaneously solve his own problems. What was it his English friend, Malcolm Samuels, had once said when they'd discussed the possibility of making an investment together? No risk, no reward?

The buzzer sounded. Well, finally. He got up and let Ben in.

The man looked like hell. Unshaven. Hadn't brushed his teeth apparently. Clothes looked like he'd slept in them. Or perhaps not as the case may be.

He grabbed his friend by the shoulders, looked him in the eye.

"Ben, you look terrible. Get your butt into the bathroom and take a shower and wake up. We've got a lot to discuss and I need you functioning, not looking like a pile of warmed-over dog shit."

Thirty minutes later, they sat facing one another in the living room, Ben holding his second cup of coffee, his dark hair combed straight back from his forehead, eyes halfway alert. Some borrowed clothes from Felix's closet had halfway fit his somewhat smaller frame.

The dance could begin.

They'd known each other for a long time. And there wasn't much each of them didn't know about the other. At least, Felix had always assumed that that was the case. But thinking you know someone doesn't automatically mean you really *know* that person.

He discovered in the next two hours that he'd been seriously off the mark with his assumption that he knew just about everything about his friend Ben. He didn't. Not even close to it.

Anulka had been absolutely right. Ben was a real number.

Felix got right into it, describing to Ben his relationship with Anulka, his meetings with her, and her proposal to him. No perfume. No flowers. Nothing left out. Straight facts.

He emphasized the fact that *any* decision, either for or against, would have to be one made and agreed to by the both of them. In a neutral voice, neither asking for nor expecting support, he told Ben everything he knew or could remember, the money Anulka would get, the risks of the operation for everyone concerned. Why the amount to be taken needed to be 5,000,000 Euros to equalize in some way those risks. The division of the money: 1,250,000 Euros for Ben and 1,250,000 Euros for himself. The rest for Anulka.

Not a word from Ben. He just sat there, occasionally

smiling, occasionally nodding, several times burping up some gaseous remains of whatever he'd had the previous night to eat.

Disgusting, thought Felix.

"That it?" Ben asked when he'd stopped talking.

Felix nodded. "Yup, you've heard it all."

Ben smiled. He got up, walked out onto the terrace, leaned over the plants to look down at the park, then came back into the living room, looking Felix in the eye and, with a mischievous grin on his face, spoke the unexpected.

"Beautiful. What a chance!"

He moved back to his chair and sat down, leaning forward while rubbing his two hands together.

He was definitely awake now. He looked Felix in the eye.

"When do we start?" he asked.

Felix looked at him. Speechless. Not believing what he'd just heard.

Then it started. No formal consulting-speak. No office double-speak. Just down-and-dirty consternation and down-and-dirty street language.

"Wait a minute there, Ben. What the fuck! Are you telling me you're willing to go in and pop that damn bank for five million Euros? Just like that? No problems. Just 'let's do it? No doubts. No concerns. No questions. Shit, can I believe that? Are you sure you heard everything I said? Is somebody home there in that head of yours? Damn it, this is serious stuff and we need to talk seriously about it. And I mean seriously, you understand that?!"

Ben looked at him, his eyes flashing.

"Yes, damn it, I heard everything. And I understood everything and, yes, my brain is functioning. And, by the way, your questions and your attitude are really pissing me off. So back off, Felix."

He stood again and walked to the terrace door, looking out for several seconds, then turned back to him, angrier than Felix had ever seen him.

"Now, my friend, you listen to me for a moment, damn it. I heard you loud and clear. With all respect, your problem is that your mother and her death and your need to clear up things in Zurich are starting to twist your brain cells around in your head. I can understand that. But since you've asked, let me give you straight out my reasons for answering the way I did."

"There are a lot of them so you better be patient and listen damn carefully."

"First of all, what the hell do you think I've been thinking about the last days with this whole matter of the Handelsbank and all the uncertainty surrounding it and no idea how it's going to shake out and you off screwing some Swiss action all the time? The pressure of not knowing how or if the insurance company will handle the whole mess—and how the bank will react to what Heinz is proposing to them—has me really worried."

Ben started pacing back and forth in front of Felix. Then he stopped and stared directly at Felix.

Definitely pissed.

"Secondly, how the hell do you think I feel about the firm's reputation and my reputation and my image with some of my old Gulf contacts who gave us those consulting assignments way back when? What the fuck do you think I'm thinking when I look at our monthly profit and loss statement and see only red, red, red? And that every month for the last eight months."

"And then there's an expense report lying on my desk showing almost three thousand Euros in expenses from your recent little fuck trip to Paris. Not including airfare. That bill is apparently still outstanding. Probably paid for with another one of your numerous, continually maxed-out credit cards."

"Here's another big question for you, Felix. What the hell do you think I've been thinking when I look at my future in this firm and what I need to do to protect myself? Both financially and legally, which I'm sure you can understand, because you're in the same shitty situation I find myself in. But with one big difference, my friend. I know what I'm going to do. I have a plan."

"When I look at you sitting there, trembling about the proposal Anulka has made to you, worrying about what to do when you haven't really got much in the way of alternatives, then I see someone who doesn't have a clue about where he's going and how he's going to get there. And my comment to that is one word. Shit."

Ben now even more agitated.

"You look at me like I'm crazy or something. Well, let me tell you something."

He paused. "No, let me tell you everything. First of all, I'm going to resign from the firm as soon as we get this thing with the Handelsbank completely taken care of. Also forget Paris and that little deal you've got going over there. No Paris consulting. No nothing. In fact, you can have my verbal resignation now; a final effective "last day", if you will, can be arranged when the bank problem—and my responsibility with it—has been resolved. And, oh, yes, you can also have my little pile of shares in the firm. Gratis."

"Second, I'm thinking of moving back down to the Gulf. To Sharjah to be exact. I've been offered a really interesting position with the same bank I used to work for, you know it, the Banque Sharjah Denier, probably starting in their Corporate Acquisition division where I worked years ago."

He smiled to himself. "They're also making noises about sending me to the Far East at some point in the future since they want to expand their business there. Or whatever. All very interesting and a hell of a lot better than where I am right now, Felix. Yes, we have a close friendship, a long history together, but, as you've probably noticed by now, that friendship does have a few limits to it."

Volume still high.

"Third, what the hell do you think I've been doing all the time here in Frankfurt? You know, I came here to work with you to restore some sanity to my life after the high-pressure cooker of my ten years in Sharjah. I was burned out. I needed to decompress after all I had been through and done. And thanks to you, I was able to at least get back some of that sanity. But now I'm done. And I mean done. Over and out done."

Ben paused for a second, regarding Felix closely before he continued to speak.

"Apropos those ten years in the Gulf. What do you think I was involved in down there? Maybe playing tiddlywinks or going to long lunches or dodging the hot sun? No, I'll tell you *exactly* what I was doing. I was getting rich, Felix. Savor that word, my friend. Rich. Filthy, fucking rich."

"Ben, I really don't think . . . !"

"Shut up, damn it, this is all stuff you need to know! I've had it with all the bullshit so let me finish."

Ben stared at Felix, then took a deep breath and plunged right back into it.

"Do you know the amount of dollars in cash that pour into the Gulf from Afghanistan or Pakistan or other parts of that region every week and every month? Cash, Felix, major cash. Millions and tens of millions of dollars from the stupid American spooks and their allies trying to push their weight around by buying or trying to buy influence with some of the local ass-kickers or tribal chieftains or local governments or whatever these kind of people call themselves. These guys take the money, say thank you, and then off it goes out of the country. All of it flowing from East to West. It never stops."

"Roll that word 'millions' around on your tongue for a minute, Felix. Do you know how most of that cash money gets from those countries to the Gulf and then into the banks there? How it then becomes 'legal tender' in a safe haven, meaning bank account, for use in buying or paying for no matter what in this world? Do you know how that kind of money is physically transported? And who's doing it? And getting a damn good piece of it, legally or, sometimes, by force? Or because everybody else involved in transporting it got shot up and killed. Not your normal slave, I can tell you that."

He leaned in closer. "Now, I ask you, who the hell do you think was involved in—and profiting big time from— that little game? And flying his ass around all over the place in that godforsaken region, sometimes in the middle of the night? Landing on some air strips you wouldn't even consider categorizing as a halfway suitable dirt road. Or being shot at. And sometimes even shooting back. And hitting some people. Even killing them. Or sweating out some piece of shit border control idiot, smiling his ass off because he wanted a nice little payoff, who'd decided to take a look at what that little private jet with Ben sitting in it had just brought with it from some hellhole in the region? Do you think the Fairy Godmother was doing all of that, Felix? Fuck no, she wasn't!"

Ben was now spitting the words out. Firing them at Felix to make him finally understand his friend and what drove him.

"Another question for you: do you know how many Pakistanis and Indians live and work their asses off in construction on the Gulf? Do you think all those guys have bank accounts? Well, I'll tell you. They don't. You want to know what do they do with all the money they earn building those beautiful buildings you see in all the pictures of Dubai and Abu Dhabi? They transfer it to somewhere else in the region. Or even further away."

"To do that, they have a system, my friend. '*Hawala*' it's called or 'chit'. Not a formal system. An age-old system, built on one thing only, on the trust between the people involved."

"Do you know how that informal underground 'banking system' works? I bet not. So, I'm going to tell you what it is. It's the perfect money laundering machine. No bank involved. Functions under the radar. Cash on one end, cash on the other, and only communication and trust in between. Really a good system because it's cost effective, built on trust and connections, and, under normal conditions, uses no negotiable instruments for the 'money transfers'."

He paused for a second, weighing his words once more.

"What the hell do you think I was doing when I was running around in the souks or in those people's barracks or on their job sites in that fucking heat, sweating my ass off, talking and visiting and building trust and learning some of the language from all those guys working there? Or loaning some of them money for their use within the Hawala system and then profiting from the business they did every day, multiple times a day?"

"What, Felix, what was I doing? Looking for a bathroom or an outhouse to dump all that strong black coffee shit those people like to drink all day long? Hell, no, I wasn't," he shouted.

He stopped for a second, his face red. Still more to say.

"I'll tell you something. When I think about those times, I can tell you, I'm not even telling you the half of it. Screw that. Not even a quarter of it. Hell, I probably broke more laws in one year than have been written in the last ten years."

"I've got four, or maybe it's five, false passports lying in a safe deposit box in Sharjah. And two loaded 9mm Glocks with extra magazines lying on top of them. Beautiful weapons. Damn things are useful, I can tell you. The one thing I haven't done is murder. And, of course, rape. When I think about it, I never had to—or wanted to," he said, laughing quietly to himself for a moment.

"Nevertheless, I'm sure my soul will probably roast in hell one day. But right now, I'm living, my friend, living, and I intend to keep on doing that as long as I can. And running and playing hard as long as I see possibilities to make the big plays, to grab a hunk of all that change out there for myself. That's what I do. And I have no intention of stopping . . . , that I can assure you."

Ben smiled at Felix. Not a mean smile. Not a friendly smile. Just a smile. Voice an octave lower.

"I live high, Felix. You know it. Or, on second thought, maybe you don't. Let me give you just one more little example. You remember my telling you about my vacations down on the Cote d'Azur? You probably thought I was renting a little shithole, one room apartment somewhere up on the Grande Corniche near Nice and just holing up there for two weeks while I was blowing around the area, chasing some of the Nordic action that had come down to the Cote for the summer. And mostly walking or using a small bicycle because I couldn't afford a rental car. And eating at the French version of McDonalds."

"Well, I can tell you. It isn't so. And it never was so. Rich does what rich does, Felix. So here's the story. I own a four-bedroom penthouse apartment on Cap Ferrat, right next to where the cruise ships come into the harbor and drop anchor. The women love it."

"You know that area. Right next to Villefranche-sur-Mer and its harbor. The apartment's all paid for. Beautiful old three-story, Art Deco building high up on a small hill out toward the end of the Cap. And on top of it, my penthouse. It had been partially renovated and rebuilt when I bought it, but I tossed out all that tasteless shit, and had it completely redone."

He smiled at the thought. "It has a great view directly along the coast to Monaco and Menton—and in the other direction toward Nice. You couldn't buy it today for under twenty-eight million Euros. Over eight thousand two hundred square feet of heaven. Got some great furnishings and art and stuff in there. Nice big swimming pool with that infinity negative edge on it out on the terrace facing the west."

"Know what I got parked in the garage down on the lower level? A black Porsche Speedster convertible. Had that baby fitted out for racing. Six speed stick. Big tail pipes. Great sound. One hot machine, I can tell you. Should get yourself one sometime. And what do I do with it? I drive up and down the Croisette in Cannes at midnight on a hot summer night."

"The women, they love that shit," he added, with just a slight touch of acid in his voice. "Just can't fit them all into the car at the same time."

"So, Felix, your little deal with the Bankhaus Finsler? Let me make sure you understand what I'm thinking here. It'd be a damn nice diversion if done right. Probably net us all a nice sum of money."

"So why shouldn't I be sitting here and telling you, yes, okay, let's do it? Money is money and I can always use more. Besides the whole deal sounds good and doable, and even like fun, so why not? And when I say that, don't think that because I use the word fun that I'd treat the mechanics of this pop in a cavalier fashion. Believe me, you will never ever see me as focused and concentrated as I am when I know some fucking hot money deal is going down. Particularly when I'm personally involved in making that hot deal happen."

"Your deal? No, pardon me, Anulka's deal, is a good deal. I don't even hesitate with something like that."

He looked away for several long seconds, then turned back to Felix again, his voice now softening a degree or two.

"One last thing. Don't be disappointed in me or be surprised at what I've told or said to you this morning. I regret that I didn't tell you all of this much earlier. And perhaps I was a little too rough in the telling. I'm sorry for that. But know one thing, Felix. I've been loyal to you all these years, and I remain that today. In spite of everything that has happened, and is happening. And in spite of my intentions to put a different spin on my life in the future. That you can and must believe. Because it's true."

Felix stood up and walked in stony silence out onto the terrace. Ben watched him go, then decided he needed another cup of coffee in the kitchen.

He'd known it all along and yet he hadn't known it. Those hot irons he'd always thought Ben had in the fire? Hell, the guy had huge steel girders heating up in its flames. And it wasn't just a fire.

It was a damn conflagration.

Okay. Decision made, he thought. We do it.

And I live with Ben the way he is. Besides, even if he doesn't really need the money, *I* need the money. That's for damn sure.

His thoughts turned to Ben's tirade. Disappointed? Not really. Friendship gone? Not really. Just different now. More honest? Perhaps. Still built on trust? Probably most of it still intact. Enough for what we are planning to do? Most likely. Still more work to be done to get back to where they both were before this morning? Definitely.

Some short-term planning issues flashed through his mind. We likely have no future. But we have to make it possible for the rest of the consultants to finish their current work. And then we liquidate the firm. Clean and neat.

Paris. I'll convince him we need to take care of that as long as it goes.

The Handelsbank issue isn't going to go away soon, he thought. Maybe a couple of months, if not more, until we see some, if any, resolution there. Plenty of time to do the job in France. And keep up the sham of being busy while we do what we've decided to do in Zurich.

After that? Black hole. Or maybe back to Switzerland to set up my tent. And maybe do some part-time consulting. Hell, I could even move into my mother's old apartment and keep all of her furniture instead of giving part of it away.

Why not? Not a bad idea at all.

Felix went back into the living room. Saw that Ben was back from the terrace, sitting at one end of the couch.

He plopped down at the other end, met his gaze and held it.

"Damn it, Ben. I'm sorry. I didn't mean to set you off like that. But what you just told me? Man, that's just damn unbelievable. I had no idea."

He turned his body more to his right, studying his friend for a moment more closely.

He spoke softly, intensely. "You know, I thought I knew you well. And now it seems, I didn't really know you at all. I think that's really sad. But no matter. It's better that I know how you really feel instead of the way it was before. I can deal much better with the truth and reality than you might think, my friend."

He paused, reflecting for a moment. Then he spoke again, his voice now even more soft and even in tone.

"God, Ben, what a hot life you've led. Funny, I always sort of suspected you had a real program going. But I had no idea what you were really doing down there in the Gulf. And then that you hit it big-time rich with all that stuff? No real word for that, Ben. Just wow!"

"No, really. Don't give me that raised-eyebrow look. I congratulate you, I really do."

Felix looked at him closely. Ben still waiting for a serious reaction to his comments on Anulka's proposal.

"And as far as the Finsler bank deal goes, I can tell you honestly, and I mean this, I'm glad you've said yes. I told you, it had to be the both of us together. Or nothing. Now, it's a go. And I'm fine with that."

Ben smiled, then nodded. "Good."

He wasn't in the mood to say anything more. Or to ask any more detailed questions. That could come later, he thought. It was the concept that counted now.

A loose end needed clearing up.

"There is one more thing I do want to say, Ben. It concerns your resignation. And I'm going to say it formally. I'm damn sorry our working relationship is going to end. It makes me very sad to think that what we've built together hasn't lasted. But then, I have to admit, I'm certainly much more to blame for that than you."

"As far as putting an official stamp on everything is concerned, we can shake hands on that right now. What does one say? I accept with regret . . . yeah, that's it. With deep regret. Yes, Ben, certainly that."

He stood. Ben followed him up. They shook hands. And then they hugged each other. Both knew the game and how it was going to have to be played. Two old friends taking the first tentative steps toward trying to find their way back to what had been, less than an hour ago, a deep friendship based on trust and confidence. And respect.

Both of them sat down again. Felix turned to Ben, studying his face.

"You know, Ben, I am curious about one thing. If you have that kind of money, why take the risk of doing something that could possibly blow up in your face? And perhaps ruin the good life you're leading. Why that, tell me?"

Ben smiled that Cheshire cat smile of his and, in a very quiet voice, answered the question.

"That's a fair question, Felix. And I'll give you a serious answer. You've been listening to me talk a great deal this morning about my life. I don't think I left any doubt in your mind that I am not your typical modern guy. I take risks. That's my game. That's what I love to do."

"I judge the facts, I balance the risks and the rewards, and if the latter outweigh the former, then I go for it. Your deal with Anulka? I think it's doable, in fact, very doable. It's the kind of risk I like, not just an in-and-out deal, but a real operation over time. A bank, an inside track, a dependable partner, the money? Hell, that's a deal that really gets me going."

"Risk? It's been my best friend for a long time. And that will always be the case. Never going to change, that's for damn sure."

They looked at each other. Everything out on the table. Everything discussed.

Everything decided.

28
Autobahn 13
Bad Ragaz Exit
Bad Ragaz
Switzerland

November 24   The same year   11:08 am

Anulka was going to be late for the meeting. Taking the Bad Ragaz exit off the A 13, she'd suddenly had to stop. A multiple rear-end collision about a hundred yards ahead of where her car stood. Her arrival probably delayed by at least twenty to thirty minutes, if not more. And no call possible to alert Giovanni.

Too dangerous without a throwaway.

Well, he can just wait, she thought. He knew she could run into traffic coming from Zurich. Well, it wasn't traffic. It was an accident. But not one in which she was involved. That would have screwed up the meeting for sure.

She looked with distaste at the corner of the small package lying on the seat next to her. One of its corners peeked out from underneath the jacket she'd thrown over it when getting into her car in Zollikon. 80,000 Euros in 500 Euro notes packed inside, the first down payment on the 480,000 Euros she still owed Giovanni and his gofer.

She opened the driver-side window. A fresh, late-autumn smell came into the car.

She glanced anew at the package lying next to her, thought about how she'd managed to reach the point where she'd been able to tap into another client's money, money from a German client, a client who, through contract and price manipulations, had allegedly fleeced the Greek defense authorities of millions and millions of Euros.

The persons responsible for the contracts they had concluded with him long gone into Greek prisons, the perpetrator, the client, still free, occasionally running around the Aeolian Islands, a volcanic chain of small islands just north of the coast of Sicily, showing up occasionally in the Italian social press during the summer with the one or the other scantily-clad "beach candy" on his arm.

They'd chosen him because of his propensity to transfer his money from the island of Cypress in the Mediterranean directly to his account in Zurich. With one exception, he had never been to the bank in Zurich for a visit.

Another "perfect" client.

She smiled, remembering the day in August when Felix had let her know that both he and Ben had agreed to accept her proposal. A good day, a serious day, a fateful day.

The prep time for the run at the bank had gone smoothly.

With Felix and Ben spending most of their time in Paris, it had taken a little longer to get everything ready. However, by the end of September, all parts of the plan had been discussed and agreed upon. Required documents had been provided for and all potential risks identified and planned for.

She opened a small bottle of apple juice she'd bought at the last autobahn service area. Taking small sips at a time, she thought about how different the second run at the bank had been compared to the first one. To begin with, she'd not been in love with Felix as she'd been with Giovanni. Or thought she'd been. And Felix was certainly not a man who preyed upon her dark energies, using them to his advantage as Giovanni had done. This was a pure business arrangement, even though Felix's demeanor indicated to her that he saw their relationship in a different light.

Second, Felix had a whole set of problems he needed to solve. Not the case with that greedy bastard, Giovanni. She also had a set of problems she needed to solve. Itches getting itched. Bottom line: a win-win for both with, of course, an occasional side benefit thrown in. She smiled at the thought.

Third, she'd known exactly who would be coming to the bank. He wasn't an unknown factor like the first time. Although his partner had played the role of bag man, Giovanni hadn't revealed a single detail whatsoever about his partner or where he came from.

Certainly, a smart move at the time to protect her—and him as well. It made the meetings she'd had with him in the bank totally neutral. No danger of familiarity. No pre-knowledge of the other person which could perhaps color the discussion and potentially endanger the process.

That gofer guy had really been one strange piece of work, she thought. And obtuse. Like a robot. Uncertainty in the air every time he'd come to visit. Underneath it all, implicit in his direct gaze, was a threat of the unknown, of perhaps physical danger, or worse, if she made any mistakes. Or stopped the deal from taking place.

With Ben, it was entirely different. And it had also worked perfectly even with knowing him and having coordinated with him in advance the mechanics of each meeting at the bank.

Ben had made his first visit at the beginning of October. He'd arrived at the bank, having called eight days in advance for an appointment. Underground garage. Welcome. Conference Room upstairs.

She'd been extra careful not to give any sign she knew the man who intended to withdraw five million Euros in tranches from "his" account over a period of several months. One misstep and the whole deal would have gone south in a hurry.

What had surprised her was the job he'd done in matching his appearance to that of the real client. Eye color correct. Hair color with the right "aging". Regional German accent perfect. Something stuffed in his cheeks to make him look heavier and fuller in the face. Middle gray, double-breasted suit with a green-patterned BOSS tie against a striped blue shirt. A three-day beard.

He'd handled the forged signature on the required documents without any hesitation whatsoever. Excellent facsimile. His false passport was of German origin, a Hamburg professional, he had said, when they had discussed it in one of their meetings. The real client's German passport was on record at the bank. Perfect fit.

But it was the character of the meetings they'd had that had really surprised her.

During the whole time he was in the bank, his eyes had continually signaled his amusement at how they both were handling everything. At one point, she'd almost laughed at his facial expression. He hadn't said anything out of place, but the impression he'd made on her was astounding. He'd actually enjoyed the whole damn process. Cool as cool could be, she thought. Not a hair or nerve out of place.

Definitely a player. And, definitely, the better man.

She drank the rest of the cider, then put the empty bottle on the seat beside her. Despite her anxiety about the imminent meeting with Giovanni, she smiled for a second, reflecting on how unique and interesting life could be sometimes.

One day after Ben's first visit in the bank, they'd all met at a lonely picnic area along the Swiss side of the Rhine outside of Zurich to divide up the first tranche. No one around. Bad weather and a chill matching the lateness of the season.

She'd watched, bemused, as Ben had stuffed his 25 percent share of the money into a small white pillowcase he'd apparently brought along for that purpose. "Stole it from my hotel," he'd said, with an innocent look on his face, as he arranged the notes carefully inside its folds.

Anulka and Felix had looked at each other, then looked down at the over-the-shoulder messenger bags each of them had brought with them. Normal money-carrying equipment, so to speak.

But a pillowcase? All of them had had a good laugh at that.

As they'd divided up the money, there'd been no averted eyes, downcast looks, sideward glances, or nervousness. Not a bad conscience anywhere in sight. It was almost as if they were there on the river enjoying a Sunday picnic lunch.

That made it easier for all of us, she'd thought.

Afterwards, she'd observed the both of them, standing several steps away from her near the edge of a small cliff, looking down at the slow-moving Rhine river. She was astonished at how relaxed they appeared.

She'd also felt a calmness she'd not known for a long time. Perhaps it was because she was finally on the way to solving her problems. Whatever had been causing that feeling in her that day, she'd known it was all good.

As she'd stuffed the Euros into her messenger bag, she'd thought about what she would do with her fifty percent share of the money. The major part of it would go into her safe deposit box where it would join the rest of the money already there. The rest, exactly 80,000 Euros, she would keep separate.

She had a client meeting planned in Bad Ragaz. And she was looking forward to enjoying a hot bath at the Tamina

Thermal in town, then walking around the spa park with its several large Sequoia redwoods.

It was also on the grounds of that park that she intended to arrange a meeting with Giovanni and give him that money. If he wanted it, he could damn well drive up from Milano and pick it up.

Felix had his safe haven at a bank in Thalwil. She'd been there in the village one day, having coffee with him at the local cafe, when he'd pointed out a building across the street.

"I have a nice big safe deposit box in the lower level of that bank", he'd said.

She'd looked at him, questioning his decision to keep the money in Thalwil. He'd explained to her that he hoped to move to Switzerland as soon as possible and to live in his mother's old apartment. That bank was close to where he would live.

His reasoning for the move was understandable. Because of all the negative publicity in Germany relating to his person and his firm, that country no longer represented a viable, long-term, future business opportunity for him.

Just before they'd gone to their respective cars, Felix had asked Ben where he'd be safekeeping his money. Ben had laughed and said he'd rented a small unit at one of the self-storage facilities near Kloten Airport.

A self-storage unit?

Felix spoke first. "That's really crazy. And, besides, is that really safe?"

"No, believe me, it isn't." he answered.

"But, you know, doing something like that is actually very simple," Ben said. "I just walked in and spoke to the guy at the front desk. I told him I was working as a consultant in Zurich and didn't want to cart all my files back and forth to Frankfurt where I live. I said I would need the unit for six months. Signed the required documents. Paid the rent in cash for the first three months. Done."

He grinned at them, enjoying the telling. "Then, I went to a local builder's market, bought myself a small combination lock for the door and now I'm all set. In fact, when we're finished here, I'm going to be going directly there."

She'd just stared at him. He would be parking hundreds of thousands of Euros in cash, eventually, if everything worked out, 1,250,000 Euros inside a simple, self-storage unit? All that money in a pillowcase?

With one single schlock lock on the outside door to keep it all safe?

Crazy. Absolutely crazy.

Anulka's opinion of him had a small additional qualifier in it, reflecting how impressed she was by him and his attitude: crazy, maybe, but, if so, genial crazy.

Later that same evening, she'd sat in the living room of her apartment, preparing to set the machinery in motion: the time had come to contact Giovanni in order to arrange a meet with him. She anticipated it would be the first of several she would need in order to get all the money to him.

There was desperation, a feeling of deep hopelessness in her. Even though she was still intensively involved with her myriad duties within the bank, she knew those obligations had a limited shelf life. She wanted only one thing, a life in sync with the person she really was.

She wanted out.

She'd trembled as she'd grasped the throwaway phone, flashes of fear shooting like electric darts through her whole body.

God help me, she'd thought, I can endure anything in the world but this. Having to talk to him again. And then having to see him again.

She remembered well the drill she had to go through in order to reach him. Use a throwaway phone. Call his number. Let it ring a total of three times. Hang up. Repeat the same procedure again. Call back again exactly five minutes later after the second call. Wait for him to pick up.

Pacing back and forth in her living room, and then on the terrace, she'd done exactly that. He'd answered on the fifth ring.

Her whole body had started to shake as she heard his voice. No how-are-you. No long-time-no-hears for her. The heat of her hatred pushed back down deep inside.

The words had rushed out of her mouth. Haven't got much time to talk. Here's the deal: I'm going to be in Bad Ragaz on November 24th for a visit with two clients. Won't take the whole day. Got some time left over in between. How about a short walk in the spa park and a coffee afterwards. I know your birthday is coming up and I would like to give you your present personally.

His answer had been yes.

She hadn't expected anything less.

He'd played the game. He'd said he had two or three meetings to attend in Chur, not far from where she would be. He would schedule them around that date so he could meet her in Bad Ragaz at the same time she'd be there.

He'd understood fully what she was really saying. She'd understood fully what he was really saying. He didn't have one single damn thing to do in Switzerland, not one single appointment, but he would come anyway because he knew what was in play.

She was going to get them the rest of the money.

"What time?" he'd asked her. She'd told him, hurrying on, heading for the final goodbye as quickly as possible.

Will look for you on the main path of the park when I arrive. Could be late because of traffic, but coming in any case. Gotta go. Bye. Click.

Dial tone.

Despair. Sweat on her forehead. Her stomach had signaled to her it was about to send back upstairs everything she'd had for dinner. She'd just barely made it to the toilet.

Afterwards, she'd lain on her bed, trembling, a foul taste still in her mouth. From what her stomach had disgorged. But also, from having had to listen to his voice on the phone, even for so short a time.

But the deal was done. Her trip toward freedom had finally started. At least that.

Or so she assumed.

29
Spa Park Next to the Park Hotel Bad Ragaz

Bad Ragaz

Canton St. Gallen

Switzerland

November 24   11:31 am

An ambulance siren howled up ahead of her. The police had made one-lane movement of traffic possible. The rear-ender was a multiple mess of twisted car parts and steel.

She slowly inched forward past the location of the accident, then drove directly into the center of town.

After several minutes of cruising back and forth, she finally found a parking spot on the Flora Weg, just outside the Park Hotel's grounds, and only a few steps from the park. She would check in later.

She put the brown package into a MIGROS plastic shopping bag. She took the main path into the park, the hotel just visible through the bushes lining the park boundary.

When she'd been younger, she'd stayed there several times with her parents. It hadn't been fancy then, and it still wasn't fancy, but she remembered walking down a narrow path from the street to the front of the hotel, thinking it was the most beautiful thing she'd ever seen.

She looked around, scanning the park, seeing but not seeing the trees, the towering sequoias, the neatness of the flower beds, the beauty of it all.

Suddenly, she saw him, fifty yards away, standing at the crossroad of two paths. He was looking directly at her.

In spite of the warmth of the day, a sudden, ice-cold chill coursed through her whole body. Her skin seemed to crawl back into itself. She wanted to turn and run. She felt faint.

Rational thought drove her forward. Do what you came here to do, she thought to herself. Give him the package, then turn around and walk away. Fast.

He didn't move as she approached him. No friendly look on his face. Just a mask. No smile. No handshake. No you-look well comments. Or how-are-things or have-a-good-trip here questions. A simple hello on both sides. Nothing more.

They stood facing one another, two paces apart. She wanted it over with.

Yesterday.

She broke the heavy silence. "Let's get this done, Giovanni. This is what I have to tell you. I'm going to say it once. And that's it. I'm not interested in a shouting match with you in the middle of this beautiful park. So, listen carefully and don't interrupt me."

He looked at her, impassive, studying her face. "Okay, I'm listening."

She met his gaze, her eyes locked onto his.

I can do it, she thought. I'm not afraid.

"One night, long ago, you and I sat eating dinner in Cannes and started talking about stealing money. I've never been able to forget that time because it was the beginning of something that has caused me an enormous amount of pain and suffering. And sadness, if you want. Yes, I did agree to do our little deal. Yes, I even looked forward to it. Yes, together we took a lot of money out of the bank. All okay. But, as you well know, the whole situation has radically changed. You know exactly what I'm talking about so don't try to rationalize it. Or discount it. Or look innocent. Or perhaps say you're sorry when I know very well that that's not at all how you really feel."

"I'm not going to dwell on all that has happened or hasn't happened. I don't want to think about your treachery. And I'm certainly not going to dwell on the blackmail you may think you've successfully pulled off because I've come here with money. You haven't."

He took a step closer to her. He countered, speaking quietly to her.

"Wrong. There was no treachery. And no blackmail. You're just too stupid to see it for what it all was. We had a deal and you walked out on that deal. All we wanted was for that deal to be completed. That's it."

Anger rising in her. "Shut up, you bastard. You interrupted me. Do you want me to explain things? Yes or no?"

He threw his right hand up in the air in a sign of frustration. Touchy little bitch.

"Ok, have it your way. Carry on."

She increased the tempo of her words. "Yes, we had a deal and, for your information, I intend now to do my best to honor that deal. But not because of your silly little games or because you think I owe you that money in any way, shape, or form. I intend to have a life. And that life is not going to include you or any thought of you or of what you or I did or of what was once upon a time."

She looked directly at his face, saw his hateful look.

"Or, for that matter, any of your threatening facial expressions which only diminish you because they're so infantile. You know, you really are a despicable human being. And seeing you here standing in front of me like this makes me feel sick."

He stepped toward her, his face unreadable. "Anulka"

She stood her ground. She couldn't believe how angry she suddenly felt. Here she was, perhaps still in danger, yet she was attacking him as if that possibility didn't exist. The years, the hatred, the frustration, the sadness, the torture, the brutal murder of Luca, the nightmare of worry that had been her life pushed her forward, kept the fire burning hot, fed with the oxygen of the thousands and tens of thousands of breaths she'd continually had trouble drawing to sustain herself during that hell.

"Don't talk to me, Giovanni. You just listen, damn it."

She held the MIGROS bag up for him to see. "There are 80,000 Euros in this bag. I'm in the process of trying to get more money that, if you want to put it that way, belongs to you and that Frankenstein friend of yours. I intend to have the rest, you know damn well that means 400,000 Euros, in about four to five months. It's not possible to do it all at once. So, live with it. Those five months are a reasonable period of time for what I consider to be the height of unreasonableness. I'll call you when I think we should meet again. Afterwards, you can go straight to hell as far as I'm concerned."

She extended her right hand towards him with the shopping bag hanging from it. He just stood there, a smirk on his face.

He made no move to take the bag.

Easy, she said to herself. You know what he's trying to do. Games and intimidation. Neutralize it.

"Giovanni, you look grotesque when you have that kind of a look on your face. Ever looked at yourself in the mirror when you do that?"

She looked down at the shopping bag. "Okay. If you won't take the bag, then pick it up from the ground."

She let go of the bag. With a soft thud, it hit the graveled path in front of him.

Nothing more to say. Get out of here. She turned to go.

He took a step toward her, the bag still on the ground, not picked up.

"Ok, Anulka, stop right there. You've had your say. Now listen to what I have to say to you."

She slowed her step, then stopped and turned to face him. Why not? Let's see how far he goes with this.

He looked around the area to see if anyone were within hearing distance. No one. He regarded her with a poisonous look in his eye. His words whispered, but like an unsheathed knife, striking her repeatedly, slicing into her.

"You are one stupid bitch. You should never have cut off the deal. We had a good chance to finish it. But you got yourself all in an uproar about being caught or whatever other bullshit was going through your head at the time."

"If you'd carried on, we wouldn't be standing here today. But no matter. It is as it is. You've apparently found a new way to get money out of the bank. I assume the money I see here on the ground comes from the bank. And, of course, from some other client you're screwing with. Or whatever you're doing. Bottom line: you're into big money again. Congratulations."

He leaned right into her face. "This is what we want. And don't give me any lies about not being able to do it. And don't screw me around here, Anulka. I heard what you said. I don't want to hear any teary-eyed version of your best-effort bullshit."

He mocked her. "What did you just say? 'In the process', I think were your words. Oh, yeah, and 'try to honor our deal' was also in there somewhere. Screw that."

His pinched face full of hatred, saliva at the corner of his mouth, he leaned even closer to her.

"You can and you will do this, you bitch. First of all, just so you know, I'm pissed that you've only brought 80,000 Euros with you. We thought you'd be bringing the whole amount. Well, you haven't and that's really the shits."

"So, we're going to start a new game. New conditions. First of all, we still want the rest, the 400,000 Euros, money that's apparently coming out of your new scam. But we also want something on top. From the same scam. *Moltissimi soldi di piu.* Major additional money. That means you're going to have to hustle your ass a little bit more than you planned to."

"I repeat my words so there's no misunderstanding. *Moltissimi soldi di piu. Capisci?* Got that? And I warn you. It'd better be somewhere well into a six-figure amount. Let's just say, at least another three to four hundred thousand Euros. Minimum. Should be easy for you, knowing the system the way you do. And the fact that you're very clearly right back in business. Our original business. Only, as of now, we're not benefiting from any of the extra goodies from your 'new' business."

He twisted his head to the side, looking more closely at the expression on her face.

"Don't look so surprised. Hell, it's your own damn fault. Do I care about your feelings—or anything to do with your getting that money together? Not one iota, not so much."

He put his two fingers together with just a crack of light between them to show her what he meant.

"I don't give a damn how you do it, but the next time we see each other, I want to see all that money wrapped up in one nice neat little package. After that, but only after that, are we quits with one another."

A tight smile. He mocked her. "Got your little brain wrapped around that little concept, *mia cara?*"

She moved back away from him. She wasn't looking at a human being. She was looking at the devil incarnate. And she feared for everything dear to her. He wasn't going to let her go. The blackmail was going to continue. She would never be free.

She couldn't answer. Didn't want to answer.

He continued, not waiting for her to react. "You may hate me. Frankly, I don't give a good God damn whether you do or you don't. But I hate you even more for what you've done and for how you've cheated me. Yes, cheated me. And cheated us. And screwed around with us. So, don't get that little innocent look on your face."

He paused for a second, looking away at the trees. Turning back to face her, he smiled slightly, and then spoke again, each word hitting her with the force of a fist.

"There's something else you should know that you're not going to like, but I'll say it anyway because I want to be sure that you understand what's in play here. Maybe then you'll realize how serious I am. Because I'm damn serious, believe me."

"Your life means nothing to me. *Niente.* Frankly, I don't care what happens to you. If you don't do what I'm telling you to do, then you're running a great risk. Professionally, that's for damn sure. But what you're really doing is putting your own damn life at risk."

She stared at him. And swallowed hard. What was that he was saying?

"You heard that right. It's your life that's in play here, damn you. Don't think I'm just playing here. You remember that evening in Magliaso? Do you think for one moment that the Lugano police were right when they thought your Luca had been involved in some business deal gone bad? He wasn't. I can tell you. I know he wasn't."

"He died for one reason. Because of you and your stupidity and your stubbornness. I pulled the trigger that night, Anulka. I killed your little paramour and I can pull that same trigger again." He lowered his face to look at her, his eyes burning into hers.

"I saw you running to him. I saw your face. But I wasn't aiming at you then. Now it's different. If I have to take another shot some time, then I advise you not to doubt my words here for one minute. It would be you then that I'd be looking at through that scope. And not even saying goodbye to when I feel the recoil from the shot I'd take."

"So, don't think you can screw me around. I'd get in real close just like I did the last time. Your pretty head right there in my sights. I enjoyed it then and I'd enjoy it even more this time. With a big bright smile on my face. You want to know why that smile? Because that poor bastard Luca did nothing to me, but you, you've double crossed me. And, by

God, you bitch, you'll pay for it if you don't toe the line the way I tell you to."

"So, get the hell out of my sight. Go back to Zurich and do what you have to do. Then call me. Four months. Five months. Okay. But that's it. Any longer then you can kiss your ass and your life goodbye."

Death threat. Straight out. No wiggle room anywhere.

A death sentence if she didn't perform.

She looked at him. What to say? Luca. Dead. Shot by this bastard. Something I just knew. Just knew it. Now I know it. Oh, my God.

The horror of it. How could she react to his hate, to his demands, to his threatening her life? She shuddered; her heart raced. She hadn't expected something like this, something so evil, so totally debased.

She steadied herself. Hurt everywhere, but also the conviction, the determination, the strength. He was not going to have his victory.

She knew what she had to do.

She looked him straight in the eye, said simply, "Five months," then turned and walked away, not looking back, feeling the hatred in his eyes boring into her as she moved away from him. Fighting the urge to scream at him, to do or say something more to him, but knowing that the cool-headed retreat was the better—and smarter play.

He didn't call after her. He let her go.

Straight ahead along the remaining stretch of path to the edge of the park. Not running. Not walking slowly, sure steps with her head held high. Knowing that by not directly reacting to his evil, she'd temporarily trumped him—and his threats.

Inside of her a Category 5 storm. In the middle of that maelstrom, hearing the buzzing in her head that wouldn't stop, she finally spoke to herself.

"Five months you give me, you bastard? And you killed Luca? My beloved Luca. And now you want to kill me? You piece of shit, no way that's going to happen."

She reached her car, opened the door, and got in. She grasped the steering wheel with both hands. Knuckles turning white. She heard her short, ragged breathing.

She couldn't stop.

Luca. Luca. Killed by that scum. An innocent bystander in a battle, the existence and dangers of which had been totally unknown to him. Dead because of her.

Tears ran down her cheeks, the salt contained in them the sad but familiar taste as they reached her lips. She remembered the carved chess figures, the king and the queen, both of whom had stood there, side by side, on the chessboard that night in the Villa Visconta. She saw that tragic scene now as if she were still sitting there. The same massive rage she'd felt that night came rushing back, coursing, tumbling its way through her veins, heating and fueling her determination— and her intentions.

She remembered the plan she'd originally conceived that July evening in her apartment, a plan designed to settle once and for all the score with Giovanni. Short term, pay him off. Long term, somehow get revenge.

She grabbed the sun visor and yanked it down, shoving the little cover back hard to expose the mirror hidden behind it. She looked at her image in the mirror. Her green eyes flashed sparks back at her from its shiny surface.

A thought struck her. Blackmailers never let go until they're forced to let go. Maybe there's a way to find that force, that ability to push back.

But what can I do? I haven't found anything that would work besides giving him the money.

Thoughts shooting off in every possible direction.

Throw the fear of discovery at them? Make it real for them? I've already discarded that idea. The law would show no mercy. And I'd be right in the middle of it with them as well.

What about murder? No, she thought. No. God, no. First of all, I wouldn't know how to do it. Besides, I'm just not the kind of person who can decide to kill someone and then go and do it. Or have someone do it for me. That'd be a different kind of hell for me.

Run for it? I can't do that yet. I'm not ready. And they'd hunt me down like a dog if I did.

In the emotion of the moment, she couldn't identify any acceptable course of action that would help. Frustrated, angry at herself for her lack of ideas, she sat back in her seat, breathing heavily.

God knows, I've done all I can alone. I need help. And I need some good advice.

One of her favorite phrases in German was an old but oft-used one: *kommt Zeit, kommt Rat.* Give things time. At some point, you'll have your answer.

She'd thought often about the value of that old saying when she'd faced difficult investment decisions at the bank and had waited until the passage of time had given her the answer. Now it was time to use that very same phrase to achieve that very same result in her personal life.

She needed an answer, even if she had to wait for it.

Otherwise, she'd no longer have a life.

30
Lounge/Bar Terrace
Hotel Eden Au Lac
Utoquai
Zurich
Switzerland

February 21   The following year   10:52 am

A sunny, late winter morning in Zurich. Unusual weather for the end of February. But nonetheless, a welcome respite for the citizens of Zurich from the cold and dreary winter and its week-long foggy weather. The thermometer measuring almost 69 degrees Fahrenheit. In the sun even warmer. Reason enough for the lounge staff to start up limited-service operations on the hotel's lounge/bar terrace with its view of Lake Zurich and the Alps.

Anulka had invited Ben to have a coffee on the terrace.

"Such a lovely day," she'd said. And if he had time for something to drink, it would be nice to be able to offer him that as well.

Nothing unusual in such an invitation. Theoretically, Ben was one of the bank's most important clients. He hadn't even been given a lunch at the bank or in a local restaurant during his past visits. But this was certainly not her fault. During every visit to the bank, he'd been all business and no pleasure and declined every lunch invitation she'd extended to him.

The sun warm in their faces, they sat facing each other, chatting and drinking the coffees they'd ordered.

For his part, Ben was enjoying the view—and the company. Part of that enjoyment came from the fact that the last tranche, a total of 800,000 Euros, was packed away in a case lying right next to him on an empty chair. Dangerous and risky to have that kind of money just lying around, considering a major part of it didn't even belong to him. But that was Ben. Forever on or near the red line.

She didn't particularly care about the whereabouts of the money. She was busy doing other more important things, like considering her options.

She knew very well that, at some point, the ground on which she stood was going to get hot. She didn't intend to wait for that to happen even if she could maintain when push came to shove, perhaps even credibly, that she hadn't known the client, that his documents and person had been in order, that she had seen no reason to deny his request for the money from his account. That might work at the beginning, but for how long? At some point, there might be too many questions and her eyes, her demeanor, might at some point desert her and tell them she'd known all along he wasn't the real client.

That had been part of Giovanni's original plan. Dumb idea, she thought.

She knew she had to start preparing and packing now. It was definitely not part of the plan to have someone walk into her office one day from the state attorney's office, or from Finsler management, or from the auditors, or from the offices of FINMA in Bern and accuse her of fraud or embezzlement, or however else they chose to define what she'd done.

She knew it could be years before the whole scheme was discovered. Nevertheless, she wanted to be long gone and well-established somewhere far away before any alarms went off.

Subtracting the 80,000 Euros she'd given Giovanni last fall, but including her 50% share of the last tranche, she'd calculated she'd soon have a total of almost 10,400,000 in Euros stored away in her safe deposit box. Or over 11,500,000 US dollars. Tax-free. Her own little pile of dirty money.

It was a heavy amount of money looking for a home. Both figuratively, but also literally. And that was indeed the problem she faced.

Her mind was racing. Giovanni's death threat had really changed her thinking. The conclusion she'd reached that day in Bad Ragaz was still valid.

If she wanted to be free, she needed help.

Now, sipping her coffee, she knew she had to be very careful in how she tried to enlist that help. And then, afterwards, what she would try to do with that help.

At least on paper, the whole matter of leaving Zurich

looked simple. In order to disappear, she needed to successfully execute a three-point plan. First step: Find a permanent
home for the money she had. Second step, resolve, in some
still-to-be determined fashion, the issue of Giovanni and his
partner. And third, resign from the bank and go somewhere
else with her new identity.

Somewhere where she'd be free of the fear of being identified and then arrested. Or found by those bastards in Italy.

Before she could address that final issue, she had to
make sure she had a secure financial basis. That was the
reason the money issue was number one on her agenda. She
had to get all the cash physically out of the country and into
a safe haven.

It was way too dangerous—as well as too cumbersome—
to try to convert even a part of the money in Switzerland
and then take what she had bought with it, be that gold,
or some other valuable asset, out of the country. Buying
diamonds might be a choice, but the head of the Wealth
Management division of a major private bank buying heavy
caret diamonds in Switzerland with cash? Not feasible. And
big-time suspicious.

It was also way too dangerous to risk taking the money
itself, even in smaller tranches, on repeated trips over the
border into France, Italy, or any other European country.
Border patrol people have long memories and they are trained
to be suspicious of the same people repeatedly showing up at
the one or the other border crossing.

Even if she were able in some way to get the money out

of the country, simply carrying it into any bank abroad, and then asking to open an account, was also very problematic. Laundering cash money had become a very risky sport at many a bank in Europe as well as in many other financial institutions in other parts of the world. Banks were on the watch-out. So were the fiscal arms of the governments who supervised them. And they would be particularly vigilant in her case if she were to resign, leave the country. and, at the same time, try to get the large cash hoard she had out of Switzerland.

She'd been back and forth on the money issue. At the end, she saw only one real alternative. She had to get all that cash not only out of Switzerland, but also completely out of Europe. And do it when all was still quiet.

She knew it wasn't so much the needing-to-be-done issue that was sticky. That was clear. It was the how-do-I-do-that part of the plan which was still causing her problems.

She assumed that Ben had the same problem. Namely the money end of the stick. The man couldn't just leave all his cash forever in the self-storage unit he'd rented near Kloten Airport. He needed it out of Europe as well if he were ever going to be able to use it.

She turned away from the view and looked at him, smiling.

"Ben, thank you again for coming along for the coffee. I want to be very open with you about something. I have a problem and I think you might have the same one I have."

"May I speak openly?", she asked.

"Of course, Anulka. Always!"

"Okay, fine. Thanks."

She looked at him, her eyes now boring into his. "So, here's the situation as I see it. We both have a substantial amount of cash stashed away. Yours in your little hideaway. And mine in a safe deposit box."

A slight smile at the corner of her mouth. "By the way, I hope that lock you bought for your storage unit is a good one."

"Don't worry, the money's still there," he said, amused at her concern. "And the lock works fine. Believe me, nothing is so unlikely to raise suspicions as a place to hide money as a self-storage unit. I'm good with it."

She laughed. "You know, I believe you. Believe me, I really do."

Another sip of coffee. She took a breath and then plunged back into it.

"Ben, I need to get the cash I have out of the country. Not to another European country, but into an account somewhere *outside* of Europe. If I may say so, that's probably the same problem you have. I can't imagine you'll want to leave that money in Switzerland forever. Or that you'd just want to get it over the border into some other country here in Europe."

"Certainly not, Anulka. Carry on."

"If I remember correctly," she continued, "Felix once told me that you'd worked for an international bank in the Gulf, I think he said it was Dubai or Abu Dhabi, I don't remember exactly. Is that correct?" she asked.

"Yes, that's precisely right. But it was not in Dubai or Abu Dhabi, but in Sharjah, right next to Dubai. And, yes, I worked at a bank there."

"Okay. Sharjah."

"Yeah, well", she mused, "Having my money in an account in the Gulf would be ideal for me."

She looked directly him. "Might be difficult, however. I would imagine there are residency and other requirements that would probably block me from getting something like that done."

A small hook now out on the table, but you're still dancing around, damn it. You need this. Time to get real. Fast.

"Ah, what the hell, Ben. I'm just going to put my whole problem on the table for you."

She leaned in closer to him. "Frankly, it's all a bit more complex than just acquiring an account outside of Europe. In actual fact, I not only need an account, but I also need to find a way to transport the money and put it into that account. Have you given any thought to how you're going to solve that problem for yourself? Assuming, of course, that what I'm telling you is also a problem for you."

He had himself a good laugh. "Anulka, why are you so cautious about telling me what's really on your mind? Just tell me straight out: Hey, I need some help. Please do me the favor. Help me with my problem. That's the case, isn't it?"

"Well, of course, it is," she said, somewhat peevishly.

"Listen carefully," he said. "This is such a beautiful day. And such a beautiful view. And the company is beautiful, too. So, I'm not going to destroy all that by playing around or pretending that I don't understand what your real needs are. You're right. I have the same problem. Exactly the same problem."

"However, in contrast to you, I have a solution."

She looked at him. Slowly but surely, he was starting to really annoy her. Green eyes can communicate hellfire and damnation.

Ben, to his credit, saw that look and reacted. He leaned over, closer to the side of her head, speaking softly into her ear.

"Relax, Anulka. Take it easy. I think I may be in a position to make my plan your plan. Listen to me for a minute."

She nodded. I'm waiting.

He sat back up and smiled at her. "I know someone who works at the Banque Sharjah Denier. That's the name of the bank where I worked before I went to Frankfurt. He's not a middle-management guy. He's one of the top three executives in the bank. He's also one of the owners. And, what's most important, he's a close personal friend of mine. Been that for years and years."

A sip of coffee. A smile.

"About every six to eight weeks, he travels to Geneva and Zurich on business. He does a little of this and a little of that while he's here in Europe. Smart guy. Helpful guy. By the way, this is definitely not the kind of guy who is going to fly commercial. He has his own jet, a Bombardier BD-700. Carries eight people and can fly over 7000 nautical miles without refueling. A beautiful plane. I love it."

He leaned in closer to her. "So, now listen carefully. That jet with him on board will be arriving in Zurich in approximately seven days. That's a Wednesday. Friday evening, he'll be returning on that same plane to Dubai."

"What's my plan? Well, to begin with, I intend to be on board sitting across from him when it takes off from Zurich to go back to Dubai."

"I have to be in Paris the following Monday morning to continue my consulting work with Felix. My friend has kindly offered to have his jet bring me back to Zurich the previous evening. That would be the Sunday evening. Don't ask me what his motive is for doing that. And don't ask me why he's being so generous with the plane and the costs involved. Just accept it. He's doing it. At the moment, you don't need to know anything else about him or his name. That's secondary. What *should* interest you, however, is how I may be able to help you."

She looked at him. Damn, the guy's enjoying this.

"Here's what I plan to do. A week from this Friday, I'm going to visit my little storage unit, grab the pillowcase full of nice cash, put it into a leather case, then take that case with me directly to Kloten Airport and get on that plane. I've made this trip a number of times for business reasons in the past years. Never had a problem with security or baggage checks."

"You know all about this, I'm sure. The type of person coming into Zurich or leaving Zurich by private plane, particularly some of the major hitters you know from the news, or those that don't want to be in the news, wouldn't stand for it. So, he and I don't need to get hung up on any excessive controls or checking in or what-not."

Ben had to smile. "My friend comes here very often, so he's well-known to everyone at the executive jet terminal. We can walk onto that plane with no problem. And little or no baggage inspection. Just flash our passports at the nice man at Passport Control. Baggage gets loaded. The pilots will have already filed their flight plans. The tanks will be full. And off we go."

"By the way, just so I can get you smiling a little bit, you might find it interesting to know that I'll not be traveling that evening under my real name. I'll be using another identity, something I do at times when I feel it politic to do so."

"The damn videos are so bothersome at airports so I'll also have changed my appearance somewhat so that it matches the photo in the passport I'll be using. Amuses me no end to do stuff like that," he said, leaning back and stretching his arms over his head to release an increasing tension in his back muscles. Butt hurting as well. Damn these hard terrace chairs.

"Once I'm on that plane, I'm going to have a nice dinner with my friend while we fly to Dubai. Everything is already arranged with him. He usually leaves Zurich in the evening. Flight time to Dubai about five hours plus or minus."

"About four hours in, that plane will reach Saudi Arabian airspace and then the northern and the central portion of the Emirates. From 42,000 feet, I'll be looking down at something quite extraordinary, something one sees often in the Middle East, namely the way oil companies burn off the natural gas from their active oil wells."

"When you look at that, Anulka, you might say what a waste of natural resources. Yes, it is, but I tell you it's fascinating. Huge fires burning permanently on top of innumerable drilling towers or vertical feeder pipes dotting the barren desert landscape as far as the eye can see. My friend looks down at that spectacle just like I do. At night, it's quite a sight."

She smiled at his casual approach to what she considered to be a very serious subject. Talking about natural gas when the real issue was a totally different one. Definitely a man for all seasons, she thought, but also a man with an almost childlike fascination for the world and what's in it.

What an explosive mixture. Totally different from Felix. And Luca also.

He drew a breath. "Ok, let's go on. When I arrive in Dubai, again no problems. I'll be holding a European Union passport, not my real one, of course, but still one from the EU. So that means I don't need a visa to enter the UAE. Baggage control at the airport? Also, no problem. My friend is a well-known and respected businessman in the Gulf. I don't think I have to paint a picture showing you what that means. General aviation terminal. Out of the plane, a smile at the nice custom officials, a quick check of the passports, and into the limo."

Ben puffed up a bit with pride. "Although I no longer have residency in the Gulf, my relationship with the bank is so good I can walk in anytime I want right through the front door with any amount of cash I have and deposit it. I've had an account at the bank for over twelve years, so I have no worries in that regard. Cash deposits? Believe me, not a problem. The bank accepts them all the time. Great big gobs of cash. No questions asked."

"How do I know that? Don't ask. I just know it."

"The only thing is, this time I'm not going to be walking into that bank through the front door. There'll be a car to meet me and my friend at the airport and bring us to the bank's private entrance. It'll be very early in the morning. But," he smiled, "again no problem. There'll be people waiting for us in the bank. My friend isn't what he is at the bank for nothing."

"There's a nice little discrete set of polished wooden doors just around the corner from the main entrance of the bank. Ring the bell. Walk in. My identification is my friend from the jet. And my face *sans* the disguise."

Looking at the expression on her face, Ben was having difficulty not breaking out in laughter.

Anulka almost gaping. Big eyes. One hundred percent tuned in to what he was telling her.

"There's a nice elevator there. Wood-paneled with Arabian music piped in. But okay. It's only a one-minute deal with the elevator up to his private office floor. I can handle that minute."

"They have a money counting machine on the 19th floor where my friend's office is located. I think it's one of those hot new counters from Cassida. They keep it in a little side room off the main reception area. Big table there to put all the cash on. They also make a hell of a fine cup of coffee in the kitchen next to his office. And they heat up and serve the most wonderful, honey-filled sweet rolls one can possibly imagine."

He paused for a second, tilting his head at her.

"I was sort of thinking, I mean, if you think it's right for you, that you might want to accompany me to Dubai. Frankly, I'd be interested in hearing your opinion on the quality of the coffee they serve on the 19th floor. There might be a honey roll or two in it for you as well. One does tend to be hungry after a long flight through the night."

He had to laugh. He was having fun at her expense. And he knew it.

"Oh, and by the way, before you answer, don't worry about getting back to Zurich from Dubai. The plane will be at our disposal for the return. We'll leave Sunday afternoon late and about five hours later, Zurich right off our rightwing tip. You can be at work on time the next morning. No problem."

She let out her breath, leaned back and relaxed. It was her turn to have a good laugh. What an absolutely crazy bastard. She'd never met anyone like him. He had everything wired. And he made it all sound so easy.

"Ben," she said, a couple of forming tears in her eyes from laughing. "Ben, I should say I'm shocked at what I've just heard. I don't know how many laws got whacked out of place by what you've just told me. But seriously, I do want to thank you for the offer. And, of course, I accept. What did you think? It's exactly, I mean, exactly the solution I had in mind. How did you guess?" she asked, with a small smirk on her face.

She studied him closely, thinking down the track to other important issues. "I do have two quick questions for you, however. You know I don't have residency in the Emirates. Am I correct in assuming I'll be able, in spite of that, to open an account at that bank and deposit a large amount of cash money into it?"

"And, second, will I have free and unlimited access to that account from anywhere in the world at any point in time when I need some money?"

He looked at her, mock astonishment on his face.

"You underestimate me, Anulka. Would I offer you a ride down to the hot sands of the desert only to tell you, once we arrive, that you can't take care of your little account and logistic problems while you're there? Come on, I'd hope you'd know me better than that."

He put his hand gently on her arm. "So please, relax. You can do anything you want with that money. There'll be no difficulties whatsoever in your opening an account and then being able to access it afterwards whenever and from wherever you wish. You have a friend in high places, and soon you'll have two. Believe me. You're going to be in very good hands."

She took his hand, pressing it to her cheek. And thanked him, her green eyes sparkling and flashing. To her surprise, she saw a trace of embarrassment in his look.

She looked out over the lake. With weather conditions

so good, there were already two sailboats out on the lake, tacking against a wind that had strengthened and, in spite of the strong sun, brought a sudden chill to the air.

She thought about their conversation. Ben is going to be using a false passport. A perfect chance for me to use the one Giovanni gave me. That should be a good test. Giovanni had asked her to give him a picture of herself that showed her with some changes to her physical appearance. A little hair color here, a small tuck there, contacts with a different eye color, small cotton balls in her cheeks to change the contours of her face, some small crows' feet wrinkles around her eyes. She'd done as he'd asked.

The picture in that passport was now over three years old. Perfect. Make the same changes to your appearance. Tone it down a little with the clothes. Remember your new name and your address. Then off you go to the airport and Dubai.

She focused again on Ben who'd taken a moment to glance at the morning headlines. The sun had now slipped behind a cloud. The wind from the lake now a bit cooler. She shivered, stood, citing the change in temperature, and suggested they discuss further details of the trip inside.

As they walked toward the terrace door, he turned to her and asked, "Did I understand correctly what you just said on the terrace? Did you just say you wanted to have access no matter where you were in the world? Does that mean you're thinking of leaving the bank, and, perhaps, Switzerland as well?"

She looked at him from the side, hooked her arm into

his, and said, just before they went through the door, "Ben, there are also several other things where I may perhaps need your advice or your help. A little early now though. Let's get the money thing taken care of first, shall we?"

She threw him a thousand-watt smile that would have melted the hardest of iron if there'd been any about.

He had one of those ready for her as well.

No question about it. Just two peas in a pod, having a late morning coffee together, plotting and planning a little bit of nonsense—along with some very serious crimes.

31
Poolside
The Eauzone Restaurant
Royal Mirage (Dubai) Hotel
Dubai
United Arab Emirates
Middle East

March 2   20:52

It had been a successful day. Ben and Anulka had arrived early that morning at Dubai International Airport and gone by private limousine to the Royal Mirage Hotel located directly on the Arabian Gulf. Halim, the owner of the plane they'd flown in, had gone directly from the airport to his bank in Sharjah. They would meet him there later in the morning, taking the same limousine they'd used for the trip to the hotel.

Normally, with all that money around, a risky move not going directly to the bank to take care of the business at hand. But tiredness sometimes wins over good sense.

Good sense indeed. Certainly not missing in this little

action vignette. Ben had taken care of the problem by telling her that Halim had ordered four of his security people to shadow them by car to the hotel and then do the same thing when they made their way over to the bank in Sharjah. She hadn't seen anyone about that looked like they were ready for war. *But what the hell do I know,* she'd thought. *Everybody looks just about the same here.*

At the hotel, VIP treatment all around them, they'd checked into their respective rooms. After a quick shower, Ben had pulled on a double-breasted, 140 weight, white linen suit and an indigo silk blue shirt, two buttons open at the neck. Dark blue suede loafers. No socks.

Anulka had removed the temporary visual identity she'd put on for passport control purposes: contacts out, makeup off, crowfeet wrinkles gone, wig fluffed up, and put away for the return flight.

He'd made a short comment about her changed appearance and the Italian passport before they'd boarded the plane in Zurich. With a slight grin on her face, she'd politely brushed off his observation, telling him she would tell him "all about it" in Dubai.

He'd smiled, his look telling her what he was thinking: "Ah, the mysterious Anulka Lorenzini."

A blue linen, short-sleeved dress, white belt, and white pumps were her choice of dress for the visit to the bank. She hung her gold cross with the heavy gold chain back around her neck. A touch of pale, purple-colored lipstick. A light application of indigo blue eye shadow.

A look in the hall mirror of her suite. Anulka Lorenzini back in uniform. Anulka Lorenzini ready to take care of
business.

The flight down from Zurich had been uneventful, the
view over the Gulf being the one exception. A clear, moonlit
night had given everyone on board a particularly spectacular
view of the natural gas burn-off in the expansive oil fields
stretching almost to the horizon below the plane. Ben's friend,
Halim, had been the perfect host. A five-course dinner on the
plane had been worthy of a couple of Michelin stars. She
couldn't believe that Halim had his own cook on board just
to serve the three of them.

She was in another world.

The plane and its furnishings the definition of pure private jet luxury. She'd been so entranced by everything; she'd
slept only a little more than an hour during the flight. When
she'd awakened, she'd found she was covered with a large
square cashmere throw, woven in shimmering variations of
green and blue-hued cashmere thread.

When she'd commented on its "absolutely delicious"
softness as well as the very courteous gesture of someone
covering her while she slept, she had been told the throw
was hers to take with her when the plane landed in Dubai. It
had been woven especially for her in less than one week by a
cashmere-weaving establishment Halim knew in Abu Dhabi.

Yup, rich was not bad. Not bad at all.

The same black Mercedes 550 limousine had picked
them both up again at eleven to bring them to the bank. On

the way there, Ben had commented to her that he'd have gone, unshaven and not showered, directly to the bank if he'd been traveling alone. But with such a charming person accompanying him, and a woman to boot, a short stop at the hotel to check in and change had been a good move.

"I have to admit I feel much better after a shower and a shave," he'd said.

Yeah, she thought, with security people posted in the hotel ready to pull the trigger at a moment's notice should any attempts be made on their persons or baggage, a long, slow shower was no problem.

She'd looked sideways at him, studying his profile and what he was wearing. And you look a hell of a lot better, too, she thought.

Arriving at the bank, she'd almost had an out-of-the-body experience.

Incredible. The sun is shining. It's hot. A couple of people walking about. Quiet, except for someone chanting something, low and throaty, in Arabic somewhere nearby.

And here I am, schlepping a major pile of money I've stolen into this bank. And so is Ben. Almost like walking into a library to drop off an overdue book. Except what I'm looking at here has definitely no relation to a library. Or a borrowed book.

She'd taken the larger case containing the money out of the trunk, then another smaller, sturdier case, its contents definitely much heavier than the one with the money in it. Ben had taken the heavier one from her as she'd turned around to follow him to the entrance. The other case with the money in it, heavy enough, she thought, but whatever. One does what one has to do.

I hope he's right about that coffee, she'd thought.

He had been. And about the rolls as well.

At two in the afternoon, having taken care of all formalities and enjoyed a light lunch with Halim in his private dining room at the bank, they'd been driven back to Dubai. Figs, dates, and some cold, sliced lamb with a green salad had not been exactly to her taste, but the atmosphere and the company had made up for everything.

Outside the car, a humid 97 degrees Fahrenheit.

Halim had offered to take them both to the "At The Top", the observation deck in the Burj Khalifa Dubai, the tallest building in the world with a total of 162 floors. Both of them had declined with thanks, the simple reason being they'd both been there on previous trips to the city. In addition, they had only one day in Dubai before having to return to Zurich. And there were other exigencies on the program.

For her, the definition of other exigencies was a very straightforward one: no visit to Dubai-Sharjah was complete without a visit to the souks.

They'd spent over an hour and a half at the textile souks located in the Bur Dubai section of the city. She hadn't been interested in the bolts of dress material. Or in having a dress made for herself.

She'd been looking for something else, something very special. Another type of material with a different structure and form. And with the colors somewhat washed out.

This was Anulka anticipating the future. She knew she'd have to leave Zurich without her furniture, most of her clothes, and a major part of the beloved art and artifact pieces she had collected over the years. No way she'd be able to ship or transport everything out of the country. Some of the smaller pieces, maybe, by car, but the others were just too big, too cumbersome, and, above all, much too risky to shoot them around the world to her new life where the authorities could perhaps find her one day.

To build a bridge to that new life wherever it would be, she wanted to buy some material she could use to make throw cushions for the new couch she'd buy someday—somewhere. Something colorful, something in silk, something unusual, something exciting.

Psychologically, this was important to her. Not only would it be a nice memento from her visit to Dubai, but, more importantly, it would be something she could look at one day and remember how significant that visit had been for her future.

The souks were a dazzling display of shops, colors and materials, with miles of narrow passageways to walk if one wanted to see it all.

She'd found the right material in a small shop, a ten-minute winding stroll into the souks from the entrance. Sitting on top of mounds of rolls of uncut fabric, the aroma from incense burning somewhere nearby, a small black coffee in her right hand, she'd felt a wave of contentment.

She was on her way.

After enjoying some baklava and another strong coffee at a cafe nearby, they'd been driven back to the hotel. Even with the coffee, she was so tired she'd almost fallen asleep in the back seat of the limousine. But she'd caught herself. There was just too much to see. The unique soaring architecture of the office and apartment buildings, the amazing Burj Khalifa soaring high over the city, the dress of the people, the clean feel of the city, the richness of the environment, the bustle of the traffic.

So far removed from slow and conservative Zurich and its staid, traditional architecture.

Later, shortly before nine that evening, she and Ben had found themselves sitting in the Eauzone Restaurant, directly next to the hotel pool, and within sight of a glass-smooth Arabian Gulf. Both of them relaxed and adequately refreshed after a short rest.

The waiter had come and gone. As they looked at the menu, she decided that she was going to splurge on something she normally wouldn't think of eating. She'd ordered Foie gras Ballotine as a starter. Australian Beef Tenderloin was her choice for the main course. Southwest France on the Gulf. Australia in the Arab world. Nothing from the Arab world.

What an interesting—and diverse—place the world is, she thought to herself.

Ben regarded her with a bemused look on his face. "You know, you're really quite a woman, Anulka. Last night in Zurich, I almost didn't recognize you when you arrived at the airport. You're a Swiss citizen, and yet you traveled down here on an Italian passport. And then you walk onto that plane with two cases, one of which is dragging your right shoulder almost down to the ground because of its weight. What the hell is that, I ask myself. But then I think, at the end of the day, it's her business what she carries around with her. So, I say to myself, let it go."

"I get something approaching an answer to my questions this morning at the hotel. First of all, the real Anulka Lorenzini pops up again in the hotel lobby. Nice and neat. Dressed, as always, to the nines. Then, cool as anything, that same woman lets me walk that heavier case into the elevator at the bank, containing, I think, something like heavy metal. And what's really in the bag? Seventeen Kilogold bars at 2.205 pounds per to be sold to the highest bidder. About $1,075,000 worth. Even Halim was surprised. And he sees some real interesting stuff every day, I can assure you."

He studied her carefully.

"But not enough. Anulka Lorenzini also puts some major cash down on the table at the bank. But it's way more than what our little deal netted her. At least, I think it's much more than what we pulled out of there," he said, looking her directly in the eyes.

"'So where did all that money come from?' I ask myself. "Of course, not my business. But nevertheless, I see a woman with many veils wrapped around her, to use a metaphor which is probably very fitting, considering where we are at the moment. Hell, I thought I was the one who played all the angles. In comparison to you, I'm starting to feel I'm still operating somewhere just south of kindergarten level. So, anything you want to admit to or tell me about?"

He was laughing. She had to laugh with him. His way of expressing himself amused her.

"Look, Ben, first of all, let's put a couple of things into perspective. You in kindergarten? Nope, you're a player. And a really good one. Champion League quality. Why do I think so? Let me just list a couple of things here. First of all, the first-class acting job pulling all that money out of the bank. There were times when I almost had to laugh. If you'll pardon the expression, that was just one cool performance."

She noticed Ben had a bemused look on his face. But he wasn't interrupting. He wanted to hear this.

"Second, the pillowcase and the self-storage unit. You ask yourself about my case and its weight? What do you think I was thinking when I saw you putting your money into a simple pillowcase? And when I heard where you intended to hide it?"

"And, thirdly, this." She swept her left arm around from right to left. "What is this? Bombardier plane? Cashmere throw? The man walks in and out of a big, important bank like he owns it. The people there look at him like he's a God or something. Halim shows deference and deep respect.

Security people all over the place. Top class treatment. What the hell is that all about?"

She smiled at him. "You know it and I know it. You don't get that kind of action going by determining that your life's purpose involves staying hidden in the woodwork somewhere."

He started to cough from laughing so much.

"Okay. Okay. I take it all back. You're right. Yes, I'm a player. But it takes one to know one. Or am I wrong there?"

She smiled, admitting to nothing.

"Have it your way, Anulka. Guilty as charged. And the large amount of money? Another game? Savings? Sold a company you owned? Cleaned out the rest of the money at your bank?"

Her face showed no expression, the eyes flashing a red-light warning.

"Okay, okay," he said quickly, "we leave that one alone. But the gold? At least tell me about that."

Her face now cut stone. Confession time.

Start spinning-the-web time.

"Look, the fact of the matter is I can't stay in Zurich much longer. I've told you that. You've told me you're planning on coming down here soon to start again where you left off several years ago. Good for you. But, of course, that doesn't solve my little problem. Like sitting there in Zurich waiting for the alarms to go off one day and then being arrested and spending my life in a cold cell somewhere. Not a pleasant prospect."

She considered her words for a second.

"And leaving in a hurry is always bad. Mistakes get made when time is short. Bad mistakes. Possibly fatal mistakes. You know that. So, think. The answer's actually very simple. I resign quietly from the bank and leave Zurich in the near future."

"That gold represented my life's savings. I couldn't leave it in Zurich and I couldn't just transfer it out of the country someplace else. That would have left a trail and would have been a really stupid move. On the other hand, I'm going to need that money in whatever future I put together for myself in this world. So, what does one do in such a situation? You're a smart guy. You know exactly what one does."

She took a sip of wine, then leaned across the table, looking directly at him, answering his question. "And why did I choose gold? The answer's simple. I like the color."

Ben pursed his lips.

She leaned closer to him. "Okay, okay. Seriously now. About a year ago, I got myself an allocated gold account, meaning, with the savings I had, I was buying and holding gold. Better investment than cash. But I didn't take gold bullion certificates where you can get cheated if you don't watch out. No. I wanted to touch the stuff. So, I went for the simple solution. Gold in bars. The physical stuff. Kept it in two safe deposit boxes at a bank near Basel."

"The firm in Basel I bought it from wasn't too happy about that because they wanted me to keep that gold on their premises. Their way to earn even more money through storage fees. With the exception of four bars I left there just to keep them interested in giving me some more good deals, no way I was going to do that."

"Those bars from this morning? I just kept them handy, waiting for an opportunity to get them out of the country. You gave me that opportunity for which I am very thankful. Simple as that"

She smiled at him and raised her glass to him, toasting him and his solution to her little problem.

He leaned back and studied her carefully. A dangerous woman. And, yeah, a fascinating woman.

"Oh, yes, one final word on the whole matter. Now that I've been able to solve the big logistic money problems, the rest will be easy. Whatever money I have remaining in my account at Bankhaus Finsler, I'll withdraw on the day I leave. The remaining gold bars I have I'll turn into cash and take that all with me as well. To hell with the border controls."

"But what really pleases me is that after today, I have almost all my money here in Sharjah to do with as I please and when I please. I really like that."

Not bad. She has everything organized, he thought.

He smiled at her. Respect. Strong woman.

Inside of himself, however, Ben was battling a different emotion. He felt curiously affected by her statement that she'd be leaving Zurich soon. Even though she was still involved with her duties within the bank—just as she had just said—, those obligations had a limited shelf life for her.

She's leaving. And nothing is going to stop her. What a damn shame. I really enjoy this woman.

"Glad I could help. Very smart of you, Anulka. Not bad. Not bad at all."

He put his thoughts and his disappointment about her leaving on hold. I'll come back to that later when I have more time, he thought. Better now to lighten things up a bit.

"What about the passport and the wig and the contacts. What the hell was all of that and where did you get that passport? I have a number of false ones and I know really good ones are not easy to obtain. Yours is damn good."

Smiling, she studied his face. Damn, I hate this, she thought. I hate what I need to do. But I have to put some worry into him, I have to, well, let's call a spade a spade, I have to trap him.

She cocked her head to the side, weighing her next step. Well, at least, I've got him thinking. And questioning.

"The passport? That's a very long and complicated story, Ben. And since you've already commented on it once before, perhaps I should tell you that particular story now."

She paused for a second, looking at him. Challenging him, waiting for his reaction.

His body had changed position. Leaning forward somewhat. Tensed a bit, like a pointer during the hunt.

"Shall I continue?" she challenged him, her eyes fixed on his.

"Yeah, go ahead. Probably a good story," he said, his eyes, however, telling another story.

What the hell is this, he asked himself?

"Fine," she answered, and leaned a little closer to him.

"Frankly speaking, I have to tell you there might be a couple of loose ends in this whole operation which, short-term, could possibly endanger our walking away from this without a scratch on ourselves. I'm talking about fun subjects like blackmail and timing issues, something I've spoken to no one about up to now. Felix knows generally about the blackmail part of it, but that's only the "what" part. The who, how, where, when, and why of it? Felix has no idea about any of that. No one knows anything about that."

His eyes opened wider, his lips reduced to a thin line.

"Yeah, bad stuff, Ben, but also solvable stuff, I think. And it also contains an answer for you on the money issue you also just referred to."

She took another sip of wine, smiled at him, studying him and his reaction over the rim of her glass.

"Question for you. I know we're about to eat, so it's not exactly the best time to get into a subject like this. Never-theless, I think it's important that you know and understand what I'm talking about. So, do you want me to continue, or do you want to wait until after we've had dinner?"

She leaned over the table closer to him. "Please. Your choice."

He chewed on a piece of bread, his eyes and demeanor serious. Poured himself some water from the small bottle of Pellegrino on the table. Looked at her again, studying her expressionless face, questioning who or what those loose ends could be.

No way I'm going to wait until after dinner after that little speech, he thought.

Damn it. I always had a feeling there might be something going on that would screw everything up. Now this.

"That doesn't sound good at all, Anulka. Why don't you tell me now. We'll talk while we eat," he said. And leaned over the table toward her to better hear what she had in mind.

He was ready to help or advise her. Whatever was needed, whatever it would take to eliminate any potential danger to the deal—and the people involved, including, in particular, himself.

Trap closed.

32
Café Sociale
Via Roma
Rural location a mile from the Village of
Castel Boglione
Piemonte
Italia

March 26   Early Sunday morning   8:02 am

Strong, cold, north wind. Very unusual weather conditions in northern Italy, particularly when one considered the fact that spring, at least according to the calendar, had already arrived.

On the other hand, the sun, still just below the horizon, was starting to rise. In about ten minutes, the front façade of the small café would be bathed in the early morning's sun rays. They'd bring, at least, a small bit of warmth to Giovanni and Saverio, the only two figures seated at the one of several, beat-up tables in front of the Café Sociale, trying to enjoy an early-morning breakfast of hot coffee and brioches.

The café, with an adjacent bakery, stood alone along the

right side of a road, about seventy yards away from the point where two narrow, beaten-up dirt roads crossed each other. If one took the road on which the café was located and went off to the left, it would lead one directly into the small village of Castel Boglione. To the right, that same road stretched up at a rather steep angle to the top of a tree-lined hill about a mile away.

Normally busy during the week with tractor and vehicle traffic, there was nothing moving in any direction—and no one walking about. No cars. No cyclists. No joggers. No nothing.

The bitter cold weather and the early Sunday morning hour were keeping everyone inside and off the roads.

An agricultural machine repair shop, closed up tight for the weekend, was located directly across the road from the café. One step above a junkyard from the looks of it. Other than that, no other buildings in the immediate vicinity.

A beat-up old car and a semi-truck were parked just off the road on the small grassy portion of the dirt parking lot located in front of the workshop. Both of them with dusty, dirty, rain-speckled windows and side panels. Looked like they'd been standing there for quite a while.

The baker had just left the two men's table, almost running back into the café to seek its warmth. It wasn't his to judge, but the impression they'd made on him was not the best. Most likely professional gangster milieu from the looks of them, he'd thought. He'd heard some bad things recently about a criminal element moving into the area.

Rumors, particularly in a small, in-grown rural location, were always something the waiter heard, but then ignored. In this region, it never paid to be too curious or to ask unnecessary questions.

Besides, he had other interests, having just gotten married the past week. God, he thought, here I am working when I could be home doing something infinitely better than heating up coffee or buttering a brioche or two for some freezing guests.

Both Giovanni and Saverio were dressed for the cold weather. Heavy jackets, wool sweaters, wool caps, woolen gloves, thick cord pants, leather boots, sunglasses. They'd arrived in Saverio's black Alfa Romeo 169. It stood parked on the other side of the road, a bit up to the right beyond the truck and just short of an old battered bus stop sign and a pile of partially bagged garbage which, in that part of the world, would probably stay there until forever or, at least, until hell froze over.

Nobody gave a damn about its existence and the fact that it would most likely never disappear. Just part of the landscape. Just part of the Italian approach.

They'd locked the car and walked the twenty or so yards along the road to the café. To hell with the bloody bus and its stop sign. The bus driver can just cool down if he has to stop short to load or unload. Besides, it's Sunday and how many times is a bus going to come along anyway? Probably not even once.

The two men sat facing each other, silently pushing

their caffeine and sugar levels back up to a level where they'd be able to speak normally without their foul moods causing them to constantly bitch and complain.

What had them both seriously pissed off had a name: Anulka Lorenzini. They'd discussed the whole situation again the previous evening over several bottles of Barbera wine. And pickled garlic sleeves.

Fact was, the two of them just were not capable of getting their acts together. The first 80,000 Euros they'd received from Anulka five months ago were already long gone.

She'd used the word reasonable in describing the time she would need in order to make them whole. Those five months were now up.

Today, she was apparently bringing the rest. Payday. And perhaps another pop on top. What was worrying them was the fact that they didn't exactly know how she was going to get the money physically across the border. The officials at Chiasso, the Italian-Swiss border station, might stop her–if that were the border crossing she'd chose—and discover the money. And then arrest her.

Giovanni had learned a week ago that she was coming with the money. She'd called and told him where she would meet him, and at what time. Then, when he'd wanted to ask a question about how she'd transport it, she'd essentially told him to shut his dirty mouth and just come and pick up the goddam money.

Then she'd hung up.

Just a damn touchy bitch, Giovanni had said to Saverio after that call.

Saverio's response, "Lot of pressure there," reflected quite accurately the situation for all the parties concerned. Not only Anulka.

But that wasn't the real problem. Sitting at the cafe, Giovanni and Saverio discussed the fact that if she didn't make it across the border with the money, it'd mean they'd waited for nothing. That would mean no money today. And none tomorrow either.

All that pressure had become a little too much for them. That was the reason they were sitting together so early in the morning. Time for a last-minute coordination and check of the overall logistics. And some hot coffee.

The meet with her was supposed to take place in a little less than two hours, twelve miles away, just outside of Bazzana, in a parking lot used occasionally by a local freight forwarder to park its empty trucks. A Sunday would not be one of those days where there'd be any movement on that property. Why the hell she'd chosen that place escaped both of them. They knew where it was and what it was, of course, but Bazzana?

"Well, what's wrong with that choice?" Saverio had asked Giovanni. Hadn't she and Giovanni eaten dinner several times in Nizza Monferrato? The town, in the middle of the Piemonte wine region, was only six or so miles from Bazzana.

"She's got to know the surrounding area well," he maintained. "The parking lot is well off the main road and several hundred yards from a twenty-four-hour gas station. You might even have gassed up your car there with her at some point," he reminded him."

"And don't forget, although it's now several years ago, she spent several long fuck weekends with you at the boutique LaVilla Hotel in Casalotto. That's also only a couple of miles from here. Hell, she might even have had a coffee with you where we're sitting right now."

Giovanni thought for a moment. "Yes, all true, but still, as far as the café is concerned, that's quite a while ago. Whatever. I really can't remember if she was the one I was here with or if it was someone else."

Saverio looked at his friend with a wry smile on his face. Usual Giovanni bullshit.

Just to be sure there would be no hiccups, both of them had decided to equalize the fact she'd determined both time and place for the meet. Giovanni's equalizer, a Glock 19 9mm pistol, was stuffed into a leather holster rig strapped tightly to his upper body under his left arm. Magazine full. One bullet chambered. Safety on.

Saverio kept his, a Sig Sauer P229 9mm pistol with silencer, tucked into the large inside pocket of his winter jacket. Two extra magazines, easily accessible in a fire fight, in the outside right coat pocket of his coat. sheath holding a six inch long knife tucked tightly into the top half of his knee-high, right boot.

Hey, one never knows. What Giovanni had said to her in Bad Ragaz had been more than clear. Brutal death threat. Maybe she'd gotten so pissed she'd attempt to organize some kind of a counter move against them. Didn't seem likely after her last phone call and it certainly didn't fit her *modus operandi*. Nevertheless, prepared is prepared. And they both were definitely prepared.

Whatever the case, they both wanted to be at the parking lot early enough to make sure no one was around who could possibly disturb them—or see something they shouldn't be seeing. The transfer itself shouldn't take Ben more than five minutes.

Giovanni also was disturbed by the fact that she hadn't reacted in any way to his additional demands for more money. In fact, she hadn't mentioned the word money at all during her call. He knew she'd understood his threat, even if she hadn't commented afterwards on anything he'd said. Only the one statement concerning timing before she'd turned away from him and walked out of the spa park. Otherwise, afterwards, no further contact.

Nothing.

Nevertheless, he didn't think there'd be any problem. She'd not only come across with the original money, but she'd also add a little to it, as he'd demanded, in order to finally put an end to the constant pressure he'd been exerting on her.

He'd put the fear of God—and the prospect of a potential sniper rifle bullet in her head—into her. The white color of her face had told him, unequivocally, his verbal barrage had hit its target. Dead center so to speak. She wouldn't dare to do anything else other than what he'd demanded of her: show up and hand over the goods.

And Luca? Her knowing since their last meeting that he was the one who'd pulled the trigger, that he was the one who'd destroyed the one really good thing in her life? Well, tough shit. And, definitely, tough luck for her if she decided to double cross them now in any way.

For today, Giovanni was prepared. As for the future, he mentally shrugged his shoulders.

"No problem anywhere that I can see. I know where she is all the time. And she clearly knows that. But she doesn't know where I am, any of the time. You know, I like that kind of setup. And those odds. And I particularly like thinking about the possibility of even another payday sometime in the future."

His stomach growled again. He stood up.

"I'm going to go inside and order up some additional brioches. That guy is probably baking a pile of them for the people coming after church. This time, I'm getting the *marmelata* version. They're not bad here. And they'll be hot out of the oven. Good sweet hit, baby. You want a couple, Saverio?"

Saverio wasn't in the mood for anything more to eat. He wanted to stay loose for the time when she showed up at the meeting place. Sometimes, he ate too much of something, then burped a lot and that got him, an hour or so down the road, a bad case of reflux. And feeling a bit sick. Wouldn't be good in a meeting like the one they had planned.

"No, thanks. But a bottle of mineral water would be fine."

Giovanni returned a minute later. They continued sitting there, the bitter cold helping to clear their wine-infested arteries and heads. At least that.

The past evening, there'd been one more subject besides the border problem that had caused a short, but intense discussion between the two of them. That was the issue of her carrying the money all alone.

It was dangerous transporting that much stuff around, Saverio had said. His point was understandable. Normally, one would want some kind of protection to guard against any unforeseen problems or other issues that could affect its safekeeping. And its ownership.

Giovanni hadn't bought that point of view—or concern. He maintained she'd handle it all alone because, if one could believe it, she was so intensely scared about her position in Zurich—and the possibility of losing it. She wanted the whole thing done and over with. Quickly. And it had to be done in secret.

"Remember her phone call," he said to Saverio. "First time ever that I heard that amount of venom in her voice."

He'd also observed that since she was such a hard-assed, go-it-alone bitch, she wouldn't even consider not doing it alone. Besides, he'd said, there's no one whom she could trust with the story about what she'd done or what she was doing. Too high a risk for her, he maintained.

And, above all, also much too high a risk for anyone else thinking of getting involved and helping her to transport the money. Fraud and embezzlement weren't exactly small-time misdemeanors. Nobody with any common sense would risk helping her with something like that in play.

No, she'll be coming alone, he'd said.

Time was moving slowly. Early Sunday morning quiet. The whole time they'd been sitting there, there'd only been one car and one truck pass slowly by in front of the café, both battered old wrecks barely able to get up any speed to transport people, or anything else anywhere.

Their order arrived. Bottle of *aqua frizzante*. Sparkling water. And three m*armalata* brioches. The baker shivering, then running back into the café.

"Damn," Giovanni exclaimed, "nothing like a warm brioche straight out of the oven."

The three he'd ordered for himself might not even be enough. "Just plain hungry this morning," he said.

Saverio looked at him and at the remaining brioches on the plate, then turned his chair slightly away from the table—and from the enthusiastic munching going on. How could anybody eat that much in advance of such a meeting?

To their left and to their right, still nothing going on. From where he was sitting, Saverio could look up the long asphalt road running off to their right in a straight line up to the top of the nearby hill. The road was lined on both sides with tall, pencil-thin evergreen cypresses which so often elegantly grace both sides of many an Italian roadway or byway.

Italy at its most attractive.

The cold was starting to get to them. They pulled their

coat collars tighter, concentrating on keeping warm, and drinking what they had in front of them.

The noise of the strong, gusting wind kept both men from hearing the putt-putt sound of an approaching Vespa with two helmeted riders perched on top of it, rapidly descending from the right down the long road from the top of the hill. It wasn't until it pulled to a stop just down to their left that they both finally noticed it—and its EU license plate. *F* for France.

Motor turned off. Vespa parked off the right shoulder of the road, the battered car and the semi-truck parked in between the newly-arrived Vespa and Saverio's car.

Both riders were dressed for the cold, the driver in front in a long leather coat, turtleneck sweater, the passenger at the back in a black, thick, pilot-type leather jacket. Both wore jeans, black leather boots, black leather gloves, and black helmets with darkened visors. Thick scarves wrapped around their necks. Underneath the helmet visors, sunglasses to cut out the rest of any brightness from the low-hanging winter sun.

Both had small backpacks strapped to their backs. The rider in the front also had a messenger bag and a small black leather case hanging around his neck, the latter, judging from its size and shape, contained most likely some kind of high-powered binoculars.

Stupid shit, remarked Saverio. What had he zeroed in on this morning? Some kind of rare bird flying around in the damn cold?

The passenger at the back, of slighter build, dismounted and stretched, then took the messenger bag from the driver and slung it over the right shoulder.

Can you believe it? Damned French tourists, thought Giovanni. He could hear Saverio muttering to himself about some fools from France out so early in the cold.

They watched as the driver checked the signal on his mobile phone, holding the phone up and turning it in different directions. Hell, thought Giovanni, don't you people know where you are? This is rural Italy. No towers out here yet. Ergo: no GPS.

The driver turned to his passenger who'd dismounted and said something that the wind pushed away down the road. He snapped the phone shut. Then he reached into his jacket, took out a map, and spread it out over the handlebars of the Vespa.

Both riders raised their visors, then leaned over it, and proceeded to discuss in rapid French something they were looking at on the map. Their voices were somewhat muffled by the wind and the helmets they were still wearing. But one didn't need to hear clearly what they were saying to know exactly what the problem was.

From all of the impatient gesticulating going on, the animated pointing in different directions, the pointing at positions on the map-obvious disagreement between the two people, each one trying to convince the other that their choice of direction was the right one-, it was clear they were looking at some dumb French tourists who'd lost their way. And couldn't help or save themselves for all the maps in the world.

No help from us here, thought Giovanni. Besides, neither of us speaks a word of French. They should just get the hell out of here and stop disturbing the early morning peace and quiet.

There was no peace to be had. The driver and the passenger, voices even louder, checking the area around them, close in and further away. Logical for two people attempting to get their bearings.

Suddenly, the smaller of the two, apparently a female passenger from the sound of the voice, threw up her hands in exasperation, apparently giving up in the face of what she considered to be pure stupidity on the part of the driver.

The woman spoke loudly to the driver. "*Merde alors. Vraiment que des conneries!*". Nothing but damned stupidities. That statement they heard all the way across the road. What she'd said they didn't understand. What they did understand was the tone of the voice.

The woman was severely pissed.

She pushed the map from the handlebars, turned her head around, saw Giovanni and Saverio sitting at the table watching them. Grabbing the messenger bag the driver had been carrying, she pushed him abruptly back, away from her.

The dark visor of her helmet snapped back down into place, she walked toward the café. He watched her as she went, then reached up and removed his helmet. He was wearing a black woolen cap pulled tightly over his head. Dark sunglasses still protecting his eyes. He waited a second or two, then took two slow steps out onto the road, keeping his distance from her.

No wonder. She'd really given him hell for a while. Just some wimpy Frenchy, they both thought.

The woman came closer.

Aw, shit, thought Giovanni. Here we go. The short back and forth on the other side of the road had been amusing, but now that bitch French woman coming over here means we're going to get involved in the whole mess.

She approached the table next to the one where they were sitting. Chair legs scraped on dirty cement as she moved one of the chairs standing around it diagonally across to where they both were sitting. She flipped the dark visor of her helmet up, then took it off, and set it down on chair next to her.

She sat down, removing and putting her sunglasses down next to her helmet. Leather gloves still on her hands. Her hair not blonde, but dark brown. Ponytail.

Impassive. Looking directly at him, hating him, wanting to hurt him.

"*Buon giorno, Giovanni. Come stai?* Good morning. How are you?"

A slight nod of recognition in Saverio's direction. Bastard.

Speechless, they gaped at her. Anulka. Pulse rates suddenly up. Question after question suddenly shooting rapid fire through their heads.

Shit, what is this? This isn't what was planned. What the hell's she doing here? What happened to the meet in Bazzana? What is she thinking coming and sitting down right across from us like that? What's she want? What's the bitch doing here?

And who is the wimpy French guy and what's he doing here? Riding shotgun for her in some way?

Giovanni checked quickly to see where he'd gone. He'd stopped following her, remaining on his side of the road. He saw that he'd moved up to Saverio's car. Frenchy standing around it, admiring it. Sighting along the lines of the car, peeking inside. Checking the width of the tire profile. Maybe harmless, but watch him.

Warning lights everywhere. Damn it. *Damn* it.

Move, Giovanni told himself. Get some distance.

He stood up, the better to try and get the situation under control. No overt proof of it, but he smelled a major problem in her showing up like this. Too cool. Too collected. Too planned. Too sudden.

She'd been able to get right up close to them—too damn close for his taste. And she'd brought company. Not good.

He glanced at Saverio, still sitting in his chair. He saw Saverio's hand running slowly down his bent right leg to his knee where the top of his leather boot lay tight against it. He knew that Saverio kept six sharp inches of steel death in a sheath stuffed between his jeans and the neck of one of his boots.

Giovanni kept his distance from her, a step away from

the table which stood between them. No greeting for her. Time to get down to business.

"*Che cosa stai facendo qui? Pensavo che fossime incontrati a Bazzana.* What the hell are you doing here? I thought we were going to meet in Bazzana. And now you're here? I don't like surprises. I don't like change of plan like this. And who the hell is the character who drove you here? Another big bad lover like the last one?" he asked, taunting her.

She thought to herself. I'm scared, I'm so scared I'm sick to my stomach. But if I don't get him off balance right from the start, he may start something we both aren't prepared for.

Good that we found the bastard here. I guessed right, she thought. Bazzana was a bad choice. This is a much better location. Right on the road. No trucks. No traffic.

She took a breath. Time to get him running a bit.

"Yeah, you're right. We were planning to meet in Bazzana. It was my suggestion that we do so. But then I remembered this café and that we once ate lunch here together. It's not far from Bazzana. So, I thought, what the hell, I'll chance it and see if you were here having something to eat before our meeting. Looks like I guessed right."

She turned and looked at Ben across the road, tilting her head with a short movement in his direction.

"That character you refer to is a friend. He was nice enough to provide the Vespa to bring me here. He has nothing to do with this whole thing. He also has no clue about the area and gets lost all the time. *Molto fastidioso.* Very aggravating. So, leave him alone. I gave him enough hell for everybody this morning. When you and I are through with our business, he's going to take me back to Alessandria. *Basta*."

Govanni stared at her, then looked over to where Frenchy was, now back down in front of the Vespa. The guy looked harmless. He saw Saverio watching him carefully as well.

Giovanni slowly unbuttoned his jacket, letting his left arm hang somewhat to his back, his right thumb stuck into the belt of his trousers right next to the buckle. The Glock still in its holster under his left arm. Still a bit of a stretch if I have to go for it quickly.

Giovanni waited. He didn't react to the lies. Her eyes told him she knew exactly what she'd done, that she was lying and playing him with all that lost-in-the-province drama because she'd wanted to get close to him. And she knew that he knew it.

What her eyes didn't tell him was that she knew that she'd thrown him and his gofer friend off balance. His body language spoke the language of uncertainty and concern. She saw that.

Advantage Anulka. Or so she thought.

Giovanni was astounded. He looked at her closely, thought after thought racing through his head.

Damn, considering what I said to her at our last meeting, she must be either stupid or naïve to think that she can determine what happens here. Or protect herself from us if we don't like what she says or does.

Look at her. The bitch is just sitting there and calmly

staring at me. Okay. Fuck her. I'm not saying anything here. Let her talk.

She looked at him, saw the venomous look in his eyes. In spite of his visible aggravation, she hoped she could convince him to accept her proposal. It was the one reasonable way to solve everything. She knew she was taking a big risk being where she was, but she just didn't believe that he'd dare do anything as serious as murder again, particularly in an open-field situation.

And she did have money for him. Just not what he was expecting.

"Giovanni, sit down, damn it, so that we can talk about things like normal human beings. Like the money I have with me. Or is that no longer a subject that interests you?"

He relaxed a little. So, she wants to talk. And she's brought money. Okay.

A slight motion of his head in the direction of Saverio. The message: stand up and move off to the left between her and the door to the café. Watch Frenchy and what he's doing. He's throwing occasional glances up and down the road. Waiting for something?

He moved his chair back away from the table and sat down. "Okay, I'm listening. *Che cosa mi vuoi dire?* What is it you want to tell me?"

She gave him an earnest look. "Listen, there's no sense in us pushing this whole thing to the limit. I told you in Bad Ragaz I hoped I would be able to bring you all of the money you think I still owe you. I said I would need five months' time. That time is now up."

She shifted in her chair, leaned in closer to Giovanni, her eyes flashing, her hatred for him pushing her on.

"But what you've demanded is not what I can deliver. I know that won't make you happy and I'm quite aware of what you said the last time. But fact is fact. You were right when you said I'd started again taking money out of a client account. But I couldn't do it in the way we did it. This time, getting that same kind of money out would have meant running a very high risk of being caught. And if that had happened, I'd have nothing to give you. And we'd all be running for our damn lives right now."

"So, here's what I have. I've been able to get together another 170,000 Euros. That's still a hell of a lot of money. You know damn well we've all benefited from this whole deal. And we're still walking around free. We should be satisfied with that. So, accept what I have with me and forget about the rest and let's let this whole matter drop. Honestly speaking, I wish it were . . . ."

She didn't get to finish her sentence. He stood, his chair falling backwards, crashing against the wall. He reached under his left arm, unstrapped his pistol and pulled it out, cocking it and pointing it directly at her face.

Café or no café. Baker or no baker. Road or no road. He didn't give a damn anymore where he was. He saw only her and her treachery.

"What're you saying? You bitch, you're lying. Just like you've been lying all along. You're too smart not to have gotten the money. You're screwing us. I know it. Damn it. I warned you. If you didn't come down here with all the money plus plus, it was going to be your life you'd forfeit."

"I've had enough of you and your bullshit. Get up. Stand up right now," he lashed at her, spittle coming out of his mouth, his face contorted with anger and hate.

She stood, trembling at the sudden danger, striking out at him, each word spoken normally, but each word designed to push him away, make him think twice about what he wanted to do.

"You son of a bitch. Do you think I've come here unprepared? Do you think I'd walk into this situation and not have arranged in advance a way to seriously fuck you over if you tried anything stupid? If I go down, then you're going down with me, you bastard. Right along with your little stupid gofer friend."

"I've got all the videos of your buddy when he visited the bank and I've got your whole life written down on paper. And you know where those things are now? They're at the bank in a large closed envelope with my name on it. Pictures of you in there, too. That envelope is lying in a locked drawer in my office desk with a note clipped to it."

"You want to know what that note says? Well, I'll tell you. If I don't return to Zurich tomorrow morning, the bank will at some point go through my things and find that envelope. *And* the note. *And* the videos. The message on it asks that the envelope and its contents be passed on to the local criminal police."

She mocked him with her eyes and the tone of her voice. And her words in French.

"*Tant pis pour toi, mon vieux. Tu serais completèment encullé, completèment visé.* That'd be bad luck for you, old boy. You'd be completely screwed, completely fucked. So, wipe those dark little thoughts out of your mind, take the goddam money in the messenger bag, and get the hell out of my life."

Giovanni stood and came around the table, grabbing her and pushing the pistol muzzle into the side of her neck. One step away from complete loss of control.

"Listen to me, you fucked-up little bitch. You've done nothing of the sort. And even if you have, I don't give a damn about what you've arranged. I don't give a damn if you've got a whole legion of cops ready to jump our asses once they see what you've prepared for them. I don't give a damn if you've got the whole Swiss Army parked behind that hill up there, ready to come down and save you. You won't be around to enjoy it. And neither will your friend."

"What a joke. We're here in Italy. We'll take care of that problem—if it ever becomes a problem. As for you, take a good look around you. You're looking at your last day on this earth."

She saw he was no longer himself. She swallowed hard. She recognized she'd misjudged totally his ability to use rational thought, to be concerned about getting caught and put in jail. He didn't care. White-hot hatred, blinding him to any concerns about where he was, blinding him to the very real danger of himself being taken down, had a firm grip on him.

There was nothing holding him back from killing again. She knew it.

She'd misjudged. And lost. And Ben with her.

Giovanni turned and spoke quietly to Saverio. "Get over to that bastard near the Vespa and then whack him. I'm going to take this bitch over to your car. Hit the clicker for me. She's going to take a little ride with us. Damn, damn it to hell. No money. Just a token payment. Can you believe that?"

Ben was already moving slowly off the side of the road where he'd been standing, back the several steps toward the Vespa. He'd heard the shouting, heard the anger in the voices, heard Anulka's words of reason and warning, seen the gun pointed at her, understood the exchange between Giovanni and Saverio, seen Saverio start to move toward him.

Giovanni kicked the table over, pushed over the chair with her helmet and her sunglasses still on it. Grabbing hold of her right arm with his left hand, he started to drag her across the road, the barrel of his pistol hard against her throat, the messenger bag with the money still hanging cross body at her side.

A low threatening growl in her ear, every word measured, every word filled with venom: "Listen carefully to me. If you say one word, if you let out one scream, I will shoot you right here. Believe me, right in your pretty face."

He stopped for a second, grabbed her face with his left hand and turned it to his. "Do you understand me, damn it?"

She didn't scream. She believed him, but she fought him nevertheless. She twisted and turned, but he was, definitely, the stronger.

To get her quickly across the road, he needed two arms and two hands. He put the pistol in the front band of his trousers, grabbed her with both hands and dragged her, both her feet now scrapping along the surface of the road, toward Saverio's car.

As out of control as he was, a small voice started to warn Giovanni of the danger of his situation—and of possible discovery. He needed to get her quickly away from the café and the whole area. Somebody might see them. And the police, finding and then identifying the head of the Wealth Management Division of Bankhaus Finsler lying dead outside a rural café and bakery in Italy, would ask some very unpleasant questions. As would the bank. No. He had to get her off to where he could "take care" of her and where she wouldn't ever be found.

Her driver would be dead at the scene. And dead men don't talk.

Saverio walked diagonally across the road to reach Ben. As he reached the other side, he pressed his car's clicker to unlock the doors of his car so that Giovanni could put Anulka into it. He heard the click up the road. Put the clicker back in his pocket.

He approached Frenchy, who was now standing directly in front of the Vespa. Ben turned to face him, the expression on his face one of disdain, his body tensed. A short distance between the two of them, eight feet Benimum.

Saverio drew the silenced Sig Sauer out of the deep inside pocket of his jacket, took off the safety, holding it loosely at his side, finger on the trigger. Not yet aimed, but ready to put it into firing position in a split second.

Ben stood still, eyes fixed on the pistol in Saverio's hand, his own hands hidden inside the two voluminous pockets of his long leather coat. He wet his lips with his tongue, balancing two immediate needs—saving Anulka, and neutralizing the very deadly danger stemming from Saverio.

A step forward. His face impassive. Sunglasses gone. Body tensed for action. His eyes, slits in the face of the immediate danger, and the dust being blown in his face from the strong wind coming down the road.

Saverio observed the change in his demeanor. He's seen the gun and still he moves toward me. Definitely not a guy who will listen to reason and leave.

Giovanni's right, he thought. We can't let this man go. Too dangerous.

No words were exchanged. It was time to take Frenchy out. Saverio moved a step closer, his pistol still at ready at his side, contemplating a head shot, the kill shot. No way I am going to miss hitting his face at this range, he thought.

Suddenly, a loud scream from up the road, then, almost simultaneously, the cranking sound of a revving truck motor, the shifting of gears from up the road. Saverio startled, turned his head to his left to glance briefly behind him. Large, junky truck, now rolling past, shifting up another gear, clutch engaged, accelerating again after having come slowly down the hill, using its engine to break its speed.

Ben had his right hand firmly around his own equalizer. Despite the confidence that gave him, he knew he might be looking at the last seconds of his life.

The noise of the truck, and its distracting effect on Saverio, gave Ben a different opening, the opening he needed. He leaped across the narrow gap separating him from Saverio, throwing his right fist, now free of his pocket and its contents, with all the emotion of life and living at the left side of Saverio's nose, right below his eye.

It was a hard, but only glancing blow because Saverio had started to turn his face back to him again. Nevertheless, his head snapped back from the weight of the blow. He swore and fell back a step, partially blinded. Now close in to his body, Ben grabbed his left shoulder and his gun hand with his hands. Raising and turning his body slightly, he brought his right knee quickly up into Saverio's groin.

Hard. Direct hit. Once, twice, three times, massive blows, still holding Saverio's body up so that he wouldn't fall immediately to the ground from the unbearable pain being inflicted upon his balls.

Ben's old wrestling moves had come back to him. His old wrestling matches, the hard scrabble nights he'd spent in Afghanistan and Pakistan, fighting to reach his plane to avoid being caught and killed, flashed through his mind. He felt the hot wind of massive anger buzzing, helter-skelter, through his body.

Even with the tremendous pain in his groin, Saverio was still half-standing. Ben grabbed his right arm in a bend-back arm lock, loosening his grip on the pistol. He reached down and ripped it out of his hand, then jumped back away from him. Watching now as Saverio fell to the ground, moaning, twisting, grinding, his legs drawn up, still holding his groin, now with both hands.

His face hard, Ben spoke to him. "You piece of shit. Let it go."

But Saverio was having none of it. He glanced up at Ben, then struggled slowly into a position where he could put his hand onto his right knee to support his standing up. There was massive pain in him, but he felt also, now, the heat of the kill in him. He knew the pistol was no longer his. He knew it was pointed right at him. But no matter. He was sure the wimpy French bastard wouldn't have the balls to use it.

Hidden from Ben, he drew the knife out of the sheath tucked into his boot at his right knee, gauging the distance he needed to negotiate in order to get blade into flesh.

With a yell, he lunged in a sudden, quick movement at him. Ben turned to the right and away, attempting at the same time to block the knife thrust with his left arm. But Saverio was fast. The knife cut through leather and cloth and skin of his left arm. Five-inch-long wound.

Saverio saw the blood spurting from the cut of the knife, knew he was going to be the victor on this killing field.

No shots had been fired in return. Saverio stood still, watching as Ben stumbled back, then fell to his knees, supporting himself on the ground with his right hand, but still holding the pistol firmly in that same hand. His left arm, however, hung useless along his side. Blood running down along the arm to the hand, a puddle of it already wetting the sand and the asphalt of the road.

In spite of his pain, Ben warned him once more. But they were words aimed at ears deaf to anything but the message coming from his brain: "Kill the bastard. Cut him to pieces."

Ben knew there were only seconds remaining in which to act. He felt for the safety on the pistol. It was off.

He started to struggle to his feet again, pointing, as he did, the barrel of the pistol in the direction of Saverio's body, hoping to keep him away. The pain from his wound made his body and the pistol in his hand shake. He saw the hatred in Saverio's face. And he knew what was coming.

Saverio still felt the waves of pain from his groin cascading through his body. But he had the knife ready, felt the slippery hold on its handle from Frenchy's blood. He saw Ben take several deep breaths, weakened, and white in the face. He moved his right leg into a push-off position for the final lunge with the knife. He saw the black dot of the pistol muzzle now again pointed at him.

No problem. Frenchy hadn't shot the first time. He wouldn't shoot this time either.

He lunged again at him, this time intending to gut him and finish the job.

Less than six feet. Close range. Ben pulled several times on the trigger. Phut/click-clack. Three quick muffled shots tore into Saverio's upper chest and stomach. Hollow points ripping deadly holes in flesh and bone. The loudest sound coming from the mechanical cycling of the slide as it ejected the spent round and reloaded the chamber after each shot.

The force of the bullets stopping Saverio, still lunging at Ben, right in his tracks.

Two more quick shots, fired almost blindly in Saverio's direction. At that short distance, Ben knew there was little chance they would miss. He saw the hits, saw the entry wounds in neck and face.

The bastard.

Gasping, moaning at the horror of the situation, he took one step forward, at the same time watching as Saverio slammed back against the grill of the old car parked just up from the Vespa, then slid down to ground, his body crumpled together.

Ben moved over to where Saverio lay, looked down at him, taking in the blood already seeping out of the bullet holes in his body onto the dusty shoulder of the road. He looked at his eyes, sightless, his face still reflecting the hate he had felt, his body twisted in death.

His breath came in short, ragged gasps. He looked down at his arm. The flow of blood seemed to have increased. He looked at big drops of it falling to the ground. He looked down at the hand holding Saverio's pistol, his eyes still wild. Seeing, then unseeing, then focusing again.

He noticed the silence, the incessant cold, then the wind howling, and the dust being blown high in the sky.

And then, suddenly, he remembered.

Anulka.

She'd heard the shots. Ben was gone. She'd screamed, desperate sounds, knowing finally that whatever she did or didn't do, she was also going to be killed. Giovanni was fighting to put her into the car. He had the back door of the car to the street side open. He pulled his pistol again out of the band of his trousers. Put the barrel against her throat, threatening her, pushing her down so that her head would clear the top of the car door.

Looking now at her almost inside the car, half-sitting on the back seat, no longer fighting. He had her now. He just needed to get her feet inside and then he could shut the door. Pistol headed back inside the holster. Damn it, he thought, where is Saverio? Frenchy is dead. C'mon!

Suddenly, a shout. Words lashing at the air.

"Giovanni, you bastard. Stop it. Take the damn money and let her go."

Giovanni turned half-right toward the sound. His name, the words, shouted, coming from near the rear of the car.

Giovanni's eyes opened wide. Recognition. Oh, shit. The French guy.

Standing six feet away next to the right back fender of the car. Holding a pistol with silencer in his right hand. Left arm bleeding badly. That looks like Saverio's pistol, he thought.

Ben stared at Giovanni. His body was trembling, shaking, his face contorted in pain. He held the pistol unsteady in his hand, the barrel of the gun wobbling back and forth.

Giovanni tried desperately to adapt to the suddenly-changed situation. Saverio? Where? Weapon? How this? Terror.

His brain signaled his right arm and hand: grab the gun and shoot the bastard.

Anulka had recognized Ben's voice. Alive! She kicked hard at Giovanni, fighting him, distracting him, but only for a second. He was quick. And focused on the danger. He had the pistol out. Two quick slap shots at Ben. Missing the first one. The second one almost sending Ben to his knees, a long, angry red stripe suddenly visible on his neck below his right ear.

Grazing shot, just missing the right carotid artery on his neck.

Ben felt the immediate pain of the wound, the heat of the bullet that had seared his skin, the blood starting to run out of its long, raw redness down onto his shirt.

Giovanni yelled at him: "How do you like that shit, you bastard. What the hell do you think you're doing here?"

Ben moved slowly back and forth, moaning from the pain of his two wounds. He was having difficulty standing. His brain had started to shut down the thought processes that would help him survive. Giovanni took a step forward to make sure he didn't miss. It was time to finish this, to kill him and be done with it.

He grasped his pistol more firmly, avoiding, just barely, Anulka's wind-milling legs still reaching out from the back seat of the car in an attempt to stop him from shooting again. She was screaming. She couldn't see Ben, but she sensed he was hurt. And thought he was defenseless.

For Ben, there was nothing left. And yet there was something: two lives needing to be saved. Through the hurt and the fear, seconds from possible terminal blackness, he heard her, he saw her legs churning, he heard her scream, he smelled his own blood, he heard his heart beating, he felt the cold spring air.

He wanted to live.

Blind anger and the human drive for self-preservation pushed the pistol in his right hand quickly up into shooting position. Phut//click-clack. Two quick shots. Then three more, one after the other. This time taking aim and making sure.

Giovanni slammed back against the open back door of the car. Body shots, two head shots, the head exploding with the impact of the hollow points. Blood spurting out onto his face. The window of the rear car door shattered. Blood streaked down the remaining shards of glass still left in its frame.

Body tilting over to fall face down lifeless onto the asphalt pavement.

The metallic pings of the empty brass cartridges ejected from the pistol, caroming off the back fender, pinging as they hit the hardness of the smooth, asphalt pavement.

Then, sudden quiet. Nothing. No sound. Wind. Dust.

Suddenly, a voice in German. *"Maedel, die Vespa. Lauf. Schnell. Du musst fahren.* Girl. The Vespa. Run. Quickly. You have to drive."

Aware of the danger of being observed. Possible vehicle traffic coming along.

Move.

Baker still inside the building. Front door to the cafe tightly shut to the outside. Door to the adjacent bakery closed. Before coming, a worry for the both of them—wanting the short meet to go down quickly, uneventfully, without witnesses. The one risk they hadn't been able to really calculate or eliminate.

Anulka, knowing from a previous visit in the cafe that, on Sunday mornings, the baker, a one-man show that early in the morning, would have only one thing in his head: bake and bake and then bake again. Lots of guests would be coming later, walking along to the café from the village after church. Best brioches in the whole region.

Before descending from the hill, Ben had observed through his binoculars the baker coming out of the café to bring the two men their second order. The Vespa had been rolling the one mile down the hill the second he had finished serving them and was on his way back into the warm indoors.

Let those guys freeze outside had been the baker's singular thought. He had other problems to take care of. The oven was full of trays of freshly-made brioches. He'd already burned the first batch. A second time and he'd lose his job.

A good roll of the dice. The baker had heard nothing.

He'd seen nothing. A war outside and his was an island of peace. And wonderful aromas.

Ben was panting hard. A quick glance around. No one. He slipped the pistol into the outside pocket of his leather coat. Using his good right arm, Ben grabbed Giovanni's cell phone from the inside of his jacket, then ran to the café on the other side of the road and scooped up Anulka's helmet and sunglasses from the ground. She was already on her way to the Vespa.

Ben ran for the Vespa, putting the cell phone into the same deep pocket of his coat where he'd put the pistol.

They arrived at the same time. Ben fitted his helmet onto his head and fastened it, moaning at the pain in his arm. Anulka on board, revving the engine, sunglasses and helmet back in place, messenger bag still hanging cross body at her side.

Time to disappear. *Subito.* Right now.

Ben wrapped his right arm tightly around her waist. She had the Vespa already rolling toward the small crossroads near the café. Five seconds later, the raspy sound of its exhaust and its passengers were gone, covered up by the wind, and by the dust clouds blown high from the dirt along the sides of the narrow country road behind them.

Ten miles away, on another deserted crossroad, the Vespa slowed to a stop. The pieces of the disassembled Sig Sauer pistol, wiped clean of fingerprints, were dropped into each of several large colored garbage bins allocated respectively for the collection of wet garbage, bottles, and cartons.

No bullets in the magazine. She'd thrown them and the silencer earlier over the railing of a bridge into a deep, fast-moving stream below. Nothing traceable. Nothing incriminating.

A slight pause, then she saw Ben go back to the first two orange-painted garbage bins along the road, dropping two more dull metallic objects into their respective round openings.

She caught her breath. Her heart jumped. Good God, she thought. Ben had had his own weapon with him at the café. He hadn't used it. Now he was discarding it, too.

She didn't say a thing.

Before driving on, she ripped her scarf into strips and bandaged Ben's left arm. Both of them were relieved to see that while the cut was long, it was not as deep as they'd thought it might be. The wound still oozed some blood, but it was already starting to coagulate. With some water from a bottle she had in her backpack, she'd wet one of the strips and, with it, cleaned the other wound on his neck as best she could. Thankfully, the bleeding there had already completely stopped.

Another thirty miles further, in the center of Alessandria, and still protected from the cold by their clothing and their helmets, they parked the stolen Vespa in the broader portion of a street near the railroad station, blocked off and reserved for two-wheeled "vehicles". Standing there, the Vespa was indistinguishable from the many hundreds of other motorcycles, *bicyclettes*, scooters, and other different model Vespas left parked there by rail passengers or inhabitants of the town taking a Sunday walk in the area.

They'd taken care of an important matter at that location the day before when they'd been busy preparing and checking everything necessary for the meeting. On all four corners around the parking area, no video surveillance.

They could use the lot for their purposes without worry.

They left nothing behind neither on nor in the Vespa. It was squeaky clean from front to rear. No blood traces anywhere. No fingerprints, no hairs, no threads. Nothing. When found, the rightful owner was going to be happy with its completely pristine condition.

The investigating authorities, once they finally got their hands on it, wouldn't be.

No one took notice of the two leather-clad figures wearing sunglasses, wool caps pulled down tightly, helmets dangling from their arms, walking slowly along several streets afterwards to an old quiet residential cobblestoned side street. Just two motorcyclists, like many others, on the way to pick up their motorcycles—or coming from them.

A common daily occurrence, not only in the streets of northern Italy, but everywhere else in Europe as well.

Their gait was unhurried. Halfway down a side street, just under a large tree, bare of leaves, and next to a narrow driveway, a black two-door Alfa Romeo MiTo, with tinted windows and Italian plates, was parked. No traffic. No video cameras anywhere on the street. They dumped what they'd carried with them on the Vespa into the trunk of the car, then got into the car and strapped themselves in.

She in the driver's seat. For a moment, not a word was spoken. Ben winced, then moaned at the pain in his arm. He touched the side of his neck. No bleeding. But she knew the wound hurt like hell.

A short, whispered sentence. She would drive them across the border—a little over an hour and a half away—into Switzerland, and then go to a private clinic she knew through her father, citing a spill from a motorcycle as the reason for his injuries.

Ben nodded, his face relaxing somewhat.

She turned to him, put her right hand gently on his left shoulder, then reached across behind him to grasp his right shoulder, slowly pulling him closer to her, looking him intently in the eyes. "*Danke.* Thank you," she said softly, then kissed him.

Ben looked at her, tears welling in his eyes. He swallowed hard. Whether it was from the pain in his body or from the tenderness of the moment, he wasn't sure.

Ten seconds later, the Alfa Romeo drove off at a slow speed, accelerating only slightly after it had turned the corner at the bottom of the street. There was still the cell phone that needed to be taken care of, but that would only take a couple of minutes. They would break it down into pieces and put a small but heavy dose of acid on the chip before they tossed it. Even if the authorities were able to obtain all the numbers Giovanni had previously dialed or the previous call-ins to that phone from a third party—she knew she could handle any questions that might arise should her phone number show up on that list.

She knew the drill. Right down to the last raised eyebrow.

Giovanni Vincoli? Old and very public relationship. But long over and done with. The calls? God, the guy just never gives up. Nice enough time with him but. My answer to him: no, thanks. Why are you asking? What is that you're saying? Probable professional hit? Many shots? Face hits? Possible revenge or payback killing? God, I can't imagine something like that. How awful.

She flipped down the left sun visor. Pushing the little cover aside, she looked at her face in the small vanity mirror. Unbelievable, she thought to herself. She'd almost been killed. Giovanni would have taken her somewhere and then killed her. Of that she was certain.

She breathed deeply. She knew the terrible need to stop Giovanni and Saverio by killing them was something they hadn't planned. But then it could just as easily have gone the other way. South. Permanently. For both of them. A horrible thought.

They were safe. Thank God for that.

And thank God for Ben.

She looked out the window at the nondescript apartment buildings passing by, then turned and looked at Ben. His face a mask, both hardness but also pain in his eyes.

She thought of the messenger bag in the trunk of the car with the 170,000 Euros still in it. Giovanni would never see that money, never be able to use it, never be able to enjoy it. Fuck him, she thought.

She lowered her head slightly, and then raised it, looking in the mirror once more. The morning's horror was written all over her face. But it was over. At least the hard part was. Or was the hard part going to be the rest of her life living with the morning, and the fact that she had been involved in the death of two people?

No answer for that yet. Maybe there never would be.

She reached for Ben's left hand and found it. He squeezed hers gently. It was time to go home.

33
The Office of Herr Dr. Graesser
Member of the Management
Supervisory Committee
Bankhaus Finsler & Co AG
Adlerstrasse
Zurich
Switzerland

April 19   The same year   17:42

Anulka was almost hyperventilating as she walked along the corridor on the sixth floor of the bank. She had an appointment with Dr. Graesser in his office at 17:45.

Both her previous two appointments with him had had to be cancelled due to her having suddenly to travel to Vienna, and his having had a short, but strenuous, spring cold, which had kept him at home in bed for three days.

Anulka Lorenzini was ten, maximum fifteen, minutes away from resigning her position at the bank. Every step she took on the polished floor of the hall resounded like the cadenced beat of a tight drum in her head. Like a march to an execution.

He'd been for many years her mentor, her promoter, her father *in camera*, her motivator. His office had been a refuge for her as once her real father's office had been. With him encouraging her, she'd been able to pour out her concerns or her fears to him, his two hands holding hers tight afterwards before she left his office, having, through him, recaptured her energy and motivation to press on with the job at hand.

He'd enriched her life in ways he would never know. While he'd merely warned her about potential professional dangers, she, on the other hand, had known exactly how those dangers could have been costly for her and her career at the bank. Now, she was getting ready to leave him and all that he had meant to her through almost all her adult life.

She hurt inside at the thought she'd never see him again. She'd never be able to feel the strong warmth of his caring for her again, never be able to talk to him again, never be able to ask his advice, or hear his voice again. He wasn't at fault, she was, and the hurt she would cause him would be monumental in its all-pervasiveness.

Yes, she'd known all along he was part and parcel of what she felt was an immoral business model. Yes, he had certainly been and was complicit in the bank's activities, but he was also human. Her human. And humans make mistakes and sometimes make compromises they're not proud of. Maybe he had done something exactly like that.

Whatever.

At the end of the day, he was a fine human being, a gentleman, what one would call a Renaissance man. One had to respect and honor someone like that.

She knew her resignation would rob him of a part of himself. She knew he'd always seen in her the daughter he himself had never had. They'd never discussed this, but she knew he felt that way. It was going to break his heart. And in the process of doing that, of disappointing him, break her heart as well.

She sighed deeply. One day he'll discover that I'm not the woman he always thought I was. She regretted to the depth of her soul the hurt he would certainly feel. Not so much because of the damage to the bank or his reputation—that would hurt on a business level, but because she'd cheated him professionally, and had cheated him as a human being as well.

She knew he'd never be able to forgive her for that.

She could not influence that happening or not happening. All other things being equal, she thought, at least he still has some time before that might happen. As for me, I've already died my little death.

The words she intended to use came haltingly into her head again. She'd silently practiced, over and over again, how she would tell him. And gone through the reasons she would give for a decision she could not alter or reverse. In the end, she knew there was only one effective way to handle the whole thing: straight-out statement of intent, the truth only partially in sight.

As she approached his office area, she noted that his secretary was already gone for the day. She went directly to the office door behind his secretary's desk and knocked. Muffled, she heard his voice bidding her to come in.

She felt it as she closed the door behind her. This had been her refugium, her charging station, here she had been happiest. Now, it would be scene of separation, of sadness, of finality.

Looking to her left, she saw the rectangular seating group in the corner where they'd be sitting, two double couches separated at their corners by a large blue Chinese vase lamp and a polished round teak side table she knew he'd bought in Beijing on his last trip there.

The table lamp was already turned on. There were some strawberry petit-fours on a small plate next to a still-empty coffee cup on the coffee table. He never ever forgot what she liked.

He was sitting at his desk. He stood, formally, as he always did when she came to see him. They greeted each other, looking directly into each other's faces, smiling at the thought of being able to spend some time together and chat about business. And what-not.

Her heart hammered as she sat down. The last normal greeting, she thought, the last few minutes with him before the sky falls on his head. She fidgeted with the watch on her left wrist, turning the band back and forth, as she watched him pour the coffee and offer her cream and sugar. He knew she took both in her coffee.

"So, we seem to have finally found a moment to sit together without you being in Vienna or I being home sick in bed. How are you? How was your trip?"

"Ach, Dr. Graesser, it was fine. The usual problems. The usual discussions. But when I look at you, I'm happy to see you well again. I can't remember the last time you were home sick with anything. What did you have?"

He smiled at her warmly, recognizing her concern. "Just a cold and an upset stomach. Actually, I was quite happy to have a few days off. We're so busy and growing so fast. I must confess to you—but don't spread it around, please—I actually enjoyed staying at home. I finally had a chance to rest, to read some files I'd been saving for a plane trip somewhere, and I also started an interesting new novel. I like female anti-heroines in thrillers and this is a good one. A Swedish author. If you wish, I can give you the book afterwards to read."

"I'd love to have it when you're finished with it, thank you," she said, taking another sip from her coffee.

Okay, a lie, but a small one. Nothing compared to the big one still coming.

"So, Ms. Lorenzini, you obviously have something on your mind you wish to discuss with me. We've known each other for so long. Let's hear what my favorite executive in the bank has to say for herself," he said, smiling at her.

Her breath was coming in short little jolts. She remembered the warning she'd given herself. Hold onto your emotions. Keep your hands under control. Keep your sentences short, tell him as much of the truth as you can, give him your reasons, and make sure he understands your decision is irrevocable.

And that was exactly what she did.

He didn't say a word. He listened to her with his arms folded across his chest. She watched them moving rapidly up and down as he breathed and realized what she was saying, what the words meant. She saw his face flush. She saw his eyes behind his glasses cloud over.

"I know what you're probably thinking, that a sabbatical would perhaps be the best for me instead of resigning. I know the bank would give me that. One year away and then I return to Zurich and my responsibilities. But the problem goes deeper than that, Herr Dr. Graesser. I'm burned out and I've lost my drive and it has affected my love for the business. I don't know why that happened, but it has."

She drew a breath. "It was not a sudden thing. This change in me has been going on for a long time. The matter with Luca, about which you and I have spoken several times, has only accelerated my wish to take some time off, to go out into the world, without any duties or obligations whatsoever. And then to start something new in my life."

"Banking has been wonderful to me. You have been more than wonderful to me. I cannot begin to tell you in how many ways you've shaped and enriched my life. I am so thankful to you, so very very thankful. But it's time for me to move on. And, frankly, I'm glad to do so. I'm looking forward to it."

She smiled and dropped her eyes, making a weak attempt to put some lightness into her words. "A new. A new adventure in the life of Anulka Lorenzini."

Her last words with some truth to them, but also under-cut by the lie she was telling.

He leaned forward, drank some water out of the small glass standing next to his coffee, then settled back and took off his glasses. He was breathing heavily. He lifted both his hands to cover his face, drawing them from his forehead, across his eyes, his cheeks, and down to his mouth.

She looked at him, saw the unimaginable. There was wetness on his cheeks, tears he'd pulled from his eyes. She couldn't breathe.

He was crying.

He turned to her and looked deep into her eyes. The look of absolute anguish on his face, the depth of the feeling she saw in his eyes, broke her heart.

He stood suddenly and walked slowly over to one of the tall windows facing out to the city and beyond it, the Alps. He remained there for several long minutes, next to the drapes, looking out the window, slowly wiping the tears from his cheeks with a tissue, not saying a thing. Then he turned to face her.

He started to speak, softly, a slight tremble in his voice.

"Once upon a time, Anulka, and I choose to use your first name now because it's finally the right time to do so, once upon a time," he said, his voice catching and breaking.

He breathed in heavily, took a moment, found somewhere the strength to get his feelings under control, then continued speaking.

"Once upon a time, a young woman, you, Anulka, came into this bank. You will remember I was one of the people who interviewed you for your first job here. I remember sitting across from you. I remember thinking what extraordinary luck this bank has had to have such a fine and promising and energetic young woman asking this bank to hire her as a starting cashier. I remember our discussion as if it were yesterday. You asked such intelligent questions. Your eyes were so clear and trusting. I was totally enchanted by you and your abilities."

"We hired you and I think it's one of the best things this bank has ever done. You did everything I expected of you and more. It wasn't long before not only I, but also many other people here, recognized in you something special. I had the honor to become something of a mentor to you, not because I was appointed to do so, but because it just seemed somehow to work out that way."

She noticed those last words had had a strange effect on him.

"I cannot begin to tell you how proud I was, I cannot tell you what a joy it was to sit and talk with you and to guide your career here at the bank. Even though you earned it yourself, to see you promoted to the position you have today was for me one of the crowning moments and achievements of my career."

He paused, looked up at the ceiling, then turned slightly more towards her and continued.

"But I must tell you something you don't know, something, I'm sure, will surprise you. Many years ago, almost at the beginning of your time here, there was a point, before I became your mentor, when I stood at a crossroads with you."

He paused and looked across the room at her.

"You look at me with a question in your eyes. Yes, crossroads, Anulka. You see, I have to confess something to you that may shock you. But it's the truth and it's important that you know it."

She sat back on the couch, scarcely comprehending what he was saying to her. Everything around her ceased to exist. Only his words held her transfixed.

He took a deep breath. "You see, I fell in love with you those many years ago. Surprising, isn't it. Yes, I have to tell you, I loved you, Anulka. An impossible situation, as I'm sure you can understand with my being married and working directly and closely with you here at the bank. Twenty-two years age difference was also a factor that caused me to pause when I was considering, at that time, what to do with my feelings. And, of course, there was also you to consider, still young, with everything in the world in front of you."

"It was hard for me, very hard for me to live with, on the one hand, my constant desire to hold you and tell you how much I cared for you, and, on the other hand, to remember my duties and obligations as a professional and as a husband...."

He turned in the direction of his desk.

"You see that chair behind my desk? I have used that chair since I've worked here. Thirty-seven years this year. It's hard for me to believe when I look at it now standing there, but I sat in that very same chair sixteen years ago and took a decision I've adhered to up to this very day. I determined not to take my feelings for you one single step further. I determined never to let you know what was really going on inside of me."

He smiled slightly at her. "Instead, I decided to assist you as your mentor, as if you were my own daughter. As you well know, I never had a daughter, and I knew you'd lost your beloved father in your teenage years, so I was determined to be as circumspect and as caring in that role as professionally possible. It was not an easy decision, but it was the correct one. So, I worked with you, hoping you would one day become what I hoped you would become."

He looked at her, a note of pride in his voice. "You are that now what I'd always imagined you would be, Anulka. And I say to you, well done."

Soft words, caring words washing over her.

He looked down at the floor again for a moment, then up again at her, across the room. His face muscles under control.

"But, secretly, I loved you every day of every one of the years we've spent together. I'm afraid that your resignation today and its effect on me has told me that those feelings I've had for so long just never lost their original intensity."

His voice caught. "Of course, I tried to deny them, I

pushed them back down inside of me for all the reasons I just mentioned to you. I guess what I'm trying to say to you is that I seem to have lied to myself all these years. You were always there. In my heart and in my thoughts. Always . . . ."

She couldn't move. She felt her heart beating; she sensed its rapid pulse in her neck. She was transfixed by his confession. And by the turmoil of the feelings he was expressing to her.

He spoke even more softly. She had to lean forward to hear him.

"You telling me what you have today has somehow released me from that decision I made so long ago. And has finally given me the opportunity to talk with you as I've so often wanted to. Some people say one doesn't know what one has until one day one doesn't have it anymore. I can tell you, Anulka, that does not apply to your old mentor. That I can assure you. "

He took a deep breath, then expelled it. He drew himself up to his full height, buttoned his suit coat, then walked back to the couch and sat down.

His facial expression serious. In spite of his feelings, still a professional through and through.

Seconds passed. "Don't worry, Anulka, it's not necessary that you say anything about what I've just told you. I'd understand completely if you didn't say anything. I know you're surprised. I hope you're not offended."

She couldn't talk. She shook her head emphatically in answer. No offense.

"Well then, let me be a bit more formal here for a minute or two. I understand you completely. I respect your decision to reshape your life. But I'd be lying if I didn't also tell you it breaks my heart to do so. In every way, both professionally and personally."

He studied her carefully, hoping as he did so she wouldn't be taken aback by his penetrating look.

"Don't concern yourself, I'm not going to try and talk you out of leaving the bank. You've quite clearly already made your decision. I know you well enough. Nothing I can say will change that. I might try, but I know what you'll say. So, I have no choice. I must accept with the deepest of regret your resignation. And that is what I will do."

He crossed his legs, then leaned back into the couch and the cushions spread along its back. "I'm sure you understand your wish to leave by the middle of August does not leave us much time to appoint your successor and arrange for a transfer of responsibilities. But I do think the man you've suggested for your position, Herr Weber, is a very competent and appropriate candidate. I think the management supervisory board will probably agree with me on that as well."

She nodded, agreeing with his comments. But she was still unable to speak. The look on her face told him more: She was deeply affected and moved by his words and his description of his feelings for her.

And so terribly sad.

He smiled at her and waved his hand, wanting to

quickly conclude the remaining formal matters relating to her resignation.

"Details on all of this we can discuss at another time. Perhaps next Monday afternoon if that fits your schedule. I think that would be more appropriate—and also, I think, easier for us both as well after the upheaval of these last minutes. Do you agree with me on that? Is that okay with you?"

He looked at her from the side, a gentle, intense look, his eyes fixed on hers.

She breathed a barely audible "yes" to him in return, still looking at him, surprise, shock, sadness, but, above all, tenderness in her eyes. Remembering—and recognizing—suddenly in that brief moment—that same intense feeling she'd seen once or twice in those same eyes so long ago.

He took a deep breath. "But I will tell you, Anulka, it hurts. It hurts so very badly to lose you; in every respect it just hurts so much . . . ."

He attempted to smile at her again, the fingers of his hands moving slowly back and forth along the two sharp creases on his suit trousers. He blinked several times, then lost the battle.

"I'm so sorry."

His eyes filled again with tears and he put his hands up over his face to cover it from her, embarrassed, in spite of everything, that he felt so intensely, and regretted her leaving so profoundly.

She was disconsolate. She felt her own tears coming

and she let them come. Flow freely, she thought. Wash my guilt out of me if you can. Never in her whole life, except for days and weeks after the death of Luca, and the death of her father, had she felt the same deep despair that she felt in that moment. She took some tissues out of the box on the side table and tried to wipe away the wetness on her face and her chin.

The tears kept flowing.

She looked at him, the soft light from the lamp on the side table illuminating his features. And his pain. As fine a man as a woman could ever wish for, she thought to herself. Honest, a man of high integrity, professional, caring.

At least he can still be that kind of a human being, she thought. I've walked away from that. And it hurts me to know that. And to know that I can never go back to being that young innocent woman who sat across from him that day so long ago.

That woman is forever gone. It hurts. God, it hurts to know how deeply he cared for me. And that he carried that hurt around with him for so long, never telling me. How he must have suffered—and how he must be suffering now.

She stood up, now more in control of herself, and stepped over to where he was sitting. She sat down next to him and put her left arm over his shoulder, pulling his head gently to rest on her left shoulder. She could feel the intermittent shuddering of his body as he struggled to win back some control over his feelings and the hurt inside of him.

She questioned how much sadness she could still endure,

how much hurt she could still cause others for whom she so deeply cared.

She stood again, bending directly over him. She took his head into her two hands, lifted his face to hers, and kissed him slowly and tenderly on both of his cheeks.

Her two thumbs softly rubbed away the tears still forming, but now finally more slowly, at the lower lids of his eyes. She looked deeply into them. Green like hers.

She'd never noticed.

She spoke quietly to him, feeling the weight, measuring the cadence of every single word she uttered. "You have no idea how sorry I am, Thomas. No idea," using also his first name for the first time since she'd known him.

He stood, taking her with him. He wrapped his arms gently around her, and she hers gently around him.

And for a while after that, in the deepening dusk of an early Zurich evening, they stood as one in his office, saying goodbye to one another.

34
Arrest in A Fraud Case
Article in the *Helvetia Nachrichten*
Zurich
Canton Zurich
Switzerland

May 23   **The same year**
   VERHAFTUNG IM BETRUGSFALL

May 23

ar-The District Attorney for the City of Zurich, Dr. Hans Mein-ert, announced, yesterday afternoon, the early morning arrest of Dr. Peter Renauer, founder and owner of the renowned interna-tional finance and trustee group, Renauerr Treuhand AG, at his home in Zurich. Renauer surrendered peacefully to the arresting authorities. According to the District Attorney's office, the charges to be brought against him will include suspicion of breach of trust as well as suspicion of fraud and embezzlement.

Dr. Renauer's company offices, in Zurich and Winterthur, as well as his private quarters in Zurich and in Davos, where he has a winter retreat, were thoroughly searched during the morning hours for possible evidence associated with the alleged crimes.

Observers at the scene in Zurich and Winterthur reported seeing a large number of cartons and material being carried out of and put into official vehicles parked in front of the firm's two offices. Computers in the private offices of Renauer as well as those found at his home and in Davos were also confiscated by the authorities.

Numerous electronic storage devices found at the Florastrasse company location, apparently from a private security system under the control of Renauer, were also included in the items impounded.

Dr. Renauer was brought for processing to the Winterthur Prison in Winterthur where he will be held until his arraignment on Monday next before the magistrate court in Zurich.

According to an announcement made yesterday afternoon after the arrest, the District Attorney's office in Zurich received an anonymous package in early February of this year containing extensive and detailed information indicating possible fraudulent management and misappropriation of client monies placed under Renauer's fiduciary management.

The District Attorney's office submitted this material to a detailed analysis, determining after its completion that there was sufficient evidence to justify the immediate arrest of Dr. Renauer. Sources wishing to maintain their anonymity indicate that the clients allegedly affected by the embezzlement are primarily those associated with the Winterthur side of the business. The client assets allegedly involved belonged exclusively to deceased clients of the firm.

The Zurich District Attorney, Dr. Meinert, was quoted as saying that "the arrest today of Renauer serves to hinder any possible further misappropriation of client assets within the Renauer Treuhand AG. Currently, we have no reason to believe that client monies under management at the firm's location in the Florastrasse address have been similarly affected by the same practices allegedly prevalent in Winterthur and for which Renauer was taken today into investigative custody."

Because of the alleged gravity and extent of the crimes committed and the possibility of Renauer attempting to flee the country, legal sources in Zurich see little chance that he will be released on bail.

Friends and business acquaintances of Dr. Renauer uniformly expressed shock and astonishment at his arrest. Reached at his office, one of Renauer's close friends and a long-time business partner, requesting anonymity, characterized him as a "nice, quiet guy. Very hard to believe the things he's alleged to have done."

Another business associate, requesting anonymity, cited the possible effect his arrest might have upon him personally: "He was always a loner, and didn't really care about what others thought about him and his firm. However, I could imagine that now that he is faced with possible public scorn and humiliation that that experience might affect him in a very grave manner. Somehow, I feel sorry for him."

As of late yesterday afternoon, there had been no official announcement made by the Renauer Treuhand AG firm concerning to legal representation for Dr. Renauer. When questioned about the case, the managing partner of one of Zurich's leading legal groups stated that it would probably be the same legal firm represented by Dr. Lawrence Probst, five years ago, when he was accused, then convicted, of malfeasance and breach of trust in his duties as trustee of private client monies under his firm's management.

Probst is currently serving a fourteen-year term at the Poeschwies Prison in the Canton of Zurich for fraud and embezzlement. After his conviction, the prosecution had sought a sentence of 17-19 years. Probst is due to be released from prison in 2025.

35

The Autobahn near the city of Baden-Baden (A German spa)
State of Baden-Wuerttemberg
Germany

June 25   14:21

The small town of Baden-Baden is located in the western foothills of the Black Forest in Germany. A short drive to the west lies the river Rhine and, on its westside, the border to France. Its sister town is Menton, a Mediterranean city on the coast east of Nice. A strange combination: the one, a quiet health spa with historical significance, and the other, a vibrant, sun-washed elegant city on the French Riviera near the Italian border.

Baden-Baden is also located almost halfway between Zurich, Switzerland, and Frankfurt, Germany, with a direct autobahn connection between the two. A two-hour drive either from Frankfurt or from Zurich will put one in its town center or, alternatively, in front of the Kurhaus or Pump Building near the city's extensive gardens and parks.

Anulka had finally reached Felix in Frankfurt on his cell phone the previous week. She'd known he'd be returning there for several days in order to sign the final settlement papers of the compromise restitution agreement reached between himself, his insurance company, and the NHF Handelsbank.

"The insurance company paid part of the agreed-upon restitution. The firm had to pay the rest not covered by our insurance. In total, a significant sum of money, I can tell you. But, thank God, no further legal implications or problems for me or the firm. Our lawyer did a beautiful job. It's all finally behind us", Felix had told her.

She'd been pleased for him. She knew how much he'd suffered.

Thus, it had been a very relaxed and relieved Felix on the phone, agreeing, at her suggestion, to meet in Baden-Baden for the day. They hadn't seen each other for a number of weeks what with her traveling in Europe on business, and his spending almost all of his time on a second—and very difficult—follow-up client assignment in Paris.

In the preceding months, she'd not let the relationship between them advance emotionally any further than it already had. Now, however, she had a serious subject on her mind, one that required a face-to-face sit down. It definitely wasn't a meeting she was looking forward to.

The emotional discussion with Dr. Graesser had completely drained her of much of her remaining sangfroid and energy, something she hadn't had much of anyway after she and Ben had returned from their little excursion to Italy in late March.

Another strenuous and emotional event landing on top of all that which had already happened would be almost too much to bear.

In spite of her relief at the result, the morning near Castel Boglione had left some serious marks on her.

The intense worry caused by the danger of a possible miscalculation in their plans, the risk of sudden and unexpected brutal death, the constant fear of possibly losing control over the whole situation, the incredible hatred she'd felt for Giovanni, his uncontrolled rage at her and rejection of her offer, the loud, pinging sounds of the many empty brass cartridges striking the back fender of Rittero's car and the road in rapid sequence, the two dead bodies sprawled in unnatural positions, like two large soft stuffed dolls thrown there hard from a distance, the shocking cold of the morning air on her flushed face as the Vespa raced away from the crossroad, after every frame of those moments, the finality of it all, both for Giovanni's and Saverio's lives as well as for the future of her own life, everything connected with that morning had affected her emotional and physical balance more than she'd ever imagined or assumed it would.

Anulka had changed. She'd become more somber. She no longer had that certain lightness to her step, to her laugh, to her way of expressing her thoughts. Memory fragments of what had happened that day would sometimes unexpectedly enter her consciousness, crashing around in her head like the numbered balls in a fast-revolving lottery machine.

At such moments, her body tensed, she gasped for breath as she remembered what had happened in the seconds before, during, and after each fragment. She prayed for the quick passage of time so that those memories might be finally dulled along with the hurt they always brought with them.

At least, there was a certain peace in the knowledge that she was now forever free of the threat posed by Giovanni and Saverio.

She thought of Ben who'd been shocked and dismayed at the violent end. She was forever thankful that he'd not run in the face of danger, but had stayed, and in doing so, had not only saved his own life, but hers as well.

A recent call to him in Paris had confirmed that the knife injury on his arm had healed well. He would have a long white visible scar just underneath his right ear where the bullet had creased the skin of his neck.

Her biggest worry had been that the authorities in Italy would find something that would connect her to Giovanni and Saverio. But there'd been no call from anyone in Italy. No contact at all.

Several weeks after that Sunday, the newspaper, the *Corriere della Sera* in Milano, had reported again on what appeared to be a professional hit leading to the apparent shooting execution of two Italian citizens near Castel Boglione. An intensive, week-long investigation of the two men's backgrounds as well as a search of their domiciles had resulted in no additional information as to a motive for the two murders. The authorities assumed it was most likely the result of some kind of Milano underworld payback for a deal gone sour.

The newspaper had also reported that the police had no "persons of interest" currently under investigation.

How strange—and blessed—life is at times, she thought. The whole thing could have gone in an entirely different direction that day. And afterwards.

Her days in the bank had become long and tough. Even though she would be soon starting a new phase of her life, the thought of leaving the bank and her colleagues after so many years was not an easy one to live with.

Her movements were also slower, more measured. Her sentences, and the manner with which she spoke, no longer pounded the senses of those listening to her. Now, her words marched to a quieter and slower beat: *piano, adagio,* and *moderato.* No sign of *allegro*, a rapid overpowering of the auditory senses that had often left her listeners little or no time for individual consideration or thought before her next sentence arrived.

She even found herself occasionally having to ask her colleagues to repeat certain words or sentences she normally would have heard, but hadn't because she was long gone somewhere else with her emotions and her attention.

Her eyes often clouded over when she thought about the evening of her resignation from the bank. She remembered green eyes filled with tears, she remembered the deep sadness of Dr. Graesser, and the immense hurt she'd inflicted upon him. That moment, that final dose of toxicity in her life, wouldn't go away.

Often, in the evenings, she'd sat alone in her apartment or took walks along the bicycle path which ran along the lake below her apartment house, a reduced, almost bent-over figure, walking along, stopping occasionally to rub her foot in the hard sand surface, speaking to herself, trying to make sense of what she'd done with and to her life, trying to sort out the wreckage she'd created with her actions, the deaths she'd caused, thinking about her cold-hearted clients, trying to understand their cold and calculating manner, their trickery, trying to understand the elusive darkness, the horrible suicide of her father and all he'd stood for, trying to understand all those things that had created that motor for her hate, her desire for some form of revenge, for her double dealing, for her egocentric actions, for her greed.

Twice, she'd looked death in the face. Twice, she had gone to hell and back.

She hated herself for what she had been, for what she had done, for what she was.

At the same time, slowly, one small step at a time, something happened during that long exhausting process, during those many walks, during the back and forth of an emotional voyage through the wreckage of her past. She'd slowly made a discovery, something so uplifting, but also so desperately logical that, as she'd thought about it, as she'd finally recognized it for what it was, had caused her to sit down on a bench and have a good long cry.

They were gone. The toxic parts of her character, the negatives, the resentment, the hate, all things which had so long driven her, misled her, tortured her, endangered her life, were gone, used up, washed out of her, rejected, discarded.

No longer a part of her, no longer her. Burned up, their effectiveness, their seductiveness, their wrongness, destroyed by the intensity of all that had happened.

The slate was clean.

The softness in her, the caring her father had instilled in her, the gentleness of spirit, her empathy, her selflessness, her heart, the source of the many tears she'd shed, parts of her character that had always been there, that had, at times, impacted positively her actions and reactions in the course of her career, but had, sadly, more often than not, been held captive or neutralized by the darkness in her, all those good things in her had finally won the day again, pushing out all the negatives, dominating now her thoughts and actions as if nothing bad or destructive had ever happened.

A miracle, she'd thought. I'm free.

And then there was also something else, something important, she recognized.

She knew now the only way she could live with all she had done and with all the money she'd stolen would be to listen to and let herself and her future, in whatever direction she chose, be guided by those very changes, by a new ordering of her character, one she'd thought lost and was now reborn, by a new approach to life and the human spirit, by a concentration on producing and promoting good in a world needing as much of that good as one could give it.

She didn't intend that there be any mistakes along that future way.

Nor, practically speaking, for there to be any short-term problems, like some moment of suspicion at the bank or logistical screw-ups that would upset everything before she could leave Zurich.

To that end, she'd also been busy resolving the matter of the contents of her apartment. It was an emotionally-debilitating task, nevertheless, a necessary one if she wanted to have all her departure arrangements completed by, latest, the middle of August.

For months after she'd moved into her apartment, she'd poured all of her creative talent into decorating it, purchasing just the right furniture for it, and hanging the art she liked on its walls. It had been her refuge, a place of quiet and solitude, but, also, a happy place for her, filled with friends and her memories of Luca. And those horrible cigars he'd smoked there.

Now, she was slowly but surely selling off or giving away all that the apartment contained. And as each single object or item went out the door, she sensed that a part of herself, a part of someone she'd known her whole life, was leaving with it. Her special "babies", the couches, were going to her friend, Michaela, in Wolfratshausen. She and her husband would be coming the next weekend from Germany with a truck to pick them up.

The table lamps she'd sold to her neighbor on the floor above her.

Her little sales promotion effort in the other apartment buildings in her neighborhood had brought a gratifying response—and quick sales. The apartment was rapidly emptying.

But it was okay. The decision to go was the right one.

The silk material she'd bought in Dubai for the new couch cushions she would have made one day was already packed in a small wooden trunk. Lying carefully folded on the bottom, it would serve as a soft depository for items that were more fragile. The trunk itself still had enough room for her to put additional things into once she'd finished selecting and wrapping them carefully in bubble-wrap.

Lying directly on top of the silk material was a small leather etui with individual pockets and button flaps. One of those pockets contained the gold cuff links she'd removed from Luca's shirt cuffs as he'd lain on the ground in the bushes the night he'd been killed.

She'd never cleaned them. They still had the small smeared smudges of blood on them caused by her touching them with her bloodied fingers after she'd cradled what was left of his head in her arms, physical reminders of the horror of that night, horrible symbols of what her cheating and lies had done to her life—and her happiness.

At the same time, small reminders of a love so deep, a

love that had been and still was such a dominant factor in her life.

Several small cardboard boxes containing those effects she planned to take with her stood in the entrance hall. The picture of her father and her as a young girl lay in one them, carefully wrapped in bubble wrap to protect the frame which held it. She'd piled several small cardboard boxes on top of each other along the wall where once the map had hung that Luca had given her in Paris that morning so long ago. Now packed away, she realized she would not see it again until the questions of somewhere, somehow, sometime had been answered satisfactorily.

Actually strange, she'd thought, as she wrapped up a small silver picture frame, containing an old photo of her mother and father.

I know what I'm leaving behind, I don't know yet where I'm going, or to what.

At least not yet.

36
The Pump Building
The Spa Park
Baden-Baden
Germany

June 25   14:28

She was so deep in thought that she drove right by the Baden-Sued exit on the *Autobahn*. Not a problem. It was only a short three miles further north to the Baden-Nord exit. She would take that one to leave the autobahn and travel the short, five-mile distance over to the town center.

It was a beautiful, warm spring day, the fresh green foliage of the trees contrasting with the blue sky, flowers already poking out of the ground on the side of the autobahn, a sign that even poisonous car exhaust can't extinguish nature's force and drive.

Suddenly, a picture of Felix looking at her in the near-darkness of his room in Paris popped into her head. Why am I thinking about that right at this moment, she asked herself?

No matter. When she thought about that aspect of her relationship with him, she experienced the same surprise she'd had that night. The sex with him had been much better than she had expected. She'd also enjoyed his company during the preceding months. Though she knew there'd been a self-serving motive on his part for the help he'd given her during that time, she was thankful he'd been willing to do so.

She'd never forget that part of it.

What she also couldn't forget, however, was that, basically, the whole relationship had been little more than a necessary evil. No, stop, she thought, that's not right, that's not fair. And it's way too hard.

Let's call it a necessary arrangement, giving herself and her previous actions a bit more honor and dignity than the word "evil" would have done.

She left the autobahn as planned, but now someone in the car behind her had started to honk at her. She looked in her rear-view mirror and saw Felix waving at her. She waved back. She stuck her hand out the open window and pointed with it in the direction in which they were driving. Follow me and I'll find us both parking spots for our cars.

He signaled to her that he'd understood.

Ten minutes later, they were walking together, her arm hooked into his, toward the Pump Building, the source of the waters one "took" in a spa town like Baden-Baden. They found a bench to sit on to the left of its entrance.

They sat for a few minutes, enjoying the scene, admiring the flowers in the flower beds stretching out in front of them, a rainbow of color. They chatted about the drive to Baden-Baden, some minor traffic problems, about the number of people walking around in the park. Was anybody out there working anymore?

He told her about the final meeting with the bank and his impression of the bankers as they'd watched him sign the final papers. She spoke to him of the burdens of her job, of her disenchantment with the banking business. And her increasing demotivation.

Felix turned to her. "Listen, it's not that I'm not enjoying the view and the chit-chat, but I have something serious I'd like to discuss with you. I can see in your face that you're under great strain. So, let me talk to you a bit and perhaps remove some of that strain and worry from your life. Okay?"

She looked at him. Could he perhaps already suspect why she was here?

"Felix, I am under strain. And it's bad. How kind of you to recognize that. Please go ahead. What is it you want to say?"

He took her hand and squeezed it for a second, then laid his arm along the back of the bench as he spoke.

"Anulka, you and I have had a wonderful relationship. I'm not going to lie to you and tell you that I didn't fall in love with you. Because I did. Being with you as I have, experiencing you and the kind of woman you are, doing what you and I and Ben have done, in spite of its being something very wrong, wakened something in me, did something for me, that you perhaps—and I certainly—would never have suspected."

"It has given me for the first time in years a renewed

feeling of being alive, of having the strength to influence and master my fate, of being able again to shape positively the things in my life I encounter instead of letting them shape and—sometimes—torture me. Or, even worse, lead me astray."

"I've not been very smart in my life. I've also frankly wandered off the line more than I would like to admit. You know that very well. I don't regret having done that, but at the same time, I'm not at all happy about it. I want to do things differently in the future. I must do them differently. And I can do them differently now, thanks to you."

He noticed she was looking at him and smiling. A kind smile.

He took a breath and continued. "The fact of the matter is and please try to understand me when I tell you this—, I don't believe you and I are meant for a long-term relationship. On the one hand, that makes me very sad. That also doesn't mean it wouldn't be great fun to try. But, on the other hand, I recognize the differences in where we're going, no, wait a second, let me express that somewhat differently, where we're going to have to go because of the circumstances of the situation we both find ourselves in."

He studied her face carefully. "I think I know you pretty well, Anulka. And that's why I want to say this to you. If I were you, I would have come to Baden-Baden to tell me, we must part, that you cannot be responsible for having me involved in anything that would endanger me and my freedom."

"I know you know that the more imminent danger of discovery lies with you, and that, if we were together, you'd be drawing me into that, and the possible actions you might want or would have to take to escape that discovery. If that's your thinking and I think it is, then it honors you."

"Tell me honestly. Am I right in what I'm saying?"

He looked intensively at her, staring at him, tears now forming in her eyes. Those green eyes he'd found so beautiful so long ago.

Wiping the tears away with the back of her left hand, she took his hand to her cheek and smiled at him.

He knew.

And he was so right.

"Oh, Felix, you're such a wonderful person. And, yes, I do want to say something to you as well. And perhaps confess something while I'm at it. I hope you'll understand me and not look at me as someone despicable. Or unworthy of your caring."

He looked at her, a question in his eyes.

"When I met you for the first time at the bank last year, I saw certain things in you that I liked. Our dinner the following evening indicated to me that there was more. I discovered similarities in our characters, unfortunately, not exactly the finest similarities, as we both know. And yes, I decided to take, I will use that word, advantage of those similarities."

She kept her eyes right on him. "I didn't think you'd really consciously admitted your shallow weaknesses to yourself as much as I'd admitted those I have to myself. In a selfish way, I saw that I could use your weaknesses to help me solve my problem."

"I must tell you, I regret that. I'm sorry I had to do it, but, at the time, I felt I had no other choice. As it turned out, even though it was wrong, it was the right thing to do. I think I can also safely say that both of us—and Ben as well—have profited from my doing that. Each in our own way. And I'm not talking about the money side of things."

She paused for a second, and then looked directly into his eyes. The expression on his face very serious, his eyes fastened on hers.

"Are you offended by my use of that word profited, Felix? Please don't be. I mean it in every way in the positive sense. And please forgive me that I had to be so hard in how I viewed you."

He waved a hand over his shoulder, indicating that there was no problem. He smiled at her.

"No, Anulka, I'm not offended. I know what I was then and what I am now. And you don't have to say you're sorry. It's okay. Believe me. It's okay."

She continued, her voice now somewhat softer. "I needed help and you gave it to me. I am so very grateful to you for that, Felix. You've just told me how you profited from our little operation in the bank. I knew that. I've seen that in you. You've changed. You've become stronger. More balanced. More confident. And that makes me very happy.

"I remember watching you on the banks of the Rhine the first time we met to divide up the money. I could see what was happening to you. I saw it in your face. I heard it in the way you spoke."

She studied his face. "However, believe me when I tell you this. What I didn't count on with all of the back and forth 'profiting' that was going on was the fact that I not only liked you, but I also very much enjoyed you and being with you. Starting with Paris, and all the times after that."

She looked at him, seeing he was about to stop her from talking.

"Please don't interrupt me. I really need to say this to you. Let me finish here and then we can talk about it."

He nodded to her to continue. "In spite of everything, I have to say you're right. We have in fact come to a point where our ways must part. I have my reasons for saying this. I want you to know and understand them because they're important for you and your well-being."

She thought for a minute about her meeting with Dr. Graesser. A hollow feeling settled in her stomach.

She swallowed hard.

"I've resigned from the bank. My resignation has been accepted. I will be leaving Zurich sometime around the middle to the end of August. I don't know where I'm going, but I'm going. Somewhere to a new life, somewhere where I can give my life meaning. I only told you a little about my childhood and my youth and the problems I had with the business of banking and the clients I had to deal with day-in and day-out. There are multiple levels to the story of your Anulka that I can never tell you. Just please accept that fact and leave it at that."

"I'm totally burned out and I'm so very worried the

bank might discover what I've done. I'm going away. In that decision, that future I've chosen for myself, you are absolutely right, there is no place for any relationship, no place for you, no place for us. I'm sorry, really sorry to have say it this way, so directly, but I think it's best to be one hundred percent honest with you."

He looked at her, his face impassive, but his eyes full of understanding and acceptance.

She knew how her words would affect him, would hopefully help him to understand. And accept.

She chose carefully. "There's something I really want. I want you to be happy and free to live your life, Felix, unburdened by what we've done. I want to know that you're smiling when you look across the lake and think of me. I want you to take that new-found confidence and positive attitude you now have and put it to work. Believe me, I want nothing more than that, your continued safety, and your newly-won happiness."

She took his hand and held it tight.

"I guess what I really want to say to you is thank you, my dear Felix, for all that you've been for me. Accept what I have just told you because that's my way of showing you how much I care for you. And accept also, for God's sake, that you'd be endangering yourself in ways that are just too extreme if you were to push for any other solution. That is something I could never bear. So please, …"

He raised her hand and kissed it, then held it to his cheek. He looked into her eyes, smiling at her.

"It's okay, Anulka. I hear you and I understand you completely."

"You don't have to worry about me. I'm a grown man. Please don't think I didn't consider the fact that you might be taking advantage of me. It's alright. Both of us knew somewhere deep inside of ourselves what was really going on. I don't regret one thing that happened. Believe me, not one single thing."

"You're a wonderful woman, a unique person. You've enriched my life and given me new energy for the future. And, yes, I accept what you've said. Frankly, I'm not surprised at all. First of all, it's logical. And secondly, it fits you, and as I said before, it honors you that you think that way. And I thank you again from my heart for that. For your feelings and your caring."

He paused. His voice trembled somewhat, caught. He looked at her.

"Am I sad about all of this? Of course, I am. Nothing like this is ever easy."

He looked down, somewhat embarrassed, at the footpath in front of him, rubbed his right shoe back and forth along its sandy surface.

She turned and put her arms around him and hugged him. He kissed her cheek and wished her well. She recognized what she'd done and been for him and she believed profoundly in the good she'd be doing for him by going away from him. Good that had actually come from her when she'd almost started to believe that there was no more of it in her.

She felt a feeling of relief—and satisfaction—inside herself. At the same time, she felt the tug of the unknown growing stronger in her.

For the first time, she could feel the thrill of facing an uncertain future. Felix had spoken true words to her on that bench, but he'd also accomplished something else at the same time, something he'd never know he'd done. With his simple words and his act of kindness, he'd given her a stronger peace. And, along with it, a stronger feeling of resolve and a feeling of hope she'd never again let go.

She squeezed him the tighter for it.

She breathed in deeply, looking up at the early summer sun, letting its warmth strike her face and warm her skin. And wend its way into her open heart.

And she smiled at the wonderful, multi-faceted colors of the park, at the deep blue of the sky, at the vastness of the world all around her, at a world waiting for her, damaged as she was, but, nevertheless, its arms open to her.

37
Indicted Wealth Management Manager Found Dead

Article in the *Helvetia Nachrichten*
Zurich
Canton Zurich
Switzerland

November 30   The same year

ANGEKLAGTER TREUHAENDER TOT AUFGEFUNDEN

November 30

ar- The District Attorney in Zurich, Dr. Meinert, announced yesterday evening at a hastily-called press conference at its offices in Zurich that Dr. Peter Renauer, renowned finance manager and trustee, had been found dead in his cell at the Winterthur Prison, where he was being held pending the beginning of his trial, scheduled for May 25 of next year.

Based upon several items and utensils found in Renauer's cell, the prison medical authorities are assuming that his death was caused through direct ingestion of a toxic poison. The poison will be analyzed at the laboratories of the medical examiner for type and toxicity. An autopsy will be performed and the results made public at an appropriate time.

The Director of the Winterthur Prison, Dr. Steinmann, who also took part in the press conference, expressed his regret at Renauer's death. He announced that he'd ordered an internal investigation into the possible manner in which he'd been able to procure, and then use poison to take his life.

Normally, prisoners and their cells are subject to routine searches every 24 hours. The last search had taken place the day before at ten o'clock in the morning. According to prison records, nothing suspicious or unusual was found by the responsible personnel during that search. Based on this unfortunate circumstance, a review of the procedures used to conduct such searches will be carried out in the near future, Dr. Steinmann announced.

Questioned about Renauers physical and mental condition, Dr. Steinman did confirm that he had been in treatment for depression and sleeplessness. According to informed sources friendly to Renauer, he was suffering from the shock of losing his firm, from the loss of his image and his reputation, as well as from the public pillorying he was being subjected to by the local and international press.

As this newspaper has reported in the past, Renauer was to be tried for breach of trust, fraud, and embezzlement in connection with the disappearance of an estimated seventy-five million Swiss francs in client monies. His arrest in June of this year set off an avalanche of lawsuits against his firm, the Renauer Treuhand AG, as well as a sister company, the Kunst Treuhand AG.

Bankhaus Finsler & Co has also been rumored to have had a decade-long association with the Renauer Treuhand AG. To what extent the bank might be involved in the alleged crimes of the Renauer Treuhand AG will be a matter for the courts to decide, Dr. Meinert said, during an informal presser at the end of the formal press conference.

For the last four months, a court-appointed, forensic accounting firm has been combing through the records and accounts at both Renauer company locations, this, in an effort to determine the full depth and breadth of the alleged fraud. Final findings and recommendations are due to be presented for review by the Prosecuting Attorney's office in Zurich in the first week of March. In this regard, Dr. Meinert emphasized that "there will be no delay in bringing this unhappy chapter to a best-possible conclusion, in particular for the clients and their families affected in such a serious manner by Renauer's crimes."

Sources close to the District Attorney's office emphasized that office's particular interest in the analysis work currently being done on the storage devices found in Renauer's office in the Florastrasse. Dr. Meinert gave a brief overview of the importance of this work during the press conference: "More than 173 DVDs, which were taken from the firm's offices on the first day of the operation, have had to be registered and catalogued. A complete and thorough analysis of their respective contents will continue well into the first quarter of the coming year. However, the initial results of our investigation show that Renauer was using a video/ audio system in his private office to record many of his private conversations with the firm's clients as well as other parties involved with the firm. There is also some evidence that the contents of some of the DVDs could have been used for purposes or blackmail or other criminal acts."

"Unfortunately, a small number of the DVDs are of lesser quality due to the parties being too far away from the microphones or the sun hitting the lens at a certain angle which essentially blocked the visual recording during those few minutes. Nevertheless, working with a local company with relevant experience in the examination and analysis of DVDs, we are confident we will be able to recapture most, if not all, of the audio and film data affected by these two circumstances."

"We want to emphasize to the general public, and, above all, to the clients of the firm, that we will follow the trail or trails we find wherever they lead us. It is not our intention to discontinue this work until every fact, and every issue, has been identified, and every possible criminal act has been discovered, properly examined, and resolved."

Just before the close of the press conference, Dr. Meinert announced that the District Attorney's office still had no official information as to the names of the person or persons who had anonymously sent the original package with the first incriminating information relating to Renauer and his firm. Dr. Meinert expressed the hope that this person or persons would at some time make himself or themselves "available" to provide further information on the case, and in doing so, contribute to a positive resolution of all outstanding matters and issues in the case.

38
New Development in the Custodian Scandal surrounding Dr. Renauer

Article in the *Helvetia Nachrichten*

Zurich

Canton Zurich

Switzerland

February 17   The following year

NEUE ENTWICKLUNG IM RENAUER
TREUHANDSKANDAL

February 17

ar-The District Attorney's office in Zurich announced today several new developments in the poison/suicide case of Dr. Peter Renauer, the well-known financial advisor, trustee, and owner of the Renauer Treuhand AG. Dr. Renauer committed suicide in the Winterthur Prison on November 29. He had been facing trial for breach of trust, fraud, and embezzlement in connection with the disappearance of approximately seventy-five million Swiss francs from the accounts of his deceased clients.

The District Attorney's office in cooperation with the medical examiner's office, and based on Article 254 of the Swiss Code for Criminal Procedure, has applied for permission to exhume the body of Ms. Chantal Hofmaier, formerly of Thalwil, Canton Zurich. Ms. Hofmaier was employed for more than two decades at the Renauer Treuhand AG in the Florastrasse in Zurich, the last seven years of which she spent as private secretary to Dr. Renauer.

In previous proceedings, the interim managing director of the Renauer Treuhand AG had testified to the existence of a long-term, personal relationship between Ms. Hofmaier and Renauer, a relationship which had continued up to her death two years ago in May. Her passing was originally ascribed to a severe heart condition that allegedly suddenly worsened, causing her untimely death. No autopsy was performed after her death due to an alleged lack of ambiguity concerning its medical cause.

New information available to the District Attorney's office, including the exotic type, and extreme toxicity of the poison used by Renauer to take his life as well as two recent anonymous letters addressed to that office, have raised several serious questions in the case that need to be answered, Dr. Meinert, District Attorney for the City of Zurich, announced yesterday afternoon.

According to statements made by Dr. Meinert, there is also concrete information available that points to the possibility that Ms. Chantal Hofmaier was, in fact, the original source of the anonymous client account information that led to the subsequent arrest and imprisonment of Dr. Renauer.

He also indicated that his office is interested in clearing up a number of possible irregularities relating to the demise of Ms.

Hofmaier. Based on new information now available, the District Attorney's office wants to determine whether her death was due to the alleged natural causes, or the result of some other internal or external cause.

In this connection, sources close to the District Attorney have confirmed that Dr. Meinert recently spoke personally with the son of Ms. Hofmaier, Felix Hofmaier, a resident of the Canton of Zurich. The meeting had been scheduled with him in the hope that he could shed additional light on the cause of his mother's death as well as on any possible role Renauer might have played in her death.

The results of the overall investigation will be made available to the public in a second press briefing tentatively planned for Friday of next week.

39

The Tiara Chateau Hotel
Mont Royal Chantilly

Route De Plailly
La Chapelle-En-Serval
France

December 13   A year and a half later   22:17

Felix sat at the desk in his junior suite with his laptop open, scanning the news on the Basel newspaper website. He was tired, but it was a tiredness mixed with a feeling of satisfaction.

His consulting work in Switzerland and in France –including his continuing engagement for the same, now long-time, client in Paris—had been keeping him busy. Even more so than he had originally planned, anticipated, or even wanted.

Nevertheless, it all represented a positive development in a life that had calmed down considerably after the events of the past several months and years. He traveled during the week, mostly to France. On the weekends, which he spent in

Zurich, he always seemed to be busy: opera, theater, eating his beloved crab cakes at the Ermitage, visits to the Thalwil cemetery, an occasional date.

All in all, life was good. And most importantly, it was good in a positive way, just as Anulka had said she wanted it to be for him.

Of course, there were still the wounds from the past, wounds that were only slowly healing. His firm in Frankfurt long dissolved and gone. His reputation in Germany gone. A major amount of money gone to settle the whole Handels-bank matter.

His mother gone. Anulka gone. And Ben gone, some-where off in the Far East—was it Singapore or Djakarta he'd mentioned once upon a time?—doing whatever Ben did when he had enough gas in the tank. Which, of course, he always did.

Renauer dead, but no tears or regrets there. He'd gone down as he'd deserved, hurting all the way. Hopefully, the bastard was roasting in hell.

A soft bong. His computer signaled the arrival of an email. A subject message that could only have come from one person.

The title: *Wagners redux.*

Damnation. Ben. Long time, no hear, my friend, he thought, as he clicked on the mail.

Felix glanced for a second at the word "From" at the top of the email. Strange email address. Had Ben been in an

Internet Café when he'd sent the message? No way to really tell. No clue as to his location.

Ah, what the hell. Doesn't matter. Let's see what he's got to say.

The main text of the email contained a small collection of nice-to-hears and nice-to-knows. All business, and, as always, a lot about his more recent activities in the finance area. No need to worry about Ben, he thought.

Doing just fine, thank you very much.

He was moving on again shortly. Retiring from business was the word he used. No information on where he was going, just that he was going. And the new location? It would be a permanent one.

Typical Ben, he thought. He'd always had that wanderlust gene in his DNA.

He finished reading the main part of the email—some surprisingly deep and detailed philosophical musings from Ben about life in general and his change in attitude in particular—, then turned his attention to a postscript at the end.

Its short contents pushed his pulse rate up dramatically.

PS. How could I forget to tell you the good news. As I mentioned above, after all the years of running around the world, and all the false starts and stops, I'm finally settling down permanently. Not only geographically, as I mentioned above, but also, and more importantly, personally.

Curious? You probably guessed it. I recently married, can you believe it? My wife intends to found a non-profit school for disadvantaged children. She anticipates she will have about one hundred to one hundred fifty students from the town where we will settle as well as a smaller number from further away. She wants also to teach English several days a week in addition to her other duties. It will be wonderful to watch her. I tell you, the best thing in the world is to love and to care for someone.

 I guess it happens to most of us when we least expect it. I can assure you I certainly hadn't. I hope very much you'll have the very same experience one day, Felix. You deserve it in spades, old friend.

 But here's also even more important news! We're actually doubly blessed, my wife and I. Not only through our being together, but, in addition, by something really special. We have a baby daughter who is almost two months old. The joy of our lives, I tell you.

 We call her Annie.

 M.

Felix swallowed hard. He looked for a moment into the distance, seeing nothing. His eyes clouded over. A moment of doubt. Did that message contain what he thought it did? Would Ben, knowing Felix's former situation as he did, have written something like that? Yes, after so long a time, yes, I think he would have, he concluded.

He would want Felix to be happy for him.

Felix had made his own decision that day, accepted her leaving, knowing her need to be her own woman. Nevertheless, since then, there'd always been unanswered questions in the back of his mind. Where was she? How was she?

Well over two and a half years gone by, and now, finally, it seemed, he had an answer. For a moment, sadness and disappointment coursed through him. And yet, at the same time, the knowing better than what had been the past, the not knowing. Slightly annoyed at perhaps an element of dishonesty in her actions. But forgiving definitely the better reaction. Because he cared for them both.

Smiling gently, he looked again at the name of their baby daughter.

Annie.

He knew the name in Polish.

Anulka.

40
Conference Room B10
Bankhaus Finsler & Co AG
Adlerstrasse
Zurich
Switzerland

December 15   The same year 9:35 am

Director Anton Weber hurried along the carpeted corridor to the wing of the bank that contained a number of additional conference rooms. The main building had the most such rooms, but they were unfortunately all reserved, or already in use. He'd asked his young assistant to take Mr. Sala, one of the bank's top wealth management clients, to Conference Room B10.

Something to drink, rolls, whatever.

"He asks for it, you go get it," were his instructions to his assistant.

Weber, the Director of Wealth Management at Bankhaus Finsler & Co, and successor to Anulka Lorenzini, was somewhat concerned as he closed the double doors to the conference room behind him and turned to greet his guest.

Sala had called him the previous morning, and, in a booming but very friendly voice, told Weber he was in Zurich and would be spending several days in town on business before flying back home to Rome. He wanted to visit the bank, something he'd last done almost eight years ago. Too busy with other things, he'd said, but I know your bank does its job.

At the time, those statements hadn't meant anything more to Weber than what they apparently were: Sala informing him of the time of his last visit to the bank and his opinion of the bank's performance. Nothing unusual there. Standard behavior for an older client, particularly for the type of client Sala appeared to be, a man who would, very likely, have not one but several eight figure accounts at different financial institutions spread around the world.

Long periods of time between visits. Only called when they wanted something or wanted to know something. Otherwise, they just simply remained silent for longer periods of time.

An appointment had been made for the next morning at 9:45. Sala knew the drill. He was not required to divulge any bank or account-related details over the phone.

A courteous request: "When you visit tomorrow, please be so kind as to bring your account information with you as well as your personal identification documents. It's just a formality, of course."

"No problem," was the answer.

Would Mr. Sala have time enough to go to lunch after the meeting? Sala's answer to that invitation was clear: "*Sono Italiano. Pranzo andra bene.* I am Italian. Lunch will be fine."

Looked like it was going to be just another nice meeting with a nice client.

But then again, perhaps not. The problem was several things Weber had found in Sala's client file after the call. First of all, a note to file right on the top, signed by Ms. Lorenzini, stating that Sala had, most likely, brought dirty money to the bank, that he was very likely guilty of tax evasion, since the frequent and large deposits made at the bank years ago had been all in cash. In addition, there were rumors that his various businesses, particularly along the west coast of Italy up near Genoa, were not exactly the type of businesses that would survive the light of day were the finance or judicial authorities to take a closer look.

Weber thought briefly, no surprise there. Often the name of the game here.

The visitor logs in the file, certainly much more important for resolving the situation at hand, seemed to show that Sala had visited the bank frequently over a period of ten months, all this before his last visit which had taken place in August, a little less than three and a half years ago, and not eight years ago as he had mentioned on the phone.

According to those records, Ms. Lorenzini had been his sole contact during that whole period of time. Apparently, no one else had been even partially involved in the meetings, since a short protocol of each meeting as well as other documents signed during that time only showed her and Sala's name. The records also showed that during those visits, he'd withdrawn a total of 13,300,000 Euros in cash from his account.

Something, Weber surmised, any normal person would certainly not forget.

Each visit and its date had been noted and registered on a separate sheet on the inside flap of the file. Her signature was also on the request forms showing the client had requested X number of Euros during each visit. Copies of the receipts for the monies received—each of them signed individually by Sala—were also in the file.

A lot of money to take out in cash, Weber thought, as he'd looked at the total amount withdrawn. But that wasn't the real problem. For him, the real and, now, intensely-worrying problem was the time discrepancy between what Sala had told him, and what the bank's records were now indicating.

How could Sala have possibly forgotten his frequent visits of three-and-a-half to four years ago? Did I hear him correctly when he mentioned the number eight years, he asked himself? Or am I completely wrong here? Whatever it is, he thought, that's something we need to check with him when he arrives tomorrow for the meeting.

What was also in the file were copies of a change of address form filled out by Ms. Lorenzini and Sala at the time of his first visit. Apparently, Sala lived in Bologna. No mail or communications whatsoever to be sent to that address. Only the normal bank greetings at holidays were to be sent to his former address in Rome where, apparently, he usually spent important times of the year.

That's strange, Weber had thought. Hadn't Sala mentioned that Rome was his home? What had happened to Bologna? Had he moved again?

Very curious. And very suspicious. The man could be an imposter. For such situations, the bank had a Security Department. Weber had asked two of the people in the department to meet with and check the credentials of Mr. Sala personally upon his arrival at the Private Customer entrance to the bank. He'd had his secretary take down to them a note with the particulars on it he wanted checked.

Sala walked briskly into the bank the next morning and was immediately approached by the two men, who, courteously and diplomatically, guided him into a small meeting room off the main reception area. They knew the drill from A to Z.

Full name. Correct. Check. Passport Italian. Check.

Picture likeness appears somewhat older. Looks okay. Check.

Same full name in the passport as the name Weber had given them. Check.

Everything fit, except for two things: the number on Sala's passport was different from the passport number given them by Weber. The Rome address in the passport did not match the address in Bologna Weber had written down on the note.

Inconsistencies requiring answers.

Questioned about the passport number, Sala told the security guard that he'd had to get a new passport since his last visit to the bank. He'd unfortunately lost the old one on a recent trip to the Far East, and had had to get a new one at the Italian Embassy in Singapore. Understandably, the new passport had a different number from the old one.

Please also check the date of issue. Then you'll see what I'm saying is correct.

An acceptable explanation for the difference in the passport numbers. The Italian Embassy in Singapore as the issuing authority. And the recent date.

Check.

Sala repeated his Rome address. The lead security guard knew there'd recently been a number of internal administrative foul-ups involving some of the bank's client addresses. He didn't make a big issue of the matter.

Let Director Weber take care of that, he thought.

He called Weber immediately after clearing Sala, reaching him in his office. All details concerning the security check and its findings were passed through the phone. Weber confirmed he'd personally check the address situation with him.

Sala was not the kind of man who liked or accepted the use of overbearing regulations or controls. He knew who he was. He'd been a client of the bank for a long time. He knew he had an almost nine-figure Euro balance in his account.

Damn it, where was the respect?

Before Weber's assistant left the conference room, Sala expressed his displeasure at a security procedure he felt had been both totally unnecessary, as well as personally insulting. The assistant, a young man with a year and a half at the bank, mumbled his apologies, citing the need to protect the client and the bank against any attempts at fraud or embezzlement.

That explanation didn't sit too well at all with Sala. Definitely wrong choice of words. What really pissed him off was the fact that the bank seemed to be assuming he might be an imposter. He paced back and forth along the length of the conference table, waiting for Weber to arrive.

He didn't touch his coffee. He looked at the sweet rolls. To hell with them, too, he thought.

He was just getting ready to go out and make some real noise about having to wait when the outside doors to the conference room opened, and Weber stepped into the room. One look was enough for Weber. One of the most important clients of the bank was not in a good mood.

The men shook hands, with Weber apologizing for the slight delay and that Sala had had to submit himself to the security check upon his arrival. His reason was the same his assistant had given ten minutes ago. With a little more diplomacy and explanation thrown in.

Sala waved it off with a short brush-off movement of his right arm over his right shoulder. Some guttural comment Weber didn't understand accompanied his body movement.

No sign of a bad mood. It was worse. Sala was seriously pissed off.

Weber gave it another shot. "Mr. Sala, I really do appreciate your understanding the need for that small greeting this morning. I can assure you, it was not meant in any way as a personal snub nor was it directed in any way toward questioning or doubting your integrity."

Sala nodded, folded his arms, and leaned back in his chair. His eyes closed down to slits. Fuck 'em. He wasn't going to make it easy for anybody. After listening to Weber throw around a few more desultory comments about his visit to Zurich and the bank's alleged appreciation of his status, Sala shut down the audio.

Weber looked at him and saw he'd gone off line. This was not going to be easy. He *had* to know.

He decided to tack in a different direction. A small, white lie would have to do. He shuffled some papers lying in front of him.

"As we do for all of her clients, Mr. Sala, we always like to make sure our records are current and up to date. An administrative matter."

"Unfortunately, we've had some recent computer problems with client address records here at the bank. I'm concerned your address may have been affected. According to our files, you currently live in Bologna."

Here comes the bomb, Weber thought.

"It appears that that Bologna address replaced a Rome address we'd originally recorded when you opened your account with us. On the phone yesterday, you told me that Rome is currently your place of residence."

Weber looked directly at Sala. A pleasant expression on his face.

"Could you kindly enlighten me here, please, Mr. Sala? If the Bologna address we have is incorrect, then what is your correct home address at the moment and how long have you lived at that address?"

A very exasperated Sala dictated his address to Weber, his words clipped and knife sharp.

"I am not pleased about this, Herr Weber, but I'll give you an answer. I have lived in a penthouse apartment in the Via Archimede in the Parioli area of Rome for the past 34 years. Nowhere else. Only there."

"That is the address I gave this bank when I opened my account here, and that is the address you should still have in your records, damn it."

"I've never changed my address and never lived anywhere else. A Bologna address is impossible. How the hell did that address get into my file and into your records, can you tell me that, Herr Weber?"

Weber started to breathe a little more heavily. There was definitely something wrong here. At the hairline above his forehead, small beads of perspiration started to appear. He felt warm. If he'd been alone, he would have immediately taken off his suit jacket and hung it on the chair next to him.

He had to be careful. He couldn't say anything that would cause Sala to start worrying about the bank's professionalism. Or, worse, the safety of his money. Nevertheless, Weber knew he had to ask another question. The only question that really counted. And it had to be posed in a subtle fashion, almost as an afterthought.

First, the answer to Sala's question.

"Mr. Sala, I'm not sure how the Bologna address got into our records. It must have been an administrative mistake. As I told you, we've had an issue or two of similar nature here at the bank in the recent past. I apologize for this *malheur*. I can assure you we'll reenter the correct address in your file as quickly as possible."

Nice little white lie. He looked closely at Sala.

"By the way, Mr. Sala, do you happen by chance to remember the name of the person you met with when you last visited us here at the bank?"

Sala opened a small black book, flipped a couple of pages back and forth, then found the right page, and read the information written on it to Weber.

"Just a second, please. I keep a record in here of everything relating to my visits to Zurich."

A moment's silence. "Ah, here's what I've been looking for. As you probably see in your records, my account number here at the bank was changed in the early Nineties. Subsequently,—you see it?—, I came to Zurich over, I think, a period of just about two years and put large amounts of cash into that account. After that, I stopped coming. Wasn't necessary. You people were doing all the right things and, frankly, I didn't need the money."

"My last visit was eight years ago. I was here in July of that year. I remember that particular visit very well because my young niece accompanied me to Zurich. She'd just turned fifteen and the trip was a birthday present for her."

Sala was definitely not happy. No smile at the thought of his niece.

He added quickly, using a somewhat sharper, almost sarcastic tone. "I'm sure you'll also see from the file that I opened my first account here in the Eighties, but it was just small potatoes at the time. I wanted a different account later, so I got it and then came all the deposits. So that's the whole story. Does that match the data you have in your records, Herr Weber?"

Oh, oh. Lots of aggression there, Weber thought. He nodded emphatically a yes to the question.

Sala looked directly at Weber with unfriendly eyes, his voice edged with a touch of sarcasm.

"I assume you will also be asking about it, but am I correct in saying the account number I was given at the time is still valid? SUT15778-00864?"

Weber answered yes to both questions.

He shifted his position in his chair. This is not only bad. This whole thing's going in the wrong direction, he thought. A disaster.

Sala continued, reading the information directly out of his little black book.

"During my last visit here, I spoke at the beginning of my meeting with a Herr Dr. Graesser. I didn't note down his first name. Nice gentleman. Senior executive at the bank."

"There was also a young woman who came with him to the meeting. Her name and title were, can't read my handwriting so well, ah, yes, now I have it, a Ms. Anulka Lorenzini, Assistant Director of Wealth Management."

"If I remember correctly, she was obviously someone he thought very highly of because he left the meeting after about ten minutes, leaving her to continue the discussion. I think she even gave me a recommendation for a good Italian restaurant just outside of Zurich. I don't like to lose such things. I still have the address she gave me here in my little notebook. But that's it."

"No further visits here at the bank after that. That is, up until today."

Shit. Weber took a deep breath, then thanked Sala for the detailed information he'd provided. He told him Ms. Lorenzini had been a very competent director of the bank before she'd resigned to pursue other interests in her life.

"I respected her a great deal. We were very sorry to see her go." And then he stopped talking.

An uncomfortable silence descended upon the room. Sala fumbled around with his little note book, checking whatever else he wanted to check at the moment.

For Weber, however, the alarm bells had been long sounding off loud and clear in his head. Absolutely no further visits after the last one eight years ago?

He knew exactly what his next question should be: are you sure you weren't here between then and now and are you sure you didn't take out a total of 13,300,000 Euros in cash from your account during your visits at that time?

He couldn't do it, couldn't pose that question, the all-important, finally confirming question.

The horror of it was that Weber already knew the answer. Sala was the real thing. The bank also had his original signature on file, the one he'd put on all the required forms when he'd opened his account so many years ago. And then there were "his" signatures on the receipt confirmations for the 13,300,000 Euros. All of them would have to be carefully examined by forensic specialists.

However, Weber had no doubts after looking more closely at both sets of signatures. At first glance, the more recent ones looked okay, he had to admit. But, even to his inexperienced eye, he saw there were several differences between the new ones, and Sala's original signature on the signature card he'd had signed when he'd opened the account.

Clear and disturbing differences. Fatal differences.

At the beginning of the meeting, Weber had stolen a quick glance at the copy of the picture that Ms. Lorenzini had copied out of Sala's passport when he'd supposedly visited the bank less than three and a half years ago. Now, he took a closer look at that same picture, then glanced up to gaze—as innocently as he could—at Sala.

Similar look and appearance, but I don't think it's the same man, he thought.

Additional confirmation that, in all probability, someone else, using Sala's bona fides, had come to the bank and withdrawn, slowly and systematically, all those Euros without

Sala's knowledge, but, and that was the real stickler, with the full support of the bank.

Weber stood up slowly. He buttoned the jacket of his suit. No rapid movements, one step at a time.

He told Sala he wanted to pick up the latest account information for him from his secretary. The information she'd given him for Sala this morning was unfortunately from the end of the previous month. He felt sure that Sala would be interested in seeing up-to-date information, captured as of yesterday evening.

Would he please excuse him for a moment? Sala nodded, and told him he would be pleased to see that data, thank you very much.

Weber left the conference room, hurrying along the corridor to the reception area located near the elevators.

"See that data. Is that what he said? Good God, save us from what he will say when he sees what funds are missing from his account", he said to himself.

Worse. We have almost 6000 clients in our Wealth Management Division now. Could there be other irregularities like this one among other clients which we don't know about yet? Red flags and hurricane strength winds swirled around inside Weber's head.

He swallowed hard, then took a deep breath. He reached for the phone standing on the desk at the reception and carefully dialed the private office extension of Dr. Graesser.

Graesser picked up on the second ring.

Weber gathered every bit of courage he possessed and spoke, in a somewhat shaky but low voice, into the phone.

"Herr Dr. Graesser, *Guten Morgen. Hier spricht Herr Weber*. Good morning. This is Director Weber. Please excuse this unfortunate but necessary disturbance. I'm currently meeting with one of our wealth management clients in Conference Room B10. His name is Mr. Sala. From Rome. I regret to have to disturb you, but I think it would be advisable if you could immediately come downstairs to meet with us."

"Unfortunately, there appear to be some serious issues involving unexplained large withdrawals from his account that require your immediate and personal attention."

Particular emphasis on the words "unexplained" and "large" and "immediate".

Graesser understood very well the tone of Weber's voice. And the words he was using. He wasn't going to question one of his best people about the potential seriousness of the problem at hand. If Weber called and asked him to come to his meeting, then there certainly must be an important reason, or reasons, for him to do so.

He asked Weber if it were possible for him to wait for thirty minutes or so. He was in an important meeting and really couldn't leave immediately.

Weber went looking and somehow found even more courage in himself. He needed it. Graesser was his boss. He was one of the major stockholders of the bank and a member of its management board, but the momentary situation called for extraordinary measures.

"Herr Dr. Graesser, please accept my apologies for my having to be so direct with you. But, frankly, with all respect, I don't think you should care too much at the moment about who you have sitting across from you. I ask you, please come down here. It's extremely urgent. I need you now. Please."

He put down the phone as gently as he could and took a deep breath. I hope I won't have lost my job by the end of the day because of that little tirade, he thought.

Weber turned to go back to the Conference Room B10. As he did so, he glanced at his watch.

It was 10:42 in the morning, the precise moment when the intact world of Bankhaus Finsler & Co AG changed forever.

About the Author

NEIL GIARRATANA is the author of *CEO Priorities*, an influential contribution to the art of successfully managing and leading international-based operating companies. *CEO Priorities* continues to be sold twelve years after its publication around the world.

Neil is a graduate of Stanford University with a degree in International Relations. He has an MBA from Harvard Business School. Fluent in German and French, he spent the major part of his business career in Europe managing both American subsidiaries as well as stand-alone European companies.

The crime thriller BANKHAUS is the author's first novel, spanning multiple European and Middle Eastern financial capitals.